MOSES
V.
TRUMP

A Contemporary Novel

David Dorsen

Collusive Publishing

Published by
Collusive Publishing
3501 Davis St., N.W.
Washington, DC 20007

ISBN-13: 978-0-692-12506-9
ISBN-10: 10: 0-692-12506-X

To Kenna

Chapter 1

"It was a nice funeral, dad."

Judge Jay Jason shifted his eyes to his only child, Vernon, who stood not five feet away looking out the study window. The view was a good one – Central Park from the tenth floor. The kid was what, forty-three, forty-four? Jesus, how had it happened?

"Bullshit!"

Rumpled and tired well beyond his seventy-five years, Jason picked at a slight tear in the fabric that covered the arm of the chair. He'd often told his wife Audrey that he wanted to be buried in the chair, so it made no sense to spend money to fix it. She had only laughed at his jest, as she had so many times. Her laugh had been one of the first things that attracted him. The first of so many. He needed to remember their good times, not the horror of her last months. He sank deeper into the chair and stared at the ceiling.

"No, dad, really, it was nice."

"There's no such thing as a nice funeral. If it's someone you liked, it just adds to the pain. If it isn't, it's a waste of time. If it's someone you hated, it's an anticlimax and hypocritical. This one . . . was pure and simple pain."

Vernon left the window and slowly sat down on the sofa next to his father's chair. His large frame and surplus pounds did not make for agility. He turned to his father. "At least no one repeated mom's dying words."

"What do you mean? There were just the two of us in her hospital room."

"Don't you remember? You walked into the waiting area and repeated what she said, 'Donald Trump. Donald Trump. God damn him. God damn him.'"

"I really said that?" Jason asked. "I don't remember. Who was in the waiting room?"

"Andy and Carmen, your housekeeper, two of mom's bridge partners, a couple of nurses. That's all I recall."

Jason and Vernon sat quietly. Vernon cleared his throat and looked at his father, who was slumped over in his chair. "I'm not sure it's a good idea for me to go back to Washington tonight, dad. Someone should stay with you."

"We've been through this. I'm all right, and you have your trial on Monday. Don't forget that I know something about those things."

"Sure, dad, but I . . ."

"Besides, I feel like being alone and doing some thinking. After forty-eight years of marriage, I'm going to have to get used to being alone." Jason reflexively brushed back his thinning gray hair. As a matter of fact, forty-eight years and seven months, he thought. And now alone. Damn. Damn. He wondered what the rest of his life would be like. He didn't relish what he saw. He had recently realized that his legs almost always ached slightly when he walked. Not a serious ache, but an ache nevertheless. He was an old man. A lonely old man.

"I'll stay one more hour. You'll have plenty of time alone after I leave."

Jason turned to Vernon. He noted an edge in Vernon's tone. When had that started? Jason could not tell. He had long known he had not been a particularly good father when the kids were growing up. He had spent long hours at the office and taken frequent business trips. When he wasn't traveling, he brought work home from the office. He had left the upbringing of his children to his wife. Could Vernon's relentless weight gain be a silent reprimand to his athletic father? Jason had no idea. He had not considered that before.

"What are you going to do, dad?" Vernon watched his father struggle for words, which were slow in coming.

"I'm not sure. I'll stay away from the courthouse for two weeks. A few things I must do right away, including getting documents and tax stuff ready.

"Oh, there's the notes to people who sent flowers, and of course, memorials to her foundation." Jason looked toward the window. Night was falling fast, and the wind was picking up. April weather could be so fickle.

"Sue can take care of most of those," Vernon said, referring to Jason's long-time secretary. "Just give her a list, and I'm sure she'll handle everything."

"There's so many to thank. People were very kind," Jason said, "but yes, that's a good idea."

Vernon nodded his head. "By the way, did you notice the tall, blonde, older woman who came into the Temple after Mom's service had started? She sat in the back, left early and spoke to no one. She was striking, well dressed." Vernon added. "Very fit for her age. I wonder who she was. Probably a friend of Mom's we never met. Mom knew practically everyone, it seemed."

Vernon straightened his tie and sat up straighter. "After you take some time, what are you going to do?"

"I don't know what you mean. I'll go back to judging, of course. What else am I going to do?"

"About your future, dad, the best thing to do is to take your time. Don't do anything precipitous."

Just like Vernon. Always cautious, well, almost always. At least we're not arguing.

"Spoken like a tax lawyer," was all Jason said.

Being a district judge was a good life, and being a senior district judge able to control one's own workload was a better life. He took senior status when he turned seventy, as soon as he could. He could quit tomorrow and receive the same pay for the rest of his life. The intellectual challenge was not large, but there were the occasionally difficult issues, the nimbleness required to settle cases, and the pressures of trials to keep him involved. Especially in recent years the work had been less important than his life with Audrey.

After a while, Vernon went to the kitchen and returned with mugs of coffee for both. The late afternoon shadows superimposed patterns on the Persian rug.

"It's too bad Robert isn't here."

Vernon's statement shocked Jason. Jason could count on the fingers of one hand how often he and Vernon had talked about his deceased brother in the past twenty years.

"Yes. He would have given us both comfort," Vernon said slowly.

Jason shook him off. "I'm fine, son. Fine. It's been a long day, and yes,

Robert's presence would have made your mother's final months more bearable for everyone. She never got over Robert's death, you know."

Five years older than Vernon, Robert had gone to Harvard College and Harvard Medical School and, to his parents' delight, graduated near the top of his class at both. Dark and with good features, his only blemishes were ears that stuck out and his less-than-average five-foot, eight-inch frame. He was athletic, and he was good enough to play soccer for Harvard.

Tragedy struck, however, and everything changed. Celebrating their graduation from medical school, Robert and a classmate drank too much. Their car crashed into a telephone pole, killing them. That the classmate was driving made the matter worse for Audrey. Robert had been an innocent victim, not an accomplice to his death.

Vernon looked more like Jason. Initially lean, Vernon had gained wait slowly over the years. He was not obese, but he carried the weight badly. He moved slowly and always seemed tired. Like his father, he had brown hair, which was rapidly graying and slowly thinning. The temples were now almost entirely gray. An average student who seemed to emit an aura of disappointment, he had graduated in the middle of the class from Cornell College, his father's alma mater, before moving on to Fordham Law School, a good but not top-tier institution. In the top quarter of his class he obtained a master's degree in tax law from N.Y.U.

The silence continued. Neither father nor son had more to say. Besides, it was time for Vernon to catch the Acela to Washington. Vernon told his father he could get more work done by taking the train than by flying. More work meant more hours billed to clients.

"Please take some food, son. And double check that you have all your things."

A few minutes later, Vernon gathered his things and said goodbye to his father.

After Vernon left, Jason's thoughts of his son took him to his relationship with his own parents, which he had slowly come to realize had been unsatisfactory. Immigrants from Romania, his parents had devoted their lives to his older brother and him, making extraordinary sacrifices during the Great Depression and early war years. They were depressingly demanding of their getting good grades and not getting into trouble. They were simultaneously overprotective and remote. He and Audrey had tried not to make the same mistakes. They figured that they had no right to put that kind of pressure on their children. Had it made their sons Robert and Vernon happier? Jason had no idea.

Jason walked to his liquor cabinet, which was an unusual 1820 cylinder roll-top desk, his and Audrey's most valuable piece of furniture, by far. That was where he kept his private stock of exceptional cognacs and Armagnacs. Dining on superb food and drinking great wines and brandies were among his few extravagances, indeed, perhaps his only one. He hesitated, and then reached for his best bottle, Delamain's Reserve de la Famille cognac.

"But now what?" Jason spoke in a normal speaking volume as he paced the room. "I'm in good health with at least one good decade ahead of me."

Jason poured another cognac and, at a loss of what else to do, he turned on the television set. He would postpone, until tomorrow, a decision on whether to accept the dinner invitations extended at the post-funeral reception. In the meantime, he would take a leisurely ride on his stationary bicycle, probably too slowly to help much with his heart, but enough to remove the pangs of guilt over his recent sedentary life.

Jason found himself barely peddling as he watched an episode of *Law and Order*, perhaps for the third time, although he did not notice. Even Jack McCoy and Lenny Briscoe couldn't entertain him tonight. The news channels were all Trump and all depressing. Questions were being raised about Trump's inner-circle relationship with the Russians, which Trump repeatedly called a witch hunt. Trump was tweeting furiously, attacking both Democrats and Republicans on the Senate Intelligence Committee for doubting his word. At times it was comic, but not now. Jason turned off the set and dismounted the bicycle.

He turned off the lights, lay down, and stretched out his arms in both directions, without reaching the edges of the king-sized bed. "I can sleep in the middle," he said to himself. He was challenging the demons of darkness, which he feared would creep into his bedroom. He would defy them, although his mind wandered to his and Audrey's thousands of nights together, most of them happy or at least warm and comfortable.

Most of all, Jason missed his talks with Audrey before they slept. Strangely, it was the only time they spoke freely about their needs, frustrations, and youthful indiscretions. Jason enjoyed the intimacy of sharing the bed and missed his wife's presence.

————————

It took Jason two hours to fall asleep, even with the aid of a sleeping pill his internist had prescribed. "Take sleeping pills until you don't need them," was the doctor's unhelpful advice. But tonight, even with the meds, he couldn't fall sleep.

Jason did little the next several days, growing more and more bored, and not seeing any reduction in his grief over the loss of Audrey. He accepted a dinner invitation for Friday. A few people came to see him. A college classmate, a former law partner, one of his former clients with whom he had maintained a social relationship, and a few former law clerks all seemed to merge, mostly because the conversations with each of them were almost identical. He kept the visits short, because reliving the good old days did not help; in fact, it made him feel worse. The telephone calls were no better. He found himself not listening and repeating the same things over and over.

Someone had said, Jason could not recall who, that reliving the life of a dear departed one would help recovery. Actually, it didn't. It never had for him, whether it was his parents, his brother, or anyone else. He pondered what a friend had told him a long time ago. You don't make old friends any more. It was not an original thought, but he'd take one day at a time.

Then came Thursday evening.

Chapter 2

Jason flicked on the television to MSNBC. He listened to Chris Matthews speak.

"Good evening. Courtesy of the Trump Administration, we have a remarkable story even by today's elevated standards. United States Attorney Francis X. McGoohey from the Southern District of New York has just announced that a grand jury has indicted Secretary of Commerce Kate Kruiser for perjury."

Jason was confused as well as surprised. What kind of perjury? Kate Kruiser, once the darling of the Administration? The solid voice of anti-immigration and bringing American jobs back home?

Jason turned up the volume. This was easily the biggest story of the week.

How could the case be brought in the Southern District of New York? The Constitution required that a prosecution be brought in the district in which the crime occurred. How dumb could McGoohey be? Jason took a sip of cognac, one of his medium-quality brands.

"This is McGoohey's first major indictment and it is a beaut, at least according to my guest, whom we'll hear in a minute." Sitting next to Matthews was MSNBC's favorite Harvard Law professor.

"Kruiser was head of Mountain States Women for Trump," Matthews continued, "which was why she was appointed to the Cabinet, according to most commentators. She was a housewife with seven children who had led an anti-immigrant movement – her major qualification – even though immigrants were scarce in her home state of Wyoming."

Jason remembered that when she went on the campaign trail, her husband, who is a plumber, delighted audiences with tales about his work. Jason preferred husband Sam to wife Kate Kruiser.

As Matthews recited the details, Jason realized what the case was about. In one of the stunts orchestrated by the Republicans, the Senate Commerce Committee held a hearing in an auditorium on Wall Street, supposedly to emphasize the importance of free enterprise to Trump and the American people, or so Trump said.

Kruiser had been prepped to be the star witness in a carefully scripted hearing. Instead, she shocked everyone by testifying under oath that illegal immigrants are good for the country's economy and that illegal immigrants commit fewer crimes than legal immigrants or native-born Americans, because they were afraid of being caught and deported. Trump was furious, but had done nothing, perhaps because of the large turnover in his staff and Cabinet and Kruiser's popularity as a middle-class housewife in a Cabinet of male billionaires.

Jason groaned. The Trump debacle was now extending its reach to the courts. Trump was ruining everything – the environment, minorities, immigration, health care, civility, and now his life's work, the courts. Jason wondered why he still wanted to be a judge. "What the hell is happening to this country?" Jason muttered.

Meanwhile, Matthews had covered more ground. "A final development. Late this afternoon President Trump fired Secretary Kruiser. He tweeted: 'My Administration does not include perjurers and liars. Kruiser goes. Sad. Drain the swamp. I won't have a coddler of criminals on my team.' When we come back, I'll be talking to one of the most knowledgeable people in the world. Remember, this is Hardball."

Jason watched an insurance commercial. The quacking duck was mildly diverting. The Kruiser news only added to his depression. His world was collapsing. Did he even want to return to work? Right now, he doubted it. How would he function without Audrey? She had done the organizing while Jason had meandered down the carefully manicured lawn she had cultivated. He had always expected to die first. He was unprepared for the future.

Jason suddenly had an idea. He would call his son Vernon. He had almost never called Vernon in the late evening without an important reason, but why not? What better than speaking to a son at a time like this? Vernon, however, was just a weekend away from his trial. He had plenty to do. He might still be working at his office. Then, of course, he would not answer his home phone. What the hell. Jason picked up the phone and dialed.

One, two, three, four rings. Vernon's recorded message instructed the caller to leave a name, number and short message.

Jason's disappointment surprised him. "Son, this is your father. I was calling to see how you were and how the trial is progressing. Nothing important. We'll talk soon."

Jason rarely talked politics with Vernon, who was a Republican. Vernon had ridiculed Trump and had supported Marco Rubio until the unseemly end. Vernon despised Hillary, so when Trump was nominated, Vernon had accepted him, and had even contributed to his campaign, although less than he had given to Romney and McCain. Unlike his parents, Vernon did not see the election of Trump as a giant step towards the end of the world. After all, he was a Republican. Jason accepted that anyone who saw his job as making the rich richer through the manipulation of the Internal Revenue Code would never be a liberal.

Audrey's passionate dislike of Trump and work for Hillary Clinton had created tension between her and Vernon. She repeatedly told Jason that Trump would destroy the country, a view he came to share. She campaigned door-to-door, which was not like her. Jason, of course, could do nothing; he was a federal judge. He encouraged her. He was not sure his encouragement was legal, but who would know?

By the time Trump had won the nomination, illness had halted Audrey's campaigning. After the election she turned against Hillary and blamed her for losing. Why had Clinton continued to use her private server? Why hadn't she given up the Clinton Foundation? Audrey had become fixated on what she called Hillary's recklessness. "It runs in the Clinton family," Audrey had said. But Trump remained the despised ogre.

The commercials were over. Once again, Matthews's rough features filled the screen. Jason turned on the sound. "Professor, what do you make of all this?"

The Harvard professor adjusted his glass and spoke slowly. "To use a description that we don't employ very often at Harvard Law School, this is nutty. McGoohey must have learned his law at the Stephen Bannon School of Law." Matthews interrupted to explain that Bannon was a Trump's firebrand supporter, whose aggressiveness was legendary. He had been Chief Strategist in the White House, but no longer. "Bannon the Barbarian," some called him.

"Even if the prosecution can prove the facts about illegal immigrants," the professor continued, "to convict Kruiser of perjury McGoohey has to demonstrate intent to deceive. Kruiser explained at the hearings in detail why she changed her mind on the illegal immigration issue. That alone should have prevented an indictment. This is indeed nutty. But it is also serious. The legal profession has to stand up to President Trump and his pawn, Attorney General Jeff Sessions."

"Professor, some liberals are saying that Trump's firing her violated her First Amendment rights. Is that right?"

"Actually, no, Chris. As a member of the Cabinet she serves at Trump's pleasure, although that may not be the right word. Sorry." A self-conscious grin lit up his bearded face. "More fundamentally, an employer can fire an employee for making derogatory statements that relate to her duties even if the employee has some sort of tenure. She owes a duty of loyalty to her employer. So, it seems that Trump's tweet was correct."

"For once. Thank you, Professor, for coming on Hardball." Matthews looked back at the camera. "Hardball will continue on another enticing subject right after these announcements."

Jason switched off the television. Hearing about the indictment depressed Jason, but it also energized him. How could he sit at home and feel sorry for himself while the courthouse was boiling with the Trump Administration's latest fiasco?

Jason showed up at the Andy and Carmen Smith's Greenwich Village apartment punctually at seven. Even though it was Friday evening, Jason's doorman had gotten him a cab on his first wave. He had been at Carmen Smith's home several times before with Audrey, although not recently. Andy opened the door.

Andrew Smith's résumé was top-notch. Holder of a Rhodes scholarship, president of the N.Y.U. Law Review, clerkships with Court of Appeals Judge Pierre Leval and Supreme Court Justice Stephen Breyer, a brief term as an Assistant U.S. Attorney in Manhattan, Fordham Law School recruited him for its faculty, and he soon became a full professor. He was one of the school's most popular faculty members. Nearly twenty years ago President Clinton appointed him district judge as he turned forty.

Smith's passion for bicycle riding kept him thin, almost gaunt. He kept a stationary bicycle in his chambers and spent hours at a time reading briefs and cases while peddling. A profile of him in the Daily News reported that he had considered replacing his chair in the courtroom with a bicycle. His white shirt, open at the collar, hugged his body. His rather long, brown hair was gray at the temples.

Carmen was an interior designer. Her penchant for the art of India was obvious, and she sometimes dressed the part. Tall, slender, and with dark skin and black hair, she could even pass for an Indian, at least with people who were not Indians themselves. Dozens of miniature paintings from Rajasthan to

Madras, some only inches tall and wide, papered the walls.

"How are you doing, Jay? It's so good of you to visit with us."

Hearing Carmen's sympathy helped. She made him feel that he was the only person they wanted to see. They gave him the most comfortable chair in the living room and treated him like a maharaja. Seated with a glass of Sancerre in his hand, Jason stretched his feet out and relaxed, as much as he had been able to in the past few months. Being with the Smiths tempered his ongoing anguish. Audrey had particularly liked their company because they didn't remind her of most other judges and their wives, whom she called tight-assed.

Jason and Audrey had enjoyed most of all Andy and Carmen's lack of pretense. They lived pretty much as they had when Smith had been teaching law. They kept most of the same friends, including academic and artistic types. They said they had nothing to prove to anyone, and they acted that way. Hell, a job for life with removal only by impeachment and conviction was even better than tenure at a university.

Tonight, the three spoke at length about Audrey and the many good times they had shared with her. "We really liked her," Carmen said. "Audrey was so authentic and passionate about life." Carmen smiled. "She genuinely liked people. I was always afraid that if I complimented her about something she was wearing or some doodad at your home, she would insist I take it."

"She said the same about both of you." Jason was not enjoying the conversation. He was relieved when Carmen changed the subject. He took another sip of the white wine as he listened to Carmen.

"I hope you are taking care of yourself. I'm glad you're keeping the housekeeper. This is not the time to make changes. That's what Audrey would have wanted." Carmen looked at her watch. She then looked at both men. "Time to go into the kitchen and get things ready." She picked up the empty dish that had held the appetizers. "Now, don't talk about anything important until I get back." She leaped to her feet and practically sprinted to the kitchen.

Jason and Smith reminisced about the time they first met, when, a few days after he started as a federal district judge, Smith had called and asked if Jason would see him. "Of course," Jason had replied, "come right over."

"I need help," Smith had said pleadingly as soon as he arrived. "I am basically an academic. How the hell do I do this job? No one tells me anything."

Jason did his best to educate Smith about the practical aspects of judging, which were different from theoretical issues that captivated law professors, such as the jurisdiction of federal courts and old English property law. Jason had given Smith the basic information needed to be a respectable judge, including not getting behind in his case load. Among the rules, "Don't lose your temper; call a recess instead" and "Don't make jokes in the presence of the litigants. They want a stately judge; they're not here to be amused." On the other hand, a good judge tries to engage the jurors or at least sympathize with them. They are often angry they must serve as jurors. At times they become bored with the proceedings and feel left out when the judge huddles with the lawyers. To his surprise, every year or two Jason repeated his introduction to judging to a newly appointed judge who sought his counsel.

Smith entertained Jason with stories while Carmen finished the couscous. Jason was bursting with questions about the Kruiser case, but he knew it would be rude to attack the big issue while Carmen was cooking, even though her husband had certainly told her about it earlier. Carmen would give them both hell. She did not like to be slighted. Amid the warmth of the visit Jason suddenly felt overwhelming sadness.

"I'm so sorry," Jason said. "Sometimes . . . you know, it just hits me."

"It's okay, Jay, I understand. Really." He poured some more of the white wine into Jason's stemmed glass, and then his own. He continued speaking, hoping to cover an awkward, if understandable, moment for Jason. Smith tapped Jason's knee to get his attention. When Jason smiled, Smith spoke.

"Here's a story that one of our colleagues, I forget who, swore happened to him. A lawyer before Judge Whatever was unable to ask a proper question, and the judge repeatedly corrected and berated him, finally sternly saying, 'Aren't I right?' The lawyer hung his head and muttered, 'Yes, dear.'"

Jason chuckled. He was not in the mood for jokes, but he knew that Smith was trying to entertain and distract him. The joke was amusing. When Carmen arrived in the dining room with a platter, the conversation topic abruptly switched, as the two men walked to the table, although not in the direction Jason expected.

"I've made a decision," Carmen announced, as she sat down. "Trump fears and hates women. Sexual assaults are the way Trump and similar fucked-up men relate to women. For one reason or another, some men cannot have mature and trusting relations with women, so they attack them sexually in desperation. It's the furthest thing from equality and real communication. They don't like and don't respect women. Those men are emotionally retarded. A lot of bluster and force, but no human feelings. What pleasure does a man get by grabbing a woman's crotch or tit? The way they attack women sexually shows they're afraid of them."

The two men look at one another and said nothing.

"I'm sorry I touched on a sensitive subject," Carmen said, shaking her head sideways. "I'll stick to cooking." Another second or two passed. Jason wondered why Carmen had raised the subject when she did.

"Please don't get started on Trump's castration complex, dear," Smith said.

"As I said, I'll stick to cooking."

"Guess what? The prosecution in *United States v. Secretary Tampon* has been assigned to yours truly," Smith announced.

Kate Kruiser endeared herself to Trump and his supporters when early in the campaign she joined his call to stop the bleeding of jobs going abroad from the United States. Later when she became Secretary of Commerce, one liberal blog picked up Kruiser's stop-the-bleeding comment and started

calling her Secretary Tampon. While not repeated in main-
stream media, the name stuck. Given Trump's crude language,
few Trump antagonists had any qualms about using her
nickname. Jason knew Carmen thought it clever and Smith was
obviously playing to his wife.

Jason had missed the announcement in the newspapers
that the case had been assigned to Smith, assuming it had been
reported. "That's great, Andy, I think. What's the lowdown on
the case?"

"I don't know any more about it than you do. I have a copy
of the indictment and that's all." Smith ate a forkful of the
couscous. "I do know who is representing Kruiser, though. It's
Ira Moses."

Nothing more had to be said. Kruiser had retained Ira
Moses, one of the most experienced criminal defense lawyers
around, who had served under the legendary United States
Attorney Robert M. Morgenthau in the 1960s as head of the
Criminal Division and worked as a criminal-defense lawyer in
New York City ever since. Semi-retired, he was spending most
of his time living and practicing law in Wyoming, where he had
grown up. Moses was well known and respected in both New
York and Wyoming.

"Who presented the case to the grand jury?" Jason was
engaged. "Who signed the indictment for the government?
Was there a signature from someone in Washington?"

"No, only McGoohey signed the indictment," Smith
answered. "I don't know who presented the case to the grand
jury. Probably McGoohey or one of his assistants did. Strange
that no one from Justice or the Administration was in sight when
it came time to announce the indictment at a press conference.
It was all McGoohey, but they had to be in on it one hundred
percent. He doesn't have that long a leash. Or the balls, I
should add."

"Is McGoohey as bad as the press reports say? I know
almost nothing about him. I haven't had any cases with his
office since he took over."

"I know him," Smith said. "He was a student of mine. He

was in a seminar of mine on negotiating.

"Really?"

"All he was interested in was making money. He went into a real-estate firm that represented Trump's interests. You know all the stories about how Trump stiffed everyone and then let his lawyers grind down anyone who dared to sue. Trump's lawyers were pricks, perhaps by definition, and McGoohey was the worst."

The conversation drifted towards Trump and his apprentices before returning to *United States v. Kruiser*.

"Andy tells me that this case is crazy." Both she and Jason looked over at Smith to see if she was repeating something he had not wanted mentioned. He shrugged. Carmen shared Smith's political and social views but had not been interested in politics. At times Jason felt some of her ideas on politics and government were naive. Trump's rise had transformed her, however, and she was now following events closely.

Jason returned to eating his dinner. It was delicious. Carmen knew how to cook, especially exotic cuisines from Africa and Asia.

"I imagine that Trump thinks that a New York jury will convict Kruiser," Carmen continued. "I'd bet he was behind it, but he wanted deniability. I'd love to see those tweets between Trump and McGoohey."

"Who knows what will happen?" Smith asked rhetorically. "As they say, it's terra incognita. The arraignment is Wednesday, and I'll preside. It wouldn't do to have a Magistrate Judge handle the arraignment of a member, or former member, of the Cabinet. I hope you'll be back at work soon, Jason. I need a mentor on this one."

Carmen stood and began clearing the table. "Jay, I've made extra couscous. I'll pack it up for you, along with a couple of pieces of pie. I want to make sure you're well fed. You have to take some with you."

Carmen was being her usual gracious self. No hint of self-consciousness. No wonder he and Audrey liked them, Jason reflected.

"We mean it. We need you at the courthouse," Smith said. "It's not the same without you there. I'll put it differently. I need you. You're the only one I can trust to tell me I've screwed up."

The trio moved back to the living room, where they chatted for another hour. First Jason and then Smith stood. Jason shook his friend's hand. "O.K. You've convinced me to be at the courthouse Monday morning. I'm not staying home while all of this is going on."

What had been his second home would now become his first. The courthouse gave him a refuge to escape some of the realities of his life. It was a safe place. He welcomed thoughts of seeing the familiar surroundings of the courthouse and his staff. He secretly relished the respect that courthouse employees gave him. "Good morning, Judge." "Have a good day, Judge." "Is there anything else you need, Judge?" Even when a lawyer before him snarled, "Your Honor," it made him feel needed, even essential, which, in a way, he was. He was the boss.

Jason would be there for Smith and *United States v. Kruiser*. It wasn't his case, but he might make himself useful. Of course, he'd have to be careful. The case was Smith's and the rules severely limited what other judges could offer. To hell with the second week he had planned to take off. Monday couldn't come soon enough!

Chapter 3

"Judge." Sue Winston, his long-time secretary, was the first to see Jason. "We thought you were taking off another week."

Sue, whom he had inherited from a retiring judge when he was appointed, sat in the large reception area with Jason's law clerk. Jason and Sue had grown old together. Five years younger than Jason, Sue looked years older. She had had difficult early years, including an abusive marriage while in her teens. She remained physically trim, but her face was lined with wrinkles, especially when she smiled, which was often. Her wrinkles far exceeded those of her boss, perhaps because she smiled more than he. She radiated good cheer. She lived alone in Brooklyn near Prospect Park. To Jason, it seemed that her job was her life. She never complained and would do anything for Jason. She worshipped him.

"After a week alone in my apartment, I decided I needed some conflict to keep myself going. The quiet was driving me crazy. My hands were shaking. They still are. Look. I had to get out and talk to people, flex my muscles and push a few of them around, preferably defense attorneys."

"Judge!"

Jason lifted his eyebrows at her admonition, and then he smiled. "Please call both the clerk of the court and the chief judge and tell them that I'm here. When you talk to Chief Judge Marbury or one of his law clerks, tell him that if he has anything for me, I'll do it with pleasure. Actually, don't tell him the last part." Jason hesitated. "Well, you know what to say."

He turned to his law clerk, Joe MacDonald, who had followed him to the door of his office. "Joe, give me five minutes and then come see me."

Because of his status as a senior judge, Jason's chambers, really a three-room suite of rooms, was smaller than the one he had merited as an active district judge, but were still elegant. Twelve-foot high ceilings, maple walls, and built-in book shelves were among the luxuries. Large windows flanked by cream-colored drapes looked out onto the buildings of Chinatown, eight floors down and a block away. Along with the large reception area where Sue and Joe sat, his generously sized office and a small conference room completed the chambers. His office had a mini-refrigerator, which Sue kept stocked with bottled water, Cokes for his visitors, and snacks. A private bathroom with a shower was a great convenience. The conference room, which held a dozen people, was relatively Spartan. Endless shelves in all three rooms supported the volumes that contained all the decisions of the Supreme Court and the thirteen courts of appeals around the country, over two thousand numbered volumes in tan covers with clear markings on the spine.

Jason's enormous mahogany desk dominated his personal office. Sue made sure his desktop was neat, but he kept several stacks of case files that constituted his work-load on his desk or a nearby table. A brown leather couch and a couple of brown leather chairs flanking a coffee table completed the office furnishings. One large painting dominated his private office, a portrait of Chief Justice John Marshall, the Justice who more than any other created the federal courts as the third and co-equal branch of the federal government. Marshall was dressed in a black coat with a large while cravat. His long sideburns framed a strong and intelligent face.

"Judge," Sue called from the reception area, "it's Chief Judge

Marbury's secretary. He wants to speak to you."

"One second for Chief Judge Marbury."

Marbury was from Poughkeepsie, located in the northern part of the Southern District of New York. Poughkeepsie could have been in Wyoming for all Jason shared with Marbury. Jason had always been a New York City boy. The two had had little contact before Marbury's seniority elevated him to the post of chief judge, a job of no power and a lot of paper work. Unexpectedly, Marbury moved from Poughkeepsie to the city.

Jason once asked Marbury whether he was related to the plaintiff in the seminal 1803 constitutional case of *Marbury v. Madison*, which established the supreme power of the Supreme Court. A half-hour later, Jason had learned more than he wanted about the Marbury clan in America, including that Chief Judge Marbury still held a grudge against Chief Justice John Marshall for not reinstating his ancestor to the position to which John Adams had appointed him. Jason took his leave at the first opportunity.

"How are you," Marbury's soothing voice asked, as Jason sat down, "I hope things are getting easier." Marbury was scrupulously correct. He'd probably repeat that sentiment the next five times they spoke. "I understand that you can spare some time. Mort O'Reilly called in sick, and he has a short calendar. I was hoping you could handle at least some of his calendar."

"Of course."

"I should mention that the calendar call is in twenty minutes. Is that a problem?"

"Not at all."

Like most of his conversations with the chief judge, it was short and to the point. Martin Marbury had often complained about the administrative work associated with being chief judge. Marbury was thoroughly nonpartisan and a stickler for proprieties. He resented assaults on tradition. An early Clinton appointee, Marbury could not, however, hide from his colleagues that the takeover by a new and unpredictable Justice Department offended him. Those people simply did not follow usual procedures. For them, a deadline was a suggestion and a courtesy was a distraction. Jason would do what he could to make Marbury's life easier.

Judge O'Reilly's staff told Jason that there were just two matters: a criminal defendant who wanted to change his plea from not guilty to guilty pursuant to a plea bargain he had made with United States Attorney's office and a request by another criminal defendant to fix a trial date. O'Reilly's law clerk assigned to the two cases followed Jason to the courtroom.

The guilty plea proceeded as scripted. Under questioning from Jason that he had read hundreds of times from his loose-leaf book, the defendant said he understood the charges against him, understood that he could have a jury determine his innocence or guilt, and was knowingly surrendering that right. He was pleading guilty because he was guilty and not because anyone had promised him or threatened him, among other acknowledgements the rules and the Supreme Court required. He described his two sales of narcotics to an undercover agent. The Assistant United States Attorney stated the allocution was acceptable to the government.

Jason directed the entry of the guilty plea and ordered the preparation of a pre-sentence report on which judges were dependent for the information they needed to impose sentence. He was pleased that someone had had the foresight to notify the Probation Office, so that Betsy San Antonio, one of his favorite people not only in the courthouse, but more widely, was present to explain the process to the defendant. Betsy was one of the federal civil servants who made the government work. Conscientious, indeed scrupulously committed to her job, it would never occur to her to do less than her best.

Once they were paid and the defendant was convicted or pled guilty, as almost always happened, many defense counsel lost interest in the clients they had represented. Betsy's solicitous manner raised a defendant's morale from perhaps the lowest point in his life, again often not a high priority for those defense attorneys who survived on small narcotics cases, for whom a large volume of cases filled their generally shallow coffers. Most of these lawyers prowled the corridors of state courts, but some struggled in the federal courts. Securing good representation for poor criminals was not high on the agenda of politicians, although Democrats were more engaged than Republicans. Trump was not big on due process. That was an understatement, Jason had acknowledged.

The second matter, the fixing of a trial date, promised to be similarly routine, although it proved to be anything but that. The first problem was the criminal defense attorney, J.J. Palmer, a lawyer whom Jason felt should change places with his client, and probably would one day. To Jason, it was people like Palmer on whom the system would soon rely even more now that the Trump Administration had drastically cut financing for the Legal Aid Society and other programs that provided lawyers for the indigent. Jason had not had to deal with Palmer for years, although remembered him well.

Whether consciously or not Palmer usually managed to antagonize everyone. He was seated at counsel table with his dispirited, young black client. As was his wont, Palmer seemed to confuse the courtroom with a movie set in the Victorian era. His diminutive stature and prissy manner resembled Hercule Poirot, the fussy and fictitious Belgian detective invented by Agatha Christie. Palmer wore a black suit buttoned nearly to the chin, a ruffled shirt, and a thin black bow tie. Outside of court he wore a black Hamburg. Jason noticed that Palmer had small hands and feet.

Palmer attacked the United States Attorney, the Probation Office, and finally Judge O'Reilly. "George Washington Lincoln Brown does not deserve the obloquy that has befallen him. Because of the unconscionable bail set by the Right Honorable Judge O'Reilly, he has lost his job and his wife has left him. No apology was forthcoming from Judge O'Reilly to compensate even in small measure for the blatant denial of due process he inflicted on Mr. Brown. What a lamentable tragedy."

As Palmer continued, Jason felt himself losing control. He thought he saw the bailiff rise, perhaps to try to interrupt and effect a recess to halt Palmer's insults. O'Reilly had come to court day after day while ill, and now Palmer was vilifying him. That was too much, much too much. To the astonishment of those present Jason screamed something at Palmer and stormed off the bench. He did not slow down until he had marched through his chamber's reception area into his private office and slammed the door. Startled, Sue Winston said nothing. Joe looked at him with his mouth open.

A few minutes later, Sue knocked on the door, opened it a few inches, and told Jason that Betsy San Antonio was there to see him. Betsy had an easy manner coupled with an attractive appearance. She was wearing a tan jumpsuit. Tall and dark, she was slender, aside from well-muscled shoulders that she developed as a fine high-school swimmer. A slightly crooked nose prevented her from being pretty. She had broken it on a turn while doing one more butterfly stroke than the pool had allotted. She was bright, knowledgeable, and cheerful – traits Jason admired.

They had a history. In Jason's third year on the bench, he and Betsy found themselves working late one evening on a complex sentencing set for the following morning. One thing led to another and soon they were almost naked on his couch. Everything catapulted downward from there. She froze, and he ejaculated prematurely. A devote Roman Catholic with four children and married to an equally devote Roman Catholic, John San Antonio, she dreaded the worst, both in this world and in the next.

It took nearly a year before they could look each other in the eye, but they soldiered on, eventually becoming best friends. They never spoke about that evening. Betsy's husband, like Audrey, remained unaware of the incident. The two San Antonios had attended the post-funeral reception. Jason was glad both came. Over the years he had somehow managed to ease his guilt and embarrassment when in John's presence.

Betsy spoke first: "How are you doing, my friend?" He said nothing. "That was not like you. Is there anything I can do?"

"I'll be all right."

"My suggestion? Go home and forget about it."

"I don't know what came over me."

"It could have been a lot worse. Go home and relax."

"I will, right after the judges' luncheon. I'll feel better if I stay for that."

"You'll be all right, Jay. You've been under a lot of strain. You're expecting too much from yourself."

Jason stood up and Betsy followed. "Thank you so much, Betsy. I feel much better."

She looked at him warmly. Both left his chambers. Jason headed to the judges' dining room for the weekly special luncheon.

While judges could eat lunch in the judges' dining room whenever they wanted, Chief Judge Marbury designated one day each week when they should try to attend. He liked the judges to talk to each other, something he could not readily do in Poughkeepsie. He occasionally attended the special luncheons.

The judges at the round communal table in the judges' dining room waved Jason over and he took a seat between Andy Smith and the newest judge, Malcolm Cohen. He noticed Marbury at another table with a judge whom he did not know visiting from another district.

A courtly man in his late fifties wearing a white waiter's jacket appeared at their table. "Time to order, Your Honors."

"Thank you, Charles. I'm having the deviled eggs Scalia."

"I'll have the Charles Whittaker hash."

"I'll have the Justice Jackson bratwurst mit sauerkraut."

"I'll take the lox, cream cheese, and bagel McReynolds."

"The Earl Warren sushi."

"Your turn, Judge Jason."

"Excuse me, Charles. I guess I'll try fish and chippies a la Douglas. Thank you." Jason took a deep breath, which he let out slowly and silently.

The conversation centered on *United States v. Kruiser*. After a half hour of talk Jason had learned nothing new. All acknowledged that her choice of lawyers, Ira Moses, had been a wise one, but said little about why. He was sorry he hadn't gore directly home. This was no fun. He was as morose as when he had entered the dining room.

Jason missed the lively conversations that had taken place in the spring, summer, and early autumn of 2016, when the subject was Trump's incredible run for the presidency. At the time, those discussions had appeared strange to Jason. In all his years as a judge, talk of elections and politics was eschewed. The election campaigns of Bill Clinton, George W. Bush, and Obama could have been on a different planet for all that the judges talked about them. In those years, discussing politics would have felt as weird as someone bringing up his sex life for comment.

The 2016 campaign was different. Many of the judges knew Trump and a couple had done legal work for or against him or sat on cases in which he was a party. Judges greeted the idea that Trump might be the Republican nominee, much less the president, with a mixture of mirth and horror. But as someone whom Jason could not remember said, no one got rich overestimating the intelligence of the average American. Trump, of course, was elected.

Andy Smith had said that Trump treated the Constitution with the same respect he treated a supplier's invoice. Smith had relentlessly criticized Trump. Memorably, shortly before the election Smith entered the judges' dining room and made a pronouncement. "I have just learned the real reason why Trump displays his hands to the public on television," he announced to an attentive cadre of judges. "It has nothing to do with sexual prowess. The real reason is to show skeptics that he had opposable thumbs." Everyone laughed.

Conversation about Trump had decreased once he was elected. He was, or shortly would be, the president of the United States.

"Some of us have to work. To be continued, I'm sure," one of the earlier arrivers said as he rose. At least it was better than talking about speedy-trial issues. Still on edge, Jason stood up, too.

Judge Thelma Goodson Newton, an old friend of Jason's,

stopped him in the hall. She had been out of town when Audrey's funeral had taken place, and she apologized for her and her husband's absence.

"You know how sorry we are, don't you, Jay?" she told him. When he said nothing, she pulled him into a tight hug. "Hang in there, Jay. You must come to dinner with us very soon."

"Thanks, Thelma," Jason said. "I'll look forward to it." He turned away quickly. The subject of Audrey's death distressed him.

Arriving at his chambers, he announced that he was leaving and would take Tuesday off. "Set up a status conference in the case for Wednesday or Thursday morning," he told Sue. Before she could answer, he was gone. Jason knew Sue had no doubt which case he was talking about. He would have to see J.J. Palmer once more. That and yet another reminder of his loss had been all he could face that day.

———

Jason sat in his large overstuffed chair in his living room. He punched the chair's padded arm in frustration. He had served far longer as a judge than as a practicing lawyer. Perhaps it was time to retire from the bench.

Jason had worked himself into a partnership in a prestigious firm, which meant working late most evenings and traveling often. Not so quick as some of his colleagues, he worked harder. While billing long hours was a big plus in the battle to become a partner, and the partners rejoiced when an associate logged a three-hundred-hour month, a big gap lay between being an appreciated associate and a partner. Partners must manage, and they must have clients.

Become a partner he did, but his long hours continued. He felt enormous pressure and feared exposure as a mediocrity. He was unhappy as a practicing lawyer but continued. He had no choice. Rescuing him from an unsatisfying life of private practice were the bizarre circumstances that provided him with a federal judgeship.

Jason was not political. He was a labor lawyer who diligently represented industry both by giving advice and by litigating before the National Labor Relations Board and its administrative law judges. Occasionally, disputes would take him into the federal courts, but that was rare. He was active in the bar association for New York City lawyers and joined several committees. While the bar-association work did not pay and brought no glory, it allowed him to meet and work with many fellow lawyers. It also brought in some business, a necessity.

Jason glanced at his watch. It was nearly seven. He wasn't hungry. He didn't want to watch the news or listen to his music. If this was life after Audrey, he wasn't sure he'd make it. Losing his son Robert had been disastrous. If anything, losing Audrey was probably worse. He wasn't sure he could survive a second time. He heard his telephone ring and almost shuddered. There was no one he wanted to speak to, no one. He'd let the answering machine respond. He did not even listen to the message.

Jason remembered another phone call, many years ago. He hadn't wanted to answer then either because he had a deadline, but he had, and taking that call had changed his life. District Judge Randy Beem had been on the line. He and Beem had met in law school, but were never close, although they served together on a bar-association committee.

"Jay, it's been a long time since we've spoken, but I need a favor."

"Good to hear your voice. I hope I can help you." Actually, the last thing Jay wanted was to help Beem, not if it took any time.

"I need to assign you to represent a criminal defendant in a case of mine."

Jason paused, struggling to think of something. "Really? You know I don't try cases any more. I haven't tried one in years." Jason wasn't sure about that, but he moved on. "I've tried only one criminal case in my life and the poor guy got convicted. I was afraid he would sue me."

"I assumed that, but I've run out of names. The case is

about the rackets being run by half the mob families in New York, with all sorts of conflicts of interests by law firms who do criminal defense. You know, organized crime syndicates. One of the reasons I thought of you is that it's a complex prosecution under RICO involving intricate labor relationships. You know, the Racketeer Influenced and Corrupt Organizations Act."

"I know that much, but . . ."

Beem was not listening. "The defense will need someone who knows labor law. They don't have that now."

Jason became more upset. He knew the case. It was the largest mobster case in years, with a huge cast of characters, both defendants and lawyers. He didn't think it would be helpful if he told Beem that all his clients were management.

"You'll be representing Tony Biaggio."

"But Randy . . ."

"I'm sorry, but I cannot take no for an answer. It's nothing personal." That sentence made Jason think it might have been personal, especially since the point about the defense's needing a labor lawyer was so transparently weak. The principal charge against the defendants was extortion, hardly a subtle issue of labor law.

What kind of mobster couldn't even afford an attorney, Jason mused. Nothing about the phone call made any sense. After speaking with his law partners, who were as upset about the assignment as he was, he did as he was asked and had represented Biaggio, otherwise known as Anthony the Anvil.

To shorten the story Jason was fond of telling, by asking a government law-enforcement agent on cross-examination a series of questions to which he did not know the answers and which he later acknowledged that he never should have asked, he uncovered serious government misconduct on the part of some career federal prosecutors. Beem dismissed all the charges and ordered a federal investigation, which newspapers and television gave blanket coverage. The investigation had revealed a pattern of dishonesty and corruption by an elite team of notoriously right-wing prosecutors in the Department of Justice's Organized Crime Section that had not only prosecuted organized crime and criminals, but also some innocent businessmen and labor leaders. Biaggio's parting remarks to him were, "If you ever need a favor . . ."

Jason became a hero to the liberals and to certain conservatives – so that, when a particularly insensitive and political federal judge retired a few months later and the delay in selecting his successor promised to create a bottleneck, Jason was swept into the judiciary. Part of the reason, he had been told, was that although he was a management lawyer in labor matters, he was essentially an unknown quantity with no enemies and a lot of acquaintances. He had graduated from Cornell and had a degree from Columbia Law School. He was eminently respectable. To appease the media and good-government people, the party leaders gave him one slot and then returned to their wars with a little more breathing room. President Clinton nominated him, and the Democratic Senate quickly confirmed.

What amazed him years later was the casualness with which he accepted the appointment. The amount of time he took to decide was not much longer than he took to choose what to order for dinner or for a drowning swimmer to conclude he should grab a life preserver tossed by a rescuer.

It was one month later, when Jason filled out the lengthy questionnaire for the Senate Judiciary Committee, that he had qualms. They were not about the challenge of the new job, although he was concerned. Rather, the questionnaire asked whether he had ever committed a felony or been accused by anyone of having committed a felony that had not been prosecuted. Jason knew that some candidate for a federal judicial appointment from another state was challenging the provision as a violation of his rights under the First and Fifth Amendments, along with his right to privacy. The challenge to the inquiry had not been decided. Question 27 remained.

Jason was obsessed over an event in his sophomore year at Cornell. Christine Wodjorwarski had told Jason that she had graduated from a local high school. She was a cashier at a supermarket, which was how Jason had met her. She had extraordinary breasts for a tall and thin young woman. She had long blonde hair and blue eyes, with a face that was inexpressive except for its eyes. She loved to talk and have sex.

After their first date, which was to see a movie, she told Jason not to walk her to her door. She lived with her parents on a quiet street in Ithaca. She explained that her parents were Polish, Catholic, and very strict about her social life. They would have heartily disapproved of Jason, she said. So strict in fact that Christine had told her father she was meeting her girlfriends. By then, the two were standing at the side of her home. She took his hand and they sneaked into her first-floor bedroom around the back.

Between sequences of particularly heated lovemaking, Christine confided in Jason. "I love him, you know. He's my father, but there are things about him that frighten me."

Jason could barely breathe, but he managed to ask why.

"It's what he did in the war, in 1944. I think he worked for the Nazis. I found some papers once that he had hidden." She frowned at Jason. "He had some issues with Jewish people. I was only two when we escaped to the United States. My mother said it was a terrible time, but of course I remember none of it. Evidently we almost died."

"I'm a Jew," Jason said. His head was whirling. How could this perfect creature be related to a Nazi monster? Two of his uncles had fought against Hitler. Some distant relatives died in the Holocaust. He hated the Nazis and everything about them.

Christine slid an arm behind him and moved closer. "I know but none of that matters to me. I only know that I love you." She kissed him, moved her hand lower, and Jason was lost once again.

For the next three months they had fantastic sex, of a variety and intensity that Jason had ever imagined. She said she had been a cheerleader and her athleticism reinforced her claim. In fact, they could have authored their own Kama Sutra text. He had never conceived that there could be intercourse with someone who was doing a split with her legs spread out on top of a man or enter someone who was doing a headstand

Whenever they made love, she'd whisper in his ear. "Fuck me. Fuck me." It blew his mind.

Christine also initiated Jason into oral sex. He had never imagined that anything that required him to remain seated and essentially still could be so exciting. Christine would seat Jason in a chair on one side of the room. She'd slowly undress and get on her stomach on the other side of the room, and slither towards him licking her lips. She'd open his fly with her teeth. Then, she consumed him.

Jason saw the honeymoon, so to speak, come to a crashing conclusion when Christine's father opened the door to her bedroom and found them in a remarkable, but nevertheless compromising, position. Christine's father announced that he was going to both the police and the authorities at Cornell. It turned out that Christine was not even fifteen. She was in her freshman year at the local high school, where she was trying out to be a cheerleader. Jason had committed statutory rape, a felony. A terrible situation became a potential calamity when it developed that Christine was pregnant.

In what Jason forever regarded as the most brilliant decision of his life, he telephoned his brother at Harvard Medical School. He dropped everything, drove to Cornell the next day, and met with Christine's father. They reached an agreement in which a substantial sum of money passed to the father in exchange for his silence. His brother also arranged for Christine to have an abortion, which, Jason realized, could have subjected his brother to criminal prosecution and prevented him from being a doctor. His brother refused to tell Jason any of the details, and said the less Jason knew the better.

The two were seated on Jason's bed in his small dormitory room when his brother made Jason promise never to contact Christine and never to talk about it again, ever. Jason had never seen his brother so serious. The younger brother, frightened and chastened, agreed and obeyed, even though Christine had tried to contact him several times. Jason had torn up her letters without reading them. He had promised his brother, a pledge he honored long after his brother's premature death from heart disease. But not talking about the incident did not mean that Jason was not repeatedly reminded of it, both for its carnal pleasure and for its threat to his brother's and his futures. And, he never stopped wondering what had happened to Christine.

Obviously, he had omitted mentioning these events when he filled out the judicial questionnaire. No one in his work life could ever know about the affair or the abortion that followed. Both were burdens he would never cease to carry. Only Audrey had known even of Christine's existence, although no mention had been made of her pregnancy. Jason's obvious relish over the relationship had nearly halted their engagement. Jason could never understand what led him to tell her.

While awaiting confirmation as a district judge, Jason had sat in on federal trials and sometimes asked the judges for their critiques and insights after they finished. He observed trials in the Eastern District Court in Brooklyn rather than his future home court in Manhattan; he was concerned that the extent of his observations would make some of his new colleagues nervous. Sitting in the audience, he gained empathy for jurors who suffered though long unexplained delays while lawyers conversed with the judge outside their hearing. He saw other ways to improve how trials were conducted.

Not setting his intellectual sights too high, Jason bought and studied many little volumes that law students used for cramming, such as *Admiralty Law in a Nutshell*, the McDonald's of legal scholarship. Like McDonald's, he wanted to get the basics straight and didn't want to serve up burgers when chicken McNuggets were ordered. In his first days as a judge he was prepared to get a garnish or two wrong but didn't want to commit a basic failure in understanding what was said to him or make a ruling that led to chaos.

For judges who cared, which meant just about all of them, the first year or two was an exciting and demanding learning experience, peppered with dispiriting errors. Mistakes bothered Jason, although probably less than they did his unintended victims. After some early tooth gnashing and tossing and turning at night, he had accepted the fact that he was not perfect and would make mistakes, and that all he could do was his best, even though that realization carried him only so far.

As he looked onto beautiful Central Park out of his window, Jason was miserable. It was getting dark and he was alone. After all his effort to be a good judge, look where he was. He had made an inexcusable rookie mistake in losing his temper with J.J. Palmer. He always hoped that the new judges he had briefed learned something from the orientation he had provided. Once again, he chastised himself; he certainly had not followed the advice he had given them.

It seemed time for a simple dinner of leftovers with a glass or two of wine, followed by a cognac and another episode of *Law and Order*. His experience had not dampened his appetite. Jason hoped for an uneventful evening. He got his wish and, unexpectedly, a good night's sleep.

Chapter 4

Maybe he was imagining things, Jason thought as he entered the courthouse on Tuesday morning to the usual greetings, but everyone seemed particularly nice this morning. He certainly was not looking for pity, but he could not complain. Sue was all business, more than usual, but again he had no complaints. She politely ignored his Monday statement that he would take Tuesday off. He checked his mail, external, internal, and electronic, and found nothing special. A retirement party next week for one of the court staff, a bar-association talk by a professor who usually had something interesting to say, and a couple of recent Supreme Court opinions were the meager lot. Joe, his clerk, stuck his head in the door and asked if Jason needed anything. Jason waved him off.

Jason was aware that he was not keeping his clerk busy enough. He was pleased with Joe McDonald, who looked like the prototypical bespectacled medieval scholar when he hunched over his desk. Joe had gone to Harvard College and Harvard Law School, where he was in the top ten percent of his class. In the interim between the college and law school, Joe had obtained a Master's in Renaissance history. Joe wasn't the smartest clerk he'd had, but as he aged Jason came to recognize that he needed steadiness and good judgment more than flashy brilliance. In fact, Joe occasionally surprised him with a perceptive analysis. He had been delighted that Joe wanted to stay a second year, so he was free of the task of picking a clerk for the following year.

The telephone rang. It was his personal line. He was pleased when he heard the voice on the other line, momentarily forgetting that only one person now called on this line was his son. "How are you, Vernon?"

"It seems more relevant that I ask you that."

Two lawyers talking.

"Things are going fine," Jason said.

"Sounds good," Vernon said. "The reason I called is that I'm hoping that you'll come down for a weekend, even a short weekend."

"That would be very nice. I'd like to be brought up on the latest news from Washington. I'm counting on you to fill me in. The newspapers up here don't cover congressional hearings like they do in Washington."

"Dad, that's what the Internet is for. You know you can pay to read the *Washington Post* on line, any time you want to."

"Yeah, but I'm a newspaper guy. Always have been." Jason frowned. Sometimes he really missed the old days before social media and instant everything became available.

"But you can buy a copy of the *Post* on any corner in New York, too. Or you could subscribe to it, too. It's pricey, but if it's what you enjoy, it's worth it."

Jason decided to think about it. Vernon had a point. For now, he changed the subject.

"What's your schedule like?"

"Free for the next four weekends, except the first weekend next month. By the way, a story in today's *Washington Post* says that Republicans are complaining about the slowness of nominees for the judiciary."

"Can't say that upsets me. I cannot begin to imagine what they'll be like. I'll call the first of next week."

"Promise?"

"Cross my heart and hope to die."

"Haven't heard that in a while," Vernon said.

"Maybe I'll have the bailiff try it out on the next witness. In fact, Trump might introduce a statute to require it. Talk to you in a couple of days."

"Bye, dad."

Jason and Audrey had visited Vernon a few times in Washington, although the visits were not recent. With his son divorced after a late and embarrassingly brief and childless marriage ten years earlier, there were no grandchildren to visit. Jason couldn't be sure how the divorce had affected his son. They had never talked about it except in the most superficial terms.

Jason loved certain sections of the paper, but he was still not able to bring himself to return to his pattern of reading *The New York Times* almost cover to cover, especially the Sunday *Times*. His sudden cessation as a news junky had nothing to do with Audrey and everything to do with the election of Donald Trump. While he worried that the country was going to hell, Jason's consuming interest in the news evaporated with the unexpected election results. He simply could not stand Trump and his followers, whether they were rednecks or self-absorbed billionaires, who felt that the world owed them every dime that they had and more, yet also felt exploited and cheated. Even the few adults in the Administration held no interest for him.

Jason did not consider himself a radical, but he was offended by the greed of the excessively wealthy. That Trump wanted to take away health insurance from twenty-three million people did not matter to them. Jason remembered quotations by Anatole France. "If fifty million people say a foolish thing, it is still a foolish thing" and "The law, in its majestic equality, forbids the rich as well as the poor to sleep under bridges, to beg in the streets, and to steal bread."

Still upset by Trump's choice for Attorney General, despite Trump's relentless attacks on him, Jason resigned himself to the fact that Trump's nominee to the Supreme Court to fill Justice Scalia's seat would be a right-wing zealot. He was surprised that Judge Neil Gorsuch was eminently respectable. Trump had not confined his list to people he knew. Gorsuch obviously was neither a moron nor, apparently, a bigot personally. It was just that his decisions would probably be the same if he were.

Jason had a vested interest in the law and fairness. He had become more liberal over the years as he saw the unfairness of the law and the unfairness of other judges, but that was only part of it. He respected the theoretical arguments in favor of leaving issues like abortion and the death penalty to the states, but could not accept Clarence Thomas's worship of the law as it stood in the eighteenth century. With a pin-eyed view of the commerce clause, Thomas would strike down Social Security, the minimum wage, Medicare, food stamps, and scores of other programs that Jason considered moderate if not conservative. Most of all Jason despised the cruelty of many of the arch conservatives. They would fix on any technicality to deny a defendant habeas corpus that would save his life and would viscerally deny a victim of race discrimination of her day in court. The election of Donald Trump had moved him further to the left. He was sickened by Trump's posturing, when in a just world Trump would have been in prison, himself.

When Jason called Andy Smith the following morning, he learned that he was in his courtroom conducting the arraignment of Secretary Kate Kruiser on the perjury charge. A half-hour later Smith was in Jason's chambers. Smith explained the court proceedings, starting with his first look at the parties' lawyers, Ira Moses and Francis X. McGoohey.

Moses's face looked younger than his eighty-four years, although he was bent over by the accumulation of the aches and pains of old age. He was short and could be described as scrawny. He was nearly bald and clean-shaven, albeit not entirely successfully in the latter. There was stubble on his chin and a spout of a few white hairs stood next to his right ear. His voice was reedy. A recent newspaper article described him as a superannuated Felix Frankfurter. When he was in his western home, he continued to go horseback riding daily. His wife, whom he met and married while he was in law school, had been ill for some time. No biblical Moses was he.

Deciding to handle the case himself, United States Attorney McGoohey represented the prosecution. A half-century younger than his adversary, McGoohey compensated by outweighing him by one hundred pounds. Despite his expensive suits, McGoohey seemed gross, with uncontrolled reddish hair, a ruddy complexion, and large jowls. Smith told Jason that he could not see if the man's eyes were bloodshot, but he looked like someone who enjoyed his hard liquor.

Similarities in appearance between McGoohey and Moses were confined to black suits and black shoes. Smith also mentioned to Jason that Moses should be glad the confrontation took place in a courtroom rather than in a boxing ring, although he noted that he'd bet on Moses in a foot race.

"I can't get over what's going on," Smith exclaimed. "Frank McGoohey as United States Attorney for the Southern District of New York!" He closed his eyes and shook his head.

 Smith explained that he had scheduled a conference in his chambers before the court session to get a feel for the case. "Moses wanted to make two motions," Smith said. "First, a motion to dismiss the indictment on the ground that the allegedly perjurious statements were not of the kind that could sustain a prosecution for perjury. Second, to call Donald Trump as a defense witness.

"I told Moses that of course he could make the first motion, but before I'll require the President of the United States to testify at a criminal trial, I wanted proof he's necessary to the defense's case. 'Tell me in detail why President Trump needs to be there for the defense,' I told him. I gave him a week to make his motion to dismiss the indictment and set argument three weeks from today. I informed him the motion to have Trump as a witness was premature."

"Sounds right to me," Jason said. "Moses wants to put the face of Trump on the prosecutor, although he's already more than half-way there with McGoohey's overflowing and florid countenance. The U.S. Attorney needs Trump's hair stylist."

"Actually, to have Trump as a witness on the truth or falsity of Kruiser's statement is beyond the absurd. Trump doesn't know what truth is."

Jason smiled. "I'd love to be in the courtroom when you decide that Trump is unqualified to express an opinion on whether illegal aliens are good for the economy and whether they are more inclined than others to commit crimes."

"We went to a courtroom for the arraignment. Did I tell you that I borrowed the ceremonial hangar, I mean, courtroom?"

In addition to normal-sized courtrooms assigned to individual judges, there was a huge courtroom that was used for welcoming new citizens, memorial programs for deceased judges, and the like. The builders must have leveled a maple-tree forest to construct the courtroom. Whoever had built the courthouse in the 1930s, however, apparently did not include a specialist in acoustics. The echoes were so bad they could not use the ceremonial courtroom for a trial until many years later and after they spent hundreds of thousands of dollars to cancel out the distracting echoes with baffles of the sort seen in concert halls. When technology advanced further, they installed an expensive sound system that gave the rows of attendees sitting on blond wood benches a decent chance to hear. The acoustics became marginal rather than terrible.

"The arraignment also went off without a hitch. Kruiser and her lawyer, Moses, waived public reading of the indictment, which everyone had read anyway."

"What kind of bail did McGoohey ask for?" Jason sipped his coffee. "Or did he ask that Kruiser be remanded to jail on the theory she was a danger to society because she allegedly lied to a Senate Committee?" He was enjoying Smith's update.

"I swatted down McGoohey's request for $1 million in bail and released on her own recognizance. I thought McGoohey would have a fit." Smith smirked. "I didn't even give Moses a chance to open his mouth. My guess is that people will expect a lot of fireworks when, in fact, most of the evidence will be expert testimony on whether Kruiser's statements were true or false, I mean, there will be testimony on the underlying facts about illegal aliens. Are they crooks, and do they destroy jobs? It sounds like there'll be only one interesting witness, Kruiser, herself."

Smith stood up. Jason half expected him to shake his hand. "You don't know how helpful this has been. I really need someone to talk to. Same time, same place next week?"

That evening Jason decided to eat out for the first time since Audrey's death, even though the thought of going without her to one of the restaurants they liked depressed him. He also wondered how he'd feel eating alone at a restaurant. He and Audrey would talk about solitary diners as lonely souls who had no one to share a dinner with. He had explained to her that he sometimes ate out alone when he was travelling to other cities on business, but the stigma remained in their conversations. The first question was where to go. He narrowed the list to three, Chez Maison, Spanky's Steak House, and Mr. China, three restaurants that, despite their pedestrian names that suggested unimaginative cooking, served excellent and authentic food.

All three were in the seventies on Columbus or Amsterdam Avenues, residential avenues one or two blocks west of swankier Central Park West. While all sorts of neighborhood stores occupied the street level, restaurants predominated. In a crueler world Central Park West would be called Eighth Avenue, which it was and which it became south of fifty-ninth street, where the park ended. While upscale, Central Park West did not match for elegance Fifth Avenue, which bordered the park to the east.

Jason chose the steakhouse, because he could hunker down over a veal chop or steak. Also, the lighting was brighter, and he wanted to bring something to read. He searched for a book until he found one at the bottom of a stack on a side table. It was on famous pseudo-trials in history, where the parties played the parts assigned to them, such as Joseph Stalin's show trials in the 1930s. The book's theme was finding why so many people had agreed to participate. It was not about natural disasters, which he tended to prefer as reading material, but rather about man-made ones. Jason liked the idea, but perhaps not the reality, of living on the edge.

The waiter placed the main course in front of him. Jason stared at the plate. Jason's choice for the course was a thick slice of rare prime rib, which unexpectedly repelled him. Although he had hungrily consumed the dish many times with Audrey, now it was just gross, and somehow disrespectful. To whom or what didn't matter. He couldn't read the words on the page of his book without his eyes jumping from line to line. He finished a paragraph and realized he had not understood a word of it. The chatter that emanated from the tables around made him feel like he had just been kicked out of a great party. He felt himself conspicuous, the subject of everyone's attention and sympathy. He took a few small bites, which he had trouble swallowing, and told the waiter to wrap up the rest. He left his glass of red Burgundy almost untouched. A wine that he had savored many times tasted flat. He paid the check, got up, and headed home.

Jason went to bed early. As he lay in bed, he thought about the silence before realizing that there were the usual noises from the street that drifted up one hundred feet to his apartment. He still had not grown accustomed to the absence of the small sounds that Audrey had made. He listened harder for them. Nothing.

Jason thought how he would have felt if the random-assignment wheel had assigned *United States v. Kruiser* to him. He liked the idea. Presumably, like Andy Smith, he could preside over the case impartially, despite his dislike of things Trump. He certainly would not have been bored. He smiled as he fanaticized about J.J. Palmer representing the Secretary. He realized that he felt no fear about taking over a big and demanding case. That was reassuring. Of course, he was only imagining the possibility. He figured that soldiers tend to be braver when they imagine a battle or when everyone was firing blanks in a training exercise.

Jason leaned over and turned on the light. He reached for a pen and pad on the night table and started writing. "1. Call

Andy and Carmen for dinner. 2. Have a good talk with Betsy.
3. See if there is any interesting work around. 4. Visit Vernon."
Jason felt better. He turned off the light. The muscles in his
neck and shoulders loosened. He closed his eyes. Tomorrow
would be better, he thought, as he fell asleep.

Chapter 5

One week later Smith stopped by Jason's chambers to show him Moses's motion to dismiss the indictment, which Jason skimmed. Things were moving along.

"It argues that it would be illegal to prosecute someone for saying what he believed," Smith explained. "How do you get inside someone's head? It is an interesting argument, but it proves too much. If people can lie about what they have seen, why can't they lie about what they believe? Could you prove that someone who said the world was flat was lying simply by showing how absurd the belief was considering all the evidence?"

Jason wasn't sure, but nodded agreement anyway, as he continued looking at the motion. "I wish I could say something that would solve all your problems, but the way I understand the law, the judge or jury must decide from the seats of their collective pants what's in a criminal defendant's mind. I'll give it some more thought. Sorry."

Smith thanked Jason, stood up, walked to the door, and left, obviously disappointed that Jason was not helpful.

The media reported little about *United States v. Kruiser*, largely because little was happening. Trump had even stopped tweeting about the case. Denial of the motion to dismiss the indictment generated a few stories, but little more than a mention on television.

Then, unexpectedly, Trump announced he was supporting a bill that would cut legal immigration from one million to five hundred thousand a year over a ten-year period. Was that another attempt to feed the beast of Trump supporters and maintain his base over the immigration issue? Jason had no idea. He doubted that it had anything to do with *United States v. Kruiser*, which posed no direct threat to Trump, at least in its current posture.

Jason had another thought. Trump's actions could embarrass him in the eyes of his children, who were not stupid, and this would be intolerable for him. A recent development could make it even worse. Putting out a lie in the name of his oldest son by drafting his statement and then excusing it by saying that it was like any father would do for a child demeaned Donald Trump, Jr., who was nearly forty. Was Trump's volatility and self-absorption destroying his family? His family was nowhere in sight when Trump equated the neo-Nazis with the anti-alt-right protestors in Charlottesville. When would Trump turn on his children? Could the pressure and criticism lead to a crack-up on the part of the president, who craved approval so badly that he was lobbying to have his likeness on Mount Rushmore six months into his term? No mere parade would do for him. What about Melania Trump? Either she had no illusions or she didn't care, or both. All Jason could do was watch.

———————

The following week Smith had his law clerk deliver McGoohey's memorandum in opposition to Jason. "I hope I didn't scare Smith away," Jason said to himself as he read the government's argument. Not much there either. Smith had saved himself a walk and an elevator ride, Jason concluded. Jason hoped he would learn more from the hearing or, perhaps, from Smith's description of it.

The day before the hearing Smith called, then dropped

by. "This hearing is a waste of time," Smith said. "Moses is arguing, in effect, that the jury cannot convict Kruiser because the evidence is conflicting. I find that ridiculous. Besides, I don't know what the evidence is. I'll listen to the lawyers because I've scheduled a hearing, but it's a waste of time and money, Moses's, the prosecution's, and the judicial branch's."

"You're not getting an argument from me," Jason said.

"Besides, a jury should decide this case, at least in the first instance. It is too important for a single judge to decide."

"Same answer."

"Thanks. I'll keep you posted."

Sue looked in. "Coffee?" she asked.

"Too late," Jason said.

The following morning Sue and Joe greeted Jason as he came through the door. As usual she had his coffee ready and his mail and calendar organized on his desk and computer.

"Judge Cohen would like to come by," Sue said as Jason walked toward his office. "He says it's an emergency."

"Thanks. Sue, call Judge Cohen and tell him that I'll be here, whenever it's convenient for him."

Five minutes later a distraught Malcolm Cohen was sitting in his office, with the door firmly closed. "Something terrible has happened, or rather, I've done something terrible. I may be in serious trouble. I don't know what to do. I hope you don't mind that I'm burdening you with this problem. It's terrible. Can I tell you about it? Please?"

Cohen had worked at Legal Aid for many years before one of the biggest and best law firms in the city decided to expand its criminal-defense team. Even though he had been something of a renegade at Legal Aid, the firm had offered Cohen a partnership along with a salary several times what he had been making. To the surprise of many, the arrangement had worked out well for everyone involved. Cohen enjoyed both the complexities of the white-collar defense work and the bountiful life style that his income suddenly supported. He also taught a course as an adjunct professor at Brooklyn Law School.

The second surprise seven years later was his decision to

accept the district judgeship, the last of the Obama nominees to go through in the Southern District, which reduced his salary considerably and took him from combat on the floor of the coliseum to the place higher up where the Senators sat with their thumbs poised to point up or down. Once again, he defied expectations that he would find the bench too confining, and showed signs of becoming an excellent judge, with a fine demeanor and a scholarly streak that did not seem to slow him down. He continued teaching a course at Brooklyn.

Cohen was as agitated as Jason had ever seen a judge, including himself. Normally, Cohen was as poised and good looking as the lead male in a musical. Not today. His smile was nowhere in sight. His blue eyes were wide open. He was taking deep breaths. Although he had always seen Cohen impeccably dressed, the man showed up in shirtsleeves with his tie loosened and the top button of his shirt open. He looked smaller than on prior occasions. He also looked guiltier than some of the defendants whom Jason had sentenced to long prison terms. He collapsed onto the couch in Jason's private office after shutting the door firmly.

"I am in very serious trouble," Cohen said slowly.

"Please try to stay calm," Jason said.

"I just don't know. It's so embarrassing."

"I cannot believe it's as bad as you're making it sound."

"I emailed a nearly nude picture of myself to a lawyer in one of my cases," Cohen said.

"You did what?"

Cohen was speaking quickly. "I mailed a nearly nude picture of myself to a lawyer in one of my cases. I was in a very skimpy bathing suit. I think it's like pictures that gays send to one another or use to place ads in gay magazines, although I'm not gay. I took a selfie as sort of a joke, to show myself what kind of shape I was in. I kept it somewhere, somewhere where I could find it, and I emailed it."

Jason was perplexed. What the . . .? Cohen was someone he thought he knew. Jason hated sugary soft drinks, but it was either that or liquor. He reached over to his refrigerator and pulled out and pried open a Coke. He took a sip. The last thing Jason wanted was to engage in a conversation about an inappropriate sexual adventure, but he could not think of an excuse to prevent it.

"You'd better tell me more and I don't mean about the picture," Jason said. "I gather you sent it to a woman." Jason realized that he shouldn't have said that. If it was a man, Cohen would feel alienated. Jason quickly decided he didn't give a shit whether Cohen was alienated.

"Wait, let me think," Jason said. "You may be talking to the wrong person. There's no attorney-client privilege between us. We're both judges. I cannot represent you. Do you have a lawyer?" Jason had found a way out.

"I don't think it's a crime. Not really. It was hard enough to come here. Let me tell you what I did. Stop me if you should." Cohen took a deep breath, then another.

There was no way Jason could stop Cohen, but it was a hell of a way to start the day. Jason took another sip of Coke, unaware that he had failed to offer Cohen anything to drink. As Jason stared at his visitor, he observed that his eyes were too far apart, which gave him a vacant look. He had never noticed that.

"I had this government-contracts case. It turned out to be more fun than usual, and somehow I felt that the lawyer for the contractor, a young, attractive blonde partner in a large firm – I hope you don't mind that I don't mention any names – and I sort of hit it off, at least that's what I think, thought, think. There was nothing I can point to, just a feeling of rapport, closeness. She would occasionally sort of smile into her documents. I know it sounds stupid, but I found her delightful." Jason was about to disagree, to protest, to say something, but he stopped himself and listened.

"I was a little coy, but I don't think it was obvious to others and it won't read that way in the transcript, at least I don't think so. It was a nonjury case. She was a very good lawyer, too. Oh, my God. Well, I found for her client and a week or so later, I sent her the picture."

That answered one question for Jason, but badly. Cohen

had ruled in favor of the blonde. "Some good news, some bad news, and some questions," Jason said. "The good news is that you sent her the picture after the case was over. The bad news, aside from the fact that you sent her the picture, is that she won." Jason paused. He had another thought. If the blonde had lost, she'd be mad. Since she won, she won't do anything But he was getting ahead of the facts. It was also too soon to say that. There might be other things he did not know.

"My first question is, how long ago did you send the picture? The second question is does anyone other than you and she know about this, as far as you know?"

"I sent it about three or four days ago. I haven't heard anything from her. I don't know whether anyone else knows about it. I certainly have not told anyone." Cohen was twisting his tie, making it tighter around his neck. "It's beginning to get to me. I suddenly panicked. That's why I'm here. Oh, my God." Cohen took a sharply ironed white handkerchief with a red border out of his back pants pocket and wiped his brow.

Jason was about to tell Cohen to go home and take a cold bath when his curiosity sparked a question.

"Why you did this?" Jason shook his head. This was craziness. It was suicidal. Jason's mind leapt to his decades-old alliance with Christine and his disastrous interlude with Betsy. The reason was simple with Christine. He had wanted sex. Badly. Betsy was more complicated. But that wasn't germane

"I don't know, I don't know. I was sitting in chambers working on something when I thought of her. She is very sexy, you know, beautiful, smart, poised. She had seemed attracted to me and I thought it would be fun to send her a picture. I was not thinking of doing anything. I was just kidding around. It was just a game. What would have happened if she had responded along the same lines, I have no idea. I had not thought that far in advance."

"You haven't heard from her, or for that matter from anyone else, right? That's good. It probably means that she won't do anything about it."

"You think so?" Cohen let go of his tie as his face radiated with relief.

Jason held up his hands, palms to Cohen. To his surprise, Jason was beginning to enjoy the discussion. He had always found Cohen a little too perfect. "It's just a guess on my part. As you said, I do not see that you committed a crime." Jason would not let Cohen off that easy. Besides, how could he be sure? He took another sip of Coke.

Cohen groaned.

"Maybe nothing will happen," Jason continued, emphasizing the word "maybe." "Obviously, if she calls, that may complicate things, but it doesn't sound like she will."

"Are you saying that I should do nothing? Shouldn't I send her an apology?"

"I don't want to give you advice," Jason said, "but if no one says anything it may simply go away. I for one would not increase the flow of paper. Also, she may find an apology provocative and who knows what she might do then?" Jason silently cursed himself for giving Cohen advice. Why was this happening to him? He had kept out of trouble since his liaison with Betsy, and Cohen was making him a coconspirator.

"I'm not sure I can stand the suspense, the uncertainty," Cohen said, as he narrowed his eyes and shook his head.

"You don't have many options." Jason tried to make it sound as if he was sympathetic. Something about Cohen's manner bothered him. Cohen was puckering his face as if he had a great idea. "You're not thinking of making this public on your own, are you?" Jason had no idea what made him say that.

"What would happen if I did?"

Jason was right. Cohen was weirder than he thought, and the man could not leave well enough alone. He was happy as a Legal Aid Attorney. He quit. He was happy in private practice. He quit. He is happy as a judge. Now what?

Jason stared at Cohen: "I don't see any way that going public could help you. Forget it." Now, Jason was speaking from experience.

"You're right. Besides I did something similar with students a couple of times. I'd have to mention that."

Delivered casually, Cohen's statement made Jason choke on the Coke. He stared at Cohen, who did not seem to notice. Jason could think of nothing to say.

"Thanks very much, Jay, you've been very helpful."

"All in a day's work for a federal judge. Take care, Malcolm."

Cohen jumped to his feet and walked quickly out of Jason's chambers.

Why did Cohen have to dump this on him, when he had so much on his mind? Of course, Cohen could not have imagined that his confidante had relevant experience. Also, Jason was the one who took it on himself to brief Cohen on how to be a judge. He'd have to consider whether to add something to his introduction to judging. Don't screw around with the parties or lawyers, at least not physically. No, it was not something to joke about. Was there an alternative to telling the chief judge? While he disliked dumping the problem in Marbury's inbox, it was his problem, not Jason's. Jason had taken upon himself to listen and even encouraged Cohen to talk. Could he then spill to Marbury what Cohen had told him? He didn't think he could do that to another judge, even one as stupid as Cohen had been.

In a way, Jason envied Cohen's openness. With Audrey's death, Jason had no one he could talk to, although he did not have to remind himself that his candor with Audrey had its limits. He had never told her anything about what happened in his work that was not public knowledge, and that included Betsy. Though he had told Audrey about Christine, he had spared her many of the more lurid details. His account was that he mistakenly had an affair with an underage girl. Now, many secrets compounded his indecision about what to do with Cohen's confidence. He decided that it was best to do nothing, at least at the present.

Jason found himself settling into a routine. A little work at the courthouse and then most evenings at home, whether ordering in or consuming the uncreative dinners his housekeeper prepared. Her specialty was chicken, which was fine with him. While difficult to cook well, it was also difficult to screw up too badly, at least if the timing was right. Audrey had trained her not to overcook the fowl. Afterwards, he would read or watch television. To his surprise, he found himself adapting rather well to his new routine. It probably helped that Trump's serial fiasco was in full swing.

Unlike in earlier administrations, where reading *The New York Times* was all but required to understand what was going on, Trump was far better observed on television. The *Times* was not needed because there was nothing that had to be explained. Who could imagine a character like the foul-mouthed Anthony Scaramucci as a friend and confidante of a president of the United States? Or Trump comparing his drafting a false statement for his son on an important matter of international politics with a father's helping his young son cheat on homework? Or Trump berating the Boy Scouts or telling the police to violate the constitutional rights of suspects? An editor would throw the manuscript into the slush pile.

Jason had concluded that Trump had no conception of truth. He did not understand what it meant. Not only was Trump unable to distinguish fact from fiction, he rejected the distinction. Moreover, he seemed to believe that other people could not make the distinction, at least when it was something coming from Trump. When Trump said something demonstrably false, like the size of the crowds at his and Obama's inauguration, Jason couldn't tell whether Trump thought the public would believe his distorted view or whether he did not care whether they did or did not. Trump was far past fake news. Trump was so bad that he was beyond parody. It is difficult to parody a circus.

Jason decided it was time to return to serious exercising. He had placed extra weight on his tall and usually thin frame the last few months of Audrey's life, and he did not like it. He remembered what his internist had told him on his last visit. "Old age is not for sissies." If he were going to continue working, he'd better be in good shape.

Feeling virtuous, Jason left work early and asked the taxi driver to drop him off a few blocks from his home, so he could loosen up before mounting his stationary bicycle. When he climbed out of the cab, he ran smack into Christine.

Chapter 6

"Jay," she said, as if she had spoken his name every day of her life.

He said nothing, only stared at her with a mouth and lips that refused to produce any language. She was the one he and Vernon had seen briefly at Audrey's services. The woman Vernon had referred to as fit and striking. Fifty years melted away, and they were again two kids scrambling for their clothes in a darkened bedroom with pink flounced curtains and a pile of stuffed animals that had been pushed to the floor. He stared at her. Actually, it was fifty-five years.

"Jay," she repeated. "I'm honestly not following you, well, not really. I saw your wife's obituary in the *Times*. I'm so sorry. I-I live in New York . . . since my husband died three years ago. In fact, I've outlived two of them, though my first husband, father of my children, died at 35. I moved here to be close to my daughter. My son, Gregory, lives in Washington, D.C. He works for the federal government."

"My God, Christine." He wiped his face and held out his hand. The July evening was humid, but it had nothing to do with the temperature rising within him.

She took his hand. "I hated you for a long time. Part of me still does, I suppose. You never called. But, maybe we can get through that and have coffee some time. I know you are busy, a judge, no less. But maybe coffee?"

Does a fifty-five-year-old promise still hold? Could I do this?

She dropped his hand. "Well then," she said. "It was good to see you again. Take care of yourself, Jay. I won't--"

"Give me your number," he said. "Coffee sounds good."

The trial in *United States v. Kruiser* began in the middle of an August hot spell. Luckily for all, the air conditioning was working fine throughout the courthouse. First was jury selection. It was probably true that no impartial jury could be seated if jurors answered all questions honestly, but that was probably too much to expect. Smith had arranged for Jason to get up-to-the-minute transcripts of the trial every thirty minutes once the jury was seated. It was not conducive to getting other work done, but Jason had little else to do.

To win, McGoohey first had to convince the jury beyond a reasonable doubt that illegal aliens were destructive to the economy and public safety. If proving facts about illegal aliens was a problem for the prosecution, proving that Kruiser knew the relevant statistics was tougher. And, even tougher than that was proving she believed the negative statistics about illegal aliens when she testified to the contrary before the Senate Committee. McGoohey had rushed to indictment without having thought the case through. Which Assistant U.S. Attorney would risk his or her job to tell a friend of Trump's that the indictment was crap?

It was tough going for McGoohey, but Smith often ruled in his favor. "I wouldn't have allowed that evidence in," Jason stated to himself more than once, as he read the trial transcript. Jason felt that Smith was bending over backwards to avoid criticism that he was favoring Kruiser.

There was no direct evidence that Kruiser had lied, such as an admission to a friend. Jason figured that McGoohey was saving what he had for her cross-examination when she took the stand. That could be risky. First, she might not take the stand. Second, she would have had a prior opportunity to explain adverse evidence, unlike when the opposing party reads the defendant's testimony to the jury. Of course, as much as it might want to, the prosecution cannot call the defendant as a witness.

Jason finally read what he was waiting for on page 1207.

PROSECUTION: The government rests, Your Honor.

COURT: Ladies and gentlemen of the jury. We have some legal issues to consider and this time I am happy to say you don't have to wait in the jury room. You are free to go home, but be sure to be on time tomorrow morning, as you have been each day.

The transcript segment ended there. Under the Constitution a jury cannot convict a defendant unless the prosecution presents sufficient evidence from which a reasonable jury could find the defendant guilty beyond a reasonable doubt. While the prosecution case was thin, it was enough to prevent a conscientious judge from granting the defendant's motion to dismiss the prosecution, Jason concluded. Even if it were far thinner, Jason knew Smith would not grant Moses's motion to dismiss. Both he and Smith believed that this case should be decided by a jury of twelve and not by a single judge.

The next transcript installment showed that, as expected, Smith denied the defendant's motion to dismiss. Smith then adjourned for the day. A few minutes later, he was seated across from Jason.

"Congratulations. You're doing great."

"Actually, it's been rather easy."

"What's next?"

"Moses told McGoohey and me privately that Secretary Tampon would testify and go first. She's taking the stand tomorrow morning. Defense statistics will follow."

"Moses probably wants the jury awake for her testimony. Good luck tomorrow."

Jason fingered the card Christine had given him two weeks ago and then laid it down on his desk. He had not yet decided to call her. It seemed too bizarre, too soon, yet, realistically, it was only coffee, he told himself. He went back to work.

A telephone call from Judge Malcolm Cohen interrupted

Jason's reading of recent Second Circuit opinions. Cohen had to see Jason, and as soon as possible.

Cohen was breathless. "The blonde lawyer I told you about just called. I had the good sense to tell my secretary to say I was tied up. I dashed here. This is terrible. I don't want to see her. I don't want to talk to her. I want her to go away. What do I do?"

Jason resisted the urge to throw Cohen out of his office, and instead reached for a bottle of water. "I agree it's not good news, Malcolm, but it need not be terrible news either. At least she seems to have called you first, rather than the press. I guess there are two options, call or don't call her."

"I don't want to talk to her or see her. Don't you understand?"

Of course, I understand, you idiot.

Jason took a swallow of water and composed himself. "You may not have a choice. You don't want to piss her off. After all, you came on rather strong, and she might feel that your ducking her phone call was, to say the least, rude and possibly sadistic. Remember, you were the one who started the whole thing. That might prompt her to do something destructive, to you, not herself."

"Argh."

Jason was winging it. His advising anyone as to the wiles of women was such a joke that he almost laughed out loud. He had always considered himself mildly retarded in the grand game of sexual innuendo and advances. He sounded to himself like one teenager talking to another.

"What can I say when I call her?" Cohen was clasping and unclasping his hands in his lap.

Oh Christ, why me?

"I guess either that you sent the photo by mistake or that you changed your mind based on all the circumstances, something like that. Maybe even consider telling the truth, which few people in your predicament would venture."

Cohen paused and shook his head. After a moment he spoke again, this time his vice was softer, almost sensual. "She's so delightful . . ." His voice trailed off.

Cohen frightened Jason. Jason was also finding Cohen obnoxious. He was acting like a spoiled brat. He was sorry he had given him advice in the first place. He had to extricate himself as Cohen's extra-curricular sex advisor. "I wish I could help you, but I cannot, and I am beginning to feel that I've already exceeded proper bounds. I suggest you see a lawyer and perhaps a psychiatrist. You have to talk to someone, but I cannot be that person." Jason stood up and walked to his door. The meeting was over.

"Jay, I . . ."

"You need to leave, now!"

After a moment, the younger man stood, hovering over Jason. He was furious, his face red and fists clenched. Jason opened the door and ushered him out. "Good luck, Malcolm."

As soon as the words came out, Jason realized that he shouldn't have said them. He thought it sounded like a smart ass or a chaplain on death row. Unlike chaplains, however, Jason was sure his statement would not be the last word in the matter. In fact, one look at Cohen's angry sneer on the way out the door guaranteed that.

Jason read the transcripts more closely now that it was the defense's turn in *United States v. Kruiser*. The high point of the trial would be Kruiser's testimony.

Her direct examination by Moses was slow and thorough. Moses evidently felt that the jury would warm to Kruiser, although it was not clear to Jason why. She was as far from a New Yorker as he could imagine. Maybe Moses had to erase the image of a gun-toting Wyoming cowgirl, actually a mother of seven, who helped take Donald Trump to the White House. She was, after all, bucking Trump at this point.

Kruiser recited her upbringing, education, and early career in Wyoming, including her growing up on a ranch, which Moses presented to the jury as encompassing the ideal American upbringing. Next came her successful and productive marriage. Moses's homilies made her appear more ordinary, indeed sheltered. Kruiser had never been to the east coast until her senior year in college.

Next, Kruiser testified she had long believed the worst about illegal immigrants. When Trump began his campaign by attacking Mexicans as murderers and rapists, she applauded, even though immigrants, whether legal or illegal, were not much of a presence where she was from.

"I'm not sure I knew any recent immigrants," she said to the jury, adding "legal or illegal." She interrupted a question by Moses to add. "In fact, I'm not sure I knew the difference between legal and illegal immigrants." Jason wondered whether she was laying it on too thick.

"Trump's nomination and election confirmed my conclusions," she continued. "If Donald Trump was so wrong, why did no one present facts to dispute him? Everyone claimed he ignored facts and lied, but no one gave facts that supported illegal immigrants or why they should be allowed to become citizens. I found this strange. People challenged other statements, such as global warming and foreign policy, but no one challenged Trump's attacks on illegal immigrants as a blight on the United States and the rule of law. Also, the citizens of the United States elected him. That meant a lot to me."

Jason read on. Moses took Kruiser through her nomination for Secretary of Commerce. "It happened very quickly. I had not expected anything from my work on the campaign. The first nominee withdrew his name. You remember, there was talk of a sexual scandal, another sexual scandal. The next thing I knew I was on a plane to Mar-a-Largo to see President Trump. He asked me a few questions about taxes and business. Nothing about illegal immigrants, although he had to know my position. I was told to wait outside the president's office. A half hour later he offered me the nomination and I accepted. Whew."

The transcript indicated "(Laughter)."

Kruiser described the next two weeks as "frantic." She spent most of her time with White House aides preparing for the confirmation hearings.

"They crammed me so full of facts that I felt like a cow headed for the slaughterhouse. I barely had time to use the ladies' room. They made me take reading material when I went.

When the hearings came, I still did not consider myself plumped up enough for prime, but I was getting there."

Jason wasn't sure that was how she really talked ordinarily, but it had a nice hominess to it. She also had a nice self-deprecating manner. As he read the transcript, Jason's opinion of Kruiser rose. She did not take herself too seriously and she had a sense of humor.

"Preparing me included feeding me information on immigration, but it wasn't the major event. They told me that the Democrats were playing to Latinos, and that they would assault me with my own statements on illegal immigrants. It made sense. For the first time I was taking a serious look at the problem, I confess." The transcript indicated "pause," which indicated a significant pause, but Jason could not tell what was going on. Maybe Moses needed a rest, but Kruiser's testimony continued without a recess.

"They explained to me that Obama had been tougher on illegal immigrants than Trump had acknowledged, but Obama played that down because he courted Latinos. They answered my question about why Democrats were silent during the campaign on the role of illegal immigrants – Clinton did not want to look like she was supporting illegal immigrants.

"A funny thing happened," Kruiser continued. "As the people preparing me gave me the other side of the illegal-immigration argument, so I could respond to Democrat Senators, I started questioning my position. Not totally, but a tiny bit. One preparer told me that accounts of the hardships illegal immigrants endured both in their own countries and in coming to the United States were not exaggerated. They all stressed, however, that most of them were bad people who hurt America."

Moses interrupted the narrative by having Kruiser identify a copy of the transcript of her confirmation hearing, which he introduced into evidence without objection. To give Kruiser a rest, Moses read a few questions and answers.

"All in all, the confirmation hearing went well," Kruiser responded to a question from Moses. "The Democrats did not press me on my views on immigration. I had digested the feed on most issues well enough to regurgitate answers that offended only Democrats, and then not all of them. I guess they had bigger fish to fry. If I didn't get a blue ribbon, I didn't get the booby prize either. The Republicans were satisfied that I was a team player. The White House aides told me I was in the home stretch and leading."

Jason was shaking his head. Kruiser was competing for mixed-metaphor queen. If it had been intentional, it was brilliant.

Smith declared a recess at this point. Jason waited impatiently for the next installment, which came nearly an hour later. Moses asked Kruiser what happened after she was confirmed.

"After I was sworn in, I asked to see more material on immigration, employment, and crime. I also met with delegations representing Hispanics, who impressed me. I met with a group of economists who told me that immigration was necessary for the health of the economy. They told me that the country would have serious economic problems if immigration was cut. I found out the effects of illegal immigration were far more complex and nuanced than conventional wisdom." Jason remembered Trump's shock when he learned how complicated federal programs on health care were.

"What made you change your mind? Moses asked.

"I spoke to people who worked with these illegal immigrants. They told me they were basically decent people who wanted a better life for themselves and especially their children. They asked me what I would do in their place. It was a hard question to answer. Leaving the country they grew up in, they grew to love their adopted home. It was also dangerous. What kind of parent wouldn't do that for her children? People told me that older generations of immigrants to America often broke the laws of their country when they left to come to the United States. Legal and illegal immigrants alike to the United States bribed officials from their home countries to allow them to depart. They asked me, what kind of country are we to reject these helpless and hopeless people?"

"Did there come a time when you changed your mind about illegal immigrants?" Moses, who had generally avoided the stilted language of trial lawyers, succumbed here.

"Ultimately, I became convinced of the value and decency of most illegal immigrants. Once I got over the fact that the overwhelming majority of them were not bad people, I could analyze the economic and other data dispassionately. I decided that my prior statements about illegal immigrants and immigration were incorrect. I could not reject the facts. When I was invited to testify by the Republican-controlled Senate Committee on Commerce in the hearing held on Wall Street, I concluded I had no choice but to state my new views if someone asked me. So, when asked, I testified that I believed that illegal immigrants aided the economy and that they committed fewer crimes than legal immigrants."

"How did you feel about changing your mind, Ms. Kruiser?" Jason realized that Moses referred to her as Ms. Kruiser, rather than Secretary Kruiser, presumably to emphasize that Trump had fired her. It was subtle, but it might help.

"I'll tell you honestly I did not want to change my mind. All my friends and colleagues agreed with President Trump."

"Why didn't you give the White House a heads up on your new beliefs or even tell your staff of your change in views?" Moses asked. Jason was reading carefully. This was a critical question and answer. She replied:

"It never occurred to me to tell them. I was not in touch with the White House regarding my Senate Committee testimony or much else for that matter once I was confirmed. Actually, the White House was making all the important decisions."

The transcript read: "(Laughter)."

"Also, immigration was not a major part of my concerns as Secretary of Commerce. I didn't expect to be asked about my views on immigration. Even if I were, I didn't think I would be an important witness on the subject. I really did not think my statement would be such a big deal. I'm terribly sorry if I caused any trouble, but I firmly believed that I had to testify truthfully under oath before the Senate Committee. That's what I thought I was supposed to do."

The transcript read: "(Laughter)."

"I didn't understand. First, I was indicted by a grand jury, then President Trump fired me."

"Thank you, Ms. Kruiser," Moses announced.

That closed her testimony on direct examination. Jason was impressed with how Moses handled her. What could McGoohey do? Kruiser had effectively eliminated the problem of her inconsistent statements. She had changed her mind based on the evidence.

It was not a memorable cross-examination. McGoohey jockeyed with Kruiser for hours without creating more than a dent or two in her testimony or her credibility. He hammered away at her prior inconsistent statements, reading each of them to her and asking if she made it and whether it was true. He seemed genuinely angry at Kruiser.

"You're not a stupid woman, Secretary Kruiser. You said dozens of times that illegal aliens were a blight on our country. Didn't you?"

"You've called illegal aliens parasites and crooks. Were you lying?"

"Do you expect the jury to believe that after years of saying and believing that illegal aliens were crooks and worse, a few statistics made you change your mind in a few weeks?"

"Are you that susceptible, Secretary Kruiser? Are you that gullible?"

Moses chose not to object, even though some of the questions were argumentative and possibly harassing. The jury needed to know that she could stand up to Trump and his minions and did not need his protection. Let McGoohey bully her seemed to be the strategy. Make her sympathetic. Smith did not intervene, Jason noted. Finally, Kruiser confronted McGoohey on her own.

"You keep badgering me, Mr. McGoohey. Why would I lie to get myself in trouble with the president? Sticking to my old views was both easier and in my self-interest."

Later she responded, "Do you think I stayed up nights trying to figure out a way to ruin my career? That's what your questions suggest?"

Finally, Smith addressed McGoohey. "Sir, do you have any way to force Secretary Kruiser to change her testimony?"

"No, Your Honor, of course not."

"Then why do you keep asking her the same questions over and over?"

The transcript read: "(Laughter)."

McGoohey asked a few more questions and then sat down. Moses said he saw no need to elicit redirect testimony. It was a way of saying that the cross-examination had failed to put a dent her testimony. Jason was familiar with the ploy, although in this case it certainly made sense. That ended the session.

Over the following days, the defense introduced its evidence that illegal immigrants helped the economy and did not commit crimes more frequently than legal immigrants or native-born Americans. Moses relied on expert witnesses the same way McGoohey did. It was a laborious job of presenting statistics and surveys to contradict the prosecution. The prosecution and defense seemed to be talking about different countries.

After the defense rested in mid-morning on the fourteenth day of the trial, Smith told the jury to return the next day. After they left, he announced that he was denying all motions to dismiss. Then Smith went to Jason's chambers for the first time in over a week.

"Welcome the Honorable Judge Andrew Smith," Jason said with a broad smile. "Congratulations. You should be proud of yourself. What can you tell me? Is it as clear cut as it looks?" Sue came in with a tray of coffee and soft drinks. Both judges chose coffee.

"I'd been watching the jury," Smith said, as he took a sip. "Before Kruiser's testimony I thought that the jurors, mostly Democrats who despised Trump but who had told the lawyers and me that they could decide the case fairly, were happy to see her attacked, even though her current views were ones many of them embraced. The jurors will start out disliking any Trump ally who helped defeat Hillary. But Kruiser won them over, especially one juror who had practically cheered when McGoohey stumbled on his cross-examination. I'd never seen anything like it." Smith paused. "I wasn't sure what to do, so I did nothing."

"Generally wise. Anything else?"

"Not really," Smith said. "I shouldn't say this, but I'd be totally shocked if there was a prosecution verdict."

"I don't want to hold you up, since you have work to do. Congratulations again. Maybe you'll get promoted to the Second Circuit."

"Thanks, friend, but I've stopped thinking about that."

"Sure."

The summations the following morning were passionate, but there was surprisingly little tension in the courtroom. The jurors retired to deliberate around 3:00 p.m. Jason sent his clerk Joe to sit in the courtroom. He would learn the verdict from Joe only a minute faster, but Jason couldn't bear to wait.

At 4:30 p.m. the jurors were brought to the courtroom so that a U.S. Marshal could explain the plan to take them to dinner and to a hotel for the night. They would resume deliberations next morning at 9:00 a.m.

Smith asked them if they had any questions. After a short huddle in the jury box, the foreman stood up and said they were near a verdict and would like to try to finish that afternoon. While the crowd in the courtroom buzzed, none of the lawyers said anything, so Smith sent them back to the jury room.

An hour later the jury sent a note that it had reached a verdict. The jury returned to a full courtroom, which had somehow materialized, and quickly sat down. A few jurors were smiling and were looking at Moses and Kruiser. The bailiff asked the foreman whether the jury had reached a unanimous decision on the sole count of the indictment, perjury.

"We have, Your Honor."

"What is that verdict?" the bailiff intoned.

"Not guilty," the foreman responded emphatically.

   The spectators cheered. As the media representatives fled the courtroom, Smith discharged the jury with his thanks. Dozens of friends and supporters mobbed Kruiser and Moses. Joe raced to tell Jason. Kruiser had won. Trump had lost.

Chapter 7

Liberals hailed the verdict. More than Kruiser, they celebrated Ira Moses, who added to his luster by winning yet another big case. He had the additional advantage with liberals that, unlike Kruiser, he had not helped get Trump elected. McGoohey was the big loser among Trump and his loyalists. Trump did his best to make sure McGoohey was the only loser. By a series of tweets, he suggested that a better trial lawyer would have secured a conviction. One tweet was: "Some lawyers can lose even open-and-shut cases. Why can't I get a Moses on my side? Sad." He took a different tack in another tweet that was directed at his base: "What would you expect from a New York Jury? Bigots."

Another winner, of course, was Judge Andrew Smith, who had handled himself well. Several editorials praised his judicial demeanor. Nevertheless, *United States v. Kruiser* was rapidly receding as a consuming event in the United States Courthouse in lower Manhattan.

Ten days after the verdict Chief Judge Marbury asked Jason to come to his chambers. Jason, who had no idea why Marbury wanted to see him, naturally went.

"Thank you for coming," Marbury said. "Let's sit over there. It is more comfortable."

Marbury led Jason to a pair of overstuffed chairs to the left of a massive oak desk and leather chair, where they sat down. Immediately, Marbury's secretary came in and set down a carafe of coffee, several cups, and a tray of snacks on the small table between the chairs. Marbury thanked her and then turned to Jason.

"I want to talk to you about something very private. I need your advice." Jason was relieved that the summons had nothing to do with him. He did not want another lecture on his taking care of himself. But what could it be?

"Of course, Martin."

"Help yourself to coffee and something to eat."

Jason poured a cup for himself and took the smallest pastry. "How can I help you?"

"It is about Malcolm Cohen."

Jason tried to maintain a poker face. "Malcolm?"

"I received an anonymous letter from someone who says he is in a case before Malcolm and that Malcolm was showing preference to a woman lawyer in the case."

Oh, my God. Does Martin know that I've been talking to Malcolm? Marbury's demeanor gave nothing away.

"This is not the first time I have heard something along these lines," Marbury added. The comment surprised Jason. "You are one of the most experienced judges around here. You are also sensible. I need your advice."

"Do you have any more information?"

"No, I do not even know the name of the case. I do not have much to go on, and yet I must check out any possibility this might be a valid complaint."

What should he say to Marbury about his conversations with Cohen? He couldn't just sit there any longer. Shit.

Jason lifted his hands and shook his head. "You have to confront Malcolm. I think he would resent us talking behind his back. Any judge would."

"You are probably right." Marbury set down his empty coffee cup. He had never bothered to refill it. "I will have to talk to him. This sounds serious, and if the allegations are true .

. ." He shook his head. "I hate this part of my job." He paused. "I appreciate your candor, Jay. Sorry to burden you with my CJ problems, but I needed your help."

Jason left Marbury's office feeling uncomfortable about not saying more. Would he have felt worse if he told Marbury what he knew? What would have happened? Jason also felt guilty about his own secrets. Christine's voluptuous image appeared before him. She was still a beautiful woman. Here he was advising the chief judge on how to deal with sexual misconduct. It made no sense. Neither did having coffee with Christine, but he still had her card. It was in his pocket.

On a chilly October day, a month after the trial in *United States v. Kruiser* ended, Smith visited Jason's chambers on their way to the judges' weekly special lunch. They hadn't spoken to each other since Carmen had dragged them to a Broadway show the preceding week. It had been a frivolous musical neither man had enjoyed. Even Carmen had been disappointed. Next time, they'd opt for the New York Mets. Maybe they'd take the pennant this time next year. Their 2015 win seemed a lifetime away.

"What's up?" Jason asked Smith when he sat down.

"Something strange is going on with *Kruiser*."

Jason was surprised. The case was over. "What do you mean?"

"Someone called my clerk, Charley, at home last night and asked him what he knew about Juror No. 4. Charley wisely asked who was calling. The caller said she was a reporter on a story. The caller wouldn't give her name, so Charley hung up. He told me today and I told him to speak to an FBI agent.

Jason thought Smith had overreacted but said nothing. "Who was Juror No. 4?"

"I told you about her, the one who seemed very strong for the prosecution then abruptly switched conspicuously. She was a well-dressed and handsome woman around forty years old. I don't remember her name. She was certainly the most elegant juror I've had in a long time."

"Anything else?"

"A law school friend of mine, a Republican whom we sometimes see, called me a few days ago to say that a friend of his connected with the Federalist Society told him that he heard there were irregularities in the trial. I thanked him but really ignored the call."

"Doesn't sound like much." Jason heavily discounted anything the Federalist Society, a haven for conservative and especially originalist lawyers, professors, and judges, had to say on anything controversial. Its leadership was in bed with Trump. It controlled judicial appointments.

"We'll see," Smith said without conviction.

"Time for lunch."

"Let's go."

Jason and Smith sat down at the large round table in the center of the judges' dining room. Six judges were already seated and listening intently to one of their number. "A judge from the Eleventh Circuit who hails from Alabama called me this morning and said a new federal judge, the first Trump appointee to the district court there, had crossed himself when he took the bench. The defendant's lawyer objected as a violation of the First Amendment. The judge ridiculed the objection. The jury convicted the defendant and it's now on appeal." Those around the table understood the significance of the incident. Would Trump and his people succeed in breaking down the barriers between church and state?

Jason thought how things might change in the next year or so, when Trump-appointed judges were sitting on appeals from their trials. He did not know which would be worse, judges who were incompetent or judges who were unremitting ideologues, including fundamentalists and racists. Would he even be able to hold a conversation with a district judge who thought that Medicaid was evil and destroyed the will of the poor or that judges should look to the Bible for guidance when rendering a decision or imposing a sentence? These were things that could not be dismissed as a joke. The lunch broke up.

A few days later, Jason received another call from Smith. "I don't mean to sound paranoid, but I'd like to come over. How's now?"

"Sure."

Smith arrived two minutes later. That he tied Malcolm Cohen's record for getting to Jason's office did not bode well, Jason concluded. "Sit down, Andy. Would you like some coffee?"

Unlike Cohen, however, Smith looked okay. "No, thanks." Something was definitely awry. He never refused coffee.

"I just got a call from a reporter I know. He said that Stephen Bannon's former rag *Alt-Times*, or whatever it is called now, is working on a story about the trial. The reporter asked me if I knew anything about bribery of a juror. I couldn't believe it, but he was serious. I told him the last time I heard anything about bribing a juror was when Jimmy Hoffa was on trial. He wasn't amused. I told him off the record that I didn't know what he was talking about and that I couldn't believe that something like that had happened."

It was the same magazine, or whatever, that Trump relied on in the campaign for some of his more outlandish statements, although now it was called *Total Faith*. He'd have Joe check it out immediately. Smith's chambers could not do that. "What did the reporter say?" Jason asked.

"'Thanks, and by the way, good luck.' I didn't like the 'good luck.' I don't know what to do. This is crazy."

"I'll give you the advice you gave your clerk, Charley."

"Call the FBI?"

"Exactly. Bribery is serious. I assume you have no problem giving them the reporter's name."

"Of course not," Smith said. "It was Sam Rodgers of the *New York Post*. I agree with your low opinion of the *Post*, but I've known Sam a long time and he plays it straight."

Jason knew Rodgers also. A good reporter at a dubious newspaper. "Did Sam say whether the *Post* is running a story?"

"He said his editor insisted on corroboration."

"That may be a first. Keep me posted." Jason winced at his pun. When Smith had left, Jason thought about their conversation. There was nothing he could do but wait.

Things were moving fast. Just under a week later the *Total Faith* blog announced that the next issue would be an exposé of *United States v. Kruiser*. Neither Smith nor Jason had learned anything more in the interim.

The issue appeared online to its subscribers one week later with a cover that showed a dagger at the heart of a statue of justice holding the balance scales, and with blood streaming down her front. Copies were few in the courthouse, both because no one would admit to subscribing to *Total Faith* and no one in the courthouse wanted to be seen with reading a copy of the magazine that alleged misconduct in their courthouse. Smith had found a friend of his who subscribed, who sent it to him.

The following morning *The New York Times* summarized the story on an inside page, explaining that it was just summarizing the magazine's story, which claimed that Kruiser's lawyer, Ira Moses, had bribed a juror to win *United States v. Kruiser*. The *Times's* story oozed skepticism.

Almost immediately a series of tweets from Trump lauded the *Total Faith* story. He extolled the "meticulous research" that he said was typical of *Alt-Times* and *Total Faith*. He raked over Kruiser. He blasted the judicial process in New York City. He called Moses a "crook": "We now know why traitor Kruiser was acquitted. Her so-called lawyer bribed a juror. He's a crook! Lock him up. Bad man. Drain the swamp." In another tweet Trump criticized "so-called Judge Smith" for allowing the jury to acquit Kruiser. The tweet ended: "Fake news. Fake judge. Crooked lawyer. Make America great again." Yet another said: "I told you that illegal aliens were bad. Legal aliens are not much better. It's been downhill since 1789. Make America Great Again."

With Trump on board, it was good television and it got extensive coverage for one news cycle. The serious media considered the story incredible, resembling some of Trump's claims during the campaign, such as that thousands of Muslims in New Jersey cheered when planes plowed into the twin towers of the World Trade Center, or afterward, that Obama had wiretapped Trump's headquarters.

Smith told the media he knew nothing about the story or its contents. He told Jason he had not heard anything from United States Attorney Francis X. McGoohey or, in fact, anyone else. Apparently, no one took the allegation seriously. It looked like the issue would disappear into the ether, as so many other Trump-related accusations had.

———————

Ten days later just before noon, Jason was in his office slouched in his large easy chair with his eyes closed. He wasn't asleep, and he wasn't ill. He needed to figure out how to handle the situation in which he found himself, and it wouldn't be easy. An hour earlier the clerk of the court called him to say that the random-assignment arrow had pierced his name for a libel case that had been filed that morning, *Ira Moses v. Donald Trump, Everett Mandick, Beverley Clooney, and Total Faith, Inc.*

The clerk added that the filing was immediately followed by a big press conference with plaintiff Moses and his lawyer, Reginald Whitebread. She did not have to say more; this was the biggest libel case in the country ever, dwarfing the filing thirty-five years earlier of *General William Westmoreland v. CBS & Mike Wallace* and *Ariel Sharon v. Time, Inc.*, where the commander of the allied troops in Vietnam and one of the top Israeli generals had separately sued major media for libeling them regarding their conduct relating to armed conflicts. Those two cases had been tried simultaneously in the old federal courthouse, the one next door to where Jason sat, and now used by the Second Circuit. It was a very big deal at the time. This was bigger.

Jason told Sue to hold all his calls, except the obvious ones from his son and the chief judge. He thought of adding President Trump to the list, but decided that it was not the time to make jokes with his secretary.

Jason pondered his predicament. Do I want the case? How hard will the job be? Can I handle the case physically? Emotionally? The interest in the case will be enormous. He also worried about being thrust into such a public role. Will the Trump forces investigate my background? Will they uncover my screwing around in college; the statute of limitations had expired decades earlier. But the embarrassment to him, the stain on the federal judiciary, the scandal of the statutory rape and abortion would be enormous. There was no one he could ask. Certainly not his son.

A telephone call from Chief Judge Martin Marbury interrupted his thoughts.

"Just a friendly call to see how my favorite judge is doing."

This didn't sound like the Martin Marbury he knew. He never called just to check up on how the judges felt, and jocularity was far from his ordinary tone. Obviously, Jason had to accept the statement at face value. "I'm doing fine. I'm pacing myself, but I'm looking forward to *Moses v. Trump*."

"That's good news. I want to make sure you understand that for any reason you do not want to try the case, you know you don't have to take it. Everyone would understand how much you have been through."

"It's so kind of you to say that, and reassuring." Jason was annoyed. Of course, he knew he didn't have to take the case, although it would be unusual for a judge to recuse himself and let another judge handle a big case unless there was a conflict of interest. It would raise the question of whether the assignment of the second judge was tainted. Was Marbury suggesting that it would be better if he bowed out in favor of a younger and less stressed judge? Wasn't Marbury giving him a chance to drop the case for a plausible reason? He would be safe. But is that what he wanted?

"I feel up to the challenge, but, of course, I'll think about it because of your concern. I want to decide quickly, whichever way I come out."

"I appreciate that. I just wanted you to know that we are

behind you one hundred percent whatever your decision."

"Thanks, Martin."

He decided to call his son Vernon. Father and son had not settled on a weekend for Jason to visit D.C. Now was the perfect time to check in with him. He couldn't mention his college liaisons with Christine, of course, but he could use Marbury's inquiry to get his son's thoughts. Jason rose from his chair and left the room. In the reception area, Sue sat at her computer. Joe stood behind her. Both were intently concentrating on something on the screen.

"Sorry to interrupt . . ."

Both Sue and Joe looked up. "Yes, Judge?" Sue said.

Jason had no doubts about what they had been reading. "Please get me my son. By the way, any calls?"

A couple of long seconds passed. "Twenty-three, Judge. Mostly from the press, although one from someone with a thick oriental accent named Henry Chin, another from a woman who identified herself as a college friend of yours, another from . . ."

"I-I get the picture." He took a deep breath. "I assume my son is at his office. Try him there." Jason turned around and headed back to his office.

"You O.K., Judge?" Sue asked. "Anything I can do? All these calls . . .' Her boss was rarely this brusque.

Jason stopped, and turned to his secretary. "No, I'm fine, Sue, thanks. Just distracted, I guess. I'll fill in everyone later, after I talk to Vernon." He closed the door of his office and sat down at his desk.

A few seconds later, his phone rang. It was Sue. "Your son, Judge."

Jason skipped the ordinary pleasantries. "Guess what? Have you heard that Ira Moses has sued Trump and the magazine that published the story about bribing a witness?" Jason did not wait for an answer. "The case has been assigned to me." It felt surprisingly good to share the experience with his son.

"I think that's terrific, dad. I just heard about it. Someone I know at the *Washington Post* called. It's huuuuuuge."

Jason smiled as his son imitated Trump. "I'm a little worried about the strain of a long trial." Jason decided to frame his taking the case negatively to get a more candid opinion.

"Don't be ridiculous. It's just what you need. It will invigorate you. Besides, I haven't read your name in the paper in a long time."

"It's good of you to say that."

"I mean it. I'd like to come up to see some of the trial."

"It's months away. I expect to see you before then."

"Actually, I was planning to call you. As it happens, I'll be in New York next Thursday. We can have dinner before I fly back to Washington that evening. Would that work for you?"

"Of course. I'd like nothing better," Jason replied. Vernon wouldn't even entertain the prospect that he'd step down. It was settled. He'd preside over *Moses v. Trump*.

"How would Spoleto at 7:00 p.m. be?"

"That will be great," Jason was feeling better. "I'll take care of the reservation."

When the two ended their call, Jason felt more in control, lighter, yes, invigorated, although he recognized that it would take a lot of effort to try the case. Also, the chance that someone would uncover his tryst with Christine after several decades was almost zero. He decided to table his decision on whether to call her until the case was over. But, the idea of two old friends renewing an acquaintance over cups of overpriced coffee couldn't be more innocent. After all, they had both lost spouses, and they were lonely. There was nothing else going on.

Then, faced with a difficult, but workable, situation, Jason did what any self-respecting lawyer would do. He went to lunch. He told Sue that he was walking to Chinatown. As he opened the door to leave his suite, however, he found Andy and Carmen Smith standing in his way.

Chapter 8

"We came to take you to lunch," Carmen said simply. Unlike the exotic sari she usually wore at home, today she was dressed in a red wool dress and matching coat. "We have a reservation at Forlini's. We're not giving you any choice in the matter."

"Excellent! Thank you!" Jason hugged Carmen. First Vernon and now an impromptu lunch with two of his favorite people. The day was unquestionably improving. The sunny late fall weather was also helping.

Forlini's was a New York City landmark. The Italian restaurant had stood near Chinatown's western edge for seventy-five years. Its unassuming façade hid a tiny warren of rooms that always reminded Jason of a memorable restaurant he and Audrey had found in a small town in Tuscany, not far from Sienna. No one in the City made a better ribollita. Today the three huddled in a booth built for smaller people and ordered the famed twice-cooked bread and bean soup, a Tuscan specialty. First, however, would be the signature antipasto for three.

"Isn't it ironic that the first victim of Trump's push to liberalize the libel laws to allow more suits against the media and others might be Trump, himself?" Smith said. He held up a glass of Dolcetto to celebrate Jason's assignment. "Of course, he has no chance of making it easier to sue the press. Standing in his way is the First Amendment. His next tweet will probably repeal the laws of gravity."

Carmen and Jason saluted Smith. The wine he had ordered was excellent, even though it was from the Piedmont region well north of Tuscany. Jason said nothing about the geographical mismatch. For regional dishes Jason liked wines from the same region.

"What will Trump do?" Smith continued. Not getting an answer, he tried again. "If you were Donald Trump, would you let yourself be pushed around by a district judge? Look at what happened to Bill Clinton." Smith was being his provocative self.

The three stopped their conversation to deal with the waiter who served the assorted antipasto. He topped off their wine glasses and silently retreated. Smith repeated his question.

"Trump could move to dismiss or at least postpone the trial until after he leaves office," Carmen said when Jason did not respond. "Isn't that right?" She picked up her fork. The conversation usurped the fine food in front of the trio, at least for the moment.

"That's probably a loser under *Clinton v. Jones*," Smith said. "Presidents are fair game for civil suits, the exalted nine decided unanimously. It was public knowledge that right-wing groups were funding Paula Jones's sexual-harassment suit, but that bothered none of the nine. What did they think was going to happen?"

Jason was uncomfortable with the luncheon conversation. He did not want anyone to overheard him discussing the case, although the noisy restaurant made that all but impossible. He made a sign like patting the head of a child to make the others to keep their voices down.

"Try the artichoke, darling, or the grilled red pepper," Carmen said. "Relax, this isn't a business meeting. We're celebrating, remember."

Smith squeezed her hand with his. "What could the Justices have been smoking?" Smith asked Jason in a lowered voice. "Trump would be allowing a lowly district judge to determine his fate." He paused and watched Jason help himself to a rice-filled tomato and several thin slices of prosciutto. "It's not like Trump to let an underling tell him what to do.

"I just thought of something else," Smith said. "What if Trump claims that the tweet was part of his official functions as president? He's immune from suit based on his official duties. That would not only bar the case from proceeding but end it for all time. Isn't that right?" Smith was looking at Jason.

Even though no one could hear them, Jason was increasingly uncomfortable discussing the case, which, after all, involved the president. "It's certainly something to think about." It was one of Jason's less memorable legal utterances.

Smith still had not touched his food. "Another question, how would they serve Trump with the summons and complaint?" Smith was asking good questions. He smiled at his wife, who was listening intently. "You don't just ring the bell at the White House and tell them you're a process server to serve the president," as he turned to the food in front of him. He added an artichoke heart and some cheese to his plate. He forked them in slowly.

"What did Clinton do?" Carmen asked.

"He wasn't Trump. I assume Clinton had someone accept service," Smith said. "Nixon accepted service of a subpoena for tapes made on his famous White House taping system."

"Ah, for the good old days." Jason felt he had to say something. He was, in a sense, the guest of honor. He lifted his glass. "Thank you again. This is an unexpected treat, and I am grateful to you both."

"Here, here!" Smith said as he and Carmen picked up their glasses. A waiter removed Carmen's empty plate, but left the antipasto, which they had not finished, along with the plates of Andy and Jason, who held up their hands when the waiter reached to clear the rest of the table. Jason wondered if his afternoon schedule would allow a nap. He seldom had one, much less two or was it three, glasses of wine with lunch.

"What do you do in a case like this if Trump is not served? He'd be the proverbial 800-pound gorilla not in the room,"

Carmen said. "Won't it look as though he's afraid of the case if he resists being served? But will that matter to him? He says all sorts of things that he knows nobody believes."

Carmen absentmindedly reached for a piece of the chewy bread in the bread basket, then pulled her hand back. "There isn't anything anybody can do if Trump avoids service, is there?" Carmen asked. "It's not like giving false answers to the police, which can be used on cross-examination to challenge a witness's credibility."

Carmen knew a lot more about the law than Jason realized. He smiled as he fed his fantasy of her going head to head with J.J. Palmer.

"Luckily, not the judge's call," Smith said. He pointed his fork in Jason's direction. "One thing Jay, you had better start preparing for a very unusual case and a very unusual defendant. My advice is to get the lawyers in early as possible to cut down speculation." Jason smiled. The student had become the professor.

"Why did Ira Moses file suit? Wasn't the obvious thing to do simply to ignore the article?" Carmen asked another good question.

"You'd think so," Jason responded.

Smith spoke when it was obvious that Jason would say nothing more. "Moses was originally from Wyoming, where the Secretary comes from, and he is a member of the Wyoming bar and spends a lot of time there. The bar is in the hands of people to the right of Attila the Hun, no offense meant to Attila. They're making noises as if they were going after Moses on something or other after the *Total Faith* article, I understand. The Wyoming bar association is in a world of its own, with a view of the Constitution to match. So, Moses must think that the best defense is a good offense. Better a New York jury than a Wyoming bar association."

The trio turned to the soup that the waiter set down in front of them. Carmen requested some grated parmigiana on the focaccia. Smith tore off a hunk and dunked the yeasty bread into his soup. Carmen rolled her eyes at him and Jason laughed. Smith was acting the part of a Florentine peasant with exaggerated gestures. Eating silenced the table for several minutes until Carmen spoke.

"Do you think Trump will settle?"

"No chance. Trump never settles." Smith spoke with conviction. "He did settle the Trump University suit, but that was different. This case involves his persona."

"Why would Moses hire someone like Whitebread to handle the case?" Carmen again spoke Jason's thought. "Isn't he a criminal lawyer without any experience in defamation law? That's what the papers say."

"The usual reason, money," Smith said. "Whitebread is a long-time buddy of Moses's, who took the case as a favor. It will be a war that costs each side way over $1 million in legal fees, at least if they are paying. Moses could never pay New York lawyers their hourly rates." Smith quickly ate the last of his soup and laid down his spoon. The others had already finished.

When the waiter asked if anyone wanted dessert or coffee, all declined. Gelato and biscotti were always tempting. Carmen was the first to lay her napkin on the table. She may have wanted to avoid further antics by her husband, like his gross attack on the ribollita.

"I have to get back to work, gentlemen." She pushed back her chair and stood. "One of my clients is coming in this afternoon to discuss draperies." She smiled at the men. "This conversation to be continued, I'm sure. Right, Jay?"

Jason rose with Smith. "Thanks again to both of you. Lunch with you was just what I needed."

———————

As soon as Jason returned to his chambers, Joe filled him in on recent events. The three defendants other than Trump had been served. A large international firm represented *Total Faith* and its publisher-editor Mandick, he said, while the reporter had her own counsel, a small New York firm that did some libel work. The magazine's insurance carrier was paying for both sets of defendants' lawyers, according to the reports.

"Anything regarding Trump?"

"Not a word, Judge. Should we schedule a conference with the lawyers or should we wait to see what happens with Trump?"

"I plan to keep a tight rein on the lawyers, so let's have the ones who are already in the case in early. I don't want to wait on Trump. He is just one of four defendants. Ask Sue to a notice a pretrial conference one week from today at 10:00 a.m. in chambers."

Jason circled the room. Often, he could think better when he moved, a liability for a judge whose job required him to sit and listen. Sometimes Jason got up and paced during a trial, but that seemed to disconcert the lawyers and witnesses, who tried to address both the jurors and him. It also took him out of microphone range. Joe jotted the important facts of Jason's instructions onto a yellow legal pad he always carried. Joe was very low tech.

"Start with a basic memorandum on libel law, listing what Moses has to prove to prevail. I've never had a libel case. I can tell you, I think, what *New York Times v. Sullivan* stands for. Beyond that, I won't trust myself much further without considerable help, and much of it will have to come from you."

"One question, Judge, should I work on the assumption that Moses is a public figure, or is that not clear?"

Jason was pleased that Joe had started researching, or at least thinking, on his own. Jason spoke: "That may be the biggest legal issue in the case, aside from Trump's status. If Moses is a public figure, he'll have to prove that Trump and the others either knew that the story they published was false or that they didn't care one way or the other whether it was true or not. That's a hell-of-a-lot harder than proving mere negligence. The complaint doesn't provide a clue. It asks for $100 million compensatory damages and $100 million punitive damages. Pull some of the leading libel cases from the shelves and line them up on my desk with markers to tell me what I should read." Jason knew more than he had let on. Jason also preferred reading from the printed page over reading from a screen.

Most television stations led with the story that evening. Most newspapers ran the story on page one above the fold. There was little variation or insight. The only difference was how the stories played Trump's tweets. There was an assortment of recent ones to choose from: "Why isn't anybody suing Hilary Clinton for erasing 33,000 emails or her foundation? Disgusting"; "Suing the President of the United States for calling a crooked lawyer a crooked lawyer? Ridiculous. Lock him up!"; and "Twice as many people attended my inauguration than Obama's. They want to change the subject. More Fake News."

As Jason read leading libel cases, first Sue and then Joe knocked on the door and told him they were leaving for the day. Jason had made a reservation at Spoleto, as simple an Italian restaurant as could pay the rent in the east 50's. It was a restaurant that made sense because his son had to catch the last shuttle flight to Washington from LaGuardia Airport. He would get home very late if he took the train.

———————

Over dinner, father and son talked about the case, although Jason added almost nothing to public reports. He knew a few things about the lawyers that had not been reported, but that was about it. He could shed no light on how Moses could serve Trump with a complaint and summons and force him into the case. He knew nothing about either side's strategy, which was not unusual. In most cases a judge knows only what he learns from the parties in their court filings, which is little for quite a long time, sometimes not much until the eve of the trial. Since members of the media have contacts with the parties or their lawyers, they know more than the presiding judge.

"We have some new restaurants in Washington, including Italian. I'm wondering whether Spoleto is slipping."

"You may be right," Jason agreed. He preferred this subject. "This is the first time I remember not finishing the spaghetti carbonara. It's off tonight. The pasta is almost tasteless. I don't think they put enough salt in the water in which they boiled the spaghetti."

"That was always something that bothered you." Vernon took another sip of wine. "I hope you're eating well. You'll need endurance."

"Sure am. I enjoy the restaurants. Friends invite me for dinner. I send out for meals. The housekeeper still comes in twice a week and stays to cook. It's working."

Vernon asked the waiter for a fourth glass of wine. At his father's sharp glance, he replied. "Relax, dad, I'm not driving."

The two sat silently for several minutes, each lost in memories they couldn't share, especially the big one. Jason had been alone when he got the news about his son Robert's death. Jason had spoken to Robert earlier in the evening. Robert had said he had been drinking, but assured his father he wouldn't drive. Someone else would. Vernon had not attended his older brother Robert's medical school graduation. He'd gone backpacking in Europe with college friends. He'd heard about Robert's car crash and death two days after it happened. Because of her father's heart attack, Audrey had flown to Tampa right after the graduation ceremony.

Removing the half-eaten pasta, the waiter served a veal chop to Jason and baked salmon to Vernon. The two ate slowly, Jason barely tasting his food and ignoring the excellent Brunello he had chosen. Forcing himself to put the past away and enjoy his son's company, Jason interrupted the pained silence with a funny story about Sue and Joe. Soon the two were laughing.

"Are you sure you're O.K., dad?"

"Why do you say that?"

"I don't know how to say this, but you seem too good to be true. I worry that you're ignoring the pain of losing Mom. Even though I advised you to take it, perhaps you're getting involved in this big case before you're ready. You don't have to be macho."

"I don't feel that way," Jason responded. He was feeling good because he was strong and recuperating quickly, yet his son is criticizing him for it. Why would his son do that just when there was progress in their relationship? Jason frowned.

"I wasn't finding fault with you, dad, I'm asking if you need help or want anything, whether you're trying to prove something to yourself or someone else."

"I'm sorry I jumped on you. It has been tough." Jason regretted his reaction. There was something else. He felt guilty because he was still considering calling Christine. He didn't know what to do. He was lonely and needed someone to talk to, a sympathetic woman. He could not mention that to Vernon. Vernon would think he was disloyal to his mother. It had only been six months since her death. What young people often forgot was that in a long illness, like cancer, a spouse's grief begins almost with the diagnosis. And, Jason was seventy-five. Audrey would want him to enjoy the rest of his life and not be lonely. He would certainly want that for her if he had become ill instead of her. Also, Jason was angry at himself for not asking Vernon how he was doing. After all, he had lost his mother. It was a bad note on which to end the evening. It was hard work developing a relationship with a son, especially one he had largely neglected for over forty years.

"Son, do you mind if I ask you a question? Did your mother ever ask you about your marrying again?" Vernon had married a beautiful woman when he was thirty, whom his parents liked. Only months later, however, Vernon and Sarah separated, then divorced as soon as they legally could. Vernon refused to give details, but Audrey and Jason had concluded that Sarah suffered from a mental illness. And it was serious.

"Once or twice. Actually, I've gone out a few times with different women. I'm not totally against the idea." Vernon smiled.

"Anything to report?"

"Not really."

How would you like to go out with my new girlfriend's roommate? Jason could almost hear his college roommate ask. Jerry Klein was from Cleveland and the two had met early in their freshman year. They started rooming together the following year. Jerry went out with some of the prettiest girls at Cornell. In fact, with quite a few of the prettiest girls at Cornell, since Jerry did not specialize in long relationships. It was early in their junior year.

"Tell me more."

"Like Shirley, Audrey is a sophomore. She is medium height, well-built, black hair, majoring in English, and with a father who is loaded."

"What's the catch?" Jason had asked.

"No catch," Jerry answered. "She's rather shy, or so Shirley tells me."

"Sure."

The two went on a double date, which went pretty well, or at least Jason thought so. Jason found Audrey attractive and lively, and she shared his sense of humor, but there was no chemistry. Audrey's eyes were hazel and hair auburn. She was bright and interested in many things. She was a bit short for his taste. They went out a few more times, then stopped. Christine was a tough act to follow. They picked up a couple of months later after they found themselves in the same class on American colonial history. He admired her intelligence and self-confidence, but again they went their separate ways. Jason graduated, still unattached. He went to Columbia Law School. Two years later, they met again at a Cornell alumni gathering in New York City. Audrey was working for a publishing company as a reader of fiction. This time it was different. One year later they were married at a huge event at a reform temple in New Jersey. Jason was never sure how enthusiastic Audrey's father was at the match. Whatever reservations her father had disappeared when Jason became a federal judge.

"I have to go," Vernon said. He set down his empty coffee cup and brushed off his tie. He did this automatically, especially after a meal. "Again, congratulations and good luck. The case s one hot potato. From what I understand, the president will try to stop the entire case from proceeding."

"Where'd you hear that?"

"I read it in *The Washington Times*."

"Son, you and your firm have been covered by the press, haven't you?"

"Yes."

"Did they get the story right?"

"Not really."

"My follow-up question would be asking you about the ownership and partisanship of *The Washington Times*." Jason knew it was a very conservative paper and might be acting as a sounding board for someone connected with Trump.

Vernon laughed. "I should know better than to duel with a judge. I really should be going, as much as I'd like to linger."

"Next time." Jason felt better.

Jason paid the bill, and the two men left the restaurant. The evening had turned cold and rainy. Vernon flagged a cab and insisted his dad take it.

"I'll catch the next one," Vernon said. "You take care of yourself."

Jason pulled his son into a quick hug and then patted him on the shoulder. "Thank you, Vernon. Thank you for spending time with me, thank you for listening. I appreciate it." He said the words hoping Vernon had forgiven all the times Jason had not been there to listen to him.

"You're welcome, dad. We'll do this again soon." He sounded as though he meant it. Jason wondered whether he was being too sensitive.

Chapter 9

Singly or in small groups the participants in the first conference in *Moses v. Trump*, escorted by Sue, walked past Jason's office and took seats in the conference room. Jason could just glimpse them from his desk. First was a group of four, one late middle aged, three around thirty. They must be Theodore Butt and three associates from his prestigious New York law firm, Jason concluded. Butt was a large man; his features, which tended to be rounded rather than angular, lacked distinctiveness. He would be much more impressive if he lost twenty or thirty pounds. A full head of black hair with a tinge of gray, a black suit, very light blue shirt, and red tie. Pretty much the uniform. Two of the three young lawyers seemed fungible, the third was a woman. They were little more than scenery, however, perhaps intended by Butt to intimidate Reginald Whitebread, whom he would certainly outgun.

Next to walk by his door was someone Jason assumed was Whitebread and a young associate. Tall, angling, and elderly, he walked stiffly, like a superannuated cowboy in the movies. Jason wondered whether he wore cowboy boots. His view was blocked. He'd see later. He trusted security to see that Whitebread was unarmed, or at least disarmed.

Next was Counsel to the President Anthony Crunch and a

young male lawyer from his office. Jason had seen pictures
of Crunch but had never seen him in person.   He was larger
than the pictures suggested, reminiscent of a bear, or was it
a walrus? Crunch was neatly dressed in an expensive black
suit, with a crisp white shirt, and a red and blue striped tie,
another version of the standard uniform for lawyers. Crunch's
version was upscale; everything made to order and perfectly
tailored to disguise his overweight frame. His features were
undistinguished except for the black John L. Lewis-like eyebrows
that hovered above his heavily-lidded eyes. His black hair
seemed glued to his scalp. He had a conspicuous tan. He wore
a large ring on the pinky of his left hand. Jason found the overall affect jarring.

Jason was pleased that Crunch personally called Sue to say
he was coming to the conference and that he had a statement
he wanted to make. Nevertheless, Crunch's attendance at the
conference surprised him; Whitebread had not served Trump so
Trump was not officially part of the case. Most attorneys would
have stayed away.

"They're all there," Joe said from Jason's door.

What about Frederick Rattle, Beverly Clooney's lawyer?
Jason must have missed him. Jason got up and walked the few
steps to the conference room and sat down at the head of the
table. He wore his suit jacket, but not his judicial robes. He saw
Rattle seated alone on the far side of Butt. He was thirty-six, Joe
had told Jason. He had been a federal prosecutor in the Eastern
District of New York, which included Brooklyn and Queens. Dark
complexioned with thinning black hair, Rattle boasted a trim
beard and a narrow face.   He was slender and wore a dark blue
suit with a shirt of blue and white stripes and a solid sky-blue tie.
Hah, a nonconformist, Jason joked to himself. Rattle's nose was
red, and he sniffed repeatedly, to Jason's dismay. Twelve people,
including a court reporter and Joe, filled the room to capacity.

Jason was most interested in Crunch, who had seated
himself immediately to the right of Jason. Like many other
lawyers whom Trump brought into the government at a high
level, Crunch had represented his real-estate interests. He was

not a litigator, but a deal maker and breaker. He seemed a little uncomfortable, a feature Jason observed in those who were not used to defending many of Trump's strange positions publicly. One advantage in representing Trump was that one quickly became more comfortable in being a hard-ass. Jason reserved judgment on Crunch's competence.

"Good morning, lady and gentlemen." The salutation sounded strange. Jason hated to have one woman in the room. "Please identify yourselves individually to the reporter and me, stating whom you represent." Jason had been correct on all counts. Butt and three associates from his firm represented both *Total Faith* and Everett Mandick, its editor-in-chief and publisher.

"Thank you," Jason said. "Before proceeding further, I understand that the lawyer for the president has a statement to make."

"Thank you, Judge Jason." Crunch's young colleague handed him a sheet of paper. "I am here on the president's behalf as an observer to demonstrate his respect for this court." Crunch had a pronounced New York accent, Jason noted. He remembered that Crunch had grown up in Brooklyn. "The plaintiff has not served the president with the summons and complaint. However, I am appearing specially without subjecting the president to the jurisdiction of the court. I emphasize the president does not consider himself part of this case, but obviously has a contingent interest in how it proceeds. I am not yet prepared to say whether the president will agree to be served."

Jason saw Whitebread roll his eyes, presumably at the idea that Trump would accept service. Jason had to be careful not to do the same thing. Jason was unsure about Whitebread, whom he studied more closely. He seemed very relaxed. His lanky frame looked out of place in a suit. Jason imagined him in a cowboy outfit, complete with holstered six-shooters and spurs. His demeanor oozed informality, geniality, and earnestness. Jason wondered whether he would talk like a cowboy. Or shoot from the hip with twin pearl-handled pistols.

"My first question to Mr. Whitebread is whether he will accept the status of the president as described," Jason said. "I am not sure whether the president's codefendants have standing to complain because codefendants cannot ordinarily complain about whom else the plaintiff chooses to sue, but I want to hear from them, too. Mr. Whitebread?"

"We accept my brother Crunch's proposal," Whitebread said in a deep voice. "Beyond that we are unwilling to go. Also, we intend to continue to try to serve Mr. Trump with the summons and complaint."

Jason had no idea what Whitebread meant when he said they were unwilling to go further, but he let it pass. Probably Whitebread said things to impress his clients, should they read the transcript. He would sound tough. He had spoken like a lawyer, although his accent located him far west of New York City.

"*Total Faith* and Mr. Mandick agree." Butt's associate nodded solemnly as Butt spoke.

"Defendant Beverly Clooney takes the same position," Rattle said. His hoarse tones were broken by throat-clearing coughs.

"If you have no objection, Mr. Crunch," Jason continued, "please summarize the potential immunity issue. I think that a summary might help put the case in perspective. Of course, if you are reluctant there is no need. Your client has not been brought into the case."

Crunch sat still for a long time before he spoke. He briefly leaned toward his associate beside him, listened and quietly nodded to him. Then Crunch's heavily lidded eyes focused on Jason. "I cannot discuss where that issue stands and what the concerns of the president are," Crunch said. "I really don't think I should say any more. I have been instructed to stay, provided we are assured that my participation will not be construed as submitting the president to the jurisdiction of this Court, and to say nothing. If that is not acceptable to all parties and this court, I shall have no choice other than to leave." Crunch seemed programmed. "This is a very unique situation," Crunch added.

Jason winced. "Unique" never required a modifier,

especially one so insipid as "very."

Early in his legal career Jason had prepared a memorandum for one of the senior partners in the firm where he worked. The partner, who had been first in his class at Harvard or something like that, had praised Jason's research, but was less enthusiastic about his writing. "Let me tell you something, young man," the partner had told Jason, "you think like a lawyer, which is good. But you write like a garbage man, or a sanitation engineer, to be politically correct. I don't want to see you make another grammatical error, which leaves you a choice. On the assumption that you don't want to be unemployed, I'll give you the names of some books to read on grammar."

"Thank you, Mr. Crunch," Jason said. His eyes rested briefly, first on Crunch and then for some reason he could not explain, on the pale countenance of the young lawyer beside him. "I appreciate your statement and position." In fact, Jason realized that Crunch was correct and that he had made a mistake in addressing him.

"I think we can postpone consideration of anything to do with immunity," Jason continued. "I have a few preliminary matters to discuss. I want you to meet my law clerk, Joe McDonald." Jason indicated the young man seated behind him. Unlike the others who had immediately opened expensive laptops, Joe's yellow legal tablet and a half-dozen Number 2 pencils lay on a clipboard. Wearing a brown tweed jacket and a boldly yellow and black striped tie, Joe was by far the most casually dressed.

Jason told the lawyers that he did not want the case tried in the press. Just a request, mind you, although he reminded them that he had certain weapons if things got messy. No one needed reminding of the White House's penchant for leaks or, for that matter, Anthony Scaramucci's aborted fifteen-minute campaign against leaks.

Jason glanced around the table. Everyone was engaged. Whitebread emptied his glass of water and reached for the pitcher. Crunch studied his unopened laptop and made eye contact with no one. Rattle stared at the complaint in the case.

The young lawyers typed notes frantically on their keyboards. It was like army basic training where none of the recruits wanted to make eye contact with the drill sergeant.

"I'm not sure I can do anything about this," Jason said, "but it would be messy if the president gets served on the eve of trial after discovery has been completed. No activity before Mr. Trump is in the case can affect him. He would not be bound by earlier discovery, so earlier depositions could not be used against him, which could cause confusion. There's nothing that can be done now. We'll deal with the problem if it arises."

Again, Jason scanned the group on lawyers to see if anyone disagreed. Joe was writing on his yellow pad in his own shorthand that only he could read. Jason had always admired that ability. It came in handy during meetings like these, since transcripts took time when you were not paying for expedited transcripts.

"I cannot wait very long for the president to be served," Jason said. "We have a complaint filed and several defendants have been served. I have no choice but to proceed with the case. I will delay discovery and other matters for thirty days. After that we will proceed like in any other case. I shall start the calendar thirty days from today. Jason checked with Joe. "Mark your calendars for Friday, December 15.

"I hope you can resolve discovery disputes by yourselves. If not, I am here. A party can move for a protective order if he feels the discovery is abusive. On the disposition of any motion relating to the timing, amount, or scope of discovery, I will award attorneys' fees in favor of the prevailing party, and they may approximate the costs and attorneys' fees incurred. My order will state whether the lawyer or the party shall pay the fees. Any questions?"

Jason was tired of lawyers who created unnecessary disputes to wear down their opposition. Then, when a judge found their conduct excessive and ordered fees and costs to be paid to other party, they just billed their clients for the amount. One of Jason's pet peeves was that lawyers abused the system, and their clients, not they, had to pay for abuse. Only if the lawyers had to pay the attorneys' fees would it stop was Jason's view. Of course, Jason knew from personal experience, clients sometimes do demand abusive discovery and abusive everything else.

No one spoke. A few shook their heads negatively.

"Good," Jason said. "I am setting a hearing date now for resolution of the issue of whether Mr. Moses is a public figure, so you'll have to finish your discovery on that issue and submit memoranda simultaneously ten days before the hearing date. Let's note the hearing for five weeks from Friday at 2:00 p.m. That will be December eighth." He noted all the associates now had iPhone in hands as they punched in the dates on their mobile calendars. Jason quietly closed his leather bound, monogrammed day timer, the last of over forty-five he had kept – all of them annual gifts from Audrey. Jason had assumed that the issue whether Moses was a public figure would be raised by the defendants, and no one seemed surprised when he set the issue down for a hearing.

"That leaves only one more matter to discuss today, which is the trial date, which I shall now set at six months from the start of the calendar, for the record, Monday, June 4, 2018. The factual issues are not complex. All dispositive motions will be filed no later than one month before that." It was a peripatetic schedule for a major civil case, almost unheard of in the Southern District of New York. The lawyers looked at one another, but no one objected.

Jason continued his assault on tradition. "I do not like to see more than two lawyers representing any client at a conference in chambers. Only two lawyers for a party will sit at counsel table in courtroom proceedings. I hope that is understood."

Jason was also fed up with lawyers who generated large fees unnecessarily. Clients, even distasteful ones like *Total Faith*, had rights. One of the reasons he became a judge was because he detested the economics of law practice, such as charging each client that benefited for the full time it took to prepare a memorandum, rather than dividing the cost among them. An hour's work might generate six billable hours, one to each client that benefited. Lawyers defended themselves – each client was getting what he paid for. Jason thought it was sleazy nevertheless.

Jason remembered the old joke about a senior partner dying and going to heaven. He's taken aback by the elaborate reception and asks why. God says, "it's not often we can welcome a 120-year-old man into heaven." The lawyer says there must be some mistake, that he's only 86. God replies: "You should know that we have your billing records up here."

Jason concluded the meeting. "We'll notify you of the date and time of the next conference." The lawyers departed silently. Jason watched Crunch and his associate leave before walking the few steps to his personal office.

Trump would not understand how one of many hundreds of federal district judges could order him, the president of the United States, around. Jason had to admit that the issue was not crystal clear in his mind, even though judges liked to make it seem so. True, Article III of the Constitution gave federal judges the power to decide cases and controversies. But wasn't the presidency a co-equal branch of the government with the judiciary? Why couldn't the president, whose job it was to assure that the laws were faithfully executed, likewise tell the judiciary what to do? Since everyone assumed that judges could tell the president what to do, while the president could not tell judges what to do, Jason was in no position to argue. Better minds than his had decided that.

The following week passed quickly. Speculation about *Moses v. Trump* was rampant, although usually inaccurate. Jason refused to talk to the press and told his two-person staff that a media interview was a firing offense. While he was sure there would be no problems with them, he wanted to be on record in case a leak disrupted the proceedings.

Jason's daily routine was uneventful enough that the highpoint was lunch in the judges' dining room, even on days when there was no chief-judge request to attend. He was going there more often. The lunches always buoyed his spirits. He noticed that Cohen was rarely coming to the judges' lunchroom, which he did not consider unfortunate. It was a good place to relax with his colleagues. He dallied there.

Jason found himself going out less in the evenings. So far, he had confined those solo ventures to his three favorite restaurants. He continued to receive and accept dinner invitations from Andy and Carmen Smith and Thelma and Fig Newton, two congenial judges with entertaining spouses. They were lively evenings replete with challenging discussions of world events, science, or whatever was on the minds of the participants. Jason chose his after-work company with care. He liked his stockbroker, but not enough to talk about money with him for three hours. He was not yet ready for an evening with a former law partner, now retired, whose enthusiasm for labor law and his antipathy to unions made him gag.

This evening Jason had consumed a meal delivered from an Indian neighborhood restaurant.

The television interrupted Jason's after-dinner reading with breaking news. Trump had been served with the summons and complaint! Jason closed his book. A man on a private security detail hired by Trump for Mar-a-Largo had led him to a woman with a small baby in the forefront of a group restrained by a rope. When Trump got close, the woman reached out and served him with the summons and complaint in *Moses v. Trump*. Another report said it looked as though the woman was breast-feeding an infant. Yet another account said it was not clear that the baby was real, noting that the woman, when interviewed, asserted she would not let Trump get that close to an infant.

The Secret Service and the rest of the private security detail were caught by surprise. Trump tweeted something nasty about how he was ill-served and that he would have the FBI lock up whoever was responsible. "Can't believe that the president can't be shielded from cranks. Lock her up. No transgenders in the military."

A later program on CNN added to the information. A sum of money had been paid to a member of the detail, which had been hired to supplement the Secret Service when Trump bowed to complaints about the size of the bill to pay for security for him. Congress insisted that Trump provide some of the security when it became known that he was charging the government for guest admission fees, golf carts, and food and water for Secret Service personnel at his resorts. It had not worked out particularly well. The private security detail had a history of roughing up innocent demonstrators, allegedly on Trump's orders.

Trump had been done in by private enterprise. In the age-old tradition someone had sold out to the highest bidder, CNN gloated. Trump tweeted: "Can't I count on anyone but my family and myself to do anything right? Very sad. Drain the swamp."

The next day *The New York Times* reported that a disaffected Russian oligarch who had moved to the United States had spent $1 million in efforts to serve Trump. The oligarch said he disliked Trump almost as much as Putin. He said that he wanted to help fund Congress's Russian investigation, but his lawyers told him that was illegal. The Constitution dictated that only Congress could fund government operations. Trump's tweet denounced the oligarch as part of a left-wing conspiracy to damage him, the Constitution, the country, and Putin.

Hundreds of Trump supporters gathered outside Trump Tower chanting "lock him up," holding up identical pictures of the oligarch. *The New York Times* story said its sources told them that the picture was a Russian mug shot and speculated on how the demonstrators had obtained it so quickly. One demonstrator, who held up a picture of Trump, had to run for his life. The media reported that most of the demonstrators had been bussed in from Staten Island. No one would say who paid for the buses.

By coincidence Jason had scheduled a meeting on the case the Monday after Trump was served. He was in his conference room when the cadre of lawyers, reduced by two that Butt had left at his office, arrived. "I understand there has been a recent development in the case," was Jason's low-key opener. "Anything to say, Mr. Crunch?" Crunch was slumped in his chair looking bored. He roused himself when Jason addressed him.

"I'll confirm that the president was handed the complaint

and summons, but we are exploring whether the service was legal because of the circumstances. I cannot say more on that."

A few snickers rattled around the table. "Are you referring to the fact that the baby was not real?"

"Enough of that, Mr. Whitebread," Jason said. "I am proceeding on the assumption that service was proper on President Trump until there is a motion contesting the service and I rule otherwise. I will not wait to see if Mr. Trump moves to quash the service." Jason looked at Crunch, who spoke reluctantly.

"I'm afraid my instructions preclude me from discussing the matter further, Your Honor. I can add that we are moving expeditiously." As before, the man made little eye contact. His monotone statement sounded as if it had been prerecorded from a script prepared by someone else. His New York accent persisted.

"I appreciate that," Jason said. "I'll give you one week to file a motion to quash the service; otherwise, I'm ruling that the president has been served." Jason wasn't sure he could do that, but no one argued with him. Jason also could not conceive how the service was invalid. People used tricks all the time, and those gimmicks never affected the validity of service.

"Is there any problem with our telling the media what happened today, Your Honor?" Mr. Moses asked.

"None, but I welcome restraint. Mr. Crunch, please convey to Mr. Trump my request that he not make any remarks that could reasonably be construed as possibly prejudicing the trial of the case. I am forwarding this as a request by the court. Please also mention this request to the new Chief of Staff." Jason resisted the urge to add, "whoever he may be."

"I understand that. I don't think I have to say more. My client must decide things by himself. I'm sure President Trump will act responsibly," Crunch said.

"We'll have a court session Friday at 2:00 p.m. that will deal with scheduling matters. Unless there is something else, I think we can call it a day." Jason could not detect a hint of irony in Crunch's comments. He concluded that that was probably something in Crunch's favor. He was sticking by his unusual client.

Jason looked out the window. An unusual blanket of snow had arrived in November. Jason watched the street below where people scurried along newly shoveled sidewalks. He felt good about how things were progressing on the trial.

He wondered what Chief Judge Marbury had done about Malcolm Cohen and his dalliances with women lawyers who appeared before him. Marbury had said nothing. Neither had Cohen, who, Jason thought, had avoided him the past week or two. Jason obviously could not ask Cohen and was unsure of the protocol of asking Marbury, but he had made up his mind to ask him anyway. He decided on the same basis that had influenced some of his other actions, namely, what was the worst they could they do to him. Jason enjoyed having life tenure and being immune from retaliation or discipline unless he shot a lawyer in open court. He was in the same boat as Trump. They could get rid of him only by impeachment. Actually, Jason realized, he was probably more vulnerable than Trump. He could not count on the cadre of Republican congressional sycophants.

Jason telephoned Marbury, who asked him to come right over. Marbury led him to his enormous office that Jason had concluded was larger than a tennis court. They sat next to each other on one of the two couches that faced each other, yards away from Marbury's desk. His desk was the size of Jason's, but the table on the far side of the room was larger than the ones in Jason's office and conference room combined. Jason turned down an offer of refreshments.

"I hope you don't mind my asking" – Jason was annoyed at himself for beginning that way – "but I was wondering how the Malcolm matter has worked out." Jason paused. He was having second thoughts about asking for this meeting.

"I think it's resolved. Malcolm explained to me that he had been talking to a woman lawyer while waiting for the other side's lawyer and the subject of swimming came up. Malcolm said he told the lady lawyer that he had swum for his college team and that he happened to have a picture of him from those days. He said that the other party's lawyer came into chambers when he was showing the picture and must have misunderstood. The lady lawyer won the case, which may have upset the other lawyer. He also said that he had talked to you about the matter and that you had not taken it seriously. He said it was a misunderstanding and there was nothing to worry about. I consider the incident closed." Marbury spoke unusually rapidly.

Jason was dumbfounded. *Cohen's story was an incredible distortion. He made it sound as though he had reported the matter to me and I said it was nothing. Shit. If I challenge his story, it will look like I had been covering it up with Cohen. What a mess!*

"I'm glad to hear it," Jason said after a few seconds. "I assumed you took care of it, but I wanted to make sure that you were not expecting me to do something." Jason did not know what to say about his role. He had to say something. "I'm not sure where Malcolm got the idea that I didn't take the incident seriously."

"That's not important. I should have let you know what I decided," Marbury said.

"You have plenty on your mind. I was just curious."

Jason returned to his chambers. He felt like a poker player whose opponent had just drawn an inside straight to wipe him out. Or maybe one who got bluffed and folded the far better hand. He suspected he had made an enemy in Cohen. Finally, Jason worried that Marbury was unhappy with him because he had not told him about the conversation he had had with Cohen.

Why couldn't they just leave me alone? After all, I have President Trump to worry about.

Chapter 10

Crunch called Joe to say that the president would not file a motion to contest Moses's service. That removed one issue from tomorrow's hearing. It would be a short session, but it was important that he inform the public that the case was progressing and what the issues were. Even a brief court proceeding would cut down on idiotic rumors.

The jammed ceremonial courtroom, the same one Andy Smith had used in *United States v. Kruiser*, awaited Jason, who was punctual as usual. He strode purposefully through a door in the front of the court room to his high-back chair on the dais. The awkward architecture of the ceremonial courtroom made in difficult for him to see people close to him because of a railing that partially obstructed his view. He figured out that a slightly higher seat on his chair would solve the problem, which he had installed, although at times he felt as though he were in a child's high chair.

The media filled the first three rows of benches on the left side of the spectator section. Jason recognized a few reporters who covered the federal courts in lower Manhattan, including Sam Rodgers, in the first row. Jason was pleased that the courthouse regulars were allotted the best seats. The front row on the other side was reserved for V.I.P.s. In that front row Jason recognized Rebecca Moses from a shot of her on television, a plump woman in her seventies whose hair was a disconcerting red.

The parties' lawyers were seated at three tables in front of Jason, rather than the normal two, because there were three distinct interests rather than the normal plaintiff and defendant. Whitebread and an associate sat at a table to Jason's left. Crunch and the same dour young colleague that had accompanied Crunch at earlier meetings, representing the president, sat at a table next to Whitebread's. Butt, an associate from Butt's firm, and Rattle, who collectively represented the four defendants, sat at the third. As usual, clients were not present for arguments on motions. There was no question of televising the hearing, because the law prohibited that in federal courts.

After the bailiff intoned the traditional opening of a session of the court, "Oyez, oyez, all those having business before the court draw near and you shall be heard," Jason asked, "Mr. Crunch, do you have anything to tell the court?"

"Your Honor, this is obviously an unusual and difficult situation," the large man representing the president began. "The president has been served and he no longer has the option of being a bystander. He has instructed me to file a motion to dismiss the case against him or, at a minimum, postpone his case until he leaves office in view of his position as President of the United States. We respectfully request the court to expedite consideration of that motion."

"Anyone want to respond at this time?" Jason scanned the clusters of attorneys who sat before him. No response.

"I'll give the president one week to file his motion, with responses due one week after that. We'll have a hearing on the motion on January 5 at 2:00 p.m. in this courtroom. Next on the agenda, I'll consider whether Mr. Moses is a public figure immediately after the immunity issues are resolved and the scope of the lawsuit is resolved. I'll asked the parties to exchange briefs on that issue on December 13 with responses one week later. We'll hold a hearing on the public-figure issue on January 19 at 2:00 p.m. Whether Mr. Trump wins or loses, we're going to trial as scheduled in early June of next year. Anything else?"

Silence, once again. Jason thought this was an obedient group of lawyers.

"If there is nothing else, we'll adjourn until January 5, 2018. This applies only to court hearings. The conference schedule is unaffected."

"All rise." Some people had come a long way for five minutes of activity.

Barely seated at his desk after returning from the hearing, Jason's phone rang. Sue put Cohen through. "I have to see you. Can I come over now? It's about the matter we talked about."

"I'm sorry, Malcolm," Jason said. "I'm tied up in this case of mine. I just don't have time to see you." Jason wanted off the Cohen matter. Marbury was handling Cohen, not him.

"It will just take a minute."

"I'm sorry, but I can't right now." Jason wondered if he were making a mistake in not seeing Cohen.

"When can we talk? You owe me. You can't abandon me now."

I owe him? That's crazy! "I'll give you a call."

"Thanks a lot."

Was Cohen being sarcastic? Probably. Jason knew he had alienated Cohen, but he didn't care. The man had lied to Marbury, and was doing everything he could to implicate Jason.

He walked over to the door, closed it, and returned to his chair where he sat with his eyes closed. He needed to think. Marbury told Jason the problem was over, or rather never existed. He'd have to tell Marbury if he spoke to Cohen and learned that it was still going on, and he didn't want to do that. He decided there was nothing he should or could do. The situation either would, or would not, resolve itself, but in either case he did not want to be involved in it any further.

Fifteen minutes later, the phone range. "Your son is on line one," Sue said.

"I'm sorry I haven't called recently, but I've been very busy, including preparing for a one-week trial before the Tax Court in L.A. Next week I have to go to Cleveland to meet to a client."

"How did the trial go?" Jason asked.

"Not bad, although I have no idea how it will come out. For a Tax Court case there was a lot of live testimony. The DOJ lawyer was bright, but inexperienced. It was one of her first trials with real witnesses. She had trouble with hearsay."

"You should see some of the clowns that come before me." Jason thought of a few crazy moments in his courtroom before he snapped back to the present. "How are you doing otherwise?"

"No complaints. How's the case of the century going?"

"O.K. The big issues are the ones you read about in the newspaper. Immunity for Trump is the biggest by far. There's also an issue of whether Ira Moses is a public figure." Jason realized that none of that was news to Vernon, but it was safe. Other subjects perhaps less so. Jason decided he could not talk to his son about Cohen. Talking to outsiders, even a son, about misbehavior by a fellow judge was out of the question.

"One more thing, son. As much as I'd like to visit you, I must postpone my trip. I don't want to take on too much. There's a lot to do here."

Jason was exaggerating. He did not want to go to Washington. It would be tiring, and he wasn't sure how a weekend with Vernon would work out. And December in D.C. could be depressing, even more than in New York. He was happy to work at a leisurely pace and watch whatever on television attracted him. *Law and Order* remained his favorite, even though some of the courtroom scenes made him gag. Things were wonderfully uncomplicated on television, but also unpredictable, which made it fun.

"Sorry to hear that," Vernon said.

"I'm sorry, too. We'll get together soon." Both hung up. Given the choice, Jason preferred his life to be simple at this point. He had his memories and his job, plus an occasional social outing. He thought about Christine. While he was more than intrigued and would enjoy her company over coffee and perhaps dinner, he did not want to court controversy with his son over his seeing her. Not yet.

The memoranda and responses Whitebread, Crunch, and Butt submitted on the issue of immunity added little of substance to what Joe had written, except for an interesting argument by Whitebread that there was no such thing as temporal immunity for a president being sued. Butt stated he sided with the president. Rattle filed a one-sentence memo that said defendant Beverly Clooney agreed with Butt and his clients. While unmentioned, having Trump at their side would be catastrophic for the defendants. They wanted him out of the case any way they could. In a Manhattan courtroom it would be hard to imagine a more miserable ally. The issue before Jason was a reprise of *Clinton v. Jones*, with a new cast and minor changes in the plot. The question was how it would play out.

When the case returned to the ceremonial courtroom on January 5, Jason observed that the crowd was as big as ever despite the six inches of show that had fallen overnight. Once again, it was a pretrial hearing not the main event, but one that would decide whether Trump would have to participate in *Moses v. Trump*.

Crunch had the most at stake, by far. Subjecting Trump to a trial would be not only an embarrassing loss, but also one that would place Crunch on the receiving end of Trump's fury. Trump famously did not like to lose. Likewise, he famously never took responsibility for his failures. If he had to go to trial, it would be Crunch's fault. If he went to trial and lost, it would be Crunch's fault. Jason felt some sympathy for Crunch, although not a lot. He had chosen to work for a volatile president after having worked for a ruthless businessman.

"Ladies and gentlemen, a couple of preliminary things," Jason began after the bailiff called everyone to order. The sound system was working fine.

"I have not set a time limit on this hearing," Jason said, "but I do not want to suggest that you should be verbose. I have read all the memoranda carefully, and so don't repeat yourselves."

Crunch strode confidently to the podium directly in front of

Jason, but several feet below him. "Your Honor, I recognize that I cannot argue that *Clinton v. Jones* was decided incorrectly; only the Supreme Court can amend or change its decisions." Crunch spoke with exaggerated distinctiveness. His argument was well rehearsed, and Jason could see that Crunch had pages of large-type printing in front of him in case he faltered. "Nevertheless, this is a constitutional case of the highest order and implicates separation of powers, namely, the right of the courts to interfere with the personification of another, coequal branch of this government. While the courts decide cases, the other branches of government also have the responsibility of enforcing the Constitution." Nothing controversial there, Jason thought.

"Nothing in the Constitution makes the assigned duties of the other branches less important. The president may not interfere with the courts and Congress. Congress may not interfere with the president and the courts.

"The issue in *Clinton v. Jones* was whether and when a court should postpone a trial of the president in a case that did not involve his official duties. Unlike in *Clinton v. Jones*, the president's statements here related in substantial part to his official duties, namely, the testimony of a member of his Cabinet, whom he appointed and supervised, before a committee of the United States Senate and an indictment for perjury based on that testimony. The indictment was secured by the Department of Justice, which the president also heads.

"The president is always on duty and he embodies the executive branch of the United States. Neither of the other two branches of our government is concentrated in one person. Unlike other federal officers, he cannot be indicted or tried for a crime while in office, because he personifies, he is, the executive branch. Even if the court considers the statement of the president a mixed one of official and nonofficial, that alone is enough to warrant granting absolute immunity. It is impossible to separate the official portion of his statement from the unofficial. Another constitutional branch of the government is entitled to that much deference and respect."

Jason wanted to be certain Crunch was not leaving himself

wiggle room. "Are you saying that if any aspect of Mr. Trump's communication relates to his duties he is immune, no matter how small that aspect is? Is that your position?"

"That is exactly right. If there is any element of the conduct that is official, a court's denying the president immunity interferes with the operation of another branch of the government and violates the Constitution. There is no place here for balancing of interests."

"I understand," Jason said. "But we're not here to focus on Secretary Kruiser's testimony, but on Mr. Trump's comment on an article calling her lawyer a felon. That's different, isn't it?" Jason saw Whitebread smile. "Also, hadn't the president fired Ms. Kruiser by then?" Whitebread smiled more broadly.

"It's all part of the same series of events," Crunch said. "I don't believe you can divide the scenario into thin slices. Remember, the president appointed Secretary Kruiser and she worked for him. The indictment covered a crime while she was a member of the President's Cabinet."

Jason lifted his hand and leaned closer to the microphone. "Let's assume I decide that the tweet was unofficial. You're saying if the facts were the same as in *Clinton v. Jones*, which, incidentally was decided unanimously against President Clinton, and you present strong evidence that the case would seriously distract the president from his official duties, I can grant temporal immunity?"

"Yes, Your Honor, based on new evidence. One way of looking at that case is that there was a failure of proof on the part of President Clinton. The Supreme Court said at 520 U.S. at 708, 'there is nothing in the record to enable a judge to assess the potential harm that might ensue.' We have submitted studies and sworn affidavits as part of our motion. It is indisputable that the facts here are far stronger for the president than in *Clinton v. Jones*, even on the assumption, which we dispute, that the tweet was not part of the president's official business. In this case the court has a record. That is our principal argument."

Crunch paused a second more than seemed necessary. "I

feel obliged to add that the president stands alone in this case. There was no collusion with *Total Faith* or anyone connected with it. The president played no role in the publication of the article in question."

"I understand. Anything else?" Jason saw spectators smile at the word collusion. He never thought there was collusion, at least with *Total Faith*, but Crunch made an interesting point. Possibly, Trump's claim for immunity would be tarnished if he colluded with the publisher of the article.

"I request an opportunity to speak further on rebuttal." Although he had an uphill battle, Crunch sounded confident, Jason thought. That was the sign of a good lawyer.

"Mr. Crunch, your brevity exceeded my wildest expectations. Of course, you will have time for rebuttal. I have some questions, but I want to hear from Mr. Whitebread first. By the way, Mr. Butt and Mr. Rattle, do you want to address the issue orally?"

"Thank you, Your Honor," Theodore Butt answered. "May I wait and see if there is anything I can add to what Mr. Whitebread says?"

Rattle said nothing but looked at Butt, who gave no sign.

"That's fine with the court," Jason replied. "Mr. Whitebread, it's your turn."

There was a touch of arrogance in Whitebread's manner as he almost sauntered to the podium. He glanced down at Crunch before speaking. No boots, Jason noted. Whitebread was wearing expensive black shoes with a high shine.

"Thank you. I'm not sure that I can match Mr. Crunch's brevity, but then things are a lot bigger and longer where I come from."

"Take you time Mr. Whitebread, I have nothing on my plate until dinner." Jason immediately recognized that this was not the time for jokes, especially bad ones. The case involved the president of the United States.

"Thank you, Your Honor. I've found nothing in the Constitution that mandates that the president shall report to the people of the United States as part of his official duties, much less tweet to a selected group of his followers at all hours of the day or night. It is a political act, not one of government. Members of Congress don't get immunity unless they speak on the floor of their house. Presidential power under the Constitution is great, but it should not be extended to remarks he chooses to send out to a group of his political supporters via his offhand tweets, whether at 2:00 p.m. or 2:00 a.m.

"The president is used to pushing people around and defaming them, and he should be stopped. This is as good a place as any."

Jason saw Crunch rise slowly, seemingly not sure how he should handle the insult to his client, who also happened to be president of the United States. Jason decided he should handle the situation. He had to maintain decorum.

"Mr. Whitebread, it is not my intention to limit your argument. However, I expect lawyers in front of me to respect each other and other parties. I don't think name-calling is in your interest, at least not in the Southern District of New York."

"I apologize," Whitebread said weakly. He seemed to have been thrown off stride by being called to order. He took a drink of water. He looked at his notes. "Of course, all branches of government interpret the Constitution, but the primary responsibility lies with the judicial branch. It decides cases and it must decide in this case," Whitebread stated with conviction. "That is the teaching of *Marbury v. Madison*. The law is for the courts to decide. The president cannot judge himself. The president's argument on that point is invalid." Whitebread took another sip of water.

Jason knew Whitebread had paused to allow his argument to sink in. Whitebread's argument was new, or at least expressed differently, Jason thought. "So, if a remark relates to a president's official duties, he is immune from suit. If it doesn't relate to his official duties, he must go to trial immediately? Is that it?"

"Yes, Your Honor. Exactly." Whitebread's argument had the virtue of simplicity.

"Calling someone a crook is not part of the duties and

responsibilities of the president of the United States any more
than it is the responsibility of any government official or citizen
to call someone a crook publicly." Whitebread again paused.
There was a condescending quality to the slow pace. "The
federal government, including the presidency, is a government
limited by the Constitution and laws. The president of the
United States has official and constitutional remedies. These
include firing Secretary Kruiser and referring the alleged bribery
to the Department of Justice, which, incidentally, he heads
as president. The president's role does not include inflaming
the public against citizens or demeaning them, but rather
following mandated legal procedures. I am not alone in taking
that position. The president and the government are powerfu
enough without adding more.

"One other thing. We do not accept the proposition that
a president cannot be indicted while in office. That issue has
never been resolved. Thank you."

A murmur arose from the spectators. Jason decided to
ignore it. "Mr. Butt, do you have anything to add?"

"No, Your Honor."

"Mr. Rattle?"

"No, Your Honor."

"Mr. Crunch, your rebuttal."

Crunch stood up slowly, almost wearily. He walked slowly
to the podium, shaking his head. He conveyed the impression
that it was his responsibility to dispel the ignorance of the
uninitiated. I represent the president of the United States, he
seemed to impart with his lumbering movements, which at
times resembled Trump's. Why can't you let the president run
the country? After all, that was what he was elected to do.

"I'm not sure that I have to say much more," Crunch said.
"This case involves separation of powers; the judicial branch
should intrude as little as possible on the executive branch,
especially when the president himself is involved. So, *Clinton
v. Jones* should be construed to limit judicial intrusion on a
president's actions when there are indications that the suit
will interfere with the president even when the suit does not

involve the president's official duties. As I argued earlier, this case involves the president's official duties and responsibilities, at least in part. We shouldn't have judges deciding how the president should be spending his official time. All we have to decide here is that *Clinton v. Jones* should not be extended to mixed official and unofficial statements and activities or when proof that the proceeding would interfere with his official duties has been presented."

"I've read carefully the evidence you have prepared as to the president's duties and responsibilities, Mr. Crunch, but I'm not sure that that is very probative. The Supreme Court in *Clinton v. Jones* obviously knew the duties of the president. What do you say about that?"

"There was no evidence in that case and no request that the Court take judicial notice of the all-encompassing responsibilities of the chief executive and commander-in-chief."

"Your experts do indeed portray the responsibilities of the president as awesome. But what do you say to Mr. Whitebread's statistics on how many rounds of golf the president has played since he took office? Doesn't that large and unprecedented number suggest that the president possesses the time to simultaneously run the country and litigate one law suit?"

"We seriously dispute that conclusion, Your Honor. Many of his golf games were connected to his duties. And a president should not be required to forego all leisure in performing his demanding job."

"I am not sure that you've established that the president would be unduly burdened by this case, but I assure you I shall consider your arguments carefully."

"Thank you, Your Honor."

"What about Mr. Whitebread's point that there is no such thing as temporal immunity in this context?" Jason did not want Crunch to duck Whitebread's arguments.

"That would be news to the Supreme Court," Crunch said. "They never suggested that the only choice was to dismiss or to go to trial. Their whole opinion was premised on the availability of temporal immunity. That is what *Clinton v. Jones* was all about, temporal immunity, postponing the trial until after President Clinton left office. Since there was no suggestion that official duties were involved, it would have taken the Supreme Court thirty seconds to decide the case on Mr. Whitebread's assumption."

"I understand." Jason, however, wasn't sure, but he wouldn't get much more from Crunch. "I have a couple of questions, Mr. Crunch. Please assume for the moment that I rule against your client, the president. Will the president participate in pretrial and, if necessary, a trial? I'm not saying that he will have to attend the trial. What is your position?"

The slight rustling among the spectators ceased.

"We, I mean the president, has not decided that. In fact, in the unlikely event you deny our motion, I intend to file an appeal."

"I respect your position. Let me amend my question to include denial by the court of appeals, just so the record is clear, and denial of discretionary review by the Supreme Court."

"Your Honor, the answer remains the same. The president has not made a decision on that hypothetical assumption. He's said that many times to the media and I."

Jason would have loved to give Crunch the same speech on grammar as the Harvard-trained senior partner had given him nearly a half-century earlier, but he restrained himself.

"Let me tell you my problem, or rather your problem, Mr. Crunch," Jason said. "If you told me that Mr. Trump would participate in the proceedings, as President Clinton did, you have every right to claim that participating in the proceedings would interfere with the president's duties as president. But if he is not prepared to participate if he loses his motion, how does that impinge upon performing his duties as president? Am I clear?"

Crunch waited several seconds, apparently framing his answer. His assistant pushed back his chair as if to stand, but Crunch waved him down. He leaned down and spoke quietly to the young attorney who was now red-faced with fury. Crunch stood, faced Jason, and spoke very slowly.

"I don't believe the president of the United States

should be required to risk a judgment against him to obtain a decision on his rights as president. He is entitled to that much consideration, at the very least. Suppose he participated in this case and the country suffered because of the distraction? He should not have to place the country in jeopardy to obtain a ruling from Your Honor. He cannot risk that. The country cannot risk that." Crunch seemed pleased with his answer. His associate also looked satisfied.

The president would not decide a hypothetical question that implicated his constitutional role, Crunch was arguing. Jason did not think the question was hypothetical, but he could not force any other answer now.

"I will announce my decision in open court Friday, January 12, at 2:00 p.m. I would appreciate your telling me by noon on Thursday if there any additional statements on behalf of Mr. Trump." Jason turned to look directly at Crunch. "If I do not hear from you then, I shall decide the motion based on the record as it stands. Thank you."

"All rise."

Jason exited though the door behind him. The courtroom emptied quickly.

Walking toward his chambers, Jason was almost certain he would not grant Trump total immunity for a tweet that endorsed an article in a fringe magazine that called a prominent lawyer a crook. Trump was doing enough damage to the judicial system. Jason recalled the myriad of insults to the judiciary as well as the attacks against Special Counsel Robert Mueller. He also did not want to be known as the judge who gave President Trump a license to defame citizens. He took comfort in the fact that if he ruled that way the court of appeals would make the final decision unless the Supreme Court agreed to hear the case. It would be someone else's decision. Sometimes higher-court review was nice to have. It was like a fighter pilot who had a parachute.

With Joe's help Jason began drafting his opinion that denied Trump the relief he sought. The complaint would not be dismissed. The trial of Trump would not be postponed.

Jason had another enjoyable but uneventful dinner at the Smiths' home and he accepted an invitation to have dinner at the home of Judge Thelma Goodson Newton and her husband, Figaro Newton. Dr. Newton was a nuclear physicist and the son of an English father and an Italian mother, who was a famous physicist in her own right. Figaro Newton's parents had met at the opera. Failing to consider the inevitable abbreviating of his name, Newton's opera-loving parents had named him after one of opera's most delightful characters. Jason had learned—strike that— heard more about string theory and the ninth dimension than he could imagine anyone espousing anywhere outside a scientific conference. Newton had written several books, both groundbreaking studies on the origin of the universe and popular books of stories about the foibles of scientists, which had delighted Audrey and Jason.

What intrigued Jason most of all was that Thelma Newton was a devout Catholic, and one who was married to a prominent physicist whose work seemed to negate miracles. On his and Audrey's last visit a year earlier Jason was unable to resist the temptation to ask Newton whether the solution to the mystery of dark matter and dark energy was that they were collectively heaven. He was met with icy stares from everyone at the table, including Audrey, who mumbled something about adding to the dark matter when the two of them returned home. Newton then laughed, and his wife managed a strained smile. Jason wondered whether he had struck a nerve of some sort.

Jason regretted that he was not closer to the Newtons. They would have provided good company and a distraction. Perhaps more important, he might have found speaking to one or the other comforting. But without a foundation of trust built over time he could not bring himself to impose on his colleague and her husband with his problems.

Chapter 11

With no word from the president, the following Friday, again before a full house, Jason read his opinion out loud. He concluded: "In sum, I find that President Trump's tweet calling the plaintiff a crook was not part of his official duties and receives no more protection than such a statement by any other government official or ordinary citizen, and perhaps less because of the power of the executive branch of our national government, which he heads. The president has ample alternatives to accusing a citizen of a crime in a tweet. While it is arguable that the president should not participate outside of formal channels and possibly prejudice the administration of justice, I expressly disclaim any reliance on that argument." Reading out loud in the intense circumstances tired Jason. He stood, arched his back, and walked a few steps before sitting down and continuing.

"As a result of that decision, I must now decide whether the president is entitled to have his trial postponed until after he leaves office. That is a difficult question, which involves an interpretation of *Clinton v. Jones*. After carefully reading that decision as well as the memoranda filed by the parties and by several organizations, which have filed friend-of-the-court or amicus curiae briefs, I have concluded that the trial of the president shall proceed. I construe *Clinton v. Jones* to require the denial of a president's motion to postpone the trial of a civil case unrelated to a president's official duties except in the most extraordinary circumstances."

Jason's last sentence was interrupted by loud applause from most of the attendees. He banged his gavel and the noise ceased.

"The president has demonstrated no extraordinary circumstances. Although he has brought a considerable amount of data into the record, his argument for postponement is no stronger than was President Clinton's. Indeed, unlike *Clinton v. Jones*, the facts do not seem to be seriously in dispute with respect to the president's action. Thus, the president will not be occupied in the effort to establish facts, as opposed to the law, where he is well represented by counsel. The crucial issues in this case are ones of law.

"If there is nothing else, court is adjourned." Jason closed his loose-leaf book, stood quickly, and left. The press was already fleeing from the back of the courtroom like wildlife before an advancing fire.

Jason was pleased with his effort. He was feeling comfortable. He began to see *Moses v. Trump* as the culmination of his long career as a district judge. He was tired, but it was a healthy tiredness, the kind he relished after a hard workout. He had tried not only to be fair to all the parties, but to appear fair, and he felt he had succeeded.

Late on Friday afternoon, the clerk of the district court called to say that Crunch had filed an appeal. The court of appeals would hear the case *en banc* four days later, on Tuesday, the clerk added. As far as Jason knew, this was the first time since the *Pentagon Papers Case* in 1971 that all judges of the Second Circuit would hear a case without an intervening decision by a three-judge panel. Like the *Pentagon Papers Case*, where President Nixon tried to stop publication of a candid secret report on the Vietnam War, this case involved the power of the president of the United States in the context of the First Amendment. Obviously, *Moses v. Trump* was a big deal to the

Second Circuit, too.

That evening a single tweet emerged from the White House. "Fake judges cannot boss the President. How many votes did they get? How many people showed up for their inauguration? Drain the swamp." Jason was surprised at the mildness of the language.

———————

The following morning's newspaper headlines blared: "Judge Bars Trump Stall; Tweet Trial to Proceed"; "Trump on Bill Clinton's Slippery Slope"; "Trump Had No Business Sending Moses Tweet"; and "Moses: You Shall Be Judged."

On Monday Jason told Joe to attend the argument in the Second Circuit on Tuesday morning and take notes. He wanted to go himself, but protocol precluded his attendance. Jason busied himself during the argument while waiting for Joe to return.

It was nearly noon when Joe arrived back at chambers. "The judges interrupted each other as much as they interrupted the lawyers arguing the case," Joe reported. "They couldn't wait to get their questions answered. Many of the judges seemed to like Whitebread's argument that calling a citizen a crook was not part of the president's duties, regardless of the context. One judge, I think it was Judge Newsome, pointed out that it would have been improper if the Attorney General, who heads the Department of Justice, had made the statement. He asked why logic doesn't require the president, as his superior, to adhere to the same standards."

Nice point, Jason thought. He liked Newsome, whom he knew from work on committees on which both circuit judges and district judges served.

"Also, they didn't seem to want to expand presidential power. Another thing, Crunch contested your finding that the issues were mostly legal and not factual. He emphasized the question of Trump's state of mind, whether he was negligent or possessed actual, I mean legal, malice. The judges did not seem interested in overturning your finding of fact. Do you want more detail, Judge?" Joe asked, then added, "They said an awful lot," showing his boss the pad he had nearly filled up at the oral argument.

"You've given me what I wanted, a taste of the argument. I get the picture. Thanks."

The court of appeals had promised a decision on Thursday, so Jason told Joe to schedule a hearing in the ceremonial courtroom for Friday afternoon. Jason and Joe spent the next two days working on the case while they waited for the decision by the court of appeals. Their unexpressed assumption was that Trump would lose.

Thursday morning the court of appeals announced its decision. It was 11-1 against Trump. The grounds basically followed Jason's opinion. The sole dissenter was a conservative judge from upstate New York, who reasoned that the president and no one else should decide whether the tweets were part of his official duties. He had a respectable argument, Jason recognized. He relied on recent Supreme Court cases holding that each branch of the government can set its own internal rules, such as deciding the issue of when Congress is in session for purposes of resolving what was a recess appointment under the Constitution. Congress alone would decide.

That evening a spokesman for the president stated that he would not take the matter to the Supreme Court. Jason figured that someone remembered that President Nixon had said he would obey a definitive decision by the Supreme Court on whether he had to release the secret tape recordings he made of his conversations as president. The Supreme Court unanimously ordered Nixon to turn over his tapes to the special prosecutor. Faced with an order to surrender the damaging tapes, Nixon resigned. Obviously, Trump did not want to deal with a unanimous or near unanimous Supreme Court decision against him.

Something struck Jason. Why was White House Counsel rather than the Department of Justice representing the president? That was very odd. In every case he had presided over, the Department of Justice served as counsel for the government and its officials. The reason hit Jason. Trump did not want to put his welfare in the hands of an organization headed by Jeff Sessions, whom he was trashing at every opportunity. A man with Herculean suspicion, Trump would assume Sessions would screw him. While Jason rejected that possibility, it probably explained why Anthony Crunch was representing Trump.

An hour later, Trump tweeted again. "Judges, judges, and more judges. What do they know? The people know who's right. I am. What's happening to our democracy? Tragic. Drain the swamp."

White House leaks reported that Trump was furious with Crunch. One report said that Trump inquired whether corporal punishment was legal.

The usual crowd of spectators and lawyers greeted Jason Friday afternoon when he took his seat on the elevated bench. It promised to be a short, but important, session. "Mr. Crunch, I understand that the president is not seeking review in the Supreme Court. That removes the only legal impediment to proceeding with this case. Am I right so far?"

Crunch stood and walked to the podium. He did not seem to be his previous confident self. "Yes, Your Honor," Crunch said.

"As I suggested previously, if the president participates I will endeavor to grant him every possible courtesy. I will respect his schedule so that he will not be inconvenienced. With that in mind, has the president made a decision on what he will do now that his motion either for absolute or temporal immunity has been denied?"

The spectators were totally silent.

"Yes, Your Honor." Crunch's assistant handed him an opened loose-leaf notebook. Crunch pointedly read his answer and in a monotone. "The president of the United States respectfully informs the court that he will not participate in the proceeding. He will not be judged by one of hundreds of similarly situated district judges who are far down the ladder in the judicial branch of a co-equal branch of the government, which he alone embodies. It would be as if any member of Congress could command him. He alone is responsible for the operation of the executive branch, a very different situation from the other two branches. The president means no disrespect to the court, but a president cannot be at the beck and call of hundreds of members of another branch." Crunch closed the notebook and remained standing, staring at Jason.

Everyone in the large audience seemed to have something to say to his neighbor on the subject. A dozen reporters fled the courtroom. Jason banged the gavel with moderate strokes, enough to demonstrate his authority, but not enough to suggest that he was intolerant of some audience reaction.

Crunch seemed impervious. Jason searched for Crunch's personal reaction to the president's decision, but found none. He stood at attention facing the bench where Jason sat. Crunch's associate's demeanor, however, gave a lot away. He was sitting with his head in his hands, but briefly raised his head to glare at Jason. Trump had obviously overruled Crunch's recommendation to fight Whitebread. The take-no-prisoners faction of the White House, once headed by Stephen Bannon, had obviously won. Jason concluded that someone should tell the associate how to handle himself in the courtroom. He made a mental note to ask Joe, his clerk, to check his background. "Please continue."

Crunch reopened the notebook and read: "The president has instructed me to attend all court conferences and hearings as a courtesy and to show respect to the court, but to do so only as an observer. I or deputy White House counsel shall sit in the spectators' section in this courtroom. If there is something consistent with our position that we can do, we shall be available." Crunch took a sip of water and waited.

The large crowd was quiet throughout Crunch's statement, but started talking when he paused. Jason again gaveled the audience to order.

"I want to emphasize that the president and I intend no disrespect to you or to the Second Circuit." Crunch stood a little taller. "The presidency is the equal of the other branches of the government. He has his own obligation to construe the Constitution and he is doing so here.   To do otherwise would be a long step toward destroying the Constitution as the Founders wrote it. Consequently, I leave counsel table and take my seat among the other spectators."

There was a spattering of applause. The U.S. Marshals and a few spectators hushed them. Jason tapped his gavel lightly.

Jason had spent considerable time framing his words should Trump decline to participate in the case. He decided his statement would be short and colorless. He had written it out himself. "In view of these statements by the attorney for the president, I am entering a default in *Moses v. Trump* against defendant Trump on the issue of liability. I shall leave open the other issues, such as damages. I shall instruct the plaintiff not to notice the president's deposition or send him interrogatories in view of the position taken by the president. I do not want harassment of the president. I also do not want inflammatory questions that he will not answer being reported in the media and possibly poison the jury pool. Does each of you understand that? Please identify yourselves one by one and state your answers on the record. There is no need to stand."

"Mr. Crunch, that is correct, Your Honor." Crunch spoke without emotion.

"Mr. Whitebread, correct, Your Honor."

"Mr. Butt, I do, Your Honor." Butt was smiling, although circumspectly.

"Mr. Rattle, I do, Your Honor." Rattle also spoke without emotion and without looking at Jason. He seemed curiously uninvolved. Perhaps his sinuses were dulling his senses today.

Jason had a sudden flutter in his stomach, as he realized that one flawed district judge was commanding the president of the United States to surrender his ability to dispute a law suit. While Jason did not expect to see a lightning bolt strike from the heavens, he was astonished at how ordinary it seemed. He was speaking from the bench just as he had on hundreds of other occasions, but this time his words had extraordinary import.

Another group from the media fled the courtroom. Finished

with the main issue, Jason turned to the other items on his agenda.

"The next matter is Mr. Moses's status as a public figure. I assume the parties disagree on that issue and I'll have to resolve it before the trial starts. I'm scheduling a hearing two weeks from today. Anything else? No? Good. Good afternoon."

———————

Sitting in his favorite chair at home, Jason turned on the television set to catch the news. As he expected, the big story was the default entered against Trump. To his surprise Jason saw an artist's sketch of him on the bench, hovering over a diminished Crunch, or was it Trump. He couldn't tell. It was not a bad likeness of him. The story included a Trump tweet. "Each of the hundreds of federal judges thinks he is God. They should go back to law school or go to a place I won't mention. Morons. Drain the swamp.'"

The announcer continued. "The White House issued an immediate qualification. "President Trump was not speaking of all judges, who are hardworking and for whom he was the highest respect. He was just expressing his frustration at a particular decision, just like any American might.'"

The announcer looked down at a piece of paper that had just been slid in front of him. "Breaking news. Trump has just issued a new tweet. 'Judges are morons. Period. End of tweet. End of subject. Drain the swamp.' Back with more news after these announcements."

Cable news reported White House infighting that followed the entry of default. Leakers were in full voice. One leak reported that Trump had called Anthony Scaramucci, his dismissed Communications Director but still a trusted friend, who supposedly said, "Fuck the judges. Fuck the juries." Bannon was quoted as saying: "One nuke on North Korea and nobody will give a shit about *Moses v. Trump*." All agreed on one fact. Crunch's views were irrelevant.

Jason wanted to get out of his apartment and away from

the news, almost all of which depressed him. He was surprised no reporter had called, but he didn't expect that to last. He decided to dine at Mr. China. The weather had improved somewhat, but Jason decided to take a taxi rather than walk. Henry Chin greeted him with his usual enthusiasm and led him to the table toward the rear of the dining room, which he preferred for solo dining. The restaurant was not crowded so Jason asked Chin over to his table to question him about a new restaurant in Chinatown, which had gathered several superlative reviews. Should he go there for lunch? Whom better to ask than the owner of a good Chinese restaurant?

"Judge Jay, the chef comes from a part of China not particularly well known for its cuisine. If you will excuse my frankness, it is good but not memorable." A waiter came over and asked Chin a question in Chinese. Chin held up his forefinger. He answered the waiter in Chinese in a rather stern voice.

"Excuse me, Judge Jay, some of my waiters, even some who have been with me since I opened this restaurant, cannot solve even the simplest question without asking me. I told him that I did not like to be interrupted when I am talking to distinguished guests." Chin paused. "We were talking about a new restaurant if I am not mistaken."

"No problem, Henry. But, if I may ask, why are you smiling?"

"I was thinking of how things were not so many years ago. A Chinatown restaurant would open amidst very good reviews. People flocked to it. Unknown by many diners, the food rapidly went downhill but customers, almost all American, continued to come and spend money." Chin paused. He looked embarrassed, Jason thought.

"Please don't stop. I am very curious about what happened."

"These are things we don't usually talk about, Judge Jay. But since I have started, and you are an important judge, I shall continue." Chin bowed slightly.

"Thank you." Jason was indeed curious.

"There were then only a small number of first-rate chefs

in the United States who were trained in China or, much more likely, Hong Kong. A new restaurateur would go to the owner of one of those restaurants and offer him money to borrow his chef for a few months. After favorable reviews for the new restaurant came out, the highly rated chef would return to the first restaurant. Everyone would come out ahead, except for the American diners. The Chinese figured they would not know the difference, so no harm was done."

"That is a good story," Jason said, laughing.

"But things have changed." When Jason looked quizzical, Chin continued. "There are so many good Chinese chefs these days looking for work that it is no longer necessary to use that trick."

"Ah, the good old days, Henry. What should I have?"

"Are you in the mood for a robust casserole?"

"I could be tempted."

"What would you like to drink?"

"What do you suggest?"

"I think that this is a dish that commands a good beer," Chin said. "It is not an elegant dish that warrants cognac."

"What about Tsingtao, a beer from the old country?"

"I suggest Sam Adams, Judge Jay. I have no desire to support the economy of a country that killed so many of my relatives."

"A reasonable culinary decision." Chinese have long memories, Jason recalled.

"Man does not live by fried rice alone," Chin said. "Enjoy yourself."

"Thank you, Henry, I always do."

Jason thought about his conversation with Henry Chin during dinner. Chinese restaurateurs had their elaborate code of ethics, which did not seem to protect non-Asians or, more likely, non-Chinese. They were very vulnerable, as their history in this country demonstrated. A minority in the United States, they could not build walls or exclude Muslims or anyone else. They also could not stiff-arm suppliers the way that some obscenely wealthy people like Trump regularly did. Their customs were designed to protect them from outsiders, whether majority or minority.

Jason slowly consumed the terrific dish, which included oysters, roast pig, turnips, and roasted tofu, one that so few Americans could enjoy. Jason liked that there were so many societies with such different beliefs and cultures. He wondered what the Chinese would think of the concept of a public figure, indeed, whether the concept made any sense to a foreign culture that had such different values and views of the individual and society. Americans were so egocentric. Jason forgot about the book he had brought on the typhoid epidemic after World War I, while he consumed the casserole. He had not forgotten, however, about *Moses v. Trump*.

Chapter 12

The lawyers shuffled papers and the overflow crowd of spectators talked among themselves in hushed tones while waiting for Judge Jason to appear on the bench to hear argument on whether Ira Moses was a public figure. There were just two tables in front of Jason, now that Trump's lawyers retired to the first row of the audience. The bailiff announced in stentorian tones, "All rise," while Judge Jay Jason made his way to his oversized and elevated chair.

"I am prepared to hear argument on the question whether plaintiff Ira Moses is a public figure," Jason announced. "I have carefully read your memoranda and the relevant cases. I'm sorry to deny you the chance to demonstrate your knowledge, but life is short. My understanding is that person does not become a public figure by doing his job in the private sector, however successful he is. He must do something more than work away in his profession or calling. He must reach out for public approbation. The issue is whether he seeks notice or notoriety outside the confines of his position. If he does no more than necessary to thrust himself into the public eye than his job requires, he's a public figure. If you disagree, convince me."

Jason waited a few seconds, but no one spoke. They were

looking at one another. "Mr. Butt, you argue on behalf of Mr. Mandick and *Total Faith* that Mr. Moses is a public figure. Give me your evidence in a couple of sentences."

Butt stood quietly at the podium. He closed the notebook he had opened. "Mr. Moses is a prominent attorney who voluntarily injected himself into a particular and major public controversy. He did this by choosing to represent an important public official in a case of national importance, a matter that is precisely the sort the founding fathers believe warranted full and frank discussion. Because of his stature and role, Mr. Moses has had access to channels of communication sufficient to rebut falsehoods against him. That's it in a nutshell."

So far, so good, Jason thought. "Why should the fact that Mr. Moses happened to get involved in a big case make him a public figure? In other words, why should the mere fact that a lawyer or anyone else is successful in his calling change his status from a private figure to a public figure?"

"It is important to recognize that Mr. Moses knew what he was getting into," Butt said. "The situation may be different if an ordinary case explodes. The Supreme Court has said that fortuitous events cannot make someone a public figure. If I may, Your Honor, if I recall correctly, that happened to you just before you became a judge."

Jason smiled. It was a nice point, even though Butt was heavy handed in becoming personal. It was time to hear from the other side. "Mr. Butt, please give way to Mr. Whitebread. I want to hear from him why Mr. Moses's prominence and participation in *United States v. Kruiser* are not enough to make him a public figure."

"Thank you, Your Honor. Pure and simply because Mr. Moses was a litigator who was doing his job," Whitebread said when he had stationed himself at the podium. "He did not thrust himself into the limelight by going on television, writing books, or doing those kinds of things that make someone a public figure. A plumber does not become a public figure if he fixes the plumbing in the White House."

Jason frowned. "Aren't you demeaning what this country

is about when you compare a lawsuit that goes to the heart of important issues of our government with fixing the plumbing in the White House?"

"I don't believe so," Whitebread said. "The criminal case involved a prosecution, not a debate on the policy of the Administration."

"Obviously, all these issues come up in the context of individual law suits," Jason stated. "I'm at a loss as to how you can fail to distinguish between a prosecution of a member of the Cabinet for a statement about national policy and a plumber." Jason felt his face getting red and wanted to prevent further escalation. He paused. "Mr. Butt, do you want to say anything?"

"Yes, Your Honor. Matters of government and politics have a special importance and status in a democracy, which I believe was the point the court was making. We must give people more leeway to criticize others in the context of government. That is what *New York Times v. Sullivan* is all about and it is to that case that I direct the court. The Supreme Court threw out a judgment against *The New York Times* won by a southern sheriff, a public official. The *Times* had published substantially true advertisements in good faith that civil-rights groups placed in its newspaper."

Good answer, Jason thought. Rattle spoke briefly, mimicking what Butt had argued.

"I'll take the matter under advisement," Jason said. The court adjourned.

Two days later Jason released his decision. Moses was not a public figure. He explained that aside from people whose livelihood depended on public recognition, such as actors, pop singers, professional athletes, and perhaps a few others, success in one's field alone does not make someone a public figure. Success in one's work does not mean loss of First Amendment protection. Since Moses did virtually nothing other than try a case in accordance with his profession, he is not a public figure. Ordinary citizens could not do their jobs if they became public figures simply because someone wrote about their performance. Of course, Moses still must prove that the defendants were negligent to recover compensatory damages and more to recover punitive damages. That would give the media and others sufficient protection and meet the requirements of the Constitution.

The media largely ignored the decision. It had nothing to do with Trump and it was technical.

One day later Jason sat at his desk looking at mail when Sue handed him an envelope. This was just hand delivered."

Jason withdrew the letter from the envelope. The letter was short: "I want to advise the court and counsel that *Total Faith* and Mr. Mandick are conceding, for purposes of the case only, that the article was false. We are simultaneously filing a formal notice to that effect and amending our answer to the complaint." Theodore Butt had sent it, with copies to Whitebread and Rattle.

Jason called Joe into his office and showed him the letter. "This is the first time I've ever seen a publication concede a story was false," Jason said. "That's something, especially on a big matter. Admitting that you wrote a false article can ruin a publication."

"So why is *Total Faith* admitting it was wrong?"

"Unlike *The New York Times*, *Total Faith* won't lose much if it concedes the story was false in order to increase its chances of winning overall. The religious right stays close to its friends. Everett Mandick is more interested in winning the lawsuit than losing credibility with the average citizen. Those people don't matter to him. Money does.

"*Total Faith* is something like a magazine that covers extraterrestrial affairs," Jason said with a slight grin. "The readers think everyone else is crazy. They have a different reality than other people and they are used to the fact that others reject their thinking. But there's something else that's very important for the trial. Clooney isn't conceding that the article was false. Otherwise, why would Butt send a copy of the letter to Rattle rather than have Rattle's signature on the letter? The publication and its editor are conceding falsity, but the reporter who wrote the story is not. They will be taking different positions on the truth or falsity of the article. That's something we have to think about."

Conservatives were not happy campers overall. Butt's statement that this was standard litigation strategy calmed a few, but not the bulk of the right-wing press. Some claimed Butt was a liberal whose agenda was to destroy Trump. Other conspiracy theories surfaced. There were calls on Mandick to fire Butt as his lawyer.   Trump's tweet artillery was uncharacteristically silent.

Mandick, who knew when it was time to get down to business, kept his focus on winning the suit. Much was at stake in *Moses v. Trump*. For Mandick it was survival of *Total Faith*. This was no time to screw around.

Characteristically, Mandick tried to have it both ways and, characteristically, he succeeded. He expressed his continued confidence in Butt, but bemoaned that his lawyer felt it necessary to make such a concession as a strategic decision. One ultra-right-wing Fox commentator construed the concession that the article was false as a clever gambit that demonstrated that the article about Moses was indeed true. Mandick's statement led some to praise Butt's concession as a major victory, akin to the evacuation of the British expeditionary forces from Dunkirk in World War II with only moderate losses of personnel (but loss of all heavy equipment, as arguably was the case here).

Jason followed the press reports. You rarely win wars by successful evacuations, Churchill said, and you rarely win cases by clever concessions, Jason thought.

It was Friday morning and the same lawyers sat around Jason's conference table for their last scheduled pretrial conference. "I have a question or two," Jason said to the lawyers. "The first is whether Mr. Butt and Mr. Rattle have been communicating on the issue of the falsity of the article. As I read Mr. Butt's filing, it is his and only his clients that are conceding falsity, or have I missed something? Mr. Rattle?"

"No, Your Honor, you haven't missed anything," Rattle said. Jason noticed that Rattle was dressed in a blue-gray herringbone suit that made him look very young. Without the beard he might have passed for a college student. "I don't dispute that the evidence seems strong on the issue of falsity. But even though I might believe Ms. Clooney should concede falsity, she insists the article is true. I must respect her wishes. That's my ethical obligation. Also, what would it look like if I conceded falsity and she testifies that the article is true?"

"I'd like to say something, Your Honor," Butt said. "Mr. Rattle has a gift for understatement. The evidence is overwhelming. I think any juror who voted that the article was true should be examined."

"That's a strange thing coming from you," Jason said. "Normally, I hear the plaintiff assert that his case is overwhelming, not the defendant." Jason knew that the last thing Butt wanted was to spend days on whether the article was true or false. Yet that would have to be the situation if Clooney insisted that the article was true. Jason had some sympathy for Butt's predicament.

"Well, this is not the usual case to say the least," Butt said. "Of course, we argue vigorously that we had no idea that the story was false when we published it. I have explained to Mr. Rattle ad nauseam that conceding falsity is best for everyone. It would shorten the trial and permit the jury to focus on the crucial issue."

"Your Honor," Rattle said, "I cannot in good faith deny what Mr. Butt has said, but, to repeat, I have a client who insists the story is true. I cannot describe my conversations with her, but I can assure the court that I understand the facts and that I understand my obligations."

"I'm not sure how this concerns me as the judge. Is anyone suggesting I do something?"

"Not really," Butt said. "I can only think of having another pretrial conference, one that Ms. Clooney would attend."

"I object to that," Rattle said. "I cannot be part of a gang-up on my client. I would be acting improperly and subjecting myself to a lawsuit by her and disciplinary action by the bar."

"Don't include me in this exercise," Whitebread said. "As counsel for Mr. Moses, I want no part of that and, in fact, I object to any such effort." Everyone looked at Jason.

After a pause, Jason said, "I agree that it would be unseemly to have Mr. Rattle's client here and for everyone to take turns haranguing her. I see no course other than to let in the evidence of falsity against Ms. Clooney. Mr. Whitebread can present all his evidence, subject to the rules of evidence. I'll explain to the jury what is happening."

Jason concluded the conference by reminding the lawyers that the first phase of the trial would be Moses' attempt to prove that the article was false and that Mandick, Clooney, and *Total Faith* were negligent and exhibited legal malice in writing and publishing the article. He explained that he preferred the term "legal malice" instead of "actual malice." The term malice was being given a special meaning.

Back at his desk, Jason noticed a new email. Malcolm Cohen had written, "Can I come over now?"

Jason responded, "Not a good time."

Cohen did not reply.

Jason had miscalculated. He found himself with nothing to do. In the days that followed the last conference with the attorneys, he decided that he would reread the memo on libel law that Joe had prepared for him. Several books had been written on libel trials in recent years, the best of which, he had been told, was by Renata Adler called *Reckless Disregard*, and he would try to find a copy of that on Amazon or Abebooks. He also scheduled and kept a dental appointment to have his teeth cleaned and saw his internist for his annual physical, both overdue. Aside from a moderate jump in blood pressure, which could be attributable to quite a few causes, his health was good.

In the evenings Jason usually ate at home, but occasionally

ventured to one of his favorite restaurants, especially Mr. China. Jason enjoyed Chin. One evening Chin told Jason with a sad face that a new restaurant, named The Great Wall, was opening on the next block. Jason expressed concern that it might divert business from Mr. China. Chin thanked Jason for his concern before saying, "Judge Jay, I don't think it will be a serious problem. The restaurant is Mexican." Chin smiled proudly at his joke. Jason laughed.

On Friday morning, a week after his conference, Jason called Christine. They agreed to meet for coffee that afternoon at a small café in SoHo.   Two days later they had brunch at a boutique hotel on the Upper East Side. Jason found both outings more enjoyable than anything he had done in more than a year. They had talked for hours and agreed to continue their visits. Christine's first husband had insisted that she go to college, which she did. Since she did not have to work, and they postponed having children, she was able to graduate from Queens College with a major in American history. She then obtained a degree in teaching and worked on and off as an elementary school teacher in a Catholic school. She continued teaching after her first husband died and she remarried.

Jason arrived at his chambers at 9:30 a.m. one week before the start of the trial, feeling satisfied about the case. That feeling lasted exactly one hour. Sue told him that reporter Sam Rodgers was on the phone and said it was important.

"Yes, Sam, what's up?"

"I don't know whether you've heard that Trump has started tweeting about the case. It's the usual crazy stuff he does. You know, Kruiser was a Democratic mole and she set up the indictment to embarrass Trump. She's an FBI source. The acquittal was outrageous. There's more, but that's the gist of it. I don't suppose you have a comment, Jay?"

"Sorry, Sam, but I cannot get involved. Please don't quote me. I'd rather you said that efforts to reach Judge Jason were unsuccessful, since I gather you will write a story whatever I say."

"Absolutely."

"Thanks, Sam, for giving me a heads up." Jason was disappointed that Trump would not listen to his lawyers, but not surprised. It was typical. A knock was followed by Sue's head the partially open door."

"Yes, Sue?"

"Judge, we just received this envelope from the United States Marshal's office. It's addressed to you personally and was hand-delivered a few minutes ago. It has no return address, so they opened it and made sure that it was nothing dangerous."

"Thank you, Sue."

Jason opened the envelope, which the Marshal's office had resealed with tape. The unsigned letter was typed on a computer. There was no return address. It was also short. "We know you are biased against President Trump and hostile to what he wants to accomplish for the American people. We have you on tape defaming the president. You liberal judges have no respect for the law. We can prove it. You're no judge. You have no business sitting on the case. Recuse yourself immediately. We know more than you think. Much more. We're watching."

After recovering from surprise, Jason searched his memory. He did not want to jeopardize the outcome of the trial, but he also did not want to be frightened off a case he looked forward to trying. What was worrying him most was the ending. He couldn't be sure that it wasn't a reference to Christine and her pregnancy, although he had no reason to believe it had anything to do with her. She had told him over coffee that her daughter was an assistant editor at a women's magazine based in the city. Jason and Christine had marveled over the coincidence that both their sons were attorneys who lived in D.C., but they hadn't dwelled much on specifics. The second of Christine's late husbands, an architect, had been retired for many years before his death. Nothing added up to anything questionable there. Still, Jason was concerned. He had never received a letter like this, but his current trial assignment could hardly be called a routine case.

Jason decided he could not simply ignore the letter, as much as he would like to. He needed advice. This question was beyond Smith's pay grade. There was only one person to talk to, Chief Judge Martin Marbury. But he had to be careful what he said. He picked up the phone.

"Thanks for seeing me on short notice," Jason said as he took the chair Marbury offered. "I just received this hand-delivered letter." He waited the few seconds it took Marbury to read it.

"Is there anything to it, Jay?"

"I've said some pretty negative things about Trump, but only to Audrey, to my son, and to a few other judges, who, I should add, said pretty much the same thing. I also criticized Hillary Clinton, but I don't suppose that counts for much. It really wasn't in the same league as what I said about Trump. I don't know what to do. I think I must make some disclosures, if only because the senders of the letter will know what I am doing. It would be awkward to say the least if it were released during or immediately after the trial. I would hate to recuse myself, mostly because it might delay the trial while some other judge, who may have the same problem, got up to speed." Jason stopped. He felt he had been running off at the mouth. Next, he'd be telling Marbury about Christine.

"What about the taping?"

"I cannot imagine there's a tape," Jason said. "Obviously, my family has not taped me, and I cannot believe any of the judges would do it. Otherwise, I have no idea." Jason was relieved that Marbury did not ask him about the end of the letter. He had decided that he would say he had no idea what it meant, but he felt better not having to talk about it.

"I totally agree that you cannot ignore it," Marbury said. "If you do nothing, the writer will release the letter either during or after the trial, which would make things much worse. What would you do if you had to decide on your own?" Jason suppressed a smile at Marbury's technique.

"I guess I'd call in all the lawyers in and show them the letter. Someone might make a motion to have me disqualified, which I probably would refer to a different judge. It would then be out of my hands. On the other hand, no one might move. I'd have to have Trump's lawyer part of the process. God knows what he will do. I'm pretty sure the parties think I am impartial and doing my job." Jason shook his head. He looked at Marbury. "That would count for something in the ordinary case, but who knows what that means here? Any advice?"

"What you have said makes sense to me," Marbury said and then paused. "I do not think we have to notify the FBI or do anything along those lines. No one is threatening you with harm. I do not see any crime here. Another question is whether you make the letter public. I would rather you did not. especially since it is so vague. Why give the media an excuse to start a witch hunt?"

Jason folded the letter back into the envelope. "There's one other thing. Trump has starting tweeting about the case. He's criticizing Kruiser's acquittal and demeaning the libel suit. One tweet accused liberals of trashing the First Amendment. The language was more picturesque. I'll have to call an in-chambers conference in any event to try to control Trump. I'll keep the purpose of the conference vague until they get there. Thanks, Martin. I'll keep you posted."

Jason stood and the two walked to the door and shook hands. "If you think of anything, let me know," Jason said as he left Marbury's chambers.

Jason met with the lawyers the following day with a court reporter present. Everyone was seated when Jason opened the meeting.

"Thank you for coming on short notice. There are two matters that I want to take up with you. The first involves the president's tweets about this case, which may create a problem in picking an impartial jury and otherwise. I would like to meet alone with Mr. Crunch and his associate after this conference, that is, if there is no objection. Please state for the record if you have an objection." He looked around the table. "No? Then we'll meet after the other matter is considered." Jason looked at Crunch. He took a deep breath he hoped was not conspicuous.

"The other matter is that I received this letter yesterday in an envelope with no identifying features." He held up the envelope and removed the single sheet of paper. "I do not want copies floating around, so please read the letter and pass it along. The only person other than the sender or senders who knows about the letter is Chief Judge Marbury." He said that to warn the lawyers against leaking the letter. Jason paused while the lawyers read the letter and passed it around. Joe placed it back into its envelope and laid it in front of Jason.

"I don't know who sent the letter and I don't intend to pursue that now. I don't think it is appropriate for me to explain my views or actions with respect to my political views. I can assure you that I have not spoken publicly on anything to do with this case or Mr. Trump. I believe that my personal feelings are irrelevant, and the only issue is whether I can judge fairly. That is for you to decide in the first instance. Incidentally, it may not come as a surprise that most judges in this courthouse are not enthusiastic about the new president." None of the lawyers smiled.

"Obviously, a judge cannot be disqualified because he has an opinion on major political issues," Jason said. "The issue is, can the judge can be impartial and whether the judge gives the appearance of being impartial. We can't have the public think that judges are deciding cases based on personal preferences." Jason paused.

"I have a question," Rattle said. "What are the options?"

"I see only two," Jason said. "One is to do nothing. The other is to refer the issue to another judge selected at random, who would decide whether I should be disqualified. While arguably the law permits me to decide, I would bend over backwards and have a different judge make the call. It's up to you." Jason paused again. He decided he should explain further.

"I have to put my opinion on the record. I believe that I can be impartial. If I didn't, I would recuse myself regardless of this letter or your views. It's your call."

"I assume everything would stop while the other judge decided," Whitebread said.

"That's right," Jason agreed.

"For the record, plaintiff Moses has no objection to proceeding with Judge Jason," Whitebread said.

"I have to consult with Mr. Mandick," Butt said a few seconds later. "I cannot waive a claim of possible bias without speaking to him."

"My position is the same," Rattle said.

"How long will you need?" Jason asked.

"Until tomorrow afternoon," Butt said.

"The same," Rattle said.

Jason looked at Crunch, who was staring at his hands. "Mr. Crunch?" Jason asked.

"Excuse me, Your Honor. I'll need more time than that. I'll need three days, conceivably more. The president is not at my beck and call."

"I don't see that as a problem," Jason said. "If there is no objection, we can proceed as scheduled. If there is, the trial will be delayed. Please call Joe with your answers. Then follow up with a letter. One more thing, I suggest that I seal the letter unless someone moves to have me disqualified. That means there would be no disclosure. Does anyone object?"

"No, Your Honor," Butt said. The others were silent.

"Of course, anyone who moves for my disqualification can make the letter an exhibit. Just call Joe to get a copy. Does anyone object to that?" No one did. "Okay. Thank you, all.

"I'll seal the transcript and the letter and enter an order, also under seal, barring everyone with knowledge of the letter or this proceeding from making any disclosures. Mr. Crunch and his colleague will remain. Also, the court reporter. I look forward to seeing you at the trial." Jason breathed easier.

Jason waited while the other lawyers picked up their papers and headed out of the conference room and then out the door to his chambers. He closed the conference-room door behind them. Crunch remained seated, but his associate took a position behind his boss, his shoulders back and erect. The icy stare that lit his blue eyes and sneering quality in his manner made Jason suddenly uncomfortable in the man's presence and he almost asked him to leave the room, although that would have been clearly improper. A moment later, Jason resumed his seat and focused his attention on Crunch, who seemed unaware of the decline in temperature in the room.

"Mr. Crunch, the two matters are somewhat intertwined. Both involve potential publicity by the president on the case. I know you cannot commit for the president, but I believe this discussion, which will also be sealed, can be fruitful. I see a difference between Mr. Trump's speaking out generally, which I will come to in a moment, in contrast to his disclosing something that is under seal. Do you anticipate that the president, whom I assume you have to brief fully, will reveal the contents of the letter and the discussion or attack me for being biased?"

"Your Honor, I cannot speak with certainty or commit the president, whom I'm sure you have noticed is quite independent. I have no reason to believe that he will mention the letter or make any suggestion that you are biased, at least in the context of this letter. I certainly will convey what you said."

Jason was sure all remembered Trump's attacks on the judiciary during his campaign and even after he assumed the presidency. He let Crunch continue.

"I take it that you are not entering an order against the president."

"Only the general one that bars people with knowledge of the letter or its contents from disclosing them without further order of the court," Jason said. "I don't believe that such an order is offensive or violates separation of powers. For one thing, both President Nixon and President Clinton were subjected to specific orders of a district judge." Jason paused. "I don't think there is anything else. Do you?"

"Just that once the trial proper begins I plan to spend most nights during the trial in New York at the Trump International Hotel at Columbus Circle. I can be reached there or better through my cell phone. If I must go to Washington, my deputy will take my place."

"Thank you for your cooperation. I see no problem if you want to communicate with me ex parte about the president's making comments. I think that was implicit in the consent of the other parties given earlier."

"Thank you, Your Honor."

"Have a good day."

The two lawyers left the room.

Despite the antagonism of the aide, Jason was satisfied, very satisfied, the way the conference went. He tended to discount the disruptive effect of any new Trump tweets. At least in New York City, few among the public, and that would include the jurors who sat on the case, would credit what Trump says about the case. In any event, Jason had done all he could. When three days went by with no motion to disqualify him, he was relieved. He was also relieved that there was no new letter.

Who had written the anonymous letter? Jason had no idea. Perhaps someone who had scant information and was trying to cause trouble. The country was full of people like that, he mused, especially those who voted for Trump. Who else would send such a letter? It only emphasized to him how high the stakes were in *Moses v. Trump*.

Jason needed a break and he decided that a judges' luncheon might help. Someone had placed a bouquet of daffodils on the judges' table. Charles perhaps. It was almost May. Folks often said spring was not to be missed in New York City, but this year Jason had barely noticed its coming. He joined the round table in the center of the dining room where five other district judges were sitting. It was an average crowd for a non-designated lunch day. They were not judges with whom he usually ate lunch, which for some reason made him more comfortable.

Jason talked to Samuel Sullivan, who was seated to his left. A judge who sat in Westchester and rarely came to a luncheon in Manhattan, Sullivan always seemed to smile. He seemed totally guileless. Rotund and in his late middle age, he had been a star third baseman at Tulane and had been signed to a minor league contract, but, like so many college ballplayers, found he could not hit a good curve ball. So, he became a lawyer and then a litigator, and threw them instead. His route to a federal judgeship was politics: the state's lower house, upper house, and a state-court judgeship.

"The prosecution of Kruiser is something I'd expect to happen to a state official," Sullivan said. "When you have elected prosecutors and elected judges, anything can happen."

"What do you think will happen?" Jason asked.

"To quote a Harvard professor who likes to see himself on television, 'This is nutty,'" Sullivan said.

"I saw him on Chris Matthews, too."

Malcolm Cohen's entrance interrupted the conversation. "Nothing new on Moby Trump and the judiciary," he announced. His perfect teeth and broad smile scintillated. His Italian suits enhanced his well-proportioned body. Cohen had become outspoken since Trump was elected. "The good as well as the bad news continues – his Justice Department is moving slowly on picking lower-court judges. I'd just as soon do more work than have to deal with some of the candidates for the judiciary that Trump might nominate. Can you imagine whom he'll nominate to the Second Circuit? I can't bear to think about it."

Some of the judges, even those who had serious reservations about Trump and his crew, were annoyed at the irreverence Cohen showed to the chief executive of the United States when he lumped together 9/11 and 11/8. The judges were not fans of Trump, but equating the 9/11 disaster with Election Day was more than many could take. No one replied to Cohen's comment.

Only one subject was not taboo. That was Trump's vicious criticisms of judges. His attack on the integrity of judges, however, was discussed and deplored quietly, as if Trump himself were listening to the criticisms. In contrast, Trump's appointments to fill judicial vacancies, which worried most of the judges, were not discussed. Trump's disturbing humiliation of Attorney General Jeff Sessions was likewise ignored. One judge told Jason that Trump had poisoned the atmosphere. What had been fundamentally a collegial and intellectual effort, albeit charged with major differences in views and judicial philosophy, had become infected with Trump's *ad hominem* assaults. Another judge, younger than Jason, told Jason that he was thinking of retiring. Jason had remained silent, concerned that his role in *Moses v. Trump* might be compromised.

Sullivan broke the awkward silence in his typical light-hearted fashion. "I heard a good joke about judges the other evening. There was this state-court judge. . ."

"That's a good start."

". . . who was incredibly liberal in criminal cases, you know, releasing almost everyone without bail before trial, giving almost everyone who was convicted probation. Three months ago, the judge was brutally mugged, sent to the hospital with serious injuries. For a while it wasn't even clear that he would survive, but he recovered slowly and was anxious to get back to work. He decided to hold a press conference to announce his return, and conducted one in his courtroom with television cameras and other media present. He climbed up to his chair on the podium slowly on crutches and in obvious pain. He sat down and began. 'As you know, I've just been the victim of a terrible assault. I've had a very bad spell in the hospital and I still haven't fully recovered, as you can see. But I wanted to call this press conference to announce that my awful experience wi l not affect how I judge. I plan to be just as liberal and concerned with the rights and welfare of those unfortunates who are brought before me on criminal charges as I was before.' At this point a voice from the rear of the courtroom shouted, 'Mug him again.'"

"On that cheerful note, I'm leaving," a judge said as the others broke into laughter.

"I guess we all are," Jason added.

Later at dinner he and Christine caught up on each other's lives. She had just returned from Florida where she had spent the past two months. The first anniversary of Audrey's death had come and gone. Jason still missed her with an aching anxiety that hovered at the edge of his consciousness, but he was moving on with his life. Christine, always perceptive, commented on his mood.

"You are doing better. I can tell," she said. "Life and work are keeping you busy and focused."

"Yes," Jason said. "It's been a hell of a year."

"How is your son?" she asked. "Have you seen him lately?"

"Yes, we've gotten together a few times. It's hard to find the time. He travels a lot, and now I believe there might be a new woman in his life. And yours?" He picked up his glass and sipped his wine. He was totally relaxed with her. He was glad she was back in New York. They had settled into an easy friendship neither had expected to find.

Christine sighed and put down her fork. "I don't see him as much as I would like. Just before I went to Florida we had a terrible fight, and I haven't heard much from him since. Unfortunately, we have some very different ideas. He is working on a new case, which I know nothing about. I have no idea what his work entails. He says he's working for the president, but then so do thousands of other lawyers. Isn't that right? I really worry about him. He is so angry right now." She shook her head. "I'm sorry. I shouldn't have said that. You don't need to hear about family squabbles. Tell me about your case. When do you begin with the actual trial?"

"Very soon." He was concerned about her troubles with her son but said nothing. He certainly understood. Relationships with one's adult children can be challenging. Jason noticed that Christine was very well dressed. Would that be husband one or two, he wondered.

"I guess I won't be seeing much of you after the trial begins," she said. "You'll be too busy."

He reached across the table for her hand. "No, never that busy," he told her.

Chapter 13

The trial began in early June, as scheduled. When Jason arrived the first day of trial, he was astonished at the number of members of the media and spectators in front of the courthouse; it was shades of Watergate. He ducked into the side entrance to a spirited fugue of reporters asking for comments, all of which he refused, and retired to the quiet of his chambers.

"Any word from the jury clerk, Joe?"

"Well, Judge, he says that all is well, although with the large panel things may proceed slowly."

Jason did little more than move papers among piles, so he was pleased when Sue buzzed him to say that Judge Sullivan was on the line.

"I hope I'm not disturbing you," Sullivan said.

"Not at all. They're collecting the pool of jurors and getting things set up in the courtroom."

"Just what I figured. I bet you have nothing to do. That's what happens when you're too efficient."

"Right you are."

"I wish I had a good joke, but nothing comes to mind," Sullivan said apologetically.

"There's always a first time."

"Good luck. And don't take any shit."

"Thanks." The call was very considerate of Sullivan, Jason thought.

At noon the courtroom clerk notified Jason that everything was ready for his appearance, but he was releasing the jurors for lunch. When Jason appeared at 1:30 p.m., the large courtroom was full. On the side of the aisle to his left sat scores of prospective jurors. To his right were the media, friends of someone or other, curiosity seekers, and random people in from the rain. Jason felt a little uncomfortable, even nervous. It was an unfamiliar feeling. Looking at the large pool of jurors sitting row after row, he wondered why courtrooms had benches for spectators and not chairs. Could it have something to do with how churches were designed?

Seated below and in front of Jason were the lawyers and their clients. Plaintiff Ira Moses, Reginald Whitebread and an associate were to his left, closer to the jury box. Whitebread seated Moses so he would be closer to the jurors. The table to Jason's right was larger, since it held the multiple defendants and their lawyers. From left to right were publisher Everett Mandick and his two lawyers, Theodore Butt and Butt's associate, then Frederick Rattle and his client Beverly Clooney. There was a gap between Butt's associate and Rattle. Because they were parties, Moses, Mandick, and Clooney, but not other witnesses, would attend the trial. For the time being, however, the lead lawyers were the only ones who spoke.

Jason adhered to the standard for challenging a jury for cause that knowledge of the facts did not suffice to warrant challenge for cause. When Butt continued his objection to an especially well-informed prospective juror, Jason silenced him, stating, "You are entitled to an impartial jury, not an ignorant one." Add a double entendre or two, and that was the sum of lighter moments. What qualified as humor had a very low standard in jury selection.

Jason asked the parties to stand, identified them, and asked the jurors if any juror knew any of them. No one answered. The same with the lawyers. He then named the witnesses the parties had given him and asked the jury pool the same question and received the same answer. The process was slow and boring. With the inquiry by another judge in another case of "raise your hand if you don't understand the question," one juror progressed far into the selection process before the judges and the attorneys discovered that she did not understand English. Here, a juror likewise survived the process for a while even though she was suing a Trump hotel for employment discrimination arising out of her employment in a Trump hotel.

The clerk called the jurors individually to the bench when questions focused on certain personal matters, such as whether they had an arrest record. A U.S. Marshal recognized one of the potential jurors as someone he had attempted to serve an arrest warrant and notified the court clerk. When the juror came to the bench, Jason announced that the questioning process would take place in the robing room adjacent to the courtroom. Once they were there, the Marshal arrested the potential juror. When Jason returned to the courtroom, he announced that juror panel member number 34587 had been excused for cause. Jason regretted that he could not share the details with those in the courtroom.

After three days they had picked a jury of twelve along with four alternates. It could have been a lot worse. It was a diverse group ethnically, with four African-Americans, two Hispanics, and two Asians. All but two had at least a college education, and one juror had a pair of Ph.D.'s in oriental history, interestingly not one of the Asians. Ages ranged from a recent college graduate to an eighty-two-year-old retiree who had worked all his life as a stock broker. Half were women. All but two had sat on juries before. Those cases were overwhelmingly criminal cases.

Near the end of the day the jurors were administered an oath that they would do their jobs conscientiously. Jason thanked the jury for serving. He directed the jurors to return the following morning at 9:30 a.m.

Jason began the trial proper on Thursday morning by giving a somewhat lengthier but still bland description of the setting of the case, stating that it had grown out of a criminal case in which Ira Moses had represented the defendant, Kate Kruiser, whom the jury found not guilty. He briefly described the *Total Faith* article and the Trump tweet.

Jason explained the role of the lawyers and the judge. What the lawyers and the judge say is not evidence. Evidence was what was testified to under oath from witnesses in the jury box and documents the jury saw. The judge instructs the jurors on the law; the jurors decide the facts at the end of the case. To help them follow the trial, Jason explained the difference between the issues involving truth and falsity of the *Total Faith* article and those that involved the defendants' states of mind. He saw glimmers of understanding in the eyes of some of the jurors, none of whom had previously sat on a libel case, a fact Jason had learned from the questionnaires the jurors had answered.

He explained that Moses had to prove that the charges against him in the article were false and that the defendants published the article with fault. There were two degrees of fault involved in the case. First, did the defendants publish the article negligently, which means without the degree of care with which a person in their situation should be expected to act. The concept was the same in negligence suits arising out of automobile accidents. Second, did the defendants publish the article with legal malice, which is a shorthand for knowing it was false or with a reckless disregard as to whether it was true or not. Jason explained the different positions of the defendants on the falsity of the article. The glimmers grew fewer and duller. No matter how hard he had tried to draft a short and enlightening summary, he saw nothing but failure. He soldiered on.

A sticky problem was what to say about Trump. Jason simply said that President Trump had been sued, but that he would not be part of the proceedings that would follow, at least for the time being. The jurors should not speculate why he was not part of the trial. Once again, Jason followed the adage that the less said about something complicated, the better. He would revisit Trump's status later. Besides, everyone knew what had happened to Trump.

Jason called for a brief adjournment. Eleven minutes later they were ready to start the trial proper. Jason noted that Crunch was sitting in the front row of spectators along with his angry young colleague who was busy taking notes. Joe had told him the man's name was Gregory Jeffries, first in his class at Penn and a registered Republican. No doubt the man had voted for Trump. Jason called on Whitebread.

Reginald Whitebread launched into his opening statement to the jury. He was logical and thorough, starting with Kate Kruiser's background. He barely mentioned the Trump campaign and her nomination and confirmation as Secretary of Commerce. Then, it was her testimony before the Senate Finance Committee, followed by her indictment, trial, and acquittal. The final chapter was the article the defendants wrote and published. "We will show that the evidence supporting the article was nothing more than imagination and speculation, which the defendants knew." Whitebread paused and looked at each juror in sequence.

He explained that there was no motive or reason for Mr. Moses to try to commit the serious crime of obstruction of justice. Evidence of bribery did not exist. The article was patently false. Indeed, two of the three defendants have conceded that the article was false. Whitebread took a sip of water.

"The defendants, all of them, published the article both negligently and knowing it was false or not caring whether it was true or not. You know, they didn't give a damn." Whitebread smiled at the jurors. "How could anyone believe that Mr. Moses, a prominent defense lawyer, would even consider engaging in a criminal act in such a case? Aside from everything else, it made no sense. Finally, we will prove Mr. Moses was harmed by the article and deserving of substantial damages, which we shall ask you to award.

"Mr. Moses will be our first witness," Whitebread announced. "Before he takes the stand, however, we shall read some of the questions and answers provided by Ms. Clooney under oath at her deposition that I conducted in this case. We are doing that, not because the testimony was true, quite the opposite. We shall also prove that Mr. Mandick, personally and as the alter-ego of the magazine *Total Faith*, knew that the article was false or at least entertained substantial doubts whether it was true. Thank you." Whitebread sat down.

"Mr. Butt," Jason said in a firm voice, "your turn to speak to the jury on behalf of Mr. Mandick and *Total Faith*."

Butt knew he had a problem, and he addressed it directly. "Neither Mr. Mandick nor *Total Faith* suspected that the article was false at the time of publication. It made no sense to publish a false article. It was self-destructive for Mr. Mandick to risk the future of his magazine by publishing an article on an important subject that he knew was not true. I emphasize this concession of falsity has been made only in hindsight, seven months after the publication of the article.

"The United States Constitution's First Amendment on freedom of speech, a provision we all revere, gives journalists breathing room. The value that this country has placed since its inception on the freedom of the media has caused the Supreme Court to encourage good-faith publication of news about important public events. That is what freedom of speech and the press is all about."

Jason had wondered how Butt and Rattle would handle the fact that Mandick and Clooney were very religious and true believers, if not fanatics, in the cause of right-wing politics, not the most popular of positions among New Yorkers. Butt once again addressed it directly.

"Ladies and gentlemen, it is no secret that Mr. Mandick and his magazine are avid supporters of positions that many people admire, and many people reject. Indeed, they are very religious and very conservative. What is the significance of that? A few of you might find that position abhorrent and want to penalize Mr. Mandick for holding those views. That would violate the Constitution of the United States of America and your oath as jurors. It would be offensive to the Bill of Rights that the Framers of the Constitution insisted be added to protect minorities and dissenters, and which the citizens of the United States overwhelmingly ratified in 1790, more than two centuries ago. People have the right to their views and the right to promote their views. It we are intolerant of those who disagree with us, we might as well toss the Bill of Rights out the window. This case is about the Bill of Rights." Butt held up a small copy of the Constitution for all to see.

"Mr. Mandick has the right to publish what he believes. He is also entitled to some breathing room. The freedom of speech and the press would be weak guardians of our rights if the public could second-guess reporters and publishers at every turn. We may sympathize with Mr. Moses, who I am sure suffered some embarrassment over the publication of the article, but that is not the test for libel."

Butt continued with some of the details, telling the jury not to accept automatically what Mr. Whitebread, who was going first, presented and to keep an open mind until after all the evidence was in and Judge Jason instructed the jury as to the law. He ended with a string of quotations from the founding fathers and others on the importance of freedom of the press, before thanking the jury for its attention and sitting down. Jason observed that Butt did not mention negligence. That was his prerogative. Butt wanted the jury to focus on the more difficult standard.

"Mr. Rattle, it is your turn." Jason wondered what Frederick Rattle would say about the article's being true, that at the very minimum would not come back to haunt him later.

The answer was not much. Rattle's opening statement was the model of brevity. Rattle said that the evidence would speak for itself on whether Beverly Clooney's article was true or false. He was more voluble on the issue of his client's state of mind. She was an experienced reporter, a professional, who researched the article diligently and believed every word of it. She was convinced of its accuracy as the jury will see when she takes the stand and explains. Unless Ms. Clooney was negligent or did not believe the article to be false when she wrote it, the fact that it turned out to be false on later review was irrelevant.

A few more marginally enlightening sentences, including repeating what Butt had said about the enhanced burden of proof the plaintiff had to meet, and Rattle had completed his opening. Rattle did not mention Clooney's religious beliefs. That Clooney was a professional journalist was a bigger plus in the Southern District of New York than that she was an evangelical.

Judge Jason excused the jury for the luncheon recess with the admonition that they were not to discuss the case among themselves or with anyone else or read or listen to coverage of the case. They should also keep an open mind until they heard all the evidence.   Their job was an important one.

Jason lunched at his desk. He was trying to insulate himself from the outside world and focus only on *Moses v. Trump*.

Chapter 14

"The Court is now in session," the bailiff announced when the court reconvened after lunch. When Jason surveyed the courtroom, he saw that Crunch was occupying the Trump seat in the first row of spectators. He could see that the top button of Crunch's shirt was open, not concealed by his bright red tie.

"Mr. Whitebread, you may begin."

"We will read from Ms. Clooney's deposition in this case. That is prior testimony she gave as part of the pretrial activities in the case. Your Honor, would it be permissible to have one of my associates sit in the witness box?" A young woman in a purple suit seated next to Whitebread stood up. She smiled blankly.

"That would be fine," Jason said. "Ladies and gentlemen of the jury, Mr. Whitebread will read to you a portion of the testimony of defendant Beverly Clooney in a deposition in this case. To facilitate your understanding of the testimony I am permitting Mr. Whitebread to ask the questions and have a person in his office respond with the answers Ms. Clooney gave when she testified under oath at her deposition. This testimony is relevant just on the issue of the defendant Clooney's state of mind. This evidence is not admissible on the issue of the truth of the statements in the article because Ms. Clooney was not present at any meeting that may have occurred between the juror in the criminal case and Mr. Moses." Jason looked at the jurors and saw too many uncomprehending faces. It was time for Plan B.

"To assist you I will give you an example, which is not involved in this case. Let us assume a defendant is charged with intentionally hitting someone with a stick. Part of the prosecution's case will be to prove that the defendant hit someone with a stick. Part will be to prove that the hitting was intentional. We sometimes call the latter issue the defendant's state of mind. The evidence Mr. Whitebread is about to introduce is on Ms. Clooney's state of mind. Evidence often comes in small pieces that you the jury have to assemble with the aid of the lawyers." Jason was pleased to see a few tentative smiles of understanding.

"Please proceed."

MR. WHITEBREAD: Ms. Clooney, you testified earlier that you had a meeting with a juror in the criminal case against the Secretary of Commerce. Is that correct?

MS. CLOONEY: Yes, Mr. Whitebread.

MR. WHITEBREAD: What is the name of the juror?

MS. CLOONEY: Her name is Claire Winter.

MR. WHITEBREAD: Where and when did you meet her?

MS. CLOONEY: I met her at her apartment at 152 West 32nd Street on May 27, 2017.

MR. WHITEBREAD: Was any other person present or did you speak to any other person during your visit?

MS. CLOONEY: No other person was present at the interview and neither of us made any telephone calls.

MR. WHITEBREAD: Did anyone record the interview?

Ms. CLOONEY: Well, I didn't.

MR. WHITEBREAD: How did you get into Ms. Winter's apartment?

MS. CLOONEY: I had telephoned her to make an appointment. When I got there the doorman called up and then let me in.

MR. WHITEBREAD: Had you ever been in that apartment

building before?

MS. CLOONEY: No, Mr. Whitebread.

MR. WHITEBREAD: Do you know the name of the doorman or can you describe him?

MS. CLOONEY: All I remember is that he was young, tall, and black.

MR. WHITEBREAD: Can you describe Ms. Winter's apartment?

MS. CLOONEY: It was a very nice building and she had a very nice apartment. There was a big chandelier just inside the entrance. We sat in the living room, which was to the left. There was a large red and blue oriental rug on the floor. It was very stylish, and the furnishings seemed lavish. I apologize for not being able to give a more precise description. One other thing I remember now. There was an Impressionist painting over a white couch. I could not tell you the name of the artist.

MR. WHITEBREAD: Can you provide us with the contents of the interview, what you said and what Ms. Winter said?

MS. CLOONEY: It's been a very long time, Mr. Whitebread, and I'm worried that I won't describe it exactly right.

MR. WHITEBREAD: Did you make a memorandum of your conversation with Ms. Winter?

MS. CLOONEY: I most certainly did.

MR. WHITEBREAD: When did you prepare that memorandum?

MS. CLOONEY: I prepared it later that evening. I went straight from Ms. Winter's apartment to mine and I stayed up to finish the memo the same evening.

MR. WHITEBREAD: I direct your attention to what has been previously marked Plaintiff's Exhibit 7 and ask you whether that is the memorandum to which you are referring?

MS. CLOONEY: It is, Mr. Whitebread.

MR WHITEBREAD: Is it an accurate account of your conversation with Ms. Winter?

MS. CLOONEY: Yes, Mr. Whitebread.

MR. WHITEBREAD: Is that the same memorandum that you later showed to Mr. Mandick as reflecting your conversation with Ms. Winter?

MS. CLOONEY: It is, Mr. Whitebread.

"Your Honor, that completes the verbatim reading from Ms. Clooney's deposition. I hereby move in evidence move Plaintiff's Exhibit 7."

"Admitted." Jason noted that the smiles on the faces of some of the jurors were gone, replaced by confusion. But that was inevitable in a trial, especially a long one with difficult issues. He would say something to the jurors later. Whitebread's associate straightened out the chair she sat on when she left the witness box and returned to counsel's table. Whitebread was addressing Judge Jason.

"Your Honor, I would like to read a few sentences from Plaintiff's Exhibit 7, Ms. Clooney's memorandum of her alleged meeting with Ms. Winter."

"You may," Jason said.

"'In sum, Ms. Winter told me that she met twice with Mr. Moses, both times during the trial in her apartment. She told me that at their first meeting Mr. Moses told her he was prepared to pay her a substantial amount of money to vote to acquit the Secretary of Commerce, and to try to convince other jurors to agree. She said she was worried, but that she desperately needed money. He offered $100,000. She said that the second meeting was exactly one week after the first meeting. He reached into his briefcase and took out stacks of $100 bills, which he placed on the table and left.'"

Whitebread looked at the jury, and then at Jason. "That completes the excerpt. There is considerably more in the memorandum on the subject, which I reserve the right to read later in the trial. Of course, all defense counsel have copies and it will be available to the jury during their deliberations."

"That will be satisfactory," Jason said.

"Your Honor, the plaintiff calls Claire Winter."

A tall, slender woman entered from a side door on the opposite side of the courtroom from the jury box. She walked to the witness box, where she looked first at Judge Jason, then the jury, and finally at the bailiff, who presented her with a Bible.

Placing her left hand on the Bible, she raised her right hand deliberately and confidently. She swore to tell the truth, the whole truth, and nothing but the truth.

"Please state your full name."

"Claire Peabody Winter."

Jason saw as solid a witness as he could imagine take the oath. Well-dressed in an elegant brown suit and a white blouse and minimal jewelry, she looked in complete control. Her skin was light and unblemished. Her dark blonde hair was pulled tightly into a chignon. Her thin lips, lightly brushed with red lipstick, curled upwards into a slight smile, suggesting tolerant amusement. If he had to describe Winter in one word, it would have been aristocratic.

"Ms. Winter, my name is Reg Whitebread and I represent Ira Moses in this lawsuit. We have already met, at your deposition."

"Yes, and a few other times as well in the past few weeks." A few of the spectators smiled. Winter was a stickler on truth.

"You were a juror in the prosecution of the Secretary of Commerce for perjury, were you not?"

"That is correct."

"Juror number 4, in fact."

"That is correct."

"You are the juror that Mr. Moses allegedly bribed."

"I understand that to be the case."

"Ms. Winter, please tell us something about your background."

"Certainly. I was born in New York City and grew up there. Both my parents were physicians. I went to Harvard undergraduate, where my father and grandfather went. After graduation I returned to the city and went to work at J. P. Morgan. After three years, with the encouragement of the management of J.P. Morgan, I went to Harvard Business School. I returned to Morgan for several years. Five years ago, I left them to join a major hedge fund, where I am now a partner."

Jason understood why the witness exuded confidence. She was making millions of dollars a year in a tough business. While hedge funds were not the most popular profession among the general population, it was unlikely to diminish Winter's status as a witness in New York City. Given the summary of Clooney's purported interview of Winter, Jason could see a rocky road ahead for the defendants if they had to pit their credibility against Winter's. Whitebread looked over at the jurors, then continued with his examination.

"Ms. Winter, where do you live?"

"At 131 Sutton Place South."

"How long have you lived there?"

"About ten years."

"Have you ever lived at 152 West 32nd Street?"

"No."

With that answer the air was sucked out of the courtroom. The testimony also took Jason by surprise. Whitebread had a serene look.

"Ms. Winter, does the building in which you have an apartment have doormen?"

"Yes, it does."

"How long have those particular doormen been there?"

"At least five years."

"Please describe them."

"All three are white, one is about 40 years old, the other two about 50 years old."

"To your knowledge, has the building ever had a young, tall, black doorman?"

"No." Again, a rustling among the spectators.

"I direct your attention to the woman in gray at counsel table," Whitebread said. "Did you ever have a conversation with her?

"No."

"Do you recognize her?

"No."

Now, the intensity of the silence was noticeable as Whitebread paused for emphasis and looked at the jurors. Jason found himself leaning forward in his high-backed chair. He now understood what Butt was referring to when he said the evidence of falsity was overwhelming. Whitebread looked over at the jurors with a slight smile as he arched his back and stood taller.

"May the record reflect that I have indicated defendant Beverly Clooney," Whitebread said slowly but firmly.

"It will," Jason responded.

"Have you ever met or spoken to Ms. Clooney about the prosecution of the Secretary of Commerce?"

"Obviously not, no." Winter was staring straight at Whitebread.

"Ms. Winter, I show you what is Plaintiff's Exhibit 7 in evidence. Please read it to yourself. Does that reflect a conversation you had with Ms. Clooney?"

"Of course not."

Jason wondered how many ways Whitebread would ask the same question before someone objected.

"Ms. Winter, have you ever spoken with Mr. Mandick, the editor and publisher of *Total Faith*?"

"I have not."

"To your knowledge, have you ever spoken with anyone connected with the *Total Faith*?"

"I have not."

"Do you know Mr. Moses?"

"I saw him many times in the courtroom in the Secretary of Commerce case, but I have never spoken to him and I don't know him."

"Have you ever had any communication with him about your vote in that case?"

"Of course not," Winter answered.

"Did Mr. Moses ever offer you any money, more specifically the sum of $100,000?"

"Absolutely, not." Winter looked positively offended. Why would anyone offer me money, she seemed to say.

"Was your vote in the criminal case against the Secretary of Commerce based on the evidence presented and nothing else?"

"Yes."

Jason noted the question was leading, but assumed that Butt and Rattle saw that an objection would do nothing for them.

"Have you ever been to the restaurant described in Exhibit 7?"

"No."

"Where were you on the first evening that Ms. Clooney said you were meeting with her, May 27, 2017?"

"I went to the opera with my friend, Sally Ditto. We saw 'Tristan und Isolde.' Do you want me to talk any more about the opera I saw?"

"That won't be necessary. If any other counsel wants to inquire, that is their prerogative, although I cannot think of a question that will help them." Jason gave Whitebread a piercing look to tell him to stick to questions, and he quickly moved on. "Where were you on the second evening that Ms. Clooney said that she met with you?"

"According to my calendar, I had nothing planned, so I believe I stayed at home that evening. Or, I was at my office. But it was more likely that I was home. We had just completed a major transaction and it was unlikely that I would be working late that evening."

"Your Honor," Whitebread said, "we would like to have Ms. Winter's calendar for 2014 marked as Plaintiff's Exhibit 14 for identification, and the page with the entries for the two dates identified marked as Plaintiff's Exhibit 14-A. Plaintiff moves the introduction of Exhibit 14-A."

"Without objection, Plaintiff's Exhibit 14-A is admitted," Jason said.

"Do you have serious financial problems, Ms. Winter?"

"Absolutely not. I am quite wealthy, thank you. My late husband provided amply for my needs, and my occupation also supports me." The former juror excelled at understatement.

"No further questions." Whitebread was smiling at the jury as he sat down.

"Mr. Rattle, your witness," Jason announced.

"I have no questions, Your Honor."

With that the courtroom exploded again, and Jason banged his gavel for order. It was doubtful that many heard Jason grant Butt's request for a recess. Half the reporters fled the courtroom to use their cell-phones or to head for their offices to compose their stories. Crunch also left quickly for the exit. Jason did not want to miss the excitement, so he gathered up his papers slowly. Mandick and Butt looked at Rattle with icy stares.

Jason wondered whether that's what writers had in mind when they talked about looks that could kill. Obviously, Jason thought, they expected that Rattle would have come up with something with which to impeach Claire Winter, such as that she has Alzheimer's or was recently released from a mental hospital. While Butt had conceded falsity and Rattle had refused, Jason certainly did not expect Rattle to have absolutely nothing with which to confront Winter.

Why in God's name was Beverly Clooney contesting falsity? Butt was shaking his head, presumably silently berating himself for failing to oversee Rattle more diligently on the falsity issue. Not a good start for the defenders of freedom of the press. Dominating Jason's mind was the utter craziness of what was happening. This was not how major cases were supposed to unfold. Jason was impressed by the fact that there had been no leak of Ms. Winter's testimony.

Additional witnesses on the falsity of the article took up the balance of Thursday afternoon. Called by Whitebread in succession were the manager of 131 Sutton Place South to testify that Ms. Winter has lived there over ten years and that they never had a doorman who resembled the one described by Clooney; a doorman from the apartment house who gave similar testimony; the manager of 152 West 32nd Street who testified that Ms. Winter never lived there; Sally Ditto, who testified that she went to the opera with Winter on the evening of the first interview Clooney testified she had with Winter; and two witnesses who testified that Moses had attended a black tie bar-association dinner when Clooney claimed that he had met with Winter the second time. There were also witnesses from banks who presented copies of Winter's and Moses's bank-accounts transcripts. Finally, an accountant testified that he had done analyses of the finances of Winter and Moses and found no evidence of the alleged payment. No defense attorney cross-examined any of the witnesses.

Jason was taking notes, but also reevaluating the case. There was no way this parade of witnesses would not spill over and harm Mandick and *Total Faith*. How could a juror not conclude that *Total Faith* was negligent, perhaps egregiously so, in publishing the article, or far worse?

Just before the court recessed for the day, Butt presented a short interim summation. Jason had allowed the lawyers on each side a total of ten minutes to address the jurors during the presentation of evidence. Joe would keep track of the time. Butt told the jury that all the evidence presented so far dealt only with the issue of falsity and not with whether his clients had published the article negligently or with legal malice. He also stated that his clients had conceded the issue of falsity so that none of the evidence was even remotely relevant to Mr. Moses's case against Mr. Mandick and *Total Faith*. Rattle said nothing. Butt and Rattle were not talking to each other.

Whitebread got up to say that the evidence presented absolutely bore on at least negligence by Mandick and *Total Faith*.

On that note, the day's proceedings concluded.

Back at chambers Jason returned a telephone call Marbury had made to him. Jason assured him everything was fine. "I have not gotten any more letters. I think the letter was no more than an attempt to get me to favor the defendants, or at least not favor Moses. I've all but put it out of my mind." In fact, it was not that easy for Jason.

"Good," was all Marbury said.

Jason and Joe went over the day's events. Jason could not understand why Clooney had not conceded that her article was false; she had obviously made up the whole thing. How could she possibly explain not having spoken to Claire Winter? Joe had no answer, either.

———————

The testimony of Ira Moses the next day was unexpectedly

anticlimactic, which was confirmed by Crunch's absence from the courtroom, replaced by his deputy. Whitebread stuck to his plan. It took all day for Moses to explain the details of the criminal case he had been accused of trying to fix, his reasons for believing that the prosecution's case was extraordinarily weak, which included reading and explaining excerpts from the trial record. "It was ridiculous for me to have tried to fix that case," he said several times. "We couldn't lose." The examination went slowly also because Whitebread gave Moses frequent short breaks. Moses would hold up his hand, and Whitebread would pause for a minute or two.

Moses testified that he had never talked to Claire Winter or any other juror except in open court in front of a hundred or more people. He finished, rather than began, with his personal and legal history. Whitebread's questioning moved tc a conclusion.

"What effect did the article have on you, Mr. Moses?"

"I was devastated. I was crushed. I had worked my whole life to achieve a reputation and it was being trashed. I had trouble sleeping, eating, working, everything. I was afraid to see people because I might be looking at someone who thought I was a crook."

"Did anyone call you a crook?"

"Not to my face," Moses said, "but I couldn't know what they were thinking." Jason appreciated that Whitebread was anticipating Butt's cross-examination on why Whitebread was not calling witnesses who said they believed the magazine article.

"Whom did you talk to about the effect the article was having on you?"

"My wife, my brother, my daughter, my law partner, and several others."

"Did you see a doctor?"

"Yes, I did," Moses replied.

"Did he prescribe any medication?"

"A tranquilizer and sleeping pills."

"Did they help?"

"Yes, although it took weeks for me to begin to feel like my old self," Moses said.

"How do you feel now?"

"Better, but I still worry about what people think and I keep thinking about the article."

"Thank you, Mr. Moses. No further questions."

Jason also noted that Moses had presented no evidence of any loss of income. His business probably went up because of the article, at least from liberal clients.

"It's Friday afternoon," Jason said to the jury. "I am confident that we cannot finish cross-examination today. It's been a long week, so I'm adjourning earlier than usual. Thank you for your attention. We will start at the usual time on Monday."

"Court adjourned," the bailiff announced, as most spectators walked briskly to the exits. A few partisans joined Whitebread and Moses, or Butt and Mandick. Ignored by the spectators, Rattle packed up with Beverly Clooney at his side. They remained silent and left before the others. Jason would have given a lot to know what Butt had said to Rattle.

Back in chambers, Jason considered Butt's options when he would cross-examine Moses. They were not great. Moses was essentially a fact witness on falsity. Not only had Moses adamantly denied bribing Winter, but Butt had conceded that the story was false. Was there, in fact, any point in Butt's cross-examining Moses? Since Moses made the story looked terrible, Butt had to do something. Jason struggled with that question.

Jason's long experience as a lawyer and judge taught him that it's much harder to find a solution when it's not your problem. There is a lack of urgency and energy. Samuel Johnson said that, "when a man knows he is to be hanged in a fortnight, it concentrates his mind wonderfully." Slowly the answer came to Jason. Butt would ignore what happened and would concentrate on what information Mandick and *Total Faith* had when they published the story. What the case had looked like at that specific point in time.

Jason did as little as possible over the weekend. Christine

was babysitting her teenaged grandchildren and so would be unavailable to meet. On Friday and Sunday, he ordered in dinner. He bought a steak that he grilled on the top of his stove on Saturday. He consumed good wines but did not feel it was the occasion to bring out his best. He cut into his backlog of books on disasters and watched a mini-series on World War II on DVD that he had purchased a while back but never viewed. He went for a long walk in Central Park, where he could enjoy the pleasant weather of mid-June. He remembered his long walks with Audrey and thought about some of the lesser known parts of the park they liked to explore. He also spent two hours looking at the unparalleled artwork at the Frick Collection on the other side of the park. It was one of his favorite places in New York City, where he could relax in one of the most luxurious buildings in the city. Three Vermeers in a small museum was an incredible treat. He made a mental note to ask Christine if she had seen them when he called her that night. Mostly, he took his doctor's advice not to push himself too hard. By Monday morning he was ready for more action.

Chapter 15

Promptly at 9:30 a.m. Monday, Butt started his cross-examination of Moses. Jason quickly understood that his thinking on Friday had been correct.   Butt was challenging Moses's premise that the case against Secretary of Commerce Kate Kruiser was so weak that he had no motive to bribe juror Claire Winter. Butt was arguing that it was plausible to Mr. Mandick that Moses was afraid he would lose. He went through item by item the same evidence that Moses had discounted earlier, but this time putting it in a better light, while asking Moses whether the qualifications of the various government witnesses were not substantial.

After presenting Moses with a point made by a government witness, Butt would ask, "but you did not accept that, did you?"

When the time to adjourn for the day arrived, Butt said that he had more questions to ask Moses the following morning.

Jason had been taken by surprise by the importance of the trial of the criminal case to *Moses v. Trump*. Andy's leaning over backwards in admitting some of the government's evidence and excluding some of Kruiser's had made the criminal case slightly closer than otherwise, which helped Butt's defense.

Butt continued through Tuesday morning asking Moses questions about the criminal case, which Moses patiently answered, and answered, and answered. As far as Jason could tell, it was a draw, but on something that did not really matter, like which team had left more men on base after the sixth inning. Here, the strength of the prosecution's case against Kate Kruiser was little more than a side issue, given the incredible developments. Butt had to show how complicated and difficult it was to decipher it all during the criminal trial and its immediate aftermath. Butt completed his cross-examination just before the normal time for the luncheon recess, so Jason took the occasion to give everyone ten extra minutes for lunch, as an undisclosed bonus for having endured the cross-examination.

Jason resisted the temptation to eat in the judge's lunchroom. The anonymous letter made him skittish. He wanted neither to talk nor hear about *Moses v. Trump*; he also was worried that someone might overhear something he said and repeat it, either accurately or inaccurately. That was not a problem with the great majority of his cases, which no one cared about. At least for the time being, he would stay away. He contented himself with eating a sandwich at his desk, since he also did not want to run into a juror or a reporter. He had avoided reporters, although he continued to read newspaper articles on the case. He was curious and, besides, he told himself, he might learn something.

The afternoon began with Rattle's cross-examination of Moses, a task that promised little reward. But Rattle proved to be nimbler than expected. He got Moses to admit that he had made a couple of mistakes on his direct testimony, minor, almost trivial, mistakes, but mistakes nevertheless. Moses had misstated the year of one of the trials in which he had been counsel and had wrongly described the position of one of the Secretary's assistants at Commerce. Rattle then questioned Moses about a five-year-old trial that had not been mentioned before and which seemed to have nothing whatsoever to do with the current case.

After some desultory questioning on the subject, during which it looked as though Whitebread was about to object on grounds of relevance, Rattle asked Moses whether he remembered a young woman from a minor magazine who had attended the trial and had spoken to him during a recess. Moses said he could not. Rattle asked Beverly Clooney to stand up. She was unexpectedly tall and seemed very anxious to sit down quickly. Her most striking features were her very long face and long straight brown hair. She wore no makeup.

Rattle asked Moses whether that was not the woman to whom he had talked during a recess. Moses hesitated some seconds before saying that he might have spoken to her. Since Moses had emphatically denied knowing Clooney, this testimony created a minor splash, although to what end was not clear. Why would Moses want to conceal that he had five years earlier met Clooney? With as much of a flourish as he could sustain, Rattle sat down.

Whitebread seemed uncertain as to what he should do, but ultimately stated that he had a few questions on redirect. He confined them to Moses's previous encounter with Clooney. Moses explained that he had totally forgotten the brief conversation and was reminded only when it was specifically brought to his attention. Whitebread's final question was, "Has the cross-examination in any way caused you to change your testimony on what occurred during the criminal trial of the Secretary of Commerce?"

Moses obliged by stating forcefully, "absolutely not." Moses and Whitebread returned to their adjacent seats.

After a brief recess, Whitebread announced his next witness: "The plaintiff calls Kate Kruiser." Jason would see her for the first time. A tall, slightly overweight woman, about 50 years old and with graying hair entered the courtroom and walked to the witness chair. She had a strong and angular face. Her outfit, a navy-blue suit, did not fit her well. Either she had bought it at J.C. Penny or she had gained weight, or both. Audrey would have known.

Whitebread asked her many preliminary questions, so that the jury would understand her role. Lawyers sometimes overestimate how much jurors know. Kruiser had been present at her entire trial, she said. She observed carefully. She spoke frequently with Ira Moses. Jason observed that Kruiser's answers were much less elaborate and colorful than in her criminal case. It seemed to Jason that Moses had reconfigured her for her trial. Finally, Whitebread asked her the question:

"Ms. Kruiser, at any time during your trial did you observe any evidence that your lawyer, Ira Moses, bribed a juror?"

"No."

"No further questions."

"Mr. Butt, you may cross-examine."

Butt walked to the podium, while looking at the jury. He pivoted towards the witness box.

"Ms. Kruiser, congratulations on your acquittal."

"Thank you."

"You testified at the Senate hearing the way you did because you were a woman of integrity, isn't that right."

"I like to think I am, Mr. Butt."

"You would not tolerate perjury or other criminal conduct if you knew about it."

"I would not."

"Isn't that the reason your lawyer, Ira Moses, did not tell you about his bribing juror number four, if he did bribe her?"

"Objection," Whitebread shouted, almost drowning out the end of Butt's question.

"Sustained."

"Ms. Kruiser," Butt continued in a conversational tone without reacting to the ruling, "you remember Juror Four, Ms. Winter, from your trial, don't you?"

"I do."

"Didn't she seem hostile to your defense at the beginning of the trial?"

"I guess you can say that."

"At some point in the middle of the trial, didn't Ms. Winter appear to support you and your defense?"

"I guess you can say that, yes."

"Wasn't it extraordinarily sudden and unambiguous, Ms. Kruiser?"

"Objection."

"On what ground, Mr. Whitebread?"

"It calls for an opinion. The witness is not qualified to give an opinion on that issue."

"Not all opinions require an expert. I think Ms. Kruiser is qualified to answer that question. You may answer, Ms. Kruiser"

"I believe that's correct."

"Thank you," Butt said, as he turned and walked to his seat.

"If there are no more questions, the witness is excused."

Jason concluded that Butt got the better of the exchanges. Whitehead was overtrying his case. Sometimes putting in too much evidence is as bad as putting in too little. The trick is to know when to do what. Jason remembered what his trial-practice professor told him a long time ago, before he knew it was a cliché. Trying a case is more art than science. And it takes work to become a good artist.

Whitebread then called members of Moses's family, friends and business associates of Moses's to testify to his reaction to the article in *Total Faith*, how upset he was and how his spirits seemed to have plunged precipitously. Butt and Rattle declined to cross-examine them, perhaps fearful that they would suddenly remember that they believed the article until Moses reassured them that it was false. Or else, they were afraid their questions might make someone cry. There was no way to avoid damage and it was best to keep consideration of the subject as brief as possible. That concluded the third day of evidence.

When Jason returned to chambers he checked his phone messages and found he had three hang-ups whose caller ID registered "Private Caller." That was odd since so few people had his private number. A fourth caller had left a message, and Jason was happy to learn that his son had called to say that he would be arriving Thursday morning and would go directly to the courtroom. Jason immediately called back to confirm the visit and that he assumed that his son would stay over at least Thursday night. Vernon said he was looking forward to spending a few days in New York with his dad, and no, he had not called three times before.

The first thing Wednesday morning, Whitebread informed the jury he would elicit testimony to show that *Total Faith* wrote and published the story with legal malice. He said that he would be calling one of the two editorial employees of *Total Faith* as well as Mr. Mandick himself, even though they would not be friendly witnesses, but because they were the ones who knew how the article came to be published. "They're on the other side," he said. Whitebread first called Ralph Sanderson, editor and researcher at *Total Faith*. He was a young man in his late twenties, who wore a dark brown plaid sports jacket and gray flannel slakes.

Obviously unhappy and carefully led by Whitebread who had the transcript of his deposition in front of him, Sanderson was like a mouse confronting a cat. Whitebread drew his concession that he had read Clooney's article about Moses during his role as editor and had told Mr. Mandick that he wouldn't publish it without a lot more work and corroboration. He also told Mr. Mandick that it was an important article that made serious accusations, and that he should be careful about printing it and running the risk of a libel suit. Whitebread ended his examination with the question, "Mr. Sanderson, to your knowledge, did Mr. Mandick or anyone else conduct additional research?" Sanderson, looking miserable, responded, "No."

Butt quickly rose to his feet for what was technically cross-examination, but of a friendly witness. "Mr. Sanderson, what else did Mr. Mandick say to you?"

"Mr. Mandick told me that he believed the story and that was what counted in his mind."

"Was it customary for Mr. Mandick to make the final decision on what articles would appear in *Total Faith*?"

"Without question."

"No further questions."

"One question on redirect," Whitebread said as he stood up. "Before this article, when was the last time that you warned Mr. Mandick about an article?" Sanderson paused. What a wonderful question, Jason thought.

"I don't recall," Sanderson finally said.

"Thank you, Mr. Sanderson," Whitebread said sweetly. "The plaintiff next calls Everett Mandick, the publisher of *Total Faith*."

As Mandick got up from his seat next to Butt and walked to the witness stand, Jason could only think of a variation on a quip he had heard. Mandick was Stephen Bannon without the charm and good looks. If anything could lose the case for *Total Faith*, it was Mandick. Jason realized that Mandick was the first evangelical he, and probably most of the jury, would see and hear in person. Jason never understood how these supposed people of God could accept and nearly worship as president someone who committed adultery, assaulted women, lied as a matter of course if not conviction, and passionately practiced a host of other sins and crimes. Would the jury think the same thing? Jason knew that he would be instantly disqualified and perhaps worse if anyone if anyone read his mind. Jason's job was to prevent the jury from hearing anything that would suggest these thoughts. That would be considered unfairly prejudicial under the Federal Rules of Evidence. He sat upright to watch the show. He was the wolf guarding the henhouse.

Whitebread had to make Mandick appear more than negligent to get punitive damages, which promised to be far larger than compensatory damages, if he won the case. Unlike *The New York Times* and the television broadcast networks, who defended their product to the end, Mandick was in a different category of media. Mandick was prepared to admit that he got some of the details wrong (code word for all the important facts), but would excuse himself by claiming the story was basically correct (even though it was totally wrong). He could focus exclusively on winning the lawsuit. In a word, he was like Donald Trump.

After bringing out facts about Mandick's background, including that he considered himself a hands-on editor-publisher of *Total Faith*, Whitebread asked Mandick a question that he thought had no downside risk. "You heard Mr. Sanderson's testimony about his conversation with you. Was Mr. Sanderson telling the truth?" Mandick could say yes or no. If he said no, he would be putting himself at odds with an employee of his and possibly look bad in the process, while if he said yes, he would simply be corroborating his negative testimony.

The old saying about never asking a hostile witness a question to which you did not know the answer was not true. Rather, you didn't ask a question to which no possible answer he could give could hurt you. In fact, Whitebread had analyzed the situation correctly, but he had underestimated Mandick. Mandick replied, "Yes, Mr. Whitebread, and especially his testimony where I said I believed the article."

Whitebread recovered quickly. "Are you saying, Mr. Mandick that you did not agree with most of Mr. Sanderson's testimony when he told you that the article was in his opinion wrong?"

"No, I just said I agreed with his testimony."

"You singled out part of his answer as representing the absolute truth. Are you saying, Mr. Mandick, that you have more than one level of truth?"

After the jury and the spectators laughed, Mandick acknowledged that he had only one standard of truth and that Sanderson had testified truthfully. However smart and successful, Mandick learned quickly not to joust with a good trial lawyer. Jason wondered whether Whitebread had created excessive jury expectations. Too many observers subscribe to the Perry Mason syndrome. A cross-examination is effective when, and only when, the witness collapses and recants in the face of riveting cross-examination. Most lawyers are lucky if that happens once in a lifetime.

Lounging against the podium, Whitebread asked Mandick what his options were when Sanderson told him he was worried about the accuracy of the article. Mandick replied that he could have questioned Clooney closely about the article, have someone else duplicate the research, or even kill the article. Whitebread persevered.

"You chose the former option, namely, to question Clooney, and not have anyone do more research nor kill the article, isn't that right, Mr. Mandick?"

"Yes, Mr. Whitebread."

"You believed that there was enough to print an article

declaring the extraordinary allegations made against Mr. Moses?"

"I didn't consider them all that extraordinary, Mr. Whitebread. Serious, yes, extraordinary, no. There have been all sorts of serious and true allegations against lawyers, as you well know. I don't have to remind you of the misdeeds of lawyers in President Nixon's Watergate scandal where dozens of lawyers were implicated in misconduct."

Jason smiled to himself. Give a star to Butt for coming up with a great answer. Or was it Mandick who had thought of it first?

"You don't know how many serious allegations against lawyers in articles submitted to the media never ran because it was learned they were false, do you, Mr. Mandick?"

"No, nor do I know whether the writers were as well qualified as Ms. Clooney." Mandick was good.

"Didn't Ms. Clooney tell you that she had found some mistakes in the article after she submitted it?"

"Yes, Mr. Whitebread, and that's why I went over it carefully with her. You must realize that the mistakes were not major. They were the date of one meeting between Mr. Moses and Ms. Winter and something about Mr. Moses's background."

"Your Honor," Whitebread said, "I move to strike everything after, "yes" as nonresponsive. The question I asked called for a yes or no answer."

Whitebread was technically correct, Jason, decided, but trials run that way are idiotic. Jason decided how he would handle it.

"Sustained," Jason said, then he tuned to Mandick. "Please describe the mistakes Ms. Clooney made."

A few lawyers chuckled while Mandick repeated the answer that had just been stricken. Trying not to show his annoyance at Jason, Whitebread continued.

"Shouldn't you say alleged meeting, since you acknowledge that the article was false."

"I stand corrected."

"Getting the date wrong of an important meeting of an

alleged bribery is hardly trivial, is it?"

"No, but you are taking this out of context," Mandick said. "What we are talking about here is whether a writer invented something out of whole cloth. Ms. Clooney informed me that she had made a couple of mistakes that did not go to the heart of the allegation against Mr. Moses. That struck me as something that a conscientious and honest reporter would do. I get more worried when reporters stick to every detail when they seem to have made a mistake. Nothing had happened that remotely suggested to me that she had made up just about everything in the article." Whitebread had given Mandick a chance to make a speech. Another star for Mandick.

"You didn't consider it a plus that Ms. Clooney admitted making two mistakes, did you?"

"Of course not, Mr. Whitebread. But you have to understand that I had complete confidence in the integrity and competence of Ms. Clooney from having worked with her for years."

"Your position is that despite the very, very serious charges in the article and the warning from your trusted editor you decided that nothing more was required other than to question Ms. Clooney?"

"I shall not repeat what I've said here and in my deposition," Mandick said. "If that's your conclusion, I guess you are entitled to it."

"Sir, you spoke about your confidence in Ms. Clooney. How many articles of hers had you previously published?" Whitebread was trying out another tack.

"Three, if I recall correctly." Mandick looked relaxed as he slouched in the witness chair.

"You consider that such a large number that you had this great faith in her?"

"Objection, argumentative," Butt stated, while looking at Mandick.

Jason wondered whether Butt also saw that Mandick was losing concentration and wanted to snap him back to reality. Mandick could have easily handled the question.

"Overruled," Jason ruled.

"It was enough for me to make up my mind," Mandick said.

"Am I correct that two of the articles were not controversial, one on a conservative college and one on someone who infiltrated the Tea Party movement?"

"That is your conclusion, but your description of the articles is correct."

"Are you saying the articles were highly critical of the university and the Tea Party?"

"No," Mandick said.

"So how were they controversial for your magazine?"

"I didn't say they were."

Was Mandick getting too clever? Jason found the exchanges delightful.

"That's strange. I would have sworn you had. In any event the second article was about someone who infiltrated the Tea Party, is that correct?"

"Yes."

"The article did not accuse the infiltrator of any crime or anything like that?" Whitebread asked.

"Just misrepresenting her views in order so she could join the movement."

"And that's the sum of your experience with the writings of Ms. Clooney?"

"That's my experience with Ms. Clooney's articles that I published," Mandick replied, "but I've read other things she's written for other publications. There never was an accusation that she made up a story."

"Mr. Mandick, just prior to publication didn't you describe the article on Mr. Moses to one of your largest advertisers?"

Another switch in subjects without warning, Jason noted.

"Yes, I did, Mr. Whitebread."

"What did the advertiser tell you?"

"He said that he hoped that I had libel insurance, which I took as a joke, and a statement that the article was a powerful one."

"You thought both of those things in the second after the advertiser said he hoped you had plenty of libel insurance?"

Whitebread shook his head slowly.

"That's correct," Mandick said.

"You didn't think, even a tiny little bit, that he was suggesting to you that the article could result in your getting sued and being held liable for a considerable amount of money?" Whitebread had contorted his body to make it look smaller, to the amusement of the jury and the spectators.

"No, I did not."

"Mr. Mandick, weren't you playing Russian roulette with Mr. Moses's reputation?"

"Objection."

"Withdrawn."

"Mr. Whitebread," Jason said as he stared at Whitebread, "I know Jack McCoy and defense counsel do that on *Law and Order*, and perhaps it happens on other television shows, and I am prepared to believe that it happens in state courts. However, it doesn't happen here. When a lawyer asks a question and his adversary objects, I rule on the objection. Counsel do not decide when I rule and when I don't. On Mr. Butt's objection, it is sustained. It was an improper question.

"You may continue Mr. Whitebread."

"Mr. Mandick, as you and your lawyer have said, you are conceding the falsity of the article. But isn't it a fact that for months you told the world that the article was one hundred percent true?"

"I made those public statements at a time I totally believed in their accuracy. I totally believed the article when I made the decision to publish it and for months thereafter, without question. Later, during discovery for this case, I learned some contrary things and decided, upon advice of counsel, to concede falsity of the article for purposes of this lawsuit. I did not want to waste the time of the court and the jury arguing something that I could no longer in good conscience support."

"You don't deny that your position here is inconsistent with your previous public position, do you?"

"Objection."

"Sustained. Mr. Whitebread, you've made your point."

"No further questions of Mr. Mandick at this time, Your Honor."

"Mr. Butt, Mr. Rattle, do you want to question Mr. Mandick at this time?"

"Not now, Your Honor."

"Same, Your Honor."

"The plaintiff rests," Whitebread announced.

There was some shuffling in the courtroom. A few spectators and reporters got up and left.

"Ladies and Gentlemen of the jury, we have completed the plaintiff's presentation of evidence," Jason announced. "I think we are all pleased that it took less time than expected. Because of that and because I have some legal matters to take up with the lawyers, I shall adjourn presenting evidence early today. We expect to begin proceedings at the usual time tomorrow morning. The rest of us will take ten minutes off and return to the courtroom. Spectators are welcome to stay for motions." Jason rose and retired to his chambers.

Back in the courtroom ten minutes later, Jason spoke to the lawyers in the presence of a nearly full gallery of spectators. "Mr. Butt, I assume you are ready to make the usual motion to dismiss for failure of the plaintiff to introduce sufficient evidence from which the jury could find for plaintiff Moses."

"That's correct, Your Honor."

"I don't want to steal your thunder, but there is no way I am dismissing the case. If you believe you have something that I missed or feel you have to say something for the record, please file a memorandum. I'll reserve entering my denial for forty-eight hours for that purpose and I assure you that whatever you submit I shall read carefully." Jason started to leave the courtroom by the door behind his chair.

"Your Honor?"

Jason turned to see Crunch standing at the podium. He had walked there from his front-row seat among the spectators. Jason signaled the lawyers and court reporter to the bench. He did not know what Crunch had in mind and did not want to take any risks.

"May I see Your Honor privately? It is about the subject of the last meeting I attended in chambers. I'd rather speak to you privately first and you can decide what you want to do after that. I purposely raise the question in the presence of all counsel."

"Unless someone objects," Jason said, "I think it is prudent to proceed as Mr. Crunch suggests. I shall arrange to have a court reporter present. The transcript will be preserved, whether under seal it is too early to say. Let us proceed to chambers now. Please return to your seats."

Jason addressed those in the courtroom. "Ladies and gentlemen, we are adjourning for the day."

Jason, Joe, Crunch, Crunch's associate, and the court reporter seated themselves in Jason's office with the door closed. Sue brought in coffee and shut the door behind her. "How can I help you, Mr. Crunch?" Jason asked.

"After you disclosed the letter you received to us, I of course reported the development to President Trump. As you can see, he has said nothing about it publicly and raised no objection to your continuing to preside over the case. He was, however, troubled by the letter. He does not like federal judges to receive threats of any sort. He was also concerned that if the letter became public, everyone would accuse him or his Administration of sending the letter. Or else of ignoring a threat to a federal judge. He did not want that hanging over his head."

Jason had difficultly responding. Trump objecting to threats against judges? That was almost too much to take. Jason listened.

"President Trump directed me to brief the FBI director, and I met with him and two senior aides. They listened and told me they would get back to me. When the deputy director telephoned, he said they had commenced an investigation. When I told that to the president, he waived me away, saying that if the FBI felt that way, it should go ahead."

"I apologize for interrupting," Jason said, "but am I to understand the FBI concluded that a crime has been committed? Neither Chief Judge Martin Marbury, the only person I've spoken to about this, nor I think one has been." Jason was unhappy at the turn of events. This could only complicate his life. He would not mention the unidentified telephone calls. He also resisted the temptation to ask Crunch what Trump and done and said other than to tell him that the FBI should proceed as it sought best.

"The FBI is noncommittal, or at least they have not concluded that one has been. They recognize that any threat is at most ambiguous. At this point there is no conclusion one way or the other. I think they're calling it a suspected crime."

"Thank you."

"The FBI told me not to say anything to you, because the people they were most interested in looking at were totally separate from the judiciary. They were people who might have written the letter in a misguided effort to protect the president." Crunch paused to sip coffee. "I guess I should have said on the record that this conference is highly confidential and should be sealed, but I suppose that was clear. The FBI has interviewed nearly one hundred people and has found nothing that implicates any Trump ally."

So much for keeping the letter confidential, Jason thought. *Why did I take the case? Why didn't I quit when I got the letter?*

"The FBI is broadening its investigation," Crunch continued. "This may include talking to some members of the judicial branch. We want you to know what's been happening, so you're not blindsided."

"I'm not sure I want to know any more," Jason said.

"The FBI's thought exactly."

"Shouldn't you alert the Chief Judge?" Jason asked.

"Another place where we agree. What will happen next is that someone from the FBI will call Chief Judge Marbury and set up a meeting. The FBI is running the show. The president wants the inquiry to be nonpolitical. I'm here because I'm technically in the case before you and that will be the extent of my activity. The FBI will ask the chief judge not to say anything to anyone, which will include you, so we'd appreciate your not asking him anything."

"Don't worry, I won't," Jason responded quickly. After

the events involving Trump's interference with federal law-enforcement efforts, including ousting FBI director Comey and attacking Special Counsel Mueller, Jason was skeptical about the investigation, but it was not for him to say. He didn't understand Trump's apparent timid acquiescence. Maybe he was getting worried about the Russian investigations and did not want to expand his problems.

"I'm sorry to have gone ahead without notifying you first, but I am subject to the will of the president. I'm also sorry that you are involved in this."

"No problem," Jason said. "I fully understand your position Can we close the meeting and let the reporter go? Please seal the discussion under my order." The court reporter folded up her implement and left. Court reporters were uniformly professional.

"Now that we're off the record I'll tell you that I am relieved," Jason said quietly. I don't want any responsibility for this, whatever it is. We may be talking about my friends and colleagues. Also, whatever you may have heard, I don't have an ounce of sleuth in me. My single effort ended a few decades ago." There was nothing more that Jason could say or do.

"Your Honor, can I return a telephone call from Washington? The U.S. Marshall allowed me to bring my phone into the courtroom, but told me I could not use it in the courthouse without your permission."

"Certainly. Do you want privacy?"

"I don't think so. I'll just go over there." Crunch walked to the far corner of Jason's office, while Jason sad at his desk looking at some papers. Jason could hear murmurs from Crunch, but nothing more. Then, Crunch spoke more loudly.

"Yes, sir. But I think the president is confused. He seems to think the pardon power extends to private civil suits in a federal court." A few second of silence followed. "Yes, sir. Yes, sir." A few more seconds of silence. "Of course, sir. Thank you, sir."

Crunch hung up, turned, and walked to Jason's desk. "Thank you very much for your courtesy. I hope I didn't disturb you."

"Not at all. You're welcome. Good day."

Crunch and his associate left.

Jason wondered about the call. It was as though Crunch wanted him to learn of his problems dealing with Trump. But then, didn't everybody?

Chapter 16

Butt's first witness was Clement Rapture, the managing editor of *Total Faith*. He was impeccably dressed in a dark suit, light blue shirt, and red tie, probably one of Ivanka's, Jason speculated. He was handsome and stood erect. His dark hair had a few specks of gray. He seemed nervous, however, and drops of perspiration dotted his brow. Jason wondered whether Rapture had changed his name as a career move. As Butt started his questioning, Jason saw Vernon slip into the first row of spectators in a seat he had reserved for him. Good.

"Mr. Rapture, how long have you worked for Mr. Mandick?" Butt asked.

"Eight months as managing editor of *Total Faith*, ever since he acquired it, and before that for about four years on *Alt-Times*."

"What did you do before that?"

"I worked a total of twelve years at *Forbes Magazine* and *Fortune* as an editor."

"How would you compare the journalistic standards at *Forbes* and *Fortune* with those of *Total Faith*?"

"Aside from the different scales of the operation, the standards were just about the same," Rapture said.

"Whom does the editorial staff consist of at *Total Faith*?"

"Myself and Mr. Sanderson. Mr. Mandick, of course, is involved in editing when he is in town and interested in an article."

"Were you aware of the submission to the magazine of the article that is the subject of his lawsuit?"

"Yes, in a sense I shepherded it through the publication process."

"Did you work directly on the editing of the article?"

"No, I did not," Rapture said.

"Why not?"

"I was aware of the content of the article and I asked Mr. Mandick whether he wanted me to get directly involved in the editing, which I did from time to time."

"What did Mr. Mandick tell you?"

"He said that it was not necessary," Rapture said. "It was a well-researched and well-written article and that I had better things to do."

"Are you saying that nothing in the article suggested to you that more research could just possibly result in finding substantial errors in the article?"

"Objection, Your Honor, the question is confusing," Whitebread stated, rising slowly.

"I'll rephrase it," Butt said without waiting for a ruling. "Did anything in the article or anything you learned in the preparation of the article for publication suggest to you that more research could lead to finding substantial errors?"

"No, Mr. Butt," Rapture said.

"In your experience, does Mr. Mandick make final editorial decisions based on his personal conclusions on a submission to the magazine?"

"Oh, yes, it is quite common. He was experienced, and he trusts his own judgment and, if I may add, so does the rest of the staff."

"Objection, Your Honor. I move to strike the last clause," Whitebread stated. "Nonresponsive and lack of foundation."

"Sustained." It was a good objection, Jason concluded. Without the motion to strike, Butt could have argued on summation that the entire staff trusted Mandick.

"Did you ever express to Mr. Mandick any doubts on your part concerning the content of the article?"

"Since I had none, no," Rapture said.

"Mr. Rapture, to your knowledge, has any publication you've worked for ever been sued for libel?"

"Objection, Your Honor," Whitebread stated.

"Sustained. Ladies and gentlemen of the jury, I just want to tell you that I have ruled the question improper. Whether someone else decided to sue *Total Faith* or any other publication run by Mr. Mandick proves nothing. It is easy to sue, yet people who have good cases decide not to sue for many reasons. In fact, we don't know what answer Mr. Rapture would have given. So simply disregard the question. Mr. Butt do you want to defend your question?"

"No, Your Honor, and no further questions," although Butt seemed surprised at the ruling.

"Mr. Whitebread, any cross?"

"Yes, Your Honor. Mr. Rapture," Whitebread said with a sneer, "you said you had no doubts about the article. In fact, you never checked it out, isn't that correct?"

"Yes, Mr. Whitebread, but I did read it and I saw nothing that raised doubts. Also, while I did not study Ms. Clooney's notes, I did read them, and they seemed uncommonly complete," Rapture said.

"To get back to my question, you did not investigate the article for accuracy?"

"That is correct."

"So, you have no personal knowledge of its accuracy?"

"That's correct."

"And that is because Mr. Mandick told you that he didn't want you to investigate the accuracy of the article?"

"Mr. Whitebread, I have described what happened. I see no basis for any suggestion that Mr. Mandick was trying to prevent me from investigating the article."

"But you don't know that, do you?"

"I've told you what happened, and, no, I am not a mind

reader."

"No further questions."

"Any questions, Mr. Rattle? Any redirect? Mr. Rapture, you are excused," Jason stated.

"The defense now calls Mr. Mandick," Butt announced, as his client returned to the witness box.

After describing his upbringing and education, Mandick testified that he was a self-made man who had formed a communications company soon after college and sold it for $50 million before he was thirty. He pocketed the money and led what he described as an aimless, and at time dissolute, life for years following the sale. Butt asked Mandick about his transformation.

"I was not interested in politics or religion in college or in the years when I was working sixteen hours a day on my communications company. After I sold it and became wealthy, I still had no interest in God. Gradually, I realized that I could not have done what I did alone, and that God must have favored me for some reason. I turned to the church and became a born-again Christian. It is said that converts are often the most determined of believers, and I guess that could apply to me." Mandick's smile was hardly ingratiating.

"What did you do then?" Butt asked.

"I believed that the government, and particularly the federal government, was stifling individual initiative, creativity, and inner development. Many of the people who worked in government did not have the best interests of the country at heart. I concluded that the country could be destroyed unless something was done. I also believed that people were not listening to God and were not doing His will, a course that could lead to a cataclysmic disaster.

"I decided to do my part by publishing a magazine that promoted these beliefs, which was the foundation for my first magazine *Good Faith*. I founded that magazine about five years ago. It was quite small. When Donald Trump ran for president, I was totally on board."

Jason was learning something about born-again Christians.

It was probably true for most of the New York jurors.

"Mr. Mandick, I apologize for interrupting your interesting narrative, but I have a few questions before you discuss the magazine that you run. Did you entertain doubts as to President Trump and his positions?"

"Everyone has doubts, Mr. Butt, but I rather rapidly concluded that compared to other political beliefs and movements and people, Donald Trump's was special, even divinely inspired. He respected life, including the lives of the unborn. Some of the people with whom I spoke said that they were in the Tea Party movement because God had personally told them to join. Sadly, I did not have that experience, but I believe that I am just as committed to its creed as they are. Perhaps, God does not deem me worthy to speak directly to me. The answer to your question is that at one time I entertained some uncertainty, but I soon lost these doubts and became an unqualified believer in the Tea Party and its mission. The same answer applies as to President Trump, in fact, more so. He has an extraordinary understanding of the American public and its needs. I'm not saying he's not a flawed human being, we all are, but he is someone truly special."

"Please return to your narrative, sir," Butt said.

Jason looked at the jurors, who were giving Mandick their rapt attention. Jason wondered whether the jurors regarded the witness as something of a freak. He tried to wipe the thought from his mind. The jurors would have a tough time sizing up someone like Mandick.

"*Good Faith* was moderately successful, and it reached a small but growing group of readers, largely because of our efforts and my financial support. Stephen Bannon announced right after the election that the publication department of Breitbart was for sale. He was close to Trump and was joining the Trump Administration. I knew him slightly. I purchased Breitbart's magazine, including its subscription list, changed its name to Total Faith, and continued my mission in promoting the standards of beliefs in the Tea Party movement, the word of God, and, of course, President Trump. I merged *Good Faith* into

Total Faith.

"I should emphasize that from my first day there I decided that first *Good Faith* and then *Total Faith* would adhere to the most rigorous journalistic principles, which I believe is essential to my mission. We have truth on our side and it's just a matter of finding proof for it. We have been very successful recently, and that proves that God can be revealed in a secular society, which unfortunately is what we have in this country. It is absurd to regard truth and faith as inconsistent in any way. In fact, it is inconceivable to me."

Mandick was playing to his base, Jason concluded. He was certainly not wooing the jurors, since most of them held faith and truth as polar opposites. Since Mandick would probably be delighted with a hung jury, his strategy might be entirely rational. A few might be believers.

"Sir, please tell us some of the articles that *Good Faith* and *Total Faith* have printed under your stewardship that reflect both faith and truth," Butt continued.

"Many if not most of the articles in have followed that precept. To give a few examples, there was one article that demonstrated that global warming and other natural catastrophes, to the extent they exist, are the product of God's will. I should add that I have substantial doubts that there is global warming and that puny man is responsible for anything that potentially important.

"An article explained that Hurricane Katrina was God's punishment, and that He intervened to hinder the rescue attempt. Another showed that federal programs to force people into the straight-jacket of mandated health care were inconsistent with the will of God, who valued people as individuals and wanted them to stand on their own two feet when confronted by adversity.

"Another article revealed that the federal income tax was a punishment that God visited upon the people of the United States for their sins, and that as people become more devout and accept the will of God, it should be abolished."

Jason, along with the rest of the people in the courtroom,

was not accustomed to such professions of faith. Jason saw signs of skepticism among the jurors, including a couple of incipient smiles and at least one juror who eyes were rolling upwards.

Jason thought about the dynamics operating between Mandick and Butt on the content of Mandick's testimony. Was Butt's continued employment as Mandick's lawyer contingent on his letting Mandick recount his views? Patience was a necessary quality for a trial judge, along with its companion, self-restraint. So was managing the disappointment of never finding the answer to many questions.

"Sir, please tell the court and jurors how you came to meet Ms. Clooney."

"A few years ago, I got a call from a friend of mine, Kurt Krease, who publishes a conservative magazine in California. He said he had a young woman reporter working for him, Beverly Clooney. She was tired of California and wanted to leave and go to the east coast. He said that she was first rate and that he wanted her to stay, but realized he couldn't convince her to remain, so he wanted to help her find another suitable position."

"Objection," Whitebread exclaimed. "That testimony about Ms. Clooney's competence is not admissible for its truth. It's hearsay"

"I don't believe it was offered for truth, Mr. Whitebread. Ladies and gentlemen of the jury, you may consider Mr. Mandick's testimony only on the issue of the defendants' state of mind, that is, on whether they were negligent or possessed legal malice. Please continue Mr. Mandick." Jason thought that many objections merely increased the jury's awareness of testimony, but it wasn't his job to educate lawyers.

"Mr. Krease asked her if she would like to work for *Good Faith* if it could be arranged. She was very enthusiastic. We talked for a while on the phone and I asked her to send me her résumé, which she did. I asked her if I could call her references, since I was interested in hiring her. She was enthusiastic. I called the two references that preceded her working for Mr. Krease, both of whom provided excellent recommendations.

She came to see me, and we talked about her, her work, and my magazine. I told her we'd offer her a position as a freelance senior writer with a guaranteed salary, which suited her."

"What happened next?"

"She wrote the three articles that I mentioned earlier, and each was excellent and a success. We were interested in publishing whatever she wrote."

"Mr. Mandick, please tell the court and jurors how you came to publish the article on Mr. Moses."

"I have to explain something else first. As I've said Ms. Clooney was a regular and respected writer. After one year, she told me that she needed a break, and that's when she left for Hawaii. I helped get her a job as a journalist there. She wrote me a letter or two from Hawaii, but that was it.

"One day she called me to tell me that she was back in town and asked if she could have her old position back. That must have been about a year after she had left. Without hesitation, I said yes. After a couple of weeks, she called me to tell me that she was working on an article that was perfect for the magazine and explained it briefly. I told her that my magazine was now *Total Faith* and that we would be interested. I cannot claim that I wasn't pleased by what she told me. Because of her Senate Committee testimony, I considered the Secretary of Commerce a traitor to the United States because she sought to impose policies that all but put the people of the United States into slavery to the federal government and empowered the lawless." Mandick's voice had become harsh and angry.

Jason was busy taking notes, but he also was watching the jurors. One juror put his hand over his eyes, two were shaking their heads negatively, another stared at the ceiling.

"The Thirteenth Amendment obviously meant nothing to her," Mandick said. "She was prepared to deny our liberty, just as our forefathers kept slaves. If the case had indeed been fixed by jury tampering by a supporter of the radical-left, that would help restore my faith in the citizens of New York. Kruiser should have been put in prison. I had nothing personally against Mr. Moses, although he was obviously a tool of the Secretary and the liberal establishment."

Jason was convinced that Mandick set the agenda and orchestrated defense of the case. If he wanted to win the case, he was going about it in a strange way. He was like Trump. Was it something about successful right-wing businessmen that made them self-destructive when they spoke to a broader audience? They could not restrain themselves from telling everyone how important they were. Maybe it was that they were not used to being questioned.

"When she submitted the article a week later, it was just as I expected. It was well researched and well written and explained to my satisfaction how it was that the jury acquitted the Secretary. I read it and reread the article, then I read her notes and reread her notes. Ultimately, I was totally satisfied with the absolute accuracy of the article."

"Did you do anything else with respect to Ms. Clooney and her article?" Butt asked.

"Oh, yes, I questioned her at great length concerning the article. I repeatedly challenged her, and she just as often responded without hesitation and persuasively, I should add. She explained the facts confidently and carefully. I was totally convinced."

"There has been some reference to the fact that Ms. Clooney made two corrections in the article after you approved it. Did that affect how you felt about the article?"

"It made me even more confident that it was correct," Mandick answered. "That the writer would continue her diligent search for the truth after an article was accepted and make those minor corrections reinforced my conviction that she was careful and accurate. In fact, I believe that the wrong date was a typographical error. Also, whenever she spoke to me about the article, she looked me in the eye and exhibited total confidence in and commitment to the article. I respect people who do that."

It was the sort of testimony that probably appealed to the jury, Jason thought, although it was too little and too late.

"You have heard one of your advertisers testify that he said that he hoped you had a lot of libel insurance. What effect did that have on your conclusions about the article?"

"I thought he was pulling my leg," Mr. Butt. "I did not take what he said literally, but rather that my article would hit a major nerve and that those people would go after me. They had to stop me. I never believed that he was in any way placing the accuracy of the article in doubt. He shared my view of the Secretary, and he had no personal knowledge of the events involved in the prosecution of the Secretary, at least as far as I knew."

"Did anything else contribute to your belief in the accuracy of Ms. Clooney's article?"

"Well, both Mr. Rapture and Mr. Sanderson seemed wholly supportive of publishing the article. They were and are aware of my journalistic standards I apply to *Total Faith*."

"You did not speak to the people that Ms. Clooney interviewed. Why not?" Butt asked.

"That is not how articles are written. If you don't have confidence in a reporter, fire her. Editors and publishers cannot redo every reporter's work."

"Mr. Mandick, is it your testimony that when you published the article on Mr. Moses that is the subject of this case you believed that the article was accurate?"

"Absolutely."

"Did you have any doubts about the accuracy of the article when it appeared in *Total Faith*?"

"Absolutely not."

"Then why are you not defending the truthfulness of the article in this lawsuit?"

Good question, thought Jason, certainly one that would be on the minds of the jurors. Jason looked at Beverly Clooney; she was staring straight ahead. He was getting tired and looking forward to a recess. He was sorry that Christine could not see this.

"Two reasons," Mandick replied. "It isn't necessary to win this case. The evidence of our due care and conscientiousness is overwhelming. Facts have come to my attention between the publication of the article that have made me question whether the article met the standards of *Total Faith* for publication. I do not defend something that I think is defective. That is contrary to my faith as well as my journalistic ethics."

"I have no further questions of Mr. Mandick."

"Mr. Rattle, any questions?"

"No, Your Honor."

"Before Mr. Whitebread examines Mr. Mandick we will have our morning recess."

Jason retreated to his chambers, sat down, and shut his eyes. How does a New York jury deal with Mandick and his crew, he asked himself. But maybe they are more proficient in distinguishing between charlatans and legitimate folk than judges, who sit on their elevated benches and inhabit elaborate chambers. He took a few sips from the coffee mug Sue had given him. A few minutes of relaxation before Jason returned to the courtroom to find Mandick seated in the witness box.

"Please proceed, Mr. Whitebread," Jason said after he was seated.

"Mr. Mandick, I have some questions concerning your direct testimony," Whitebread said as he strode to the podium.

"I am ready to answer them, Mr. Whitebread."

"Thank you. They concern some of the articles you mentioned on direct testimony."

"Objection. Your Honor, this trial is about the article on Mr. Moses."

"I know that Mr. Butt, but you opened the door, at least a little. If you presented testimony to show that Ms. Clooney was professional, I don't see how I can prevent Mr. Whitebread from challenging it. I'll allow Mr. Whitebread some questions on the articles." It was a silly objection that had no hope of winning. Perhaps Butt was reminding Mandick to take his time answering the questions so that Butt could object when needed. He didn't want his client to get too comfortable. Cross-examination was not the same as well-rehearsed direct examination.

"Mr. Mandick, you have testified that you adhere to standard journalistic practices with your magazine."

"That's correct."

"Doesn't that require, at times, checking and corroborating sources for an article?"

"It may, Mr. Whitebread."

"How does one check or corroborate an article that recites that God brought Hurricane Katrina to the southeast, that He did so for vengeance, and that He hindered recovery efforts by the Bush administration as part of His plan? Whom does one ask to check the accuracy of statements about God's will? I mean this very seriously, Mr. Mandick."

"You understand that God is all powerful?"

"I'm sorry, but I'm not here to answer questions."

"I'll assume to your credit that you do. Therefore, any time there is a catastrophe it is His doing. When competent and devout people like President Bush and his Administration cannot solve the problems that God willed, that is God's will. As to why God chose to punish those harmed by Katrina and why He stood in the way of President Bush, a devout believer in Him, that is something beyond our ability to comprehend."

"So, if God is involved, you don't need corroboration?" Whitebread smiled confidently.

"That's not what I said, Mr. Whitebread."

"How do you decide if a reporter is accurately describing the acts of God?"

"Editors don't go to Africa to check out what a trusted reporter writes, and I adhere to the same standards about matters that are difficult to verify."

"Wouldn't you say, 'impossible to verify'?"

"My point, exactly."

Nice touch, Jason thought, very nice touch.

"Do you believe that God created the world in seven days, Mr. Mandick?"

"Actually, it was six."

"Objection. Relevancy."

Jason wondered why Butt was objecting when Mandick was handling the cross well.   Then, he realized that Butt did not want this trial to be decided on the issue of God's role in the creation, for the simple reason that he would lose in New York City. It was one thing to defend a magazine article; it was another to challenge Darwin.

"Sustained. I think we have enough on our plates, Mr. Whitebread. I'll leave a reprise of the Scopes trial for another day."

"I'll move on to another subject. Mr. Mandick, am I right that you personally followed closely the perjury trial of the Secretary?"

"You are."

"How did you do that, Mr. Mandick?"

"I did not attend the trial, but one of the lawyers in the firm that represents the magazine attended and every day wrote a memorandum of what had transpired."

"Did the memoranda say that the trial was going well for the Secretary?"

"Objection, Your Honor," Butt stated.

"Sustained. Rephrase the question." Jason wasn't sure whether Butt's objection was the technical one that he had in mind when he sustained the objection, namely, the best-evidence rule, but there was no harm done in either event.

"What did you conclude at the time as to how the case was progressing from the standpoint of the Secretary?"

"I believed it was a close case." Mandick said.

"Sir, you were here when Mr. Moses described from the stand his opinion of the evidence. Did that cause you to change your mind on the case?"

"No, it did not. I agree that Mr. Moses made some good points, after all he is a skillful lawyer, but they were not important to one's view of how well the case was going from the standpoint of the jury. You may even agree with me that Mr. Moses was hardly an impartial judge of what went on in that trial. I frankly did not see how a conscientious jury, even one from New York, would not find the Secretary guilty."

Jason wasn't sure that the "even one from New York" line was productive, but, again, it was none of his business.

"What good points did you consider Mr. Moses made?"

"Perhaps I overspoke, Mr. Whitebread. I should have said that you were very persuasive in how you handled some of the weaker points in Secretary Kruiser's case. I admire your technique. The trial Mr. Moses described is not the one I was following."

Mandick was sharp, Jason thought.

"Did you ask Ms. Clooney what got her interested in *United States v. Kruiser*?

"I don't think I did, Mr. Whitebread, although it was hardly an obscure case."

"Did you ask her how she first heard about the alleged bribery?"

"Not that I recall."

"Do you know whether she had a source who had inside information?"

"Certainly, she told me that she spoke to a juror," Mandick said.

"How did Ms. Clooney learn about the juror?"

"I don't know. I assumed it was someone who had important confidential information about the case. Reporters have their sources."

"Move to strike the last two sentences as nonresponsive."

"Denied, the issue of Mr. Mandick's state of mind is very much in issue," Jason stated.

"Did you ask her the name of the juror?" Whitebread asked.

"No, I assumed it was a confidential source and that Ms. Clooney would tell me if she could."

"Did Ms. Clooney ever tell you the source was Ms. Winter?"

"Certainly," Mandick said.

"When was that?"

"After suit was filed."

Whitebread took a deep breath, which Jason surmised was a prelude to something important or something unknown to the questioner.

"Mr. Mandick, how do you explain Ms. Winter's testimony?"

"Objection," Butt interjected. "Your Honor, it is not Mr. Mandick's responsibility to discuss other witness's testimony."

"Mr. Whitebread, how do you answer Mr. Butt's objection?" Jason asked.

"Your Honor, Mr. Butt asked Mr. Mandick whether he agreec with the testimony of other witnesses, so why can't I?"

"Mr. Butt?" Jason asked.

"That was a situation in which Mr. Mandick had personal knowledge of the events; in effect, he was providing his account of what had happened."

"Objection sustained. Please continue Mr. Whitebread."

"Mr. Mandick, God seems to play a large role in your life."

"He certainly does."

"He also seems to play a large role in your magazine, including that the articles you listed all seem to have a divine component in them."

"It should not be surprising to anyone that we include many articles about our Savior. We live in accordance to God's will and to please God. I am only surprised that publications other than ours talk so little about Him." Mandick looked in Whitebread's eyes when he answered.

"Do you believe that God plays a role in the writing the articles in *Total Faith*?"

"I hope that the people who work for me and write for the magazine are driven by faith in God and look to God for guidance. Is that what you mean?"

"Actually, I was asking something more specific. Does God participate in the actual researching and writing of stories by other writers at *Total Faith*, Mr. Mandick?"

"Objection," Butt stated.

"I want to answer that question, Mr. Butt. We believe that God is all-powerful and that He should be a source of guidance for everyone. We believe that people should pray to God and be guided by God. Some people pray to God for mundane things, like winning a football game. We don't know whether God involves Himself in things like that. Or, if He does, how He chooses between two sets of believers that root for opposing teams. Personally, I don't think it's like a metaphysical tug of war with peoples' souls on both ends of a celestial rope."

Jason wondered how the jury was reacting to the repeated questions on God. He realized he'd find out soon enough.

"We certainly believe that He is capable of intervening and that He does so on very rare occasions," Mandick said. "But it is up to each and every individual to accept responsibility for his actions while trusting in God to lead the way to truth and a good life. If you are suggesting that when I write something, God Himself is moving my hand, I take that suggestion as very offensive. We are not nuts, Mr. Whitebread. Humans do things on their own accord under the eyes of God. They have to accept responsibility."

"Objection," Whitebread interrupted. "The answer is not responsive."

Jason shook his head. "My notes show that you asked the witness about God's participation in writing stories. Overruled. Mr. Mandick, I suggest that you end your answer shortly and let Mr. Butt ask another question."

"Yes, Your Honor. I don't think that you will find many of my faith and conviction thinking that God will send a thunderbolt down from heaven to strike a witness who lies. As I said, we hold to journalistic standards, which are human standards. I don't know whether you asked your question in ignorance or in defiance of God, but in either case, it is offensive to God and man."

As Mandick finished and sat back, obviously satisfied with his monologue, many in the audience applauded, but Jason quickly gaveled them to silence. Butt announced that he had no redirect of his client and that he was resting on behalf of Mr. Mandick. Jason declared they would adjourn for lunch.

———————

After greeting his son warmly in his chambers, Jason asked Sue to send out for a couple of sandwiches.

"You didn't tell me you were having this much fun, dad."

"I must say that I find it riveting."

"How do you instruct the jury on how they should go about

deciding which side God is on?"

"I hope it doesn't come down to that. Is someone reckless who believes in miracles and behaves as though they happen? I don't know. But I've learned to take these things in stride, although I must concede that we're going beyond anything in my experience." The two sat down and waited for lunch to arrive.

Soon, Sue entered with plates, sandwiches, and coffee, placed them down on a table, and left. Vernon unwrapped the two sliced-chicken sandwiches and handed one to his father on a plate. "What do you expect will happen this afternoon?"

"I cannot begin to imagine. Have the newspapers in Washington been covering the trial? I haven't been reading them." Jason opened his sandwich and frowned. The deli had added too much mayonnaise . . . again. No time to change it now. He scraped off what he could and then took a large bite and chewed while he listened to Vernon.

"Quite a bit, actually. The city loves politics, especially when it's spiced with sex or religion. As you can imagine, you can't find much support for *Total Faith*, excluding *The Washington Times*. It's a very conservative paper published by Sun Myung Moon, you know, the Korean spiritual leader and business mogul. While a few would not put it past a trial lawyer to fix a case, the story just doesn't make sense. It's making the Trump Administration look ridiculous, not that it would take much for most of Washington to feel that way. By the way, as a confirmed atheist, how are you taking all this?"

"No one asked me to recuse myself, although I cannot see how anyone would have a case. I'm not big on embezzlers or drug dealers, but I do my job to the best of my ability in those cases. Having said that, I find the testimony fascinating."

Father and son spoke little as they finished their lunch. Vernon stood.

"I have something embarrassing to tell you, dad. I entered an office pool. The winner is the one who guesses which member of the Trump family gets indicted first and comes closest to guessing the date on which the indictment is returned."

"You're kidding!"

"Only partially. There is a pool, but I didn't enter it."

Jason didn't know whether to laugh or cry. He did neither. He asked, "Whom would you have picked?" He instantly regretted the question, but he was curious.

Vernon looked at his father for a second, raised his eyebrows, then answered, "Jared Kushner. Like father, like son, although that would presumably also apply to Trump." Vernon paused. "Maybe we should expand the saying to like father-in-law, like son-in-law. I'm glad I'm not in that family."

Jason shrugged. "I have to get ready for the afternoon session. I'll see you back here after we finish."

"Thanks for everything, dad. I'll go to the courtroom."

After Vernon closed the door, Jason sat down at his desk. He thumbed through his notes from the morning session, making a correction here and there. His notes might be important someday.

Just before leaving his chamber he checked the messages on his private line. This time there were four hang-ups—all marked "Private Caller."

Jason closed his eyes. *I am not a believer in coincidences. For the first time in my career I receive a warning letter. For the first time in my career I received hang-ups on my private line. They must be related. Yet, why would the writer of the letter, who by now had seen that it had no effect resort to the blunter weapon of telephoning and hanging up? Wasn't there a law somewhere that made the calls some sort of crime? But that was for stalkers and others who posed a serious threat. I don't want to bother the FBI, who after all is tied up with the Russian investigation and other important matters, with a handful of innocuous calls. I also am not eager to have the FBI expand its investigation. Nevertheless, it is annoying. I'll decide what to do. One thing is certain, I'm not going to leave this case.*

Chapter 17

Back in the courtroom after lunch, a Deputy U.S. Marshal told Jason that the foreman of the jury had handed him a note containing a question from one of the jurors. The foreman, who in the federal courts was the first juror seated, was a junior economist for one of the largest mutual funds, barely thirty years old. Before the jurors returned, Jason called the lawyers and court reporter up to the bench. "Let this be marked Court's Exhibit 2. Let's see how my idea of giving the jurors an opportunity to ask questions is working."

Opening the note, Jason read: "'Why doesn't Mr. Mandick get God to zap Mr. Moses and end the case?' Not quite what I expected," as all stifled smiles. No one objected to Jason's proposed resolution, and all went to their places in the courtroom. As he sat down, Jason noticed Vernon in his front row seat. He was two seats away from Crunch, who was back attending the trial after a few days' absence.

"Ladies and gentlemen of the jury, I have received a question that after review I have concluded is not one that I can appropriately answer, but thank you. Mr. Rattle, please call your first witness." Jason had decided that he would have to make the note public if he reproached the jury. He did not want to detract from the seriousness of the trial. Also, he saw no harm in a jury with some pluck. The jurors were very attentive.

"We call Beverly Clooney." Although in the courtroom every day, she had been inconspicuous until now, aside from the moment she had been asked to stand up. Jason wondered whether Whitebread was tipping Crunch off on when to attend the trial, but that made no sense because Whitebread was seeking millions of dollars of damages from Trump.

As she walked to the witness stand, all could see that Clooney was a tall and athletic-looking woman of about thirty. Her long brown hair remained straight, and she had not put on makeup for her first day of testimony. She seemed to have the remnants of a few freckles. Her unexpressive face was gaunt and serious. She dressed simply in a shapeless navy-blue dress with a pattern featuring small red roses, with no jewelry except for a man's watch on a leather strap. She had large, strong hands and very short unpolished fingernails. She was clearly not making a fashion statement. She had the drawn look one associates with Appalachia. When she put her hand on a Bible and swore to tell the truth, it was a ringing announcement of her faith. She stared straight at Rattle when she answered his questions, except to look upwards when she said "God."

Rattle asked her about her education and early employment history, which included a bachelor's degree in journalism from a small California college and jobs at several small newspapers and magazines. She gradually began to specialize in political reporting. She won an honorable mention for a story in which she exposed the economic ties of a member of Congress to a labor union that had hired two of his children. Rattle was moving slowly and methodically through her professional life and Clooney was answering listlessly and without emotion. Perhaps she had been over-prepared. Rattle was asking his questions in a conversational tone, as though only the two of them were present. They ignored the outside world. Finally, Rattle asked her how she came to write for Mr. Mandick.

"Mr. Krease, my boss when I worked in California, recommended it. Then, a friend of mine who had written for *Good Faith* told me that it was a great place to work. Krease arranged for me to talk to Mr. Mandick, who said that he would consider any article that I would write. By then I had moved to New York City. Over the next two years I submitted three articles, and all were published. They are the articles that Mr. Mandick described."

"What was it like working for Mr. Mandick?"

"It was terrific. He was a good boss. He insisted on quality. At the beginning, he and one of his editors reviewed everything very carefully and spot-checked some of my facts and statements. He gradually gained confidence in my work." Clooney's voice reflected none of the content of the words she used. She could have been reading a shopping list.

"Ms. Clooney, how would you describe the editorial process at Mr. Mandick's magazines? How did it compare to what you experienced at other positions you have held and other magazines you've written for?"

"It was similar. Certainly, Mr. Mandick was no less careful than the magazines I had previously worked for."

"Did your political and religious beliefs come up with Mr. Mandick at any time?"

"Yes, absolutely. Mr. Mandick asked about them when I first met him. I showed him the revelatory article on a liberal Congressman I had written. I assured him that I was a conservative. On the question of my religion I told him that I was a Christian and a believer, but that I was not active in any church."

"How did Mr. Mandick react?"

"He was upset."

"What do you mean, Ms. Clooney? Was he angry or what? Did he say why?"

"He was concerned about my welfare, both here and in the hereafter. He told me that I was not a complete person without a relationship with Christ and that for my sake I had to do something about it."

"How did you react?"

"I knew that his magazines were written for religious people, but I had not thought it applied to the staff. I was confused. I told Mr. Mandick that I would welcome a closer relationship with God. He was pleased."

"What happened?"

"Nothing for a month or two, but after Mr. Mandick published my first article he called me into his office and told me that he wanted to do me a favor. He wanted me to go to a Christian retreat and that he would pay for it. He said it was run by a religious group with which he was affiliated and that it would do wonders for me. I was surprised and hesitant, but he was insistent, and he was my boss. Mr. Mandick can be very convincing." Jason noted that Clooney did not smile. Her brow was lined, almost in a frown. Her gaze did not waiver. She was concentrating on her testimony.

"So, I went, and it was a wonderful experience. It opened my eyes to all sorts of things about life and God. One thing they taught me was the importance, indeed joy, of developing a personal relationship with God. I felt very undeserving and amateurish among those people, but I made progress, slowly, very slowly. The sense of a community devoted to virtue overwhelmed me. I could feel love wherever I went. It was a wonderful, transcendental experience. My spirits soared." Clooney sat still and stared at her hands.

"I returned to the retreat after my second article, again because of the beneficence of Mr. Mandick, and I had an even more powerful experience. The hours of silence were uplifting. I felt cleansed, as though a pure stream had washed through me. I felt transformed." She suddenly raised her hands toward the ceiling. For a moment, her eyes closed. Then she lowered her hands to her lap and looked at Rattle, who was doing his best to don a beatific smile.

Rattle stumbled on his question, which tried to incorporate a portion of Clooney's testimony, then rephrased it more simply. "What happened next, Ms. Clooney?"

"I was feeling and writing much better. I started seeing a young man I had met at the retreat, and that worked well for a while. Then I felt unworthy again, that I was not doing enough for God, and that He was doing everything for me. I believed my devotion was inadequate and I kept pressing myself to do more, to feel more. This went on for a very long time. I could not sleep. Finally, I could take it no longer. I went to Mr. Mandick and told him I had to get away, preferably to a warm place. He was wonderful about it. He arranged for me to take a job with an evangelical magazine in Hawaii. Mr. Mandick did not want me to lose contact with God."

The jury was staring at Clooney. The eyes of a few widened. The spectators were also silent and attentive.

"You moved to Hawaii?"

"Yes. That was what God wanted. Like my old boss Mr. Krease, Mr. Mandick put me in touch with an evangelical magazine. I just said that, didn't I? Well, the magazine was very good, and I liked the people. And it's so beautiful there. For a while it worked fine, then Satan, I can almost see him now, you know, started taunting me."

The answer was so casual, and the absence of any reaction from the jury and spectators so conspicuous, that Jason thought he might have misunderstood what the woman said. Reluctant to interrupt, Jason nevertheless asked, "Will the court reporter please read the previous answer?"

When the reporter read Beverley Clooney's answer, this time a few spectators reacted with a short gasp. Jason was sure that also was a new one for most of the jurors. During the reading, Jason remained impassive, along with Rattle and Clooney. His mind suddenly turned to Audrey. She had occasionally attended his trials but had found them boring. She had a point. He smiled to himself as he pictured her reaction. She would have loved it, all the more because it implicated Trump. Jason told Rattle to continue.

"In what way did Satan taunt you, Ms. Clooney?"

"Satan called me unworthy and a moral coward, just the person he wanted to command. He said he had all sorts of things he wanted to show me. I was wasting my time, seeking out God, things like that." She was becoming agitated. Her hands flew to her face and then back to her lap.

"What did you do?" Rattle asked in a concerned voice.

"I resisted with all my might. I did some impetuous things, like breaking into a church late at night so I could pray, injuring myself for the glory of God, things like that. I started having visions of God and Satan fighting over my soul, with God urging me to resist Satan. I couldn't sleep because I had to be alert to prevent Satan from getting the upper hand. Finally, my doctor told me I should be hospitalized, which I naturally resisted. I knew I was distraught and tense, but I was in command of all my faculties. God was prevailing in the fight for my soul. Why should I be put in a hospital?" Here, Clooney looked at the jurors, almost imploringly. The jurors recoiled, as though an unkempt panhandler had accosted them.

"When I continued to resist, the doctor committed me involuntarily to a psychiatric hospital just outside of Honolulu. I called the editor of the magazine and told him that I was involved in a lengthy research project, and that I probably would not be in touch with him for a while. I felt that was true. He was concerned but accepted what I said."

During her response, Clooney started talking faster and her voice rose a few tones. She was clenching and unclenching her fists. Her level of agitation reached a peak when she felt God was winning. By the end of her response she seemed exhausted. She was taking long, deep breaths. She had shrunk in her chair. Rattle walked to the jury box and handed her a glass of water that was on the railing. She took several large gulps. Then she sat still.

Jason was having trouble taking notes. He didn't want to take his eyes off Clooney and the jury. Jason noticed Mandick whispering to Butt, who put his hand on top of Mandick's arm.

"What was the diagnosis?" Rattle asked Clooney.

"The doctors said I was paranoid schizophrenic, which, of course, was ridiculous."

"Did they give you medications?"

"Quite a few." She wiped her eyes. She nodded her head several times. "Quite a few."

"Did you take them?"

"Yes, they made me," she said slowly.

"Did the medications make you feel better?"

"I wouldn't call it 'better.' I became calmer and less agitated, less willing to act. I managed myself better in the institution. There were fewer temptations and distractions." Her voice, which was again a monotone, slowly increased in speed and volume. "But the medications themselves were essentially a distraction from my relationship with God. I felt I had to try harder to maintain my relationship with God. My senses had been dulled. I needed to be alert." Clooney fell back in her chair, breathing heavily.

Rattle slowed down the pace of the examination by looking at a piece of paper on his table and taking another sip of water. Finally, he asked, "What was it like in the institution?"

"It was very strange." Clooney lingered on the last word for several seconds, pronouncing it with three syllables. "Most people didn't believe me when I told them I was communicating with God and that God told me to do things, like fast one day in three, and pray for hours at a stretch for the souls of the people that had not been exposed to His light. The place was different from the retreats, where we were all believers." Clooney paused a few seconds as if she were trying to formulate a response. "Different," she repeated. She stared at her hands in her lap.

"Some at the institution listened to me," she continued, "and shared my elation at being close to God. I could not convince the others that I was the enlightened one and that everyone else was facing an eternity in hell unless they followed God's word and believed implicitly in Him. I explained to them that I was struggling to obey the commandments of God. I told the nonbelievers that I would try to help them if they wished. Some mocked me. I failed to convince so many people. So many people. Now they are eternally damned." Tears were appearing in Clooney's eyes, but the rest of her face remained impassive. She reached into her bag, pulled out a few tissues, and wiped her eyes.

While the courtroom had been hushed as Clooney told her story, a murmur grew in volume as she described her ordeal with her fellow patients. Jason asked Clooney if she would like to rest for a few minutes. She said she wanted to continue.

"How did you arrange to leave the institution?" Rattle asked.

"I didn't arrange anything. I simply walked out one day when no one was watching me. God had told me when and how to leave and I followed His specific instructions. Obviously, I had no difficulty in leaving and taking a bus away from there, since I was following the directions God had given me. I returned to the magazine's offices in Honolulu, and I told the editor that the story did not work out and that I wanted to return to New York, that my mother was very ill."

"Was that true, Ms. Clooney?" Rattle asked in an aggressive tone.

Jason was totally unprepared for the question. He stopped writing.

"God told to say that my mother was ill, so it must have been the truth. I hadn't heard from my mother in a long time, so I didn't know except for His revelation. I never checked. I didn't even know where she was. He obviously wanted me to leave Hawaii and return to New York. I believe that He saw that people were trying to separate me from Christ. God was telling me that I had important things to accomplish. God told me the first step was to return to Mr. Mandick."

Clooney touched her fingers to her lips and pointed upwards when she said that God told her to return to New York. Her action reminded Jason of how some athletes behaved after hitting a home run or scoring a touchdown. Somehow, to see that action here, in a court of law, was unsettling.

Rattle paused for a moment, as if he, too, had been momentarily stunned. "What did you do?" Rattle asked breathlessly.

"I returned to New York City and contacted Mr. Mandick. He was very receptive, very glad to hear from me. Of course, I did not tell him what happened that led me to leave Hawaii. Looking at him right now, I can see that he is shocked by what I am saying. I feel very bad now that I didn't tell him the whole truth, but I couldn't. Our God did not want me to do that." She looked at Mandick. "I had no choice, Mr. Mandick."

The jury and spectators looked at Mandick, but what they saw was not shock, but fury, which seemed to be directed at Rattle and not Clooney. Mandick's face was bright red. In a whisper audible throughout the courtroom he asked Butt whether Rattle had told him about Clooney's testimony. Butt shook his head negatively, prompting Mandick to exclaim in a stage whisper, "That son-of-a bitch." Two reporters moved quickly to the exits.

It was time to excuse the jury for a recess, which Jason announced. As he started to rise, he saw Mandick berating Rattle for deceiving him and his lawyer and destroying him and *Total Faith*. "You'll be sorry," Mandick screamed. Not sure what to do, Jason said and did nothing, but quietly left the courtroom though the door behind the bench.

As the door closed behind him, Jason heard Rattle shout at Mandick, "You'll thank me for this." Jason wondered how that could possibly be. Jason ungenerously thought that Clooney must have felt completely at home in this madhouse.

Jason sat down at his desk in his office and closed his eyes. His thoughts turned to Trump. What would Crunch be telling Trump? Whom would Trump be blaming? How was he feeling about the prospect of a multi-million-dollar judgment against him? How would the jury straighten all this out?

Returning to the bench after the short recess, Jason saw Butt trying to calm Mandick, but without success. Mandick looked as though he would kill someone, although it wasn't clear whom. Even after the jury was seated, the crowd noise continued. Jason wondered how much of the exchanges between Mandick and the lawyers the jury had heard. Since no one asked him to do or say anything, Jason simply sat down and banged his gavel. The spectators stopped talking. "Please continue with your examination, Mr. Rattle," he said.

Beverly Clooney waited patiently on the witness stand. This time her hands were knotted around what appeared to be a man's large white handkerchief. Jason wondered where she had gotten it. Maybe Rattle had it in reserve. Jason noticed her eyes were red.

Rattle stood and shuffled his notes. "Why did you write an article about Mr. Moses?"

"I had been following the Secretary of Commerce's criminal trial, but the more I thought about it . . ." she pause and dabbed her eyes, ". . . the more I felt that something was wrong. How could Secretary Kruiser ignore the wishes of President Trump? How could the jury possibly believe her and Mr. Moses, whom I saw was a liberal and a nonbeliever?" She spat out the last clause and stared at Moses for a few seconds. "I searched for an answer, until God's voice told me what had happened."

"Please explain that, Ms. Clooney?" Rattle asked in the same tone he would have employed if he had questioned her about what she had ordered for dinner. By now, Clooney's statement produced merely a murmur from the spectators.

Clooney's fingers continued their constant fidgeting. It was as if she had to fight to keep them from leaping off her lap and into the air. "I was praying, and God asked me if I wanted Him to tell me what had occurred at Secretary Kruiser's trial. It was the first time I heard his voice. I was flattered and more than a bit frightened, so I told Him that I would welcome help if He believed I was worthy of His confidence. He assured me He had been following my development and that while I still needed guidance, I was indeed worthy. He told me to be home the following night at 8 p.m. after having fasted all day. Of course, I did exactly what God commanded."

Jason wondered whether Rattle would ask Clooney what God sounded like. Given what was going on in the courtroom, that was not a major issue, Jason decided. While curious, Jason let things alone. He was trying to appear scrupulously impartial. He was being seriously challenged.

"At home at exactly 8 p.m. the voice of God asked me again if I was prepared for Him to show me what happened. I humbly said, 'Yes.' He said He would take me back in time so that I could see with my own eyes what had happened. He told me that once again I should fast all day and He would return the following night at the same time. I obviously did what He said and at 8 p.m. something entered my apartment.

"I cannot describe it, although I imagine that is what feeling yourself next to God must be like. It was an extraordinary feeling. It was simultaneously electrifying and soothing, warm and cold, wet and dry, dark and light, windy and calm. A cascade of shimmering water enveloped me, but I was not drenched. There was an overwhelming clarity about everything. It was like the bright sunshine on a clear day in Hawaii, but so much . . . better." At this revelation her fingers stilled, and a look of reverence and calm came over her face as she lifted it to scan the ceiling.

Suddenly, a commotion in the last row of the courtroom interrupted the proceedings. Several young people stood up and shouted, "We love you, Beverly" and "God bless you, Beverly" and "May the Lord protect you." Jason banged his gavel.

"Remove those people." Jason shouted. Two U.S Marshals approached the small group and signaled them to come to the aisle. They did willingly, although one continued to shout, "God will protect you, Beverly." Another threw flowers into the air. The three left the courtroom without resistance.

"That is unfortunate," Jason said almost to himself, then addressed the jury. "What just happened must have no effect on your view of the case or your deliberations. It is important that you follow these instructions."

The jurors had been watching intently. Most of them nodded affirmatively. A few were wide-eyed, staring at Beverly Clooney. An older African-American woman seemed to be crying.

Jason turned to Clooney, who was sitting quietly, with her hands on her lap and her eyes upward. "Please continue with your testimony," he said.

"Well, He, God, took me by the hand and the next thing I knew I was approaching the apartment building where Ms. Winter lived. I entered the building and went up to her apartment. Ms. Winter, Juror No. 4, was waiting for me."

Jason tried to wipe away his memory of one of the movies of Charles Dickens' "A Christmas Carol," where a ghost takes

Scrooge by hand and flies him to the home where Tiny Tim and his family were celebrating Christmas. Instead of a goose, there was Ms. Winter. Jason's mind darted into another crevice. From what he had seen Trump did not have much of a sense of humor, and he was going to need one.

"When Ms. Winter described her meetings with Mr. Moses, I felt that I was actually watching the events that I described in my notes and article, that I actually saw and heard the conversations between Mr. Moses and Ms. Winter. I saw the meetings between Mr. Moses and Ms. Winter as though I was actually present. Then, it reverted to Ms. Winter and me alone. I was able to write everything down word for word. My pen flew across the page as it had never done before. The events were seared into my memory."

Jason glanced at Vernon, who was following the proceeding with rapt attention. No dull tax discussions in this courtroom. Crunch, who was a few seats away, also seemed riveted. Jason wondered how Crunch would prepare a palatable description for Trump. That Clooney was a raving lunatic would be Crunch's fault. To Trump, everybody was incompetent, stupid, or simply wrong, except for Trump, that is. He criticizes everyone mercilessly, then expects them to thank him for that. Trump has absolutely no self-control, no self-discipline. Jason remembered his class in Cornell, Psychology 101, where the professor explained the ego, superego, and id. Jason saw Trump's cellphone as phallic symbol that he jabbed and massaged. Jason wondered whether Trump would lend his name to a host of mental illnesses. Writing books and papers about Trump's psychology will become a cottage industry.

"What did you tell Mr. Mandick about your experience?" Rattle asked.

"God had directed me to say nothing of His role until He gave me permission, and that I was to recite what happened as though He played no part in it. He said that He would surface if necessary to support my account and to prevent any harm from being inflicted on me. So, I simply described my interview of Ms. Winter, which I had recorded in my notes with complete accuracy through the help of God. Mr. Mandick asked to review my notes and I believe he did very carefully, because he later asked me some specific questions. I believe he also checked the credentials of Ms. Winter."

"Wasn't God asking you to lie?" Rattle was engaging in a fake challenge to the witness to increase the drama.

"God forbid," Clooney said. "What He said was that I was not to disclose His role unless asked directly, which no one would do unless He wanted His role disclosed. I may have left things out, but I never said a lie. Mr. Rattle, you were the first person to ask me about the source of the article in terms that required me to tell the truth."

"Can you explain that more specifically?"

"I was asked at my deposition, for example, whether any 'other person' was present when I had the conversations that I described. I did not consider God to be just 'another person,' so I answered no. God obviously did not want them to learn the truth at that time. Otherwise, he would have had the person who asked the question to be more specific. God was very careful that way."

"Have you always told the truth when you spoke under oath?" It was a leading question that no one challenged.

Jason noticed her hands were twisting the handkerchief again. He worried she might rip it apart or break a finger. Everything about Beverly was taut.

"Absolutely. I also believe that I told the truth always, even when I was not under oath. God would not want me to lie."

"Didn't you need to do more research, perhaps speak to Mr. Moses, before submitting your article?" Rattle had lowered his voice.

"If you are asking me whether I thought it necessary to fact-check God, the answer is no! No! That would be blasphemy." Clooney's voice roared the last word out over the room.

Rattle took an inadvertent stop back from the podium. A few of the jurors recoiled. "Aside from your conversations with me, have you told anyone else about God's role in your developing the story about Mr. Moses before today?"

"No." Calm returned to Clooney's voice.

"Didn't Mr. Mandick believe you had conducted an ordinary interview of Ms. Winter?"

"Objection," Whitebread said loudly. "Calls for describing the thoughts of another person."

"Sustained," Jason stated.

Rattle stood at the podium for a few seconds.

"Did you say anything to Mr. Mandick that would have led him to conclude that this was other than an ordinary interview?"

"Objection," Whitebread repeated.

"Overruled," Jason stated. "You may answer, Ms. Clooney."

"No, Mr. Rattle."

"Did Mr. Mandick say anything to you that suggested he was aware of God's role?"

"No, Mr. Rattle."

"Ms. Clooney, have you believed from the outset that your article on Mr. Moses was true?"

"Of course. How can you doubt God's word?" Tears were forming again. She hurriedly wiped them away.

"Do you believe today that your article was and is true?"

"Of course, Mr. Rattle, God helped me write it. How could it be anything but the absolute truth? I don't understand your question."

"Do you think you were negligent in not speaking to more people?

"God told me what to do. Who am I to question God?" She lifted her hands slowly; the twisted handkerchief was wet with tears. She returned her hands to her lap.

"No further questions, Your Honor." Turning to Whitebread with a slight smile, Rattle said, "your witness."

Whitebread, on his feet, screamed, "Your Honor, can I be heard privately?"

"We'll take a brief recess before the cross-examination of Ms. Clooney," Jason announced, as the buzzing in the courtroom resumed. "I want to see counsel in the robing room with the court reporter."

When the door closed, Jason asked in an even voice, "Mr. Whitebread, what is it?"

"We deposed Ms. Clooney and she mentioned nothing of this. I demand an explanation. Where did this person come from?" Whitebread angrily pointed in the direction of the courtroom.

"Gentlemen, I think we can agree that this is not how libel trials usually progress. Mr. Rattle, I want an explanation. What's going on? First of all, Mr. Rattle, did you have anything to do with the disruption?'

"Absolutely not, Your Honor. I understood that this was a sensitive matter, to put it mildly. I was not about to play games in addition."

Jason paused to decide whether he wanted to ask more questions about the demonstration. He looked at Rattle. "We are waiting for your explanation of what has happened."

"I did not learn of this development until two weeks ago when I asked Ms. Clooney how she could be so sure that she was right. That brought out what she testified to on the stand. Neither I nor any other counsel during her lengthy deposition two months ago had asked her a question that required her to say what she said on the stand. I certainly was not conscious of any dissembling on her part and when I reread the deposition, I believe that her answers were literally correct."

"Then why did you not disclose this turn of events two weeks ago?" Jason asked, a split second before Whitebread started to speak.

"Your Honor, I must say I thought long and hard about it. Ms. Clooney insisted I not. She was passionate on the subject, to coin a phrase. I considered what she told me protected by the attorney-client privilege, and that I was not allowed to say anything about it. Since she, in my opinion, did not testify falsely at her deposition, I did not feel that I was under obligation to correct anything. I believe I acted appropriately in a difficult situation. A very difficult situation." Rattle paused before adding, "Ms. Clooney is not always the easiest client to deal with."

"Mr. Butt, Mr. Whitebread, have you anything to say?"

"The plaintiff demands a mistrial."

Jason could not complain that Whitebread was pussy-footing.

"Mr. Whitebread, did Ms. Clooney lie at her deposition?"

Whitebread sat silently for a full minute. "I really cannot say at this point that she lied, but she certainly was misleading."

"Mr. Butt, do you claim she lied at her deposition?"

"My answer is the same as Mr. Whitebread's."

"Subject to further enlightenment, I shall not declare a mistrial and have everyone start all over again. My reaction is that the situation came about because neither of you asked the right question of Ms. Clooney, although I must confess that I might not have either. You will certainly have the opportunity to question Ms. Clooney on the subject. Mr. Butt, you have something to say?"

"I'm not sure that I should be faulted for not having asked Ms. Clooney whether God had been feeding her the answers, actually both the questions and answers." Butt paused. "Your Honor, I'll have to think about this, to put it mildly, unexpected development. I cannot think that fast. Could we have a recess until tomorrow morning?"

"I think that's quite appropriate. Mr. Butt. I shall give the parties until 9:00 a.m. tomorrow morning to file any motion. Absent a motion, we will proceed at 9:30 a.m. with further testimony. I want the application for a recess until tomorrow put on the record in open court."

When court resumed five minutes later with the jury present and Beverly Clooney reseated in the witness stand, Butt requested the recess, which Jason granted. He explained to the jury. "Since we are further along than any of us expected, I will grant the application and we shall resume tomorrow morning. Now, more than ever, I instruct the jury not to discuss the case with each other or with anyone else and not to read or listen to anything on the case. Unless someone has something to bring up, that completes matters for today." Jason wondered whether his explanation fooled anyone.

Back in chambers, Jason told Joe, "This is one of the very few times in my judicial career I can say I am eagerly awaiting developments tomorrow. That and the return of Donald Trump to the case." Jason was also looking forward to watching television and reading newspapers on what had transpired, although he said nothing about that to his law clerk.

"I'll be outside if you need me, Judge." Joe left, closing the door behind him.

Vernon was quiet as he walked into his father's office, but simply looked to the ceiling and rolled his eyes. "It reminds me of Shakespeare's line in *The Tempest*: 'Your tale, sir, would cure deafness.' I'll cancel my appointments for tomorrow and stick around. What will you do, dad?"

"I really don't know. Butt has a point about his not being expected to ask questions about God's role in the story, but it's not that simple. He's asking for special treatment on the basis that something unexpected came up that he was in a position to do something about. I think you understand what I'm saying. Also, Rattle should not be totally off the hook. I'll wait until somebody asks me to do something. Actually, I'm not even sure who's aggrieved more, Whitebread or Butt. Something to think about."

"All I can say is that it's more interesting than tax law." Vernon put his hands in his pockets. "What's the schedule, dad?"

"I have a few things to do, which should take an hour or so. If you brought work or have something to read, why don't you sit on the couch?"

"Fine."

Just over an hour later, they found a cab in Foley Square and went to Jason's apartment. It was a relief to be in its familiar surroundings.

"How do you feel about a drink?" Jason asked.

"A better idea no judge has had."

"How would a Prum Sonnenuhr Spatlese '86 work? You like German wines, if I recall."

"It's a great idea. I wouldn't have thought of it, although

a Chateau l'Evangile or Chateau Revelation might be more appropriate."

Chateau l'Evangile was a highly respected red wine from Pomerol, near the city of Bordeaux. "I don't know the second wine." Jason spoke slowly. He was embarrassed at the gap in his knowledge, especially in front of his son.

"That's probably because I just made it up." Vernon grinned.

Jason served the German wine. The fragrant, sweet, mellow, and low-alcohol wine, smelling of ripe apricots, which the Germans used mostly as a sipping wine before a meal or between meals, rarely found favor in the United States. It was soothing. It was perfect.

"Do you have a false floor in your office that conceals a wine cellar?" Vernon asked his father while taking a sip.

"If you don't mind," Jason said, "I'd like to stay in the neighborhood for dinner. I had intended to take you to Le Bernadin or Jean-Georges, if I could get us in. I'm finding myself a little tired. I'm getting old, you know."

"You're doing amazingly well."

"Nice of you to say that, son. Let's eat at Chez Maison, which was one of your mother's favorites. I hope you don't mind if we don't talk about the case. It's been quite a day and I want to be extra careful, in case God is listening." Jason chuckled. "I shouldn't have said that," he said with mock horror.

Seated in a corner booth, Jason put down the wine list and addressed proprietor Jean-Jean. "I think tonight calls for something special."

"Absolutely, Judge Jason. I have a bottle of Chateau Beychevelle 1970, which is a bit over the hill, but excellent," Jean-Jean said. Jason and Vernon gave their orders to the waiter. Then, the sommelier poured a thimble of wine into Jason's glass. He swirled the wine in his glass, sniffed it, tasted it, and smiled at her. She poured a few ounces into each diner's glass.

"Santé," Jason exclaimed as he lifted his glass." The two sipped the wine.

"I hear a rumor that Saturday Night Live is going to have a

skit on your case."

"Really?"

"Someone I know told me, and this is on the level, that they'll have a biblical-looking Moses and a Trump character negotiating this coming Saturday. Trump wants to trade his hotels for Jerusalem. Moses resists, and Trump keeps knocking him down and kicking him."

Jason chuckled. "I don't know if I want to see it." The two continued drinking the wine in slow sips.

"Vernon sat down his wine glass. Would you mind if I askec you about something personal? I don't want you to get angry."

"Of course not."

"I don't know how to say this, but when I saw you the last few times before today, you seemed depressed, not that you didn't have a right to be. Actually, I was worried about you. You seemed distracted and a little overwhelmed. Now, you're different. You seem excited about what's going on. You're getting a kick out of things again. I haven't seen you like this ir a long time."

Vernon paused. When his father said nothing, he continued. "It may just be the case, or maybe my imagination. I don't know. I also don't know whether to be worried or to rejoice. I probably should not be asking you this and forgive me if I shouldn't. But I felt I had to. Is anything going on? I don't mean it the way it sounds."

Jason slowly twirled the stem of his wineglass. "What you say makes sense. I didn't realize that I was acting differently. I seem to be more optimistic recently. Perhaps, it's because I am exercising. I'm sleeping better, too. Of course, this case can add a bounce to anyone's step." And there also was the unmentioned Christine.

"I'm sorry for intruding, dad."

"No, no, I'm glad you did. I also have a hard time talking about personal things, in case you haven't noticed."

"We have that in common."

Jason felt responsible for Vernon in a way he could not describe. Unlike Robert, Vernon did not shine as a child and did not seem to have had a happy childhood. He idealized Robert, who died. He never talked about his friends. He had a short and unhappy marriage. Then his mother died, and Jason couldn't fill the gaps in his emotional life. It was so difficult.

After a long dinner, the two returned to Jason's apartment. After watching the late news and part of a late-night show together, they went to bed. Jason had a good night's sleep despite the heavy meal and libation. He was pleased that Clooney's testimony got prominent coverage.

Rising early, Jason started the coffee and eagerly retrieved the newspapers from outside his apartment door. He had added a couple of newspapers for home delivery shortly before trial, including the *Washington Post*. While Vernon slept, Jason read the papers.

The morning headlines screamed: "Clooney: 'God Made Me Do It'"; "Clooney, as in Looney"; "Clooney: 'Had Help in High Places'"; and "*Total Faith's* Alternative Universe." One paper quoted an unnamed Democrat who said, "It's refreshing finally to find someone on the same wavelength as President Trump. The good people of this country are eager to learn Ms. Clooney's position in the Trump Administration." No Republican could be found who would speak on or even off the record. No tweets emanated from the White House.

Vernon joined Jason for breakfast. Together they ate while passing the papers between them. Jason's cell phone ran a couple of times, but after checking the screen he ignored the calls. He didn't recognize the names or numbers. "Telemarketers," he said to Vernon.

After breakfast, father and son headed to court together.

Chapter 18

"Your Honor, may I proceed with my examination of Ms. Clooney?" Theodore Butt inquired after the jury had been seated. No lawyers had submitted any motion and Jason saw no reason not to continue. The lawyers had submitted, however, supplemental jury instructions, which he would look at later.

"You may, Mr. Butt."

Jason watched Beverly Clooney walk to the witness stand. He noted her outfit was barely distinguishable from what she wore the previous day. Mostly, irises were the flowers in the pattern of her marginally darker-blue dress. Today, the large handkerchief intertwined in her fingers was blue. The bailiff reminded her she was still under oath.

Butt had to be careful. Although Clooney, along with Mandick and *Total Faith*, was a defendant whom Moses had sued, she could seriously damage her codefendants, perhaps more than Moses could. Her testimony on direct examination was undoubtedly better than Butt and his clients had expected, at least insofar as her testimony involved Mandick's potential liability.

"Ms. Clooney," Butt began, "you testified that you are totally committed to God and the workings of God. You allied yourself with the most devout believers. Yet you joined the effort to elect Donald Trump, who has had three wives, commits blasphemy, and appears to many not a man of God. How do you reconcile that action with your beliefs?"

"Objection, Your Honor, both on the subject matter and the characterizations." Rattle was protecting his client.

"Your Honor, the question goes to Ms. Clooney's credibility."

Jason was finding it hard to concentrate fully on the testimony. "I'll allow the question, Mr. Butt, but I instruct the jury that Mr. Butt's descriptions of Mr. Trump are not evidence. You may answer, Ms. Clooney."

"God works in mysterious ways, Mr. Butt."

"You can say that again."

"No more quips, Mr. Butt. This is not *Law and Order*."

If the jury expected more riveting testimony along the lines of the previous day, they did not get it. Butt's job was as simple as it was difficult: Convince the jury that Clooney had not said or done anything that would have put Mandick on notice that she was other than a professional reporter doing her job. Butt's subsequent questions were milder and more respectful in tone. After all, Mandick had hired her and printed her stories. Also, she had basically supported Mandick and *Total Faith's* position that they had no idea how Clooney wrote her article.

There were several objections from Whitebread and Rattle, mostly about the form of the questions and that the answers called for speculation or were asked and answered, which dragged out the examination. Jason sustained some and denied others.

Jason saw that Butt had a related goal in presenting a long and dull cross-examination. He wanted to keep Clooney as calm and normal looking as possible. That would reinforce his argument that Mandick had no reason to doubt her professionalism and sanity. Rattle's examination was designed to make her appear weird; Butt's examination was designed to make her look normal. Butt wanted the jury to see her acting normal for as long as he could. He finally finished and sat down.

"Mr. Whitebread. Any cross?"

"Yes, Your Honor," Whitebread said as he strolled to the

podium. He spent a few minutes having Clooney repeat some of her testimony about her encounters with God and Moses.

"Do you remember any details that you did not tell the jury on your direct examination?"

"I'm afraid not, Mr. Whitebread."

"You testified that God took you by the hand."

"He did, Mr. Whitebread."

"How did that feel?" Jason was interested in that question, but more interested in how God sounded. He hoped that would be Whitebread's next question.

"I don't know. I'm not sure I felt anything. I don't know." Clooney's voice trailed off.

"You're sure it was God?"

"Absolutely."

"Ms. Clooney, you have testified that you were committed to a psychiatric hospital in Hawaii, is that correct?"

"Yes, Mr. Whitebread."

"What is the name of the hospital?"

"Do I have to answer that question, Your Honor?"

"Why don't you want to answer the question?" Jason asked Clooney.

"Because the hospital may take the position that I am a fugitive from it and I don't want them coming after me and sending me back there."

"Mr. Whitebread, do you really need the name of the institution?"

"Let me see if I can proceed differently. Ms. Clooney, what was the name of the doctor who committed you?"

"It was Howard Fong, and I can give you his phone number and email if you wish," Clooney said, while tightening her grip on the blue handkerchief. She looked worried.

Jason could not understand why Clooney and Rattle would disclose the name of the doctor, but not the institution, but that was not his problem. In the overall scheme of what was going on, that was a trivial matter.

"If there is no objection," Whitebread said, 'I'll obtain that privately from Mr. Rattle. Ms. Clooney, do you have any objection to my or one of my colleague's calling Dr. Fong and his answering questions about your institutionalization."

"May I answer that, Your Honor?"

"Yes, Mr. Rattle."

"We do not, providing we can work out an agreement on the use of any information."

"I'm sure we can work that out," Whitebread responded. "Ms. Clooney, just to make the situation clear, you are concerned that if one of the lawyers in the case inquires of the hospital about you, they may track you down and have you returned to the hospital against your will?"

"That is correct."

"But wouldn't God protect you from that if you were doing His will?"

"Objection, Your Honor. Speculation."

"Sustained. Let's not go further afield than we have to."

"Do you know of any effort that the hospital may have made to find you since you left?"

"No, I don't, Mr. Whitebread, but that doesn't mean they haven't tried or won't try should they hear about my testimony."

Jason could not figure out why Whitebread was asking Clooney about her hospitalization. How would Clooney's responses help Moses win his lawsuit? It was confusing.

"Ms. Clooney, it is your testimony, as I understand it, that until you testified at the trial of this case you told nobody the circumstances of your researching and writing the article?"

"Oh, I told people at the magazine about my interviews."

"Excuse me, Ms. Clooney, I misspoke. What I should have asked you was whether you told anyone at the magazine about the role of God in your researching and writing the article."

"I did not, Mr. Whitebread."

Whitebread had to be careful, Jason recognized. Some of the jurors might be religious. A juror might react badly if he believed that Whitebread was mocking Clooney. Jason had refused requests to include questions about the prospective jurors' religious practices and beliefs in the jurors' questionnaire, so the lawyers were unable to tailor their questions to the beliefs of individual jurors.

"Didn't you think that Mr. Mandick would have been pleased to know about your closeness to God? He did send you to a retreat." Whitebread leaned over the podium, as if he needed closer contact with her.

"As I explained, it was not up to me whom I told."

"Are you saying that you wanted to tell Mr. Mandick what had transpired?"

"Objection, irrelevant," Rattled stated.

"Sustained," Jason announced. While borderline on Clooney's state of mind, Jason decided the question was too tangential. He knew that the chance of getting reversed was zero, no matter which way he ruled.

"Ms. Clooney, to your knowledge, from the time you walked out of the institution in Hawaii until, say, you spoke to Mr. Rattle about assistance you received from God, did anyone treat you differently from the way you had previously been treated? Did anyone treat you strangely?"

"Objection. Vague," Rattle stated.

"Overruled."

"No, Mr. Whitebread, not that I can think of," Clooney answered. Her brow was lined with the evidence of her effort.

Jason was more confused. Why was Whitebread seemingly reinforcing Clooney's appearance as a normal and ordinary reporter?

"You've testified of your struggles with Satan, your difficulties at the institution in Hawaii, your agitation and problems with people around you in Hawaii." Whitebread said.

"Yes," Clooney said, almost as a question.

"Did you stop taking medications after you left the mental institution in Hawaii?"

"That is correct," Clooney said.

"Then, please explain how you can say that you acted in such an ordinary and unexceptional way that no one, including Mr. Mandick, could tell that you were not performing normally?"

Clooney sat still for several long seconds. "I don't know," she finally said. Whitebread held up his palms facing Clooney and raised his eyebrows, as though he was seeking her help, but she sat still, except that her hands were twisting the blue handkerchief. Jason wondered whether Whitebread was suggesting that Clooney was an unreliable observer. If so, so what, Jason concluded. Then Jason realized that having Clooney testify that she behaved the same whether she did or did not take medications was designed to show she was faking. Too subtle, he concluded, and besides, Clooney could not be considered a reliable witness to her own behavior.

Clooney suddenly straightened her back. "Maybe that shows I didn't need the medications in the first place."

Jason was impressed. Whitebread ignored the statement.

"Ms. Clooney, did you seek psychiatric help in New York City after you returned from Hawaii?" Whitebread asked. She untwisted the handkerchief from her fingers and momentarily smoothed it on her lap. Her eyes refocused on Everett Mandick, who sat staring at her. Then she looked back at Whitebread.

Something struck Jason. While the jurors could see some of Clooney's movements, they could not see her manipulations of the handkerchief, which were blocked from their view by witness box. Unlike with Captain Queeg and his ball bearings in *The Caine Mutiny*, the jurors would not see her unusual hand manipulations.

"I spoke to one psychiatrist," Clooney said, "but I concluded that he did not believe me. That wouldn't do. I have started to look for another. It has been very difficult to find a sympathetic psychiatrist in New York, Mr. Whitebread. New York is a funny place when it comes to religious matters and religious people."

A few spectators snickered.

"I see. Ms. Clooney, I have a question about something I don't think I understand. If you feel that you were doing the will of God, why would you even consider seeing a psychiatrist?"

Jason liked the question. He glanced at the jury, which sat in rapt silence. He was unable to tell if they were sensing the peculiarity of this discourse.

"For two reasons, Mr. Whitebread. First, I want to understand how I affect people and why people would not accept me for what I was and not accept my relationship with God for what it was. Second, I was very concerned and nervous about my relationship with God, and I wanted to be able to accept what He was doing with me. I needed to do what He asked with equanimity and not become upset about it. A psychiatrist who thought as I do could be helpful."

"You mean, like Jesus Christ was able to accept God's will?"

"Objection, argumentative," Rattle interrupted.

"Sustained." Not a bad stab, Jason thought, although he was far from an expert on the subject.

"Didn't you think that what you needed was not a psychiatrist, but a minister of the faith?" Whitebread asked.

"Perhaps," Clooney responded. Her voice was increasingly monotone.

"Did you seek out a minister to talk to about your experiences?"

"No, I felt that my relationship with God did not require the intervention of a minister. Also, at that point God did not want me to talk about His role."

"Ms. Clooney, did it ever occur to you that it wasn't God who was speaking to you?"

"Who else could it have been, Mr. Whitebread?" Clooney reacted as if she were talking to a wayward child.

"I have no idea. I'm just asking if you ever doubted that it was divine intervention. For example, you mentioned that you did not consider yourself particularly worthy."

"That is true, but I am not one to challenge God's ways." Clooney looked at the jurors, then at her attorney, Rattle, then back at Whitebread. "If He wants to use me for His ends, I am enthusiastically prepared to follow His will. I am on earth to serve God. He put me here. I never doubted that I was following the will of God. Many people ask God to do something for them and believe that He does. What is strange about God asking or telling us what to do?" Clooney was far more animated than before. She took a sip of water.

"I'm sorry. I'm not here to answer your questions," said Whitebread.

"It was a rhetorical question, Mr. Whitebread," Clooney said with clipped pronunciation.

A few chuckles from the jury this time. Clooney seemed pleased with her answer, but her face showed little expression. Jason wondered whether she was capturing the sympathy of the jury. He found her politeness and ingenuousness appealing.

"Excuse me. I'm having a little trouble keeping up," Whitebread said. "You have heard a number of people take the stand and testify under oath that what you wrote was false. How do you explain that?"

"Objection," Rattle stated. "How can she know why other people said certain things?"

"Overruled. I'll allow it solely on the witness's state of mind."

"I cannot explain why these people would be confused about something like that or even lie," Clooney said. "Perhaps it was Satan that made them do that."

"Satan?"

"That's right. A lot of devout people believe in Satan. The late Justice Scalia believed in Satan and said so publicly."

"So, you still are totally convinced that your story was true?"

"Of course, Mr. Whitebread," Clooney said. "How could it not be if God helped me write the article?"

"That is a very good question. May I have a few seconds to talk to my colleague, Your Honor?"

"Yes, Mr. Whitebread." Jason sat quietly while Whitebread and his young associate whispered with animated gestures. Whitebread returned to the podium.

"Ms. Clooney, one or two more questions. Why do you think that the doctor in Hawaii had you committed to the psychiatric hospital and why do you think the hospital kept you there?"

"It was Dr. Fong. I really don't know or understand, Mr. Whitebread. People who are not close to Christ have strange views of devout people who do the work of God. I am not bitter or angry with them. They are secular people who may not know better. I just hope that God will show them the proper path as He has shown me. Over the centuries nonbelievers have punished, tortured, or killed believers. While I don't compare myself with the great Christian martyrs, my situation is not altogether different, and I aspire to greater trials and tribulations. I must accept whatever affliction God imposes on me or allows others to do. I humbly obey Him." Clooney looked upwards.

"You mean, God may have been testing you?"

"That is correct, but who am I to know?"

"Ms. Clooney, do you know of any non-supernatural explanation for the information you obtained for your article on Mr. Moses?"

"No, but then that's the whole point of a God with infinite powers, isn't it?" Clooney smiled sweetly.

"No further questions."

"Anything else, Mr. Butt? Mr. Rattle?

"Your Honor, with the court's permission, I would like to reopen my examination of Mr. Mandick to ask a few questions," Butt answered.

"Please proceed. Ms. Clooney, please go back to your seat. Mr. Mandick, please take the witness stand again. Remember you are still under oath."

Mandick strode quickly to the witness stand. He stared at Clooney when he passed her. He was angry.

"Mr. Mandick, when you published Ms. Clooney's article on Mr. Moses, did you know about her hospitalization?" Butt asked.

"No, I did not," Mandick said loudly.

"Or any of the facts related to her hospitalization?"

"No, Mr. Butt."

"Did you have any reason to believe that she, as she has testified, communicated with God in the research and writing of the article?"

"No, I did not," Mandick replied, still in a stentorian voice.

"Did you know or suspect that she had, as she has testified, the active assistance of God in writing the article."

"No, I did not."

"Or of any of the events leading up to her writing the article?"

"No, I did not."

Butt turned to the jury. "No further questions."

"Just a very brief cross-examination on the reopened testimony, Your Honor."

"Go ahead, Mr. Whitebread."

"Mr. Mandick, are there any other writers for *Total Faith* or *Alt-Times* who have had, to your knowledge, divine assistance in researching and writing articles for the magazine?"

"Objection, Your Honor," Butt exclaimed. "Vague."

"Mr. Whitebread, please rephrase the question."

"Mr. Mandick, do you know of any other writers for *Good Faith* or *Total Faith* who had, or claimed to have had, or you suspected of believing they had, divine assistance of the sort described by Ms. Clooney in her testimony?"

"No, Mr. Whitebread."

"Mr. Mandick, if you had known the facts and circumstances just alluded to, would you have published Ms. Clooney's article?"

"Objection, calling for speculation." Butt shouted.

"Objection sustained."

Jason wondered why Butt had objected the second time. Wasn't that objection, even though a valid one because of the speculative nature of the question, counter-productive if Mandick wanted to show that he followed standard journalistic standards? It then struck Jason that it was one thing for Mandick to proclaim that he followed standard journalistic standards and another to tell his flock that he wouldn't publish an article that was dictated by God.

"No further questions," Butt said.

"Any rebuttal evidence, Mr. Whitebread?" Jason was touching all the bases.

"Just, my follow up, if I decide to make it, with Dr. Fong, Your Honor. Nothing else."

"I therefore declare the record closed, subject to a request from Mr. Whitebread relating to Dr. Fong, a request I shall have to rule on if it comes before me. Ladies and gentlemen of the jury, we are adjourning now for the day. The lawyers and I have several things to take up relating to the last stages of the case. Monday morning, we shall hear summations from the lawyers, which will be followed by my instructions to you on the law, often known as the charge. You have been wonderfully prompt so far, and I ask that you do not stumble tomorrow, I mean, Monday. Thank you for your conscientiousness. Have a good weekend."

"Thank you, Your Honor. The same to you," the jurors responded almost in unison as they left the jury box to go to the jury room to pick up their belongings and depart.

"We'll take our luncheon recess and then the lawyers will reassemble in open court at 2:00 p.m. for motions, followed by a conference in chambers on jury instructions. If there is nothing else, I'll see you then."

Chapter 19

Jason greeted his son in his chambers. Sue was waiting with coffee. "One second, Vernon. Sue, please call Mr. Crunch on his cellphone and tell him that I'd like him to attend this afternoon's conference. Thanks. Guess we'll need lunch." He turned to Vernon as Sue left to make the call.

"Hope you don't mind another lunch in here," Jason said. "I don't have time to go out."

Vernon shook his head. "No problem, dad."

Sue breezed in the door and handed a menu to Vernon. "Here you go. It's from the takeout across Foley Square. We don't have time for the other place. By the way, Judge, you received a call on your private line and I picked up the phone. The person who placed the call hung up."

"Thanks, Sue. My advice is to keep it very simple, not that they have anything fancy," Jason said to his son. "Just don't give them a chance to disguise any of the ingredients. Tell Sue what you want. I'll have the usual."

He turned to Sue. "I need to see Judge Marbury for a few minutes. Would you find out if he has some time before I must return to court?"

"Absolutely, Judge. I'll set it up right away."

Vernon scanned the menu. "I'll have a turkey sandwich, but

can I get it with fruit instead of chips?"

"Done, I'll put a rush on it," Sue said as she retrieved the menu from Vernon and left the room.

"I'm afraid Judge Marbury had a dental issue," Sue said, when she returned to Jason's office. "He won't be back until late this afternoon. I left a message with his secretary that you needed to see him when he comes in. I'll be back in a sec."

"And here I was worrying that you were working too hard. I haven't had this much fun in years," Vernon said. "By the way, the last quip in Washington is that Trump couldn't make a deal if he represented both sides in a negotiation. It's no surprise to insiders, but Trump can't get anything done. He cannot even make up his own mind, much less convince others. He goes nuts when anyone disagrees with him."

"He doesn't seem to have taken advice in this case," Jason said.

"I wonder if they have a name for that."

"Stupidity? Forget I said that."

Ten minutes later Sue entered with the lunch, which she arranged on plates the chambers provided. Jason picked up and scrutinized his sandwich. "It's not Jean-Georges, but it will have to do."

"Thanks, Sue," Jason said. He smiled at Vernon. Then ate his sandwich.

Jason's major business in the afternoon was to hear motions by the lawyers in open court. Once again, the courtroom was packed. Without a jury present, the proceedings were less tense and less formal. Jason was glad of the lower stress. He could feel his blood pressure climbing during the morning session. Whoever was making those calls wanted to rattle him, perhaps to get him off the case. Once again, he forced himself to relax. He glanced around the room. First to speak was Whitebread, who sauntered to the podium.

"Mr. Whitebread, please confine yourself to the issue of falsity, which Ms. Clooney alone is contesting."

"The article is false as a matter of law and no reasonable jury could find otherwise. That would eliminate the issue of falsity from the case. The facts leave only one choice. Both alleged participants in the transaction, Mr. Moses and Ms. Winter, have denied that bribery took place. There is corroboration that they were busy elsewhere on the evenings the bribery allegedly took place. Financial records refute the allegation. There is no competent evidence that the article was true, absolutely none. I'll respond to questions from the court and would like the opportunity to speak to Mr. Rattle's opposition."

"What about Ms. Clooney's testimony?" Jason asked.

"If you recall," Whitebread said, "Ms. Clooney's account was pure hearsay. She was not present at the alleged bribes. She was repeating what Ms. Winter told her. So, her testimony cannot legally be used to prove the fact."

"Do you rely on the fact that the other defendants have conceded falsity?"

"No. I believe that was a strategic decision that is not probative as far as other parties are concerned."

"I understand," Jason said. "Mr. Rattle?"

"What's involved is credibility. The court should not usurp the role of the jury. I have not found a case that squarely presented the issue whether it would be error for a court to reject a claim that there was a miracle. We submit the court should not do so here. We request the court to leave the factual issue regarding whether there was a bribe for the jury to decide."

Obviously, Rattle did not want to defend the truth of the article. Jason realized that Rattle made a half-hearted objection rather than concede falsity because his client insisted the article was true. It was one thing to concede falsity over the client's objections and other to have a judge rule the article was false. Relying on a miracle, however, was going pretty far.

"I am ruling that the article is false as a matter of law," Jason said. "The evidence does not permit finding it was true. There is simply no evidence that the story was true and overwhelming evidence it was not. Ms. Clooney's testimony cannot establish the story is true, since she said that Ms. Winter told her about the alleged bribes after they had occurred." Rattle looked relieved.

"I do not have to rule on the general issue of miracles. I simply find that the claim of a miracle has not been established. For example, the Catholic Church has very high standards before it will accept a miracle, including corroboration. Simply arguing that there is no evidence how something happened, so it must be a miracle, does not meet the test. I now decide that the defendant has failed to meet that standard even without rejecting the possibility that another litigant could establish one."

A murmur arose from the spectators, which Jason chose to accept as approbation. He resisted acknowledging it with a nod to the spectators. "Any other motions? Yes, Mr. Butt?"

"We would like to argue that as a matter of law plaintiff has failed to present sufficient proof that we were negligent or possessed legal malice."

"I'll cut this short," Jason said. "I am denying the motion based on the entire record of the case, including the presence of multiple issues of credibility. Someone's mental state is a singularly bad issue for summary judgment or a directed verdict. The jury will decide. I will accept that you have presented full argument and have incorporated everything you previously said, so that you are protected on appeal." Jason remembered a reversal because he had allowed the case to proceed with a deficient record. Not this time.

"Your Honor, may I be heard?" Crunch walked slowly to the podium. He was sartorially impeccable.

"Of course, Mr. Crunch."

"Your Honor, on behalf of the president, I respectfully move to set aside the default judgement, subject to the verdict by the jury." Another murmur from the spectators.

"I object."

"I understand your concern, Mr. Whitebread, but I will not grant such a motion without hearing from you, so let us hear from Mr. Crunch."

"Your Honor, it is beyond dispute that the president had

no personal knowledge of the truth or falsity of the facts underlying the alleged libel. He could only have been subject to questioning on his state of mind. Thus, there is no prejudice to the plaintiff because he failed to make discovery. Since the president's information was derived from *Total Faith* and his liability is totally derivative in that sense, the judgment against him should be set aside if there is a defendants' verdict. It would be unfair if the president is the only person found liable. Furthermore, I renew my objection based on separation of powers and the right of a single district judge to exercise power over the president of the United States." Crunch returned to his seat. Jason saw his associate pat him on the arm.

"Mr. Crunch, I see your point," Jason said, "but the legal system does not permit someone to opt-out and opt-in at his pleasure. You could have stipulated, for example, that the result in the president's case would be the same as that of *Total Faith* or Mr. Mandick, at least if the plaintiff agreed." Jason looked at an agitated Whitebread. "I see Mr. Whitebread shaking his head in the negative.

"You have to play the game to win. Prejudice is not the only consideration. Moreover, we don't know what would have happened if your client had remained in the case and been subjected to discovery. Nevertheless, I shall reserve on the motion until after the verdict and post-verdict motions, since it might be mooted if the jury finds for the plaintiff. I should also mention that the law permits a jury to render inconsistent verdicts, so it could have found for Mr. Mandick and *Total Faith* and against Mr. Trump, who had not seen the evidence on which Mr. Mandick relied. As of now, Mr. Trump faces a verdict for damages, along with *Total Faith*, Mr. Mandick, and Ms. Clooney."

At that moment a disconcerting thought hit Jason. Why wasn't Trump's personal lawyer rather than Crunch representing Trump? Jason had ruled that the tweet was personal. He had entered judgment against Trump, which he would have to pay out of his personal funds when the jury set the amount. Why was the White House lawyer representing Trump, especially representing him alone, without a personal lawyer? It wasn't as if Trump had forgotten about his personal attorneys. They were all over the Russian investigation and defending sundry allegations about Trump's adultery and payoffs. They have even weighed in on the Charlottesville outrage. Was this something Jason should raise on his own or should he wait for a lawyer in the case to raise it? Jason would think about it when he had time. He addressed the lawyers and spectators.

"We will now adjourn to my chambers to deal with some legal issues."

The bailiff declared the day's session over. The members of the media and the public exited noisily. Jason and the lawyers separately walked to his chambers.

Jason greeted the lawyers seated around the conference-room table, along with the court reporter. Jason introduced Vernon, and no one objected to his attending the session.

"Let us turn to the instructions to the jury." Jason wondered whether he sounded like a minister telling the congregation to direct its attention to a certain page in the hymnal. "We've been through this several times. I will note Mr. Crunch's objection to allowing the jury to impose punitive damages against the president, which he has explained in a detailed memorandum. The motion is denied. Mr. Trump defaulted with respect to the entire complaint, which includes punitive damages. It simply does not matter whether any other defendant possesses legal malice.

"The other major issue we have to consider is the instruction on Beverly Clooney's state of mind. In other words, what it takes to find her negligent or with legal malice. I have decided not to give any special instructions on Ms. Clooney. A religious belief is one component of one's mind and character. I ruled earlier that evidence of religious belief must be considered along with all evidence. I believe that religion likewise cannot be singled out when it comes to instructions. A second reason is that there has been no expert testimony on either side on the subject. No one has given me a basis for treating religion differently from other beliefs and characteristics. I shall give the standard instruction on the state of mind and credibility of witnesses that does not mention Clooney separately. I shall also tell them that no expert witnesses appeared for either side and that they should rely on their experience and common sense in evaluating her." The lawyers grumbled, but Jason felt secure.

"You all chose to try the case that way," Jason said. "Mr. Rattle could have relied on expert testimony. Even if he didn't, anyone could have asked for the opportunity to have Ms. Clooney examined. No one did." Jason was hoping, almost praying, that no one would make a cogent objection that it was improper to leave the jury to evaluate Dr. Fong's hearsay statement without some guidance. No one did. That made reversal less likely.

Because of the president, there would be three stages to the verdict, Jason explained, with the jury to return to the courtroom after each stage. First, the question of the liability of Clooney, Mandick, and *Total Faith* under both the negligence and legal-malice standards. Second, the amount of compensatory damages with respect to Mr. Trump and any defendant whom the jury found at least negligent. Third, the amount of punitive damages against Mr. Trump and any defendant the jury found to have possessed legal malice.

As the session was about to conclude, one of Whitebread's colleagues came into the room and spoke to him privately. Whitebread told Judge Jason and the other lawyers in the room that his colleague had spoken with Clooney's psychiatrist in Hawaii, Dr. Fong. Whitebread said he saw no reason to add to the record.

Jason wished the lawyers a pleasant weekend as they left his chambers.

Vernon addressed his father. "I think I'm sticking with taxes. I'm way out of my league with cases like these." He stooped over and picked up a folded piece of paper from a chair at the conference table. "Someone must have forgotten this." He handed it to his father.

Jason looked up and took the folded paper from his son. He unfolded it and stared. It was in pencil and consisted of an elaborate doodle with curlicues and embellishments. It reminded Jason of illuminated manuscripts, the medieval renditions of the Bible in which the beginning of each chapter was a complex work of art based largely on the first letter. Jason was about to throw the piece of paper in the waste-paper basket when he made out the writing. "STAY AWAY FROM MY MOTHER!" Panic rifled through him and caught in his throat. He leaned back in his chair and closed his eyes as the pieces he'd been trying to fit into the puzzle finally fit. Gregory. Of course. Christine's son. Life's coincidences never ceased to amaze him. "Vernon," he said, "would you give me a few minutes, please? I have to make a call."

"You O.K., dad?"

"I will be, son. Wait for me, please?"

Could Gregory be behind the letter and the hang-ups? Gregory could not have written the letter. But the telephone calls might be different. There may have been a coincidence, after all. Should I mention the phone calls to Marbury? What a mess.

Twenty minutes later he joined his son in his office. Jason walked to his mini-refrigerator, which he opened. "White wine or Heineken?"

"I'll take the beer. I've developed a thirst."

Jason handed a can to Vernon and opened one himself. Each took a sip. Vernon sat on the couch, while Jason took a comfortable chair.

"Everything all right?" Vernon asked. "You look better now than you did in the conference room. I was worried . . ."

"Everything will be fine, Vernon, but I need to tell you a story. When I was at Cornell . . ." he began.

"I think I need another beer, but I'll get it myself." Vernon hadn't spoken or moved throughout Jason's recital. He had been too shocked to say anything until now. Jason gave Vernon the same bowdlerized version that he had given Audrey, one that omitted details of the sexual relation and the pregnancy. As described, it was little more than unknowing statutory rape. "You've carried this a long time. It must have been so hard."

"Your mother knew, of course. I couldn't go into a marriage

without her knowing."

"How did she react?"

"Oh, the usual things you would expect — at first disgust, incredulity, fear, then finally, gratefully on my end, acceptance, some understanding and perhaps forgiveness, though we never again ventured into that area." Jason looked at his son. "We had a good marriage. I loved your mother very much, will always love her. You need to understand that."

"I do, dad." Vernon lifted his hands. "And now?"

"And now, Christine has come back into my life. It's as though the world has come full circle and allowed me this chance to make up for my grievous behavior so many years ago. Neither of us has a lot of quality time left. We want to be friends. I have no idea, nor does she, where this will take us, but we want the chance to find out." Jason stood up and rested his hand on his son's arm. "Does any of this make sense to you? Or, am I just this befuddled old wreck of a man whom you can no longer tolerate?"

"Wow," Vernon said quietly. He stood and walked slowly around the room. "Befuddled? Not even close." He dropped down on the sofa. "It's all right, dad. I now have proof positive that you are actually human like the rest of us mortals. There were times in the past I doubted that was true." He held up his beer can and saluted his dad. "Welcome to my world. And one day, I want to meet her."

The telephone intercom rang. "The Chief Judge would like to see you in his chambers now, if possible," Sue said as she knocked and opened the door.

"Thanks Sue. Tell him I'm on my way."

"Is this a problem, dad?"

"I'm sure it's nothing. I'll be right back. Make yourself comfortable while I see what's up."

"Have a seat," Marbury said to Jason when he arrived. "As I think you know, the FBI has talked to me about the letter you received. The deputy director just left. Some disturbing news. They are not sure, but they think the sender might be a judge. They are doing some more work. By the way, I should not be telling you this."

A judge! He had joked about it, but now it might be true. "Why do they think that?"

"As I said, nothing definite. The most damning evidence is that the paper is used by the judiciary. It has a distinctive watermark."

"Is it peculiar to this courthouse or is it writing paper everyone uses?"

"No, it's standard paper the courts, probation offices; everyone uses around the country. There was also the New York postmark, though."

"Anything else?" Jason was shocked. A judge! One of my colleagues? Or could it have been a court employee? Cohen? No way. He wouldn't be that stupid! This could be career ending.

Marbury looked at his hands. "There are a few things about the language that suggests it was a judge or experienced lawyer, though the FBI is not ready to commit itself. For example, the letter says you should 'recuse' yourself. Not many people say that. Most people would say 'disqualify' or something even more colloquial. It says, 'You're no judge.' They think that most people would have a capital J. The letter says you are 'biased,' which is what the statute says. Also, it is repetitive, which the FBI thinks may be someone trying to sound uneducated. At the same time some of the letter is well written, especially, "We know you are biased against the president and hostile to what he wants to accomplish for the American people."

"Impressive, but hardly dispositive."

"True, but they're working on fingerprints on the paper, although that could be difficult."

Jason shook his head. "I made a mistake. I had the lead counsel in the case hand the letter around. That could screw up a match. The FBI probably figured that out."

"The remaining thing is that they are testing for DNA. Whoever sent the letter may have licked the flap. They have a library of DNA samples, but it is far smaller than fingerprints. There is nothing we can do but wait. I am not great at keeping secrets, especially when it is from someone who has a right to know." Marbury stood. The meeting was over. "Sorry to burden you," he told Jason as he walked him to the door.

Jason decided to say nothing about the telephone calls and hang-ups or the note found in the conference room. He was almost certain that Gregory had made the calls, just as he had written the note in the conference room. They were personal matters that did not affect the case or the FBI. The consequence of turning the FBI loose on the phone calls could create multiple disasters. In the remote possibility that he was wrong, he'd figure out what to do then. Right now, he wanted to leave Marbury with the problem over the letter and nothing more.

"I appreciate your confidence," was all Jason could think of saying as he got up and left.

Jason adjusted his jacket as he entered his chambers. He had to pretend he had not heard anything important from Marbury although there were now fewer secrets from Vernon.

"Just a personnel matter, Vernon. When are you going back to Washington? Any chance you can stay over tonight?"

"Actually, that's my plan. Does your hotel have a free room for tonight?"

Pure relief flowed through Jason. After all that had happened, Vernon still wanted to stay. Absolutely, and I'll try to find a restaurant that will take us on short notice. I'll see if my secretary can come up with something suitable for someone with your fine taste. Thank you, Vernon."

"No problem. Dinner sounds great."

Jason ended up making the dinner reservation himself, which was just as well. He was able to persuade the reservation-maker at Jean-Georges to give him a table at 6:30 p.m., with the understanding that he would guarantee that the table would be available for a pair of regulars for their 8:30 p.m. dinner. Jason knew that dinners there can take a long time. He promised "on his honor" to be finished by then. He was amused at his use of the expression. Looking forward to a great meal, Jason had not considered that he might balk at eating at a restaurant that was housed in a Trump-owned hotel, the same one at which Crunch and Gregory were staying. He probably would not have made a reservation if he had remembered, but it was silly to change the reservation. After all, Trump did not run the restaurant and he didn't know whether Donald Trump took a cut of its profits.

The dinner went smoothly, and the great food and wine were just part of it. "Remember Ted Sorensen?" Jason asked Vernon as they started on their entrees.

"Yes, he was very close to JFK. He wrote speeches for Kennedy. What made you think of him?"

"For some reason while I was talking today in court, I remembered an incident that occurred many years ago. I attended a speech by Sorensen on desegregation efforts in the South in the 1960's and how difficult it was. He spoke about the loyalty oath that Mississippi required of all demonstrators. If you did not sign it and you demonstrated, you were jailed. Sorensen had to fill out a form that asked, "Do you favor the overthrow of the government of the State of Mississippi by force or violence?" Sorensen said he thought a minute, then answered, 'Force.'"

Vernon laughed. "Funny, but I don't get the point."

Jason thought briefly that he'd bested Vernon yet again. This time though, Vernon hadn't been bothered by it at all.

It seemed to Jason that his relationship with his son had taken a significant upward turn, which made him happy. Vernon was talking about his life outside his law office, including a weekend he spent in North Carolina with a woman. While he was somewhat evasive about her, he had opened up about her presence in his life. A nuclear physicist, she had impressed the hell out of him. Vernon was talked about her attributes but was silent about how he felt about her. Jason did not ask.

"Should we have cognac in the bar?" Jason asked

"I'd prefer some Sauternes, if that's O.K."

"I have better stuff at home. I'll open something good."

"What are we waiting for?"

Back at his apartment, Jason opened a bottle of Chateau Suduiraut 1989, which had matured from its original yellow to a vibrant bronze. Its sweetness remained but was lusciously infiltrated with apricots and pineapple. It had mellowed over the years. It was a perfect wine to end the day. Jason put on a CD of Bach violin concertos, keeping the volume low.

The two men silently sipped the wine, until Jason asked a question. "Have you ever heard from Sarah?" It was the first time in a more than a decade that he had asked Vernon anything about his dreadful experience with marriage.

"No," Vernon replied and conspicuously took another sip, which he held in his mouth for several seconds before swallowing.

"Nothing?" Jason persisted. Another pause.

"I ran into a friend of hers some years ago, who said Sarah was not doing well."

Jason remained silent, his boldness had quickly vanished. He had made a mistake to talk about Sarah.

"She said that Sarah had been hospitalized for a while. Her emotional state had deteriorated."

More silence. Jason sipped the wine.

"Her friend said she was living with her mother, who had some sort of sickness. It was terminal, I believe."

"It's all very sad," Jason said.

Vernon looked devastated. "Terrible is a better word. Just terrible," he managed to say. "Despite everything, I loved Sarah. I couldn't believe that she was as sick as she was. Maybe if I had been more perceptive . . ." Vernon's voice trailed off.

"Those things happen. You cannot blame yourself. I hope things go better with your new friend."

"I certainly hope so, too. Thanks, dad."

The two men slowly and quietly finished the bottle of the Suduiraut. It took a while. A few minutes later they went to bed.

Jason lay awake thinking of Audrey, his son, Christine and her son. His mind moved on to the trial, how well it was going despite the letter, the phone calls, the egos, the surprises. He pictured the taciturn Crunch and his dour associate, Gregory, Christine's son. *Imagine, her son being a lawyer in Moses v. Trump, his biggest case!* Jason moved on to the problem of

Trump's use of White House Counsel as his lawyer.

Jason had finally figured out Trump's lawyer problem, at least to his satisfaction. Trump could not complain, because he was represented by the lawyer of his choice, the counsel to the president. It was not Trump who was prejudiced, but rather the taxpayers, who were paying a government employee to represent Trump in his private capacity. That was not Jason's problem. Also, if Trump won on appeal, at least if the court of appeals concluded that the tweet was official, his representation by the government would have been legitimate. Jason thought of the perfect description, "No harm, no foul." He closed his eyes and relaxed. He slept. It had been quite a day. In addition, he and Vernon would have the weekend together, their first in too many years to count.

Chapter 20

It was Monday morning after a pleasant and relaxing weekend. An unexpected heat wave had hit the city. Tensions were high. Jason waded through the crowd outside the courthouse to get to the entrance. As the trial progressed the people waiting outside seem more and more jovial. There was an occasional sign held high by one of those present. Today, one held high read, "Trump Has Met His Maker." Next to that was one that read, "Trump, Repent Before It Is Too Late." Jason's favorite was one that a young black man held the previous day, "Trump: Hang in There, Bro.'"

The courtroom was overflowing, but without Vernon, who had arranged to see a client so that he could charge his New York trip to business. The bar on witnesses sitting in the courtroom had been lifted because the taking of evidence had been completed. Both sides had rested. Several of the witnesses from the trial were seated among the spectators. Summations, the charge to the jury, and the verdict remained.

First to address the jury was Whitebread, who referred to the article as "the false article" to make sure the jury had the point in mind. Whitebread had a problem. If the jurors had all been liberal nonbelievers, Whitebread could have scoffed at Clooney's account and even made fun of Mandick, all in as good taste as he could muster. But, Jason suspected, there may be jurors, especially the Hispanics, who were devout, and perhaps others who were at least tolerant of religiosity. An all-out attack might offend them. Whitebread's job was to make the jurors skeptical of the defendants to the point of rejecting them and what they stood for. He tried to show that their views were outrageous without criticizing "legitimate" faith. Assisting him was the now established fact that the article was indisputably false, which he repeatedly hammered, arguing that no one could possibly have believed the article to be true.

Butt's task was probably the easiest of the three lawyers. While a strange duck for New Yorkers, Mandick was taking what some might consider a moderate position among the litigants, at least respecting his beliefs. He maintained strenuously that he followed his standard journalistic practices on the article and that he had developed confidence in Clooney. Nothing she told him led him to believe that she had acted other than in accordance with journalistic principles, at least as practiced by the responsible Christian right. Butt summed it up.

"Mr. Mandick may not be the kind of person we normally encounter, but please respect a man who has convictions and lives by them. Remember, we are sitting in the shadow of the Statue of Liberty."

Butt explained that Mandick had learned the same time as the jurors that Ms. Clooney claimed she had taken dictation from God. Mandick, Butt repeated, had questioned her closely and studied her notes before publishing the article. Butt was careful not to say that Clooney was crazy. It would sound as if he were trashing an employee whom Mandick had hired, published, and believed in. More to the point Mandick had instructed him not to. True, Mandick was predisposed to believe her when he published the story, but that, Butt, explained, was something that counted in Mandick's favor in the world of libel suits. He respected the reporting of Ms. Clooney because he knew her work and shared her faith. Butt argued that nothing presented proved that Mandick was negligent or that he doubted the accuracy of the story. That was the applicable standard and whatever one thought of Mandick and his views, everyone had to respect the Constitution.

"You cannot pick and choose among the people to whom the Constitution applies," Butt explained, "because otherwise tomorrow you may find yourselves being treated differently than others under the Constitution and laws of this country. Do your duty under the Constitution and your oath to fulfill your obligations as jurors."

Butt paused then continued: "What could be better evidence of the absence of negligence than experience in publishing unchallenged articles by the same writer. In sum," Butt concluded, "my client was neither negligent nor indifferent to the truth of the article on Mr. Moses."

For Rattle the job was to get the jury to believe that Clooney really was crazy rather than a fabricator of a story for her professional and pecuniary advantage. He didn't want to move them to the witch-burning stage, just enough to believe that she was not responsible for her actions and statements. Her account of her strange behavior was uncontradicted. Not having to defend the truth of the article made Rattle's job easier, Jason recognized. By ruling against her claim, he had helped her in *Moses v. Trump*. Rattle could imply that Beverly Clooney was hallucinating.

More in sorrow than in anger seemed best for Rattle. Perhaps even a hint that she was victimized by the religious right, but there was no mistaking the fact that she had outrageously trashed Moses, who had done nothing wrong. "Try to imagine how Beverley Clooney was thinking. Given her state of mind, no one could conceivably say she was at fault in failing to do more research."

Rattle essentially faced an overarching problem on the negligence claim, namely, that the jury had to apply an objective standard, namely, what would a reasonable reporter have done. He argued that in her community of believers, Clooney was acting reasonably. The jury could not discriminate against highly religious people. That would be outrageous and unconstitutional.

Whitebread gave a rebuttal more to have the last word than for anything he added. The subtleties of the law had little to do with his winning or losing the case, and he wanted to win, badly. He reiterated his point, which was, basically, "are you prepared to let these right-wing crazies get away with trashing a decent and honorable man like Moses?" Whitebread had to be more circumspect, so what he said was, "have you heard any evidence that would excuse the outrageous lies that these defendants said about Mr. Moses?" Whitebread stayed away from the Bible, wisely Jason thought.

The summations occupied the morning and Jason gave everyone a late and brief luncheon recess before he instructed the jury. He did not want to prolong the final phase of the trial. The jurors had agreed to eat sandwiches in the jury room.

Jason's charge did not summarize the evidence, just the law. Using their experience as men and women, the jurors would have to decide if the defendants were negligent or entertained serious doubts about the article's accuracy. Jason did his best to explain the complexities of the law to the lay jury. He hoped that the trial made comprehensible the instructions, which no longer described abstract concepts, as they were before the introduction of evidence.

Jason told the jurors that the U.S. Marshal would give the foreman a form that required the jury to answer specific questions for each defendant. Did the defendant publish the article negligently? Did the defendant publish it with legal malice? If the answer to both was in the negative, they should find for the defendants. If there was either negligence or legal malice, they should say which one or ones with respect to each of the three defendants, Ms. Clooney, Mr. Mandick, and *Total Faith*. When they decided liability, the jurors should return for further instructions.

The charge concluded with what are usually described as "boiler plate" instructions, such as the meaning of clear-and-convincing proof, how the jury should go about handling the issue of credibility, how the jury should deliberate, and the need for unanimity. He gave the instructions he had decided on earlier, including the general one on credibility and that clear and convincing proof meant that the evidence presented by the plaintiff during the trial is more highly probable to be true than not and the jury has a firm belief or conviction in it. He wished them well and sent them to the jury room to start deliberations.

Once the jury left the courtroom the atmosphere changed radically for Jason, if not the other participants. Tension born of the fear of making a mistake or having some disaster strike succumbed to a passive tension from waiting for the jury to decide. Participants in the trial faced the self-flagellation that resulted from suddenly realizing a mistake. Depending on his or her personality, a lawyer replays the trial or struggles to think of other things.

Jason remembered a conversation he had many years ago with a criminal-defense lawyer. Jason had mentioned the strain of waiting for a jury's verdict, then added, "particularly if you are convinced that the client is innocent." The lawyer responded: "Oh, I never represent innocent clients. I couldn't stand the strain." Jason wasn't sure if he was kidding.

Back from his appointment, which had included an excellent lunch, Vernon along with Joe McDonald visited the courtroom from time to time. They reported to Jason that it was very quiet, almost funereal, although Butt and Rattle seemed more upbeat than Whitebread. Crunch was nowhere in sight.

Not totally unexpected was a call from Marbury shortly after Jason finished instructing the jury. He'd like Jason to come over.

Marbury got to the point. "It looks like it is Malcolm Cohen."

"Malcolm?" Jason was shocked. Although Cohen had been one of the people he had considered, he couldn't believe it. Cohen had retaliated for what he thought was Jason's ignoring him and snitching to Marbury.

"I do not know what's behind this and I do not want to know, at least not now," Marbury said. "As you know, I have no disciplinary responsibilities over the other district judges."

"How strong is the evidence?"

"I am not really sure. They said there was a partial match on the fingerprints and a partial match on the DNA. Of course, they haven't had time to finish processing the letter you gave me last Friday."

"What do you mean, a partial match on the DNA?"

"They said that it was a match on someone who was Malcolm or someone related to him. That is all they said. It has something to do with the size and condition of the sample. It is not a billion to one that he did not do it, but it is a large number It does not look good for him," Marbury said quietly.

"We were all fingerprinted for our background checks, but where did they get Malcolm's DNA?"

"I did not ask," Marbury said.

"What will happen to him?"

"I do not know. My impression is that the FBI does not think it is a crime, but it is not their call. Because the U.S. Attorney practices in this district and before its judges, I believe that it will be handled in Washington. My initial guess was that it will not be a criminal case. There were no real threats in the letter to you. It doesn't sound like an impeachable offense, which requires strong proof of commission of a felony or something close. Other than those things, I do not know what anyone can do to him. It is really impeachment or nothing. But it's too bad."

United States Attorney McGoohey will not handle the case. That was good news for Malcolm. Jason and Marbury sat quietly, then Jason spoke. He had qualms about being involved in an investigation of a judge for sexual misconduct. Despite everything, he liked Cohen. He also readily saw that but for the grace of God . . . . Instead, he said, "I agree. Very sad. Will it become public?"

"Not officially, at least not now," Marbury answered. "A lot of people have been questioned. The DOJ in Washington will probably want to find out what else Malcolm has done. He rose. "Sorry to pull you away from your jury watch."

"Thanks." Jason couldn't think of anything else to say. "See you soon."

"I shall let you know what happens."

Jason returned to his chambers. He wondered whether

the Trump Administration would be tough on Cohen because he was a Democratic appointee. Cohen was also a dedicated, thoughtful judge. The worst Trump's people could do was refer the matter to the Judiciary Committee of the House of Representatives to debate whether to conduct an impeachment inquiry, but the referral itself would have no legal consequences. Nevertheless, that would be terrible, Jason concluded. Jason was relieved that that was the only disciplinary avenue open. No one puts a negative valuation in the file of a federal judge or docks him ten days' pay. In any event, there was nothing Jason could do.

Nothing was heard from the jury that afternoon, and they retired to a hotel for the night. Deliberations resumed the following morning. The jury sent in a note on the afternoon of the second day of deliberations. The bailiff assembled the lawyers before Jason entered the half-filled courtroom. A few minutes later, the jury, in surprisingly good spirits, entered the courtroom and took their seats in the jury box. That seemed to foretell bad news for the defendants. The jury had seemed to like Moses more than the defendants, so their good spirits might foretell a plaintiff's verdict.

"I'll mark the jury's note, which the bailiff time-stamped, Court's Exhibit No. 3." Jason opened and read the note silently. "I will now read it to the lawyers who are assembled at the bench. 'Is there any way to hold God liable?'" No one knew whether to get angry or to laugh, so to be sure the lawyers remained solemn while looking at Jason for guidance. "I'll handle it," was all he said. "Bring in the jury to the courtroom." As much as Jason would have preferred to handle the note privately, this was part of the trial and it had to be public.

Jason read the question out loud. He ignored the rustling noise from the spectators. "Ladies and gentlemen of the jury, I know that this is a strain, and I do not want you to think that we are not sympathetic to your efforts. The answer, I am sure you realize, is no. All of us, who have worked very hard on the case, request that you return to deliberate and do so diligently and conscientiously. Do any of the lawyers in the case have any comment? If so approach the bench." No one moved. "Thank you, ladies and gentlemen. You may resume your deliberations."

Jason had never had to deal with a joke on the part of jurors during deliberations, at least he assumed it was a joke. In chambers Joe could barely suppress a grin. "When you look at it as an outsider, it does have a supernatural quality. I guess a verdict against God would be a first in a United States court."

Jason replied curtly, "Yes, but Mandick is a powerful person and the damage to Moses's reputation is real. There are cases where I believed that humor was a saving grace, if you'll excuse the expression, but none of the parties or lawyers is kidding around here." Joe got the lecture because he was the only person around.

Ten minutes later the bailiff notified Jason that there was a verdict. It was obvious that one juror had made as a condition of her voting that she be allowed to ask the absurd question. That's the jury system for you. Twenty minutes later everyone had assembled in the full courtroom.

"Mr. Foreman, do you have a verdict?" Jason asked the young economist seated in the chair in the jury box nearest him.

"Yes, Your Honor," he replied.

"No one shall leave the courtroom until the entire verdict is rendered in full," Jason announced.

"On Count I of the complaint, do you find for the plaintiff or the defendant *Total Faith* on the issue of negligence?"

"We find for the plaintiff." The foreman did not look at the verdict form but stared directly at Jason.

The spectators seemed all to be speaking at once. Jason banged the gavel and asked for quiet. The noise subsided, but there was still a buzz from the room's rear.

"On Count I of the complaint, do you find for the plaintiff or the defendant Mr. Mandick on the issue of negligence?"

"We find for the plaintiff?"

On Count I of the complaint, do you find for the plaintiff or the defendant Ms. Clooney on the issue of negligence?"

"We find for the plaintiff."

"On Count I of the complaint, do you find for the plaintiff or the defendant *Total Faith* on the issue of legal malice?"

"We find in favor of the plaintiff."

"On Count I of the complaint, do you find for the plaintiff or the defendant Mr. Mandick on the issue of legal malice?"

"We find in favor of the plaintiff."

"On Count I of the complaint, do you find for the plaintiff or the defendant Ms. Clooney on the issue of legal malice?"

"We find in favor of Ms. Clooney."

Jason was relieved. He did not think the evidence supported punitive damages against Clooney, but did not relish setting aside a verdict. In fact, he was not sure that the finding of legal malice was supportable against Mandick and *Total Faith*, although he would face that issue later. About half of the press corps fled the courtroom.

"Ladies and gentlemen of the jury," Jason said, "I have to tell you your work is not done. You still must find the amount of damages, both compensatory and punitive, with respect not only to these defendants, but also against another defendant who did not choose to participate in the trial but against whom damages may be awarded. That defendant is the president of the United States, Donald Trump. With the consent of the lawyers in the case representing all parties, I am instructing you that there will be one amount of compensatory for the three defendants whom you have found liable and a separate amount of compensatory damages regarding President Trump."

That Jason's statement made no visible impact on the jurors showed Jason that the jurors knew that Trump was about to enter the fray. Jason could not remember if he told the jurors that earlier.

"I shall give you some more evidence for you to consider," Jason said to the jury. "Mr. Whitebread and Mr. Crunch, the attorney for President Trump, have agreed to the following statement:

"I am instructing you that on the same day as the story appeared in *Total Faith* the president tweeted to approximately thirty million people, and it was duly reported by all relevant media, print and electronic, that the president said, and I quote: "We now know why traitor Kruiser was acquitted. Her so-called lawyer bribed a juror. He's a crook. Lock him up. Bad man. Drain the swamp." The president repeated the charge in substance later the same day. That is the end of the additional evidence. The lawyers have stated that they otherwise have no additional evidence or argument to present on compensatory damages.

"You will first decide the amount of compensatory damages you will award plaintiff Ira Moses. I instruct you that compensatory damages are exactly what the term suggests, namely, the amount of damages that will fairly compensate the plaintiff for the harm caused by the statement that you have already found to be defamatory. This includes damage to the reputation of Mr. Moses, and pain and suffering he endured because of the statements. I instruct you that since Mr. Moses did not allege that he lost income because of the statements, you may not award him damages for loss of income. You are to fix one total amount of compensatory damages for *Total Faith*, Mr. Mandick, and Ms. Clooney. The reason is that it is impossible to separate the harm caused by the three people who worked and published the article.

"You are to fix a separate amount of compensatory damages for President Trump. In considering the amount of your award, if any, against President Trump, you may consider that his statement came after the article appeared, although very short y thereafter, and the extent of circulation of the president's statements, which were widely reported in all media in the United States and abroad. You may award the plaintiff only those additional damages President Trump caused by his tweets and media and other reports of his tweets. In other words, you must exclude from damages awarded against Mr. Trump damages that had already been caused by the other defendants' article in *Total Faith*. I will excuse the jury to allow them to deliberate." The jury filed quickly out of the jury box into their secure room.

Jason had just reached his chambers and taken off his robe when the clerk called to tell him that the jury had reached a verdict on compensatory damages. The swiftness of the verdict surprised Jason, but it was not unprecedented. The jury may have considered compensatory damages, and perhaps even punitive damages, at the same time it decided liability, something like a global settlement of the entire dispute. Jason immediately returned to the courtroom, which was not quite full, sat down, and addressed the foreman.

"I understand that you have reached a verdict on compensatory damages. What is the amount of compensatory damages in favor of Mr. Moses against *Total Faith*, Mr. Mandick, and Ms. Clooney?"

"Ten million dollars." The spectators barely registered a reaction.

"What is the amount of compensatory damages in favor of Mr. Moses and against President Trump?"

"One billion dollars," the foreman stated distinctly while looking directly at Jason. He paused and sat down. He then stared unblinking at Crunch until Crunch turned away.

A gasp arose from the spectators. Jason thought he had let out a whistle, but no one seemed to notice. After a moment, everybody in the courtroom was talking. Jason banged his gavel three times.

"Your Honor?"

"Yes, Mr. Whitebread." They were almost shouting.

"We move to conform the plea for compensatory damages to the amount of the verdict."

"Motion granted." It was a technical, but essential, request. The complaint had asked for 100 million dollars in damages, a smaller sum than one billion dollars, and the jury could not award a larger sum than requested. So Whitebread took the time-honored path of amending the complaint to seek the larger sum. It was routine, at least sufficiently routine that Crunch did not object.

Jason called the lawyers and court reporter up to the bench with the microphone off. "Mr. Crunch, this is your last opportunity to produce the president's income-tax returns."

"We respectfully decline to produce them," Crunch said

simply. No associate accompanied Crunch today. Jason noted two new faces in the VIP section. They looked like lawyers. Jason wondered whether Trump had finally accepted the need to have his personal lawyers attend the proceeding.

"Back to your places," Jason said. Important business remained.

"Ladies and gentlemen of the jury, there is one more task for you to perform, namely, for you to consider the amount of punitive damages, if any, that you award against the defendants other than Clooney. There will be a short reopening of the evidence. Mr. Whitebread?"

"Your Honor, without objection we offer the income-tax returns of defendants *Total Faith* and Mr. Mandick. That is the sole additional evidence as to them. Copies of their income-tax returns will be delivered to the jury room.

"The situation is different for the president, who has refused to produce his income-tax returns. I ask the court to instruct the jury that with respect to Mr. Trump the jury can consider his statements about his net worth, which he has stated exceeded ten billion dollars, since he has refused to produce his tax returns. I submit the jurors can also consider their knowledge of his prior statements attacking people and calling them crooks and the like on the issue of punitive damages."

"I object," Crunch stated while rising quickly, "to allowing the jury to rely on its recollection of Mr. Trump's statements." Jason could not believe that they were having this argument in front of the jury, but no one asked for the jury to be excused. "I also object to allowing the jury to consider other statements of President Trump in awarding punitive damages."

"Mr. Whitebread, what is your response?" Jason asked.

"Your Honor, I think one purpose in awarding punitive damages is deterrence. Mr. Trump's history of attacking people is relevant. On what evidence the jury may rely in this regard, I have here copies of a booklet that contains one hundred quotations from Mr. Trump that I have prepared for the jury. Each one is documented, and I have the original print or electronic statement available to show the defendants. I have no preference on which way to proceed."

"What is your position, Mr. Crunch?" Jason asked.

"We object to the entire proceeding, including the award of punitive damages," Crunch said.

"I understand that, that is on the record," Jason said, "but do you want to take a position on the evidence of Mr. Trump's statements? If you want a recess, I'll grant one."

Crunch thumbed through the pages of the booklet. "We object to the evidence."

"I shall construe that as a preference for relying on the jury's recollection," Jason said.

"I did not say that," Crunch said. "I object to all the evidence." Crunch's jaw was clenched.

"Duly noted. Mr. Whitebread, anything else?"

"Your Honor, we have nothing else."

"Done. Do you have anything to offer, Mr. Butt?"

"No, Your Honor."

"Mr. Rattle?"

"No, Your Honor."

"Mr. Crunch?"

"No, Your Honor."

Jason would have loved to know the content of Crunch's conversations with Trump. Crunch did not ask for a recess to speak to his client before the submission of punitive damages. What could Trump say that was useful? Besides, Crunch was undoubtedly spared one more diatribe.

"Does any of you wish to address the jury on the issue of punitive damages?" Jason asked. He had also considered and rejected the idea of calling a recess. No one asked for one, the jury seemed alert, and Jason wanted to finish.

Whitebread, Butt, and Crunch all requested time. Whitebread went first. "The reckless conduct of the defendants requires punishment under the law. It is as simple as that. Mr. Mandick and *Total Faith* published a false and malicious story with nothing in the way of evidence. How could they have not entertained serious doubts as to the accuracy of the story? It doesn't matter what you think of Beverly Clooney. Either way,

Mr. Mandick and *Total Faith* possessed legal malice. You know the evidence and you know the income of Mr. Mandick and *Total Faith*. I ask you to make an award that they'll remember.

"With respect to Mr. Trump, he has claimed extraordinary wealth, as much as $20 billion. His history of attacking people, including his associates, is legendary. He has been found to have possessed legal malice when he published his tweets. Once again, I ask you to render an appropriate verdict befitting Mr. Trump's actions and conduct and wealth."

"Mr. Butt?"

"Thank you, Your Honor." He turned to the jury and put his hands on his hips. "I shall be frank with you. I don't see how you found that Mr. Mandick and *Total Faith* published the article with the kind of doubt the law requires to find legal malice. I just don't understand. Mr. Mandick and the others at *Total Faith* followed standard procedures. They questioned Beverly Clooney to make sure the story was accurate, and it seemed to them to be accurate. There were no warning signs until after the article was published. Be that as it may, I humbly ask you not to award punitive damages against Mr. Mandick and *Total Faith*. You have awarded, if I may say so, extraordinary compensatory damages against them. That is enough. Thank you."

"Mr. Crunch."

"May it please the court, ladies and gentlemen, I have a lot to say, but I will try to be brief. President Trump had no way of knowing that the article was false, a fact that emerged only later. He knew *Total Faith* and he respected *Total Faith*. He has relied on *Total Faith* and its predecessor in the past and his reliance had been vindicated."

Whitebread jumped to his feet. "Your Honor, I truly apologize for interrupting, but I have to object. I do not like to interfere with the closing argument of my brother Crunch." Whitebread shook his head slowly. "Mr. Crunch, however, is arguing something not in evidence and something that is in fact false. There is nothing in the record showing that the president had ever been vindicated when he relied on *Good*

Faith and *Total Faith*. Again, I most respectfully apologize for interrupting."

Jason looked at Crunch, who said nothing.

"Ladies and gentlemen of the jury, I am sustaining the objection, but only on the first ground. You are to disregard Mr. Crunch's statement about Mr. Trump's reliance because there is no evidence in this trial that when Mr. Trump relied on *Good Faith* and *Total Faith*, the publication was accurate or inaccurate. Please continue, Mr. Crunch. In summation, lawyers can only argue based on what is in the record."

"Thank you, Your Honor." There was no mistaking the sarcasm in Crunch's voice. "I reiterate that President Trump had no way of knowing that the article was false. The only material on which he based his tweet was the *Total Faith* article. He knew of nothing else. Mr. Trump is an exuberant and outspoken man, but that is not enough to find that he acted so outrageously that he should be subjected to punitive damages in addition to the extraordinarily large compensatory damage award against him. There is nothing in the article itself that should have alerted Mr. Trump or anyone else that it was false. Mr. Trump knew none of the information that led Mr. Mandick later to change his belief that the article was true to a concession that it was false.   Ms. Clooney maintained it was true until the judge concluded otherwise. That was much later." Crunch was losing the thread of his argument. "Although he is the president, he appears before you as a citizen and litigant with the same rights as others who are sued. We ask you to treat him fairly based on the evidence in this case."

For a minute Jason thought Crunch would argue that there should be no award against Trump because no one believes him anyway. After all, there had been a flood of statements from Trump that were totally without factual support. Some claimed there were thousands. Jason doubted that such a defense would have pleased Trump, especially since Trump was still claiming that those statements of his were true. Also, that argument was not one that would encourage the jury to be lenient. Indeed, the argument was ridiculous.

It was now Jason's duty to instruct the jury on punitive damages, the last word to the jury before its final deliberations.

"Ladies and gentlemen of the jury, I shall now instruct you on the proper way to decide the amount of punitive damages, if any, that you may award Mr. Moses. As the term suggests, punitive damages are awarded to punish a defendant for intentional or reckless behavior that is outrageous and well beyond the norm. It is an unusual remedy that is imposed only for exceptional behavior beyond what should be expected in the situation. You have found that two defendants had legal malice when they made the statements, but you are not required to award punitive damages. The same is true of Mr. Trump.

"There are several factors you should consider in making any award you decide to make. The amount depends on the seriousness of the defendant's statement or conduct, whether it was isolated or part of a pattern, whether it was designed to inflict harm on the plaintiff or had other legitimate purposes, and what amount is necessary to deter future occurrences. You should consider the potential harm of a defendant's conduct to the defendant. You should also consider what is an appropriate amount in view of the economic situation of the defendant, choosing an amount that will inflict serious but not catastrophic punishment." Jason paused and scanned the jury for understanding. The jurors seemed to be following him.

"You must award punitive damages separately as to Mr. Mandick, *Total Faith*, and President Trump. You may now retire to determine the amount of punitive damages, if any, that you decide to award."

Jason knew not to get too comfortable in his chambers and sure enough, within minutes he was summoned to the courtroom. He strode to the courtroom through the door behind his chair and sat down. Everything was in place, with the foreman standing at his chair.

"Mr. Foreman, have you reached a verdict on the amount of punitive damages against *Total Faith*?"

"Yes, Your Honor, it is one dollar." The foreman looked directly at Jason.

"Have you reached a verdict on the amount of punitive damages against Mr. Mandick?"

"Yes, Your Honor, it is one dollar."

"Have you reached a verdict on the amount of punitive damages against Mr. Trump?"

"Yes, Your Honor, it is one billion dollars." The foreman sat down and again stared at Crunch.

Once more, the spectators emitted a collective gasp. Jason looked at Crunch, who seemed badly shaken, but stared straight ahead. Moses and Whitebread were grinning and shaking hands. Butt and Rattle looked relieved. Jason wondered who had advised Trump not to defend the lawsuit. Maybe Trump overruled his advisors. It had been a catastrophic call, whoever made it. Whatever the facts that emerged from White House leaks or other sources, Jason was positive that Trump would blame someone else. Jason then looked at the jurors. They seemed to be serious, but Jason thought he detected a suppressed smile on two or three. He couldn't be sure.

"Your Honor?"

"Yes, Mr. Whitebread."

"We move to conform the complaint to the verdict."

"Granted." Jason said as the audience got noisier. He paused until there was barely a murmur.

"Serves the prick right," cried a squeaky voice from the rear of the courtroom. A burst of laughter.

Then came another voice, the deepest bass than Jason had ever heard, "Fook the beegat." The sounds came from the heart of Africa. A moment of shocked silence.

"Drain the swamp, drain the swamp," a few dozen spectators chanted as the Marshals tried to restore order. Other spectators applauded or laughed. Then, there was a noise, which soon became a roar. Scores, maybe a hundred or more, of the spectators were stomping their feet and applauding and shouting in rhythm. It was mesmerizing, almost scary. Its power was palpable. Jason thought of Nazi rallies but put the thought out of his mind.

Jason banged the gavel repeatedly, but he could not be

heard. A minute went by, then two. Finally, Jason stood, waiving his gavel. The roar slowly subsided. The jurors struggled to appear somber. A few appeared frightened. Thankfully, Jason observed, none of them joined the chanters or apparently, the stompers.

"Ladies and gentlemen of the jury, I want to thank you for your calm and proper demeanor in the face of this unexpected outburst. Thank you also for your conscientious attendance and attention throughout this trial. I know that this trial has been unusual and something of a strain. The system would simply break down if jurors refused to serve or if they did not do their jobs conscientiously. I make it a practice of not commenting on a jury verdict to the jury, because that is your function, and I hope that you would not find it necessary to comment on my handling of the case for the same reason."

Jason smiled at the jury. The jurors smiled back. This was a contented jury. They and Jason appeared to be a calm island in the middle of a cyclone that was uprooting the very structure of civilization.

"While nothing prevents you from speaking to reporters, nothing requires you to do so, either. If I may make a suggestion, I would ask that each of you seriously consider whether it is in your best interests to talk to the press. I want to repeat, however, that the decision is entirely up to each of you. I am informed by the jury clerk that you are to pick up your checks in the jury room and are excused until your services are again required and you are so notified. Have a good evening. The rest of us will take a ten-minute recess and then return."

The jurors thanked Jason, stood, and filed out of the jury box. One older woman waved good-bye. A couple of them smiled. A platoon of reporters fled through the rear door of the courtroom, some to get the story on the air and some to head off the jurors. Jason wondered about Trump's possibly having to pay $2 billion for a reckless tweet, and his being honored as a federal judge. Perhaps it was his advancing age, but he was increasingly bothered by hypocrisy, his as well as others'. He calmed himself with the realization that the law did not allow damages against Trump for his other outrageous actions against the poor, the weak, and those most in need, including the ill and immigrants from persecution. Perhaps there was poetic justice in the verdict. But that was not how the legal system is supposed to work. He was most assuredly not thinking as a judge. Maybe it was time to quit. He was way ahead.

"We'll take a recess and then I'll consider motions directed at the verdict," Jason announced.

A minute later Andy Smith was seated in Jason's private office with the door closed. As soon as Smith had heard the news, which was already all over television and the internet, he had rushed over. Vernon had gone to the main floor to take a phone call from his office. Both sat silently looking at each other, until Smith spoke.

"Wow." Both smiled.

"It was a bit higher than I expected," Jason said evenly.

"Do you think the Russians will pay the judgment?" When Jason remained expressionless, Smith continued.

"I'll check on Trumps tweets. Here's one, 'I can't believe what that shit-faced judge is doing to me and the country. He thinks he was elected president. He forgets I was. Long live Trump.'"

Jason sat stone-faced.

"Here's another one. 'I'm waiting to see what kind of army that asshole Moses will have when he tries to collect his judgment from me. I'll send him back to Israel, where my friend Benjamin will have a surprise for him. Lock him up.'"

When Jason remained silent, Smith tried again. "There must be something amazing in Trump's tax returns to make him refuse to give them to the jury. What do you think it is? An offshore bank account? A fraudulent billion-dollar write-off? It has to be more serious than a return without a charitable deduction, which was the rumor during the campaign."

"I have no idea," Jason answered.

"At least he didn't offer to make a deal with you. I just thought of something. What if Trump borrowed money from some Russian oligarchs or even the Russian government? That may be why he is so nice to Putin."

When Jason said nothing, Smith continued, "One or two unsavory business deals could answer several questions. That wouldn't go over very well with the voters."

"You're right about that."

"Maybe his tax returns show those transactions. You can be sure that if Trump paid anyone a dime of interest, he'd deduct it without question. What about it?

"Maybe."

A minute passed in silence. Jason was tired, and Smith was not making things any easier. Jason wanted to think about what to do when he went back into the courtroom. He wanted to be alone.

Smith changed the subject. "Is it time to open the bottle of Chambertin that you've been hiding in your desk?"

"You're not suggesting that we should celebrate a jury's verdict rendered under the Constitution's Seventh Amendment. are you? We're judges." Jason wondered how Smith knew about the prize bottle.

"My God, no, although some might feel that the correct implementation of the judicial system is worth at least a nod. Actually, I was thinking that we should acknowledge your superb performance."

"The case is not over. I have motions to decide motions in a few minutes. How would it look if someone detected alcohol on my breath?" Jason asked. Jason was also concerned about passing out on the bench.

"I understand."

"I'll get Sue to bring us coffee. I have excellent apple strudel. That will be a more appropriate repast." Anticipating the request, Sue entered and placed coffee and strudel on the table in front of the couch.

"In a sense I feel sorry for Crunch," Jason said, as he washed down the strudel with coffee. He took a deep breath and closed his eyes. "Crunch has managed to avoid the chaos and recriminations of the Trump White House, only to be done in by a strategy he undoubtedly opposed. He's handled himself well, all things considered."

"Agreed," said Smith. "Reince Priebus, who seemed a decent man, although mousy, was ousted right after the push to repeal Obamacare failed in the Senate. That was his responsibility."

"Yeah."

"My guess Crunch will be gone in a week," Smith said. "You lose when you lose. It doesn't matter how or why. Trump has the loyalty of a viper. Screw Trump. He's stupid, narcissistic, money-grubbing, and a pathological liar. He has reduced the 'imperial presidency' to a cash cow for Trump, Inc. He deserves what he gets."

Jason frowned at Smith. "I didn't hear that. My mouth is full of strudel." Jason was wondering how he could get rid of his colleague.

Smith shrugged. "In a sense this is more pathetic than anything I've seen. Trump is a blowhard who is out of his league. He cannot be so dumb that he doesn't know what's going on. What a tragedy for the country." Smith shook his head slowly. Jason remained silent.

"I'm afraid I'll have to wait until tomorrow to get the lowdown," Smith said, as he rose from the couch. "Carmen and I have theater tickets for this evening. We're finally seeing 'Hamilton.' I'll probably cry during the entire performance. No doubt I'll catch the final round of *Moses v. Trump* on television, when we get home from the theater. Once again, my congratulations."

"My constituency awaits me in the courtroom, but first I must finish this repast."

"See you tomorrow." Smith strode out the door, almost bumping into Vernon, who was entering. Jason remained seated.

Vernon and his father quickly finished the strudel. Jason was curious what Vernon thought of the verdict, but he decided he could not properly inquire. It had to be his decision and his decision alone, with the assistance of those people the law allowed him to consult, namely, his law clerk Joe. Not even another judge of the same district court could properly participate in making the decision. Most of all, Jason wanted to go home, to his old chair and a good Cognac. He took a parting look at the portrait of Chief Justice John Marshall. It was much easier being an appellate judge than a trial judge, he thought, as he and Vernon headed to the courtroom.

Chapter 21

Seated in his elevated chair, Jason addressed the lawyers in a courtroom that was at capacity, except for the empty jury box. The reporters who had fled after the damage verdict were back in their seats. The spectators quickly settled down and waited for Jason to speak. Vernon was in the front row of spectators. Jason thought he recognized two jurors in the audience. Nothing wrong with that, he concluded, although he didn't remember it happening before. He also saw Kate Kruiser. She was loyal to her lawyer, Ira Moses. Jason liked that.

Even after the jury has spoken, a trial judge has the power, in fact, the responsibility, to set aside the verdict when it is unsupported by the evidence. Centuries of history have ensconced this important limitation on the power of a jury to render a verdict in both criminal and civil cases. Depending on the quantum of evidence, the judge in a civil case must either enter judgment in favor of the losing party or order a new trial. The losing party may then appeal.

"Mr. Butt, Mr. Rattle, and Mr. Crunch, do you have any motions at this time? Let me confine the discussion first to issues relating to liability. Remember, I was here for the entire trial and don't need you to repeat it to me." Jason could not manage his usual smile.

"Yes, we do," Butt responded. "Mr. Mandick and *Total Faith* move for a directed verdict in their favor or for a new trial. The evidence was uncontradicted that Mr. Mandick and *Total Faith* believed that the article was true. Whether or not the jury concludes that Beverly Clooney has had a serious psychiatric illness, there is no basis for a verdict against my clients, who were unaware of her hospitalization or her illness. No one has testified that she appeared other than as an intelligent and conscientious reporter. Another point is that my clients knew her very satisfactory prior work."

Butt paused to take a sip of water. What thirsty lawyers, Jason thought.

"We do not see how a rational jury could have found against our clients. Mr. Moses presented absolutely no evidence to show that Mr. Mandick and *Total Faith* didn't care if the article was true or not or even that they were negligent. Thank you."

"Mr. Rattle, I'll hear from you next."

"The evidence is uncontradicted that Ms. Clooney was hospitalized for a serious mental illness shortly before she wrote the article. She was not discharged, but escaped. No one challenged the sincerity of her religious beliefs. Whether or not she in fact had divine assistance in researching and writing the article, she totally believed in the truth of the article. She certainly had no doubts about the word of God. It was simply not negligent for a believer to accept the word of God. While the plaintiff might argue that creates a hole in the libel law that liars could slip through, it is not a serious problem. Liars are always a potential problem, but we count on juries to catch liars. Also, Ms. Clooney's life is consistent with her belief in the events she described.

"Finally, the all-important libel case of *New York Times v. Sullivan* held that a libel judgment cannot be imposed without a finding of fault on the part of the defendant by clear and convincing evidence. The Constitution protects innocently made statements. Ms. Clooney's statements were unquestionably innocent. It would violate the Constitution for you to sustain the verdict against Ms. Clooney."

Jason noted Beverly Clooney was sitting absolutely still, although he could not see her hands, which were blocked by the table. She seemed oblivious to the debate about her mental illness.

"Mr. Rattle, are you saying," Jason asked, "that if a person claims to have received the word of God and writes something defamatory, and the plaintiff does not contradict or impeach the testimony, that a judge must set aside a plaintiff's verdict?"

"I think so, Your Honor, but we don't have to go that far. We have corroboration of mental illness, in the form of the statement of Dr. Fong, plus more. No one gave a basis for questioning Ms. Clooney's sincerity or dedication at the time the article was published. We don't allow impeachment to be assumed out of thin air. The burden was on Mr. Moses and Mr. Whitebread to prove negligence and legal malice by clear and convincing evidence. They have not. The jury found no legal malice; it is up to you to find no negligence."

"Is this like the insanity defense in a criminal case?"

"No, Your Honor. One critical difference is that proving negligence is part of the plaintiff's affirmative case, while insanity is an affirmative defense on which the defendant has the burden of proof. It's more like the prosecution's burden to prove a crime was intentional when the statute requires intent."

"Mr. Rattle, what if the jury concluded that Ms. Clooney was feigning mental illness, wouldn't that provide a sufficient basis for the jury to find against her? Couldn't that have happened?" Jason noticed how quiet the courtroom was. He took a sip of coffee.

Rattle paused for few seconds before speaking. "Your Honor, that would be arguable if there was evidence from which a reasonable jury could find that Ms. Clooney was faking a mental illness. The testimony of a psychiatrist could possibly have provided that, but there was no such evidence. Nada. In these circumstances I don't see how a jury would have any choice but to conclude that she was delusional, even if a juror rejected her vision." Rattle again paused. "Another point, if I may. If Ms. Clooney feigned mental illness, that would support a verdict of legal malice. But the jury found no legal malice. So, there was no legal malice and no feigning. The evidence does not support a verdict of negligence. There is no negligence."

Rattle's last point was interesting, Jason thought. Very interesting. "Thank you, Mr. Rattle. Mr. Crunch, you have something to say on the issue of liability?" Jason was tiring. He should have postponed the hearing until tomorrow. Having started the process, however, he was reluctant to interrupt it. Meanwhile, Crunch was very agitated. Jason noted that Gregory was not at counsel table. Instead was a man that Jason did not recognize. The man was dressed very conservatively in a black suit, white shirt, and red tie with a small rectangular pattern, and wore a grim expression.

"Yes, Your Honor," Crunch said. "I shall repeat that there is nothing to demonstrate that Mr. Trump was either negligent or reckless in accepting the article in *Total Faith*. I also want to be on record that if you set aside the jury's verdict on liability on the other defendants, you should do the same with the president in the interests of justice. Please consider this a motion to set aside the default judgment. In fact, for the reasons previously stated, the court should vacate the default and default judgment against Mr. Trump. That is all I have to say, Your Honor."

"Mr. Crunch, I agree that it would be somewhat anomalous if the president were the only defendant against whom a judgment was entered. That, however, is a risk you and your client took when your conduct caused me to enter default on the issue of liability. But it's not very different from the only defendant in a criminal case to be convicted is one that pleaded guilty.

"After giving the matter extensive thought, your client decided not to defend the accusations against him. Moreover, how can we be sure that Mr. Trump did not doubt the accuracy of his tweet? For all we know, he may have told someone that. He might have admitted doubt to someone. The plaintiff may have learned that in discovery. Given Mr. Trump's record with the truth, we cannot be sure what might have turned up. But all that is speculation. Perhaps you can convince two judges on the court of appeals that you are right, but you have not convinced me today. A decision on the merits for one defendant one way does not affect a default judgment against another any more than acquittal of one defendant affects a previously entered guilty plea by another defendant in the same case. But I'll read your memorandum with care."

Crunch sat down slowly. He looked confused and helpless. Jason noticed that Crunch ignored the black-suited man seated next to him.

"Mr. Whitebread?"

"We believe that the evidence eminently supports the verdict and respectfully oppose the motions. Mr. Mandick testified that *Total Faith* followed standard journalistic practices, yet he never had anyone check out this extraordinary article. I submit that is both negligent and reckless, and therefore constitutes legal malice, or so the jury could have legitimately found. As for Ms. Clooney, it is within the purview of ordinary people to conclude that someone is faking a mental illness. Remember, Mr. Rattle presented no competent evidence of mental illness; the only evidence that was presented was Ms. Clooney's saying that her doctors told her she was a paranoid-schizophrenic and, for what it's worth, she denied it. Certainly, the jury could conclude that she was faking mental illness."

"But they didn't," Jason replied. "The jury found Ms. Clooney negligent but without legal malice, which I accept as its verdict that it believed that Ms. Clooney was not intentionally lying. Moreover, Ms. Clooney's testimony that Dr. Fong diagnosed her as mentally ill stands uncontradicted by medical testimony. Without objection on the grounds of hearsay, Dr. Fong's statement to Ms. Clooney is competent evidence. I also don't see how I can credit the testimony of a person diagnosed as mentally ill who denies mental illness over the opinion of her treating psychiatrist."

"Your Honor," Whitebread responded slowly, "if you adopt that standard, you give fanatics a free ride. It also gives pseudo-fanatics a free ride. So long as someone comes in here and says I followed the word of God, he can say just about anything. They can make extreme, unfounded charges while proclaiming that some super-natural force told them to do it. They can say whatever they want. Giving a license to such people does not facilitate the values the framers of the Constitution sought to further."

Jason shook his head negatively. He told himself to speak slowly. He was following the arguments the lawyers were making, but he couldn't rush. "I believe that is what the Supreme Court's decision in *New York Times v. Sullivan* requires. The First Amendment is more important than an occasional individual who has his defamation claim rejected. Also, how can I find Ms. Clooney negligent for, as she put it, not fact-checking God? The jury's verdict shows they didn't disbelieve her testimony."

"It's easy," Whitebread said. "Negligence is judged by an objective standard. Would a reasonable person have been satisfied with the information she had when she wrote her article?"

"But how can I ignore a person's faith in deciding negligence? That would be discriminating against religious persons. I don't see how I can do that in view of the history of religion in this country. Courts cannot do that." Jason was getting annoyed at Whitebread. He was beginning to whine, or was Jason imagining it? A whining cowboy? Jason continued.

"Let us move on," Jason said. Ignoring Whitebread, Jason gazed at the other counsel table. "Mr. Rattle, do you have something to say?"

"Your Honor, I believe everything has been said that I would want to say." Rattle had barely stood up.

"Thank you," Jason said to Rattle. Jason had questions for Rattle about the interaction of the reasonable person standard and the religion clauses, but he was tired. He could not formulate the question he wanted to ask. He turned to Whitebread, who remained seated while Jason spoke to him.

"Mr. Whitebread, you have made some points. Perhaps the Supreme Court will agree with them a year or two from now if it decides to hear your case. Meanwhile, I am bound by precedent that it has established. Moreover, I think you may have proved too much. If people go around making statements about supernatural forces and other things in which they firmly believe, it may be true that nothing in the libel law can stop them, but you must accept that no one or almost no one will believe these people. Thus, the people they defame will not be seriously damaged."

"Your Honor, you are destroying the objective standard of judging negligence. I don't see how you can do that."

"Mr. Whitebread, I am not doing that. I'm including in the concept of a reasonable person that person's attributes. You cannot ignore that a person does not speak English, that the person has a Ph.D. in a subject or that the person is blind. Likewise, you cannot ignore that a person is religious. As I said before, you may convince two judges on the court of appeals, but you haven't convinced me." Jason thought a minute, then continued.

"Let me hear from everyone on the amount of the verdict, both compensatory damages and punitive damages. I call on Mr. Butt. On second thought, we'll take a brief recess, five minutes."

As he existed from the door behind the bench, Jason signaled Joe, who quickly joined him. "Please ask Sue to bring me some more coffee." Jason felt groggy. One cup had accomplished little. Two minutes later, he was hunched over the desk in the small robing room behind the courtroom sipping coffee. He took a deep breath, then another. "I needed that," Jason said to Joe. Jason sipped slowly.

"Are you all right, Judge? Can I do something?"

"Thanks. The coffee helps a lot. I just needed that."

Joe looked inquisitively at Jason, but Jason was standing up to return to the courtroom. He clutched the coffee cup while Joe opened the door that led to the judge's chair. "All rise," the bailiff announced, as people scurried to their seats.

"Mr. Butt, you may continue," Jason said.

"The amount of the compensatory damages is greatly

excessive against Mr. Mandick and *Total Faith*. There was no claim of loss of income and no medical expenses or psychiatric testimony on behalf of Mr. Moses. We don't deny that Mr. Moses may have been upset, but no degree of upset can translate into ten million dollars for an article in *Total Faith*. That figure was pulled out of thin air. That's no basis for a jury verdict."

"You don't deny, do you, that Mr. Moses's reputation is the most important thing he has both in his personal and professional life?"

"Not at all, Your Honor," Butt responded. "If the verdict were in six figures, or even one million dollars, we could not complain. But the verdict as rendered on compensatory damages was simply crazy."

Jason wondered whether *Total Faith's* libel insurance was $1 million, but that seemed too low coverage for the magazine. "Mr. Butt, you did not object to the instruction to the jury. The libel received extraordinary coverage and repetition. I do not see how I can reverse the amount. What I'm saying is that if I do not upset the verdict of negligence and legal malice, I very much doubt that I am going to disagree with the amount of the judgment." Butt shrugged and sat down.

"Mr. Rattle"?

"Ms. Clooney wrote an article for a publication with a limited circulation. I suggest that the amount of damages in her case is even more insane."

"Mr. Rattle, the law is that the damages flow from what the defendant could reasonably foresee. This is not a case in which someone wrote another a private letter that the recipient gave to a newspaper or someone. Nor is it an article about a person that the media had no interest in. It was about a huge case and an important member of the community. There is more than its publication in *Total Faith*. These defendants knew the story would be repeated and repeated. There was no objection to the instruction. Mr. Crunch?"

Crunch rose slowly and walked to the lectern. He seemed to have shrunk a size or two. He stood for few seconds before speaking.

"Your Honor, I cannot even fathom how a verdict of one billion dollars on each of compensatory and punitive damages can survive. In fact, the verdict is so excessive that it places into doubt the jury's decision on liability. It shows that the jury was prejudiced or biased. The judgment should be set aside for that reason as well. I could go on, but there is simply no basis for such an award. It is fantastic." Crunch dropped his arms to his sides in a gesture of futility.

"Mr. Crunch, hundreds of millions of people read or heard what the president said about Mr. Moses. Are you arguing that the verdict should be reduced because they did not believe him? I'm not sure that anyone can speculate on such an argument, at least not without evidence to support it."

"Well, the president has been known to use hyperbole," Crunch said. "Also, a tweet is an informal method of communication and suggests that not every word should be taken literally."

"I don't see how you can argue that the public did not believe the president of the United States. I just don't see it. I can take judicial notice that the White House has said a presidential tweet is official. The president himself stands by them. Doesn't the verdict establish that the jury concluded that people believed Mr. Trump's statement that Mr. Moses is a crook? Hasn't the president repeatedly asserted that he is not a liar? Incidentally, what other of President Trump's tweets do you claim were false or hyperbole?"

Crunch was silent.

"Moreover, Mr. Trump has refused to produce his income-tax returns and the jury was entitled to believe his most extravagant statements about his wealth. The jury could have found he was worth up to twenty billion dollars and that he will continue to be a serial defamer. He flatly says that he will not be deterred. On those facts, I have trouble with your arguments. If there is nothing else, we shall adjourn. I didn't mean to cut you off, Mr. Crunch." Crunch was still standing at the podium, waiting to speak.

"Thank you, Your Honor. I want to make sure you understand that the hyperbole point is not my only argument. Even if the public believed President Trump's statement, how does the fact that coal miners in West Virginia, even tens of thousands of them, saw and believed the tweet, harm Mr. Moses to the tune of one billion dollars?"

Jason waited for more, but that was it. Crunch turned and walked to his chair. "I shall decide the motions this evening. I think that's in the best interests of everyone not to carry this over until tomorrow. We will take a one-hour recess." Jason wanted the whole thing to end, desperately.

————————

"Well, what do you think, Joe?" The two were seated in Jason's office. Jason had asked his son to wait in the reception area. Having his son privy to the decision-making process was improper. Judges had to live by rules.

"I really don't know, Judge, I haven't seen anything like this before." The answer did not surprise Jason. He hadn't either.

"I don't see how I or any other judge could let the verdict stand against Mandick, Clooney, and *Total Faith*," Jason said slowly. "I don't see how I can decide that a jury could reasonably reach the conclusion it did. I don't see facts that establish negligence or legal malice by clear and convincing evidence. I have to accept that a reasonable man must include a religious man. I don't see how I can decide that a reasonable man can only be a nonreligious man."

"So, you've decided to throw out the jury verdict?" Joe asked.

"Other than Trump, yes. I'm leaving Trump precisely where he put himself. He had lawyers, presumably a personal lawyer as well as Crunch, whom he concealed because it might hurt his argument that his statement was within the scope of his presidential duties." Jason remembered the many times he struggled to avoid precedent to reach a result with which he was comfortable, but still within the boundaries of the law. But this issue was not close.

Jason called out to Sue to bring some hot coffee, which she quickly did. She poured cups for both Jason and Joe. Jason avoided meeting her gaze, knowing her face would show her concern that he was exhausting himself.

"O.K., what about the damages against Trump?" Jason asked Joe.

"All I can say is that a billion dollars is a hell of a lot to compensate someone for someone saying he fixed a case," Joe answered. "That's probably more than Moses would make in a hundred lifetimes. Moreover, he's eighty-four years old."

"The question is not what you or I would decide, but whether I can say that the jury had no basis for that amount. If I throw out the billion-dollar verdict, how do I pick another number? How do I explain why $100 million is all right, but $1 billion is not? Juries have much more leeway than judges when it comes to verdicts. How do I explain any particular number other than to say the first one was too high? Of course, I could order a new trial, but that would also usurp the role of the jury. Why should I believe that a second jury would be any more rational than the first? No court has provided me with a methodology to set a lower number when I find the jury verdict too high."

Joe shrugged and returned to his desk. Jason scribbled some notes on his white pad. Five minutes later, Jason stood up. "Sue, would you be interested in seeing the end of the case?"

"That would be great, Judge."

Jason, Vernon, Joe, and Sue headed to the packed but hushed courtroom and entered by different doors. Joe and Sue sat on chairs on the opposite side of the courtroom from the empty jury box. Jason settled himself in his high-backed chair and addressed the audience.

"I have reached my decision. First, I am setting aside the judgment and award of damages in favor of Mr. Moses against Mr. Mandick, Ms. Clooney, and *Total Faith* and entering judgment for the defendants other than the president, on the ground that the plaintiff Moses failed to prove that they possessed legal malice or were negligent." Once again, there was commotion among the spectators, which Jason ignored. Mandick was embracing Butt and pounding him on the back. Clooney continued to stare straight ahead. Rattle looked lost, as everyone ignored him. Whitebread examined his hands while Moses had his eyes shut. Crunch was writing on a piece of paper.

"The Constitution requires a finding of significant fault on the part of the defendants, and evidence was simply lacking that they did not believe the story at the time of publication or were negligent to accept and publish it. Moreover, Mr. Moses had to prove negligence or legal malice by clear and convincing evidence, and I do not find sufficient evidence to support such a finding. Whether I am right or wrong would be for another court to say, if Mr. Whitebread chooses to appeal." Tired as he was, Jason was amused at his newly found respect for the court of appeals.

"I find that the unquestioned religious beliefs of Ms. Clooney prevent a finding that she was negligent. As a district judge I am not prepared to say that a person with a sincerely held religious belief can possess the fault the Supreme Court requires to impose a judgment in a libel case when she follows her religious convictions. There also was no evidence that Mr. Mandick and *Total Faith* thought the article was probably false. While they did not engage in the most rigorous testing of the accuracy of the article, the evidence falls substantially below proof of legal malice or negligence." Jason paused and surveyed the courtroom. As expected, everyone was watching him. He took a sip of coffee. He stared at the spectators for a few seconds.

"While not influencing my decision, the fact that the article was unquestionably false, admitted by two defendants to have been false, and found by the jury to have been false will serve to exonerate Mr. Moses from the most serious consequences of the allegations. Those facts will mitigate whatever harm to his reputation Ms. Clooney, Mr. Mandick, and *Total Faith* caused."

Jason looked at Mandick. "My decision cannot and should not be viewed as exonerating those defendants for having inflicted serious injury to Mr. Moses." Jason noticed how quiet the courtroom remained. He did not like Mandick and he did not like what Mandick did. Jason took another sip of coffee before continuing in a castigating voice. "I could say a lot more about the publication of the article, but I shall merely state that *New York Times v. Sullivan* and other cases provided the defendants with protection. But, I repeat, that a statement that the Constitution protects is not the same thing as a statement that is wise or true. It does not act as an affirmation of the quality of the defendants' effort or lack thereof."

Jason stood up and arched his back. He took a few steps and then returned to his chair.

"I now turn to the amount of damages the jury found against Mr. Trump. What was involved was one of the strongest and uncompromising defamatory statements imaginable about someone's professional integrity. It received enormous publicity. It is safe to say that Mr. Trump's statement reached hundreds of millions of people. It is not easy, I recognize, to decide the proper amount of compensatory and punitive damages, but that cuts both ways. It may be difficult to support a particular jury's verdict with a rigorous analysis, but then it is difficult to fault that verdict. It is imperative that federal judges give jury verdicts the deference due them. While not a basis of my decision, I shall note my understanding that at common law jury verdicts were rarely, if ever, overturned on the question of the appropriate remedy. In any event, I have no rational basis for selecting an amount different from the jury's. Therefore, I have decided not to disturb the judgment for compensatory damages against Mr. Trump."

Jason forcefully pounded his gavel. He was not finished, although more than a dozen reporters fled to the exits. He waited for quiet. Jason was feeling stronger and more confident. He took a deep breath.

"For similar reasons the amount of punitive damages is appropriate for a man of Mr. Trump's acknowledged wealth and other attributes that have been considered on the record. Specifically, we have the president's pattern of making defamatory statements, calling people liars and crooks and the like, saying that people should be locked up without indictment or a trial, and that the police should rough up innocent people. The jury could properly have considered other conduct that violated norms in fixing the amount of punitive damages.

"Without objection the jurors relied on their recollections of what the president had said in the past, which makes it even more difficult than usual for a judge to reject the jury's verdict. Mr. Trump refused to produce his income-tax returns and made extravagant claims about his wealth, I mean, he made claims to extravagant wealth. These are just some of the considerations that have led me to let the verdict stand. I am not saying that the amount of damages is a question without difficulty, but I have given the matter considerable thought, not only in the past hour, but as the trial was coming to its end. I cannot fault the jury's decision." Jason was building a record for the court of appeals.

Jason had decided that he needed to add gravitas to his ruling. "The Seventh Amendment was probably the most important amendment in the Bill of Rights, when they were adopted in 1791. The absence of a constitutional right to a jury trial in civil cases in the federal courts almost led to the defeat of the 1789 Constitution. I could go on, but the history is well known. I believe that the First and Seventh Amendments leave me with no choice." There were still two originalists on the Supreme Court, with Neil Gorsuch replacing Antonin Scalia. The case could end up there.

Jason surveyed the lawyers and the spectators. He knew where to look last. "Mr. Crunch, you want to say something?"

"Your Honor, I obviously disagree strongly with the jury's and your decision. I plan to file a formal motion for reconsideration to set aside the entry of default judgment and both damage awards. I do not think that I shall surprise Your Honor when I tell you that if you deny the motion, we plan to vigorously appeal the amounts of the damage awards as well as the entry of default judgment."

"Mr. Crunch, that is your God-given right, or at least

your right under the Federal Rules of Civil Procedure and the Constitution, which are at least as good in this court. Rest assured that I will give your written motion my undivided attention when it arrives."

Jason had personally researched the law of punitive damages. He decided it would enhance public, and perhaps appellate court, acceptance of his decision if he spoke more about the law as he viewed it. The death of Scalia removed the most uncompromising partisan of allowing juries to do whatever they wanted in awarding punitive damages. But the law remained favorable to Moses. Jason wanted both the president and the public to know that. He didn't want the media to speculate that he had acted improperly when he had arguments that supported his position. He had planned this moment.

"My instructions to the jury were far more detailed than the minimum the Supreme Court has required. I should also point out that the Supreme Court places great weight on the ratio of punitive damages to compensatory damages. In this case the ratio is one to one; in *TXO Productions v. Alliance Resources* the Court upheld an award of punitive damages that was 500 times the amount of compensatory damages." Jason paused.

"I also want you to consider some specific language in the Seventh Amendment, which reads, and I quote, 'no fact tried by a jury, shall be otherwise re-examined in any Court of the United States, than according to the rules of the common law.' Courts have read that language to mean that a United States Court of Appeals cannot reverse the amount of damages awarded by a jury, since that was beyond the power of appellate courts when the Seventh Amendment went into effect in 1791."

Again, there was an audible reaction among the spectators. Jason assumed that few attendees had remembered that clause in the Seventh Amendment, which most people view as doing no more than guaranteeing the same right to a jury trial as existed at common law. Few realized that the Amendment severely limits the power of federal courts of appeals and the Supreme Court to amend jury verdicts awarding damages, as opposed to state courts, which it doesn't apply to. Or so Jason understood.

"Maybe someone will find a way to allow a federal court of appeals to reduce the amount of compensatory and punitive damages, but I doubt it. But I suppose you know that."

Jason's glance at Crunch showed him that his sarcasm was justified. Crunch, who stared straight ahead, looked shocked. His eyes were blinking furiously.

"I will remind everyone of the short deadlines for filing motions for reconsideration." With that, Jason thanked everyone.

—————

For the final time in *Moses v. Trump*, the bailiff called out, "Please rise." Jason rose and departed for his chambers with a spring in his step. He had survived the long day.

"Judge, I've never seen two billion dollars go so fast," Joe said as Jason, Vernon, and he sat down in chambers. "How can he possibly pay?"

"Not my problem," Jason replied.

"What about his appeal? How will Trump get a $2 billion bond? Won't that mean that Whitebread could seize his business?"

"Not my problem." Joe made a terrific point, but Jason decided that it was best not to compliment Joe in the context of the $2 billion verdict. Whether he or the court of appeals relieved Trump from the obligation to post an enormous supersedeas bond could be as important as the appeal itself. Appellants must post bonds in the amount set by the court or lose the power to prevent the prevailing plaintiff from seizing his assets. Without a bond approved by the courts Moses could try to take over some of President Trump's properties while the case proceeded through the court of appeals and the Supreme Court.

"Congratulations, Judge," Sue said as she poked her head in the door.

"Come in, Sue," Jason said. "I cannot thank the two of you

enough for your extraordinary help during the trial. You've been wonderful, and I couldn't have done it without you. It was a real team effort. I shouldn't jump the gun, since Crunch and possibly Whitebread will file motions for reconsideration and then appeal. But I can't worry about that now."

"Thanks," Sue said. "It's been a pleasure, as always. Thank you for everything. If it's all right, I'll head home now.

"You're very welcome. I'm sorry you had to stay so late."

"It was worth it, Judge, every minute of it. Good night."

"Thanks again," Joe said, getting to his feet. "I echo Sue. It's been a real pleasure, and, for me, a hugely educational one as well."

"I meant what I said, Joe."

"Good night, Judge."

"Good night."

Jason looked at his son. "This is the first time in weeks I'm able to relax." Jason lowered himself in his chair and stretched his feet out in front of him. "It's quite a strain to preside over a case of this magnitude. I'm going to stay here awhile before I go home. You won't mind if I meet you at the apartment in a little bit. I feel like being alone."

"Of course not, dad. Take your time. You handled the case magnificently. I'm very proud of you." In a somewhat lower voice he added, "although the size of the verdict is shocking."

"Thanks, son. It means a lot to me for you to say that."

"I'll see you soon." Vernon got up and headed out the door. He looked back at his father and smiled.

Jason took off his jacket, loosened his tie, and sat quietly with his thoughts. He was pleased with how the case went and was satisfied with his performance. It was an accomplishment he would savor the rest of his life. His pleasure was tempered by his thoughts of Audrey, and how much more satisfying the past weeks would have been with her there. Compensating for that absence, however, was his greatly improved relationship with Vernon. He could not remember the last time he had such a warm feeling toward Vernon.

Jason's mind returned to Audrey, and her hostility toward

Trump. She would have been pleased with the way the case turned out. He smiled at the memory of some of her choice comments about Trump. He had never heard her express such hostility toward anyone. He could hear her say, "Only two billion dollars? Shame on you." He smiled.

He thought of Christine and what the future might bring. He felt comfortable with the prospect.

Relaxing in his silent chambers with the verdict in, Jason realized that he totally despised Donald Trump. Now that the trial was over, well, almost over, he could be honest with himself. The miserable selfish, egotistical ignoramus was ruining the country. "Hippopotamus ignoramus," Jason chortled. Trump was dividing the country and crushing the unprivileged and minorities, along with ruining the criminal justice system, the environment, and more. Trump got what he deserved. Fuck him.

"Relax," he told himself, "relax."

Jason suddenly had an idea. Smiling, he got to his feet, closed the blinds on all windows, and closed and locked every door to and within his chambers. He thought for a moment about turning the portrait of Chief Justice John Marshall so that he faced the wall, but decided against it. It was too heavy. Jason went to his private refrigerator and took out a bottle of 2002 Dom Perignon champagne that he had stored behind a few large bottles of sparkling water. He could not remember why he had put it there, but now he welcomed his foresight. It was a magnificent champagne.

Jason stripped the metal capsule from the top of the bottle and loosened the wires that held the cork in place against the powerful force of the natural carbonation that had been building for fifteen years. He did those tasks slowly and methodically. Then he slowly eased the cork out of the bottle with his thumbs. He wanted to do everything precisely right, which meant the cork should not explode but rather sensually ooze out of the neck of the bottle with a whoosh or a sigh. Tiny bits of foam dribbled down the neck of the bottle. He stood the bottle at a corner of his desk.

Jason removed everything else from the top of his desk to a chair or to the floor. He reached into the back of his bottom-left desk drawer and retrieved a Tiffany champagne glass from its velvet case and placed it on his desk next to the Dom Perignon. He carefully climbed onto his chair and then onto the top of his desk, resting on his knees. He reached down. Holding the tall, narrow, and exquisitely carved glass in one hand and the bottle of Dom Perignon by its thin neck in the other, he lifted himself from his knees to a nearly fully upright position, testing his balance along the way. He slowly poured the bubbly elixir from the bottle down the inside of the glass until it was three-quarters full. He straightened up. Holding the glass up to the light, he examined the tiny bubbles floating to the surface from the bottom of the glass. He sniffed the incandescent liquid in the glass. He closed his eyes and took a glorious sip, then another, then another. He opened his eyes and smiled.

"HAPPY DAYS ARE HERE AGAIN," he sang at the top of his lungs as he did a jig on the polished mahogany desk top.

About the Author

Dorsen is uniquely suited to write *Moses v. Trump*. He was Assistant Chief Counsel of the Senate Watergate Committee and an Assistant U.S. Attorney in the Southern District of New York for five years, where the action takes place. He handled two of the most important libel cases in recent memory. He represented General William Westmoreland in his suit against Mike Wallace and CBS and he represented John and Maureen Dean against G. Gordon Liddy and others. He's written books on Justice Antonin Scalia and Judge Henry Friendly of the U.S. Court of Appeals for the Second Circuit: *Henry Friendly, Greatest Judge of His Era* (Harvard University Press 2012) and *The Unexpected Scalia: A Conservative Justice's Liberal Opinions* (Cambridge University Press 2017). He taught public policy at Duke University and Evidence at Georgetown Law Center and George Washington Law School. In his spare time, he was Wine and Food Editor of *The Washingtonian Magazine* for 20 years and was an active 25% partner in a horse-breeding and racing stable, Nonsequitur Stable, LLC . Currently, he is writing a play about the Watergate's Saturday Night Massacre, a book on a case he handled in private practice, and an opera based on Hemingway's *For Whom the Bell Tolls*, for which he wrote the libretto. He graduated from Harvard College and Harvard Law School, where he served on the Harvard Law Review with Justice Ruth Bader Ginsburg and the late Justice Antonin Scalia.

www.ingramcontent.com/pod-product-compliance
Lightning Source LLC
Chambersburg PA
CBHW021218250626
47155CB00008B/2863